Praise for Lynnwood

"An exciting début from a new young writer with a dark imagination. Thomas Brown's beautifully written novel proposes a modern Gothic forest far from the tourist trail, a place filled with strange events and eerie consequences." – *Philip Hoare 'one of the world's most famous and celebrated chroniclers of the New Forest and its history'*

"It was a pretty creepy story. I kept thinking along the premise of the book 'It' by Stephen King with an English twist." – *Naomi Blackburn, A Book and a Review Blog*

"This book was great! I thought I would give it a try, but when I picked it up I couldn't put it down! It was a quick read, and the story was so creepily wonderful. I loved the author's writing style – the words flowed perfectly. Reading this was less like reading a book and more like watching the movie in my mind's eye. Fantastic! I highly recommend it! I can't wait to see what else Thomas Brown has in store for readers in the future." – *Laura Smith, Goodreads Reviewer*

"This is really rather good.

"Can we talk about the thing I loved most first? The writing. Oh, my word, the writing. It was the sort of writing that makes you marvel at how good it is, flowing and swirling and building until it's created whole worlds of dread and fear around you.

"The story itself is fairly simple, though it is given a new dimension through being told out of order, with flashbacks and the recovery of lost memories being a major part of the storytelling. *Lynnwood* wouldn't be nearly so creepy or scary if told straightforwardly, from beginning to end.

"Just trust me that this is good, and go buy it, will you?" – *Caitlin Blanchard, Reviewer, UK*

"The plot line is new and exciting, I won't say anymore about that because I don't want to give it away! But I know I was surprised more than once at what was happening. If you are looking for a good book, definitely pick up this one." – *Alison Mudge, Librarian, USA*

"An exciting, on the edge of your seat gothic that will have readers begging for more." – *Rosemary Smith, Librarian and Cayocosta Book Reviews*

Three British Mystery Novels

David Stuart Davies

Nikki Dudley

Thomas Brown

Sparkling Books

1.1

ISBN of this omnibus print edition: 978-1-907230-73-8

Also available as an e-book bundle: 978-1-907230-74-5

Individual titles also available separately:

A Taste for Blood, David Stuart Davies,   e-book 978-1-907230-48-6
print 978-1-907230-46-2

Ellipsis, Nikki Dudley,   e-book 978-1-907230-21-9
print 978-1-907230-18-9

Lynnwood, Thomas Brown,   e-book 978-1-907230-42-4
print 978-1-907230-38-7

Praise for A Taste for Blood

"Johnny Hawke breathes new life into the traditional British mystery. He's a hero with a heart." – *Val McDermid*

"A well-crafted thriller that had me gripped from the first chapter. *A Taste for Blood* far exceeded expectations with its carefully crafted plotting and characterization. So good were these that it encouraged me to read the novel a second time." – *Amazon review*

"I wholeheartedly recommend David Stuart Davies to those who enjoy a good read." – *Amazon review*

"This book by Davies is a good read for mystery followers. The characters are well sketched out and the plot will twist and turn and leave you wondering how it will all turn out – that's what you want isn't it? This is a delightful read because you are not quite sure what will happen and you are hooked enough to keep on reading. Enjoyable." – *J Robert Ewbank, author*

"Interesting mystery that takes place in the 1930's in England. Private Investigator Johnny Hawke is investigating a suicide that seems off and his police buddy, Detective David Llewellyn is investigating a bloody crime involving an escaped convict and a psychiatrist. The two stories merge for a twisted ending. The details are grisly and the main villain enjoys his victims just a bit too much. But other than that, it was a good story with an unpredictable ending – just how I like my mysteries.

"Although this is the sixth Johnny Hawke novel, you can read it and understand it without reading the previous books. Enough background is given so that you know who Johnny is." – *Donna Miller, Librarian, USA*

"I wholeheartedly recommend David Stuart Davies to those who enjoy a good read." - *Alan Semmens, Educator, UK*

Praise for Ellipsis

"From the opening sentence, *Ellipsis* is strangely engaging: what is it about a red scarf that could make someone choose someone else? And what if that choice turns out to have been thrust on the other as some premeditated plan?

"Lyrical prose intertwines with an elegiac and introspective narrative. Rather than being pretentious, there is an earthy, inviting undertone to Dudley's text, despite the curious storyline that plays with initial impressions and twists them around and around again.

"This is a work of literacy rather than prosaic shelf fodder. Think artsy, melancholic and slightly bewildering and you'll be near enough to understanding *Ellipsis*." – *Excerpt from review by The Truth About Books.*

"Well, how could I resist a novel that shares its name with the punctuation mark I overuse the most?

"*Ellipsis* is an interesting debut from Nikki Dudley that (happily) never quite settles into the shape you might expect.

"What's particularly striking about the central mystery is less the actual events of the plot than the way Dudley plays with the reader's perception; one is led to conceptualise the story in a particular way, then finds that it's not the right way – but it's hard to shake off the original interpretation, so strongly has it been established. And the ending produces a further twist that leaves us on shifting sands once again.

"As its title suggests, *Ellipsis* revolves around gaps in knowledge – in the reader's knowledge of what happens, and in the characters' knowledge of events, people, and even of themselves. And those gaps add up to an intriguing, satisfying read." – *Excerpt from review by David Hebblethwaite.*

"I wouldn't have stopped reading if my house was on fire!" – *Cas Peace, author of For the Love of Daisy, North Hampshire*

A Taste For Blood

David Stuart Davies

David Stuart Davies

David Stuart Davies is the author of six novels featuring private detective hero, Johnny Hawke, and another nine novels featuring Sherlock Holmes as well as several non-fiction books about the Baker Street detective including the movie volume Starring Sherlock Holmes. He served as a committee member of the Crime Writers' Association, editing their monthly magazine, Red Herrings, for twenty years. David is the general contributing editor for Wordsworth Editions Mystery & Supernatural series and a major contributor of introductions to the Collectors' Library classic editions.

To Alanna Knight

A lovely lady who was both a good friend and an inspiration

Also by David Stuart Davies

Johnny (One Eye) Hawke Detective:

Forests of the Night

Comes the Dark

Without Conscience

Requiem for a Dummy

The Darkness of Death

A Taste for Blood

The Further Adventures of Sherlock Holmes:

Sherlock Holmes & The Hentzau Affair

The Scroll of the Dead

The Shadow of the Rat

The Tangled Skein

The Veiled Detective

Sherlock Holmes & The Devil's Promise

Sherlock Holmes & The Ripper Legacy

Sherlock Holmes Short Stories:

Further Exploits of Sherlock Holmes (with Matthew Booth)

and many other titles

PROLOGUE

He would never forget the blood. It wasn't just the quantity – although there was a great deal of it collected in dark, shining, sticky pools on the stone floor with errant rivulets escaping down the grooves between the flagstones. It wasn't just that sweet sickly smell either, which assailed his nostrils with pungent ferocity and etched itself forever on his memory, or the crimson stains splattered on the walls and floor that had remained with him, to return at the midnight hour to haunt his dreams. Most of all it was that face, that crazed visage with mad bulbous eyes and chomping teeth. Revisiting the scene in his nightmares, these images seem to shift and spread like a living organism coagulating into one great patch of red and then from the crimson mist the giant mouth would appear ready to swallow him up.

At this juncture, he would jerk himself awake with a brief tortured sigh, his body drenched in sweat. 'Just a silly nightmare,' he would murmur to placate his concerned wife Sheila and pat her shoulder reassuringly. 'Just a silly nightmare.'

Almost ten years later, the nightmares still came. Not as often but the images were still as vibrant, as threatening, as horrific as ever. He never talked about them to anyone, not even Sheila. They were his personal burdens and he was determined that they should remain so. He certainly didn't want to reveal his secret to his colleagues and have some brain doctor try to analyse his disturbed psyche. Besides if it got out that Detective Inspector David Llewellyn was being scared witless by bad dreams it would hardly do much for his police career. So, with typical stoical reserve, his 'silly nightmares' remained private and self contained.

Until…

ONE

1935

The night was bitterly cold and the frosty lawn shimmered like a silver carpet in the bright moonlight. Concealed in the shrubbery, Detective Sergeant David Llewellyn gazed at the dark and silent house some fifty yards away. His body was stiff with apprehension and fear while his bowels churned with nervous tension. He knew he shouldn't be here. He knew he was taking a risk. He knew he was following his heart rather than his head. But he also knew that sometimes one had to take risks to achieve the right result.

The house, Hawthorn Lodge, gothic and imposing, appeared as a black threatening silhouette against the lighter star-studded sky. It rose out of the earth like a giant claw, its gables and chimneys scratching the sky, while its windows glistened darkly in the moonlight. There was no observable sign of life or occupancy and yet Llewellyn knew that there was some one in there: Doctor Ralph Northcote.

No doubt he was in his basement, a section of the house that the doctor had successfully kept secret from the officers when they had searched the premises. What he was doing there? Llewellyn preferred not to think about it at that moment. His boss, Inspector Sharples, a whisker off retirement, was a tired and sloppy officer and had not been thorough or dogged enough in his investigations. Llewellyn had been sure that a house as large as Hawthorn Lodge would have quarters below ground – a wine and keeping cellar at least – but Sharples wasn't interested. He was convinced that the arrogant and smarmy Dr Ralph Northcote was in no way associated with the terrible crimes he was investigating. How could a man of such intelligence, refinement and breeding perpetrate such horrible murders? The fiend who slaughtered those women was an animal, a beast, a creature of the gutter, not a respectable and respected medical man. Or so the blinkered, forelock tugging Inspector believed.

David Llewellyn had other ideas.

To satisfy his curiosity – at least – he had visited the local solicitor's office where he had been able to examine the original plans for Hawthorn Lodge. To his delight and satisfaction he had discovered that, as he suspected, the house did have a series of cellars. The plans indicated that these chambers were accessed by an entrance in the kitchen. However, instead of passing this information on to his superior, Llewellyn had decided to carry out some undercover work of his own. Why should he allow the old duffer Sharples take the credit for his detective prowess? He'd been sneered at and ridiculed when he'd offered his opinion, his strong conviction, that Dr Northcote was the man they were after.

Now he intended to prove it.

Gripping the police revolver in his pocket with one hand and picking up his battered canvas bag with the other, David Llewellyn emerged from the shrubbery and with a measured tread made his way across the lawn towards the front of the house, his footsteps leaving dark imprints in the frosted grass like the trail of some ghostly creature. On reaching one of the tall sitting-room windows, he knelt down in the flowerbed and withdrew a jemmy from the bag. With several deft movements, accompanied by the gentle sound of splintering wood, he managed to prise the window from its fastenings and open it a few inches. That was all that was needed. Gripping the lower edge of the window with both hands and exerting all his strength he pushed it higher, creating an aperture large enough to allow him to pass through.

Within moments he was in the house, a gentle smile of satisfaction resting on his taut features. From the innards of the bag, he extracted a torch. He had visited the house on two previous occasions in a formal and more conventional capacity with Sharples. These visits, allied to his studies of the plans, gave him the confidence to move swiftly through the dark sitting room, into the hallway and towards the kitchen.

* * *

The murders had started six months earlier. The pattern was the same in all four cases. A young woman in her early twenties was reported missing by her distraught parents and then a few days later her mutilated body was discovered in woodland or waste ground. In all instances the victim's arms, legs and breasts had been amputated and were missing. There was also evidence that the victim had been tortured. Most of the gruesome details had been held back from the press but despite that, because of the youth of the victims, the murderer had been labelled 'The Ghoul' by the more downmarket rags.

The limbs had been expertly severed and so it was suspected that a member of the medical profession was the perpetrator of these horrendous crimes. The girls had all lived within five miles of Hampstead Heath and doctors and surgeons residing within this radius had fallen under particular scrutiny. Two suspects emerged: Stanley Prince, a middle-aged GP who had been struck off the medical register some years before for conducting a series of abortions; and Ralph Northcote, a surgeon at St Luke's Hospital who twelve months earlier had been accused of assault by one of the nurses who had mysteriously disappeared before she could testify against him at a medical tribunal. As a result, the case was dropped and Northcote continued to practise.

Inspector Brian Sharples was placed in charge of the case and given one of the promising new live wires at the Yard, Detective Sergeant David Llewellyn, as his assistant. The two men did not get on. Sharples was an old hand, steady on the tiller, a great believer in doing things by the book, a book it seemed to Llewellyn that Sharples had written himself at some time back in the Middle Ages. With Sharples it was a case of softly, softly, catchee monkey. This may work in the long run, thought Llewellyn, but there may be three or four more murders before this particular monkey was apprehended. Llewellyn was a great believer in stirring up the waters and in the power of intuition. He was convinced that he had a nose for sniffing out a murderer.

Both Prince and Northcote were investigated and interviewed, but apart from their past misdemeanours nothing could be pinned on them. However, Llewellyn did not like Northcote. There was something about his oh-so-charming and rather slimy manner that set alarm bells ringing for the young Detective Sergeant. So much so that, unknown to Sharples, and any other of his colleagues, he had started to do a little digging on his own. Northcote was now in his mid-thirties and living alone, but in his youth he had been a bit of a ladies' man with, Llewellyn discovered, a string of broken engagements. Engagements which had all been ended by the girls. Llewellyn had managed to track one of these girls down and interview her. Doreen French was touching forty now, plump and comfortable looking. She had married a greengrocer and was the mother of twins. She seemed content with her lot and more than happy to talk about Northcote. She revealed nothing that was legally incriminating, but confirmed Llewellyn's impression that the man was odd and put up a false front to the world. 'In the end,' said Doreen French, her eyes twinkling brightly, 'he gave me the willies. He was... how can I say...? He liked to touch me. Not in a sexual way, you understand, but... just to touch my skin. He loved to run his fingers down my bare arm. He once gave my arm such a squeeze, it caused a great big bruise. He wasn't much of a kisser, but ...' she giggled innocently... 'he did like to lick me. On my cheek and round the back of the neck. I thought it was sweet at first. Affectionate like – but in the end... as I say, it gave me the willies'.

Llewellyn nodded sympathetically. It would give him the willies too. 'Was he ever violent to you?'

Doreen did not have to ponder this one. 'Oh, no. Not deliberately, anyway. There was that bruise I mentioned, but he never slapped me or anything like that. But I have to say, that towards the end, I just didn't like being alone with him. He just seemed odd. What had started out as endearing quirks became rather spooky. And his eating habits... ugh!'

'What about them?'

'Well, he hardly ate anything that was cooked. He liked raw steak and his lamb chops hardly sat in the pan a minute before they were on his plate, all bloody and raw.' Doreen pulled a face that effectively mirrored her revulsion.

Well, thought David, there was nothing in the interview that would provide evidence that Northcote was this Ghoul, but he certainly seemed a strange chap and it was certainly a strange chap with medical knowledge who was murdering these young girls. Now a fifth one had disappeared. Her body had not been found yet so there was a slim chance that she was still alive. Very slim, he had to admit. Sharples had refused to interview Northcote again – 'We've nothing to go on, lad. We're here to investigate crimes not cause a nuisance to respectable law abiding folk.' And so David decided to take things into his own hands.

* * *

Once in the kitchen, he examined the walls carefully for some kind of hidden door that would provide access to the cellars. His search was fruitless, however. As he stood in the centre of the lofty chamber, the beam of his torch slowly scanning his surroundings, a sound came to his ears, one which froze his blood.

It was a high-pitched scream of pain. It was sharp and piercing like nails down a blackboard. He shuddered involuntarily at the sound. Where had it come from? It was clear yet distant, like a train whistle down a long tunnel. He listened, straining his ears in the hissing silence but the sound did not come again. As he waited in the dark, he relaxed the hold on his torch and the shaft of light sank towards the floor and rested on the base of a large kitchen cabinet by the far wall. What it illuminated made Llewellyn's heart skip a beat. There were faint skid marks marking the dark wooden flooring: tiny groves that had imprinted themselves on the boards. It was quite clear to Llewellyn that these had been made by the stout legs of the cabinet as it had been pulled away from the wall.

With a tight grin, he rested the torch on the large kitchen table in the centre of the room so that the beam fell on to the cabinet and then he attempted to drag it away from the wall. Kneeling in order to obtain a more secure purchase, he tugged hard at the lower section. Slowly the cabinet moved, the feet following exactly the track of the grooves in the floor. When he had managed to create a gap between the wall and the cabinet big enough for him to squeeze himself into, he saw it.

Llewellyn's grin broadened. 'The secret door,' he whispered to himself.

He now pushed the cabinet fully clear of the wall and attempted to open the door. The handle rattled encouragingly but the door did not budge. It was locked. This did not daunt Llewellyn for although the lock was new and stout, the door was old. Retrieving the jemmy from his canvas bag, he got to work levering the door open. It was the work of a matter of moments. The wood splintered easily and surrendered to the force of the jemmy.

Gingerly he pulled the door open and with the aid of his torch he peered into the darkness beyond. There was a set of stone steps leading down into ebony void. 'Now the adventure really starts,' he muttered to himself as he moved slowly forward into the cold blackness. On reaching the bottom of the stairs he thought he heard faint, indistinguishable noises in the distance. How far away they were he could not tell. Maybe it was just the movement of rats and mice – maybe it was something else. Using his torch like a searchlight, he tried to get a sense of his surroundings. He was in a passageway with a low vaulted ceiling. He saw that there were two light bulbs dangling down but no sign of a switch by which to turn them on. He knew, however, that it would be foolish to do so even if he could. He had no intention of announcing his presence in such an ostentatious fashion.

On reaching the end of the passage, he came to another door. A thin line of light seeped out at its base. This is it, thought Llewellyn, heart thumping. Swiftly he clicked off the torch and stowed it away in his coat pocket and then pulled out his revolver before turning the handle of the door. This one was not locked. Gently he opened it and stepped inside. The first impression was of the brightness of the chamber. The walls and floor were covered in white ceramic tiles while fierce strip lights hung down from the ceiling flooding the room with harsh illumination which created dense shadows. It had the antiseptic ambience of an operating theatre.

An operating theatre.

In the centre of the room was a stone slab on which was laid the twitching naked body of a young girl. At first glance, she seemed to be coated from head to foot in some dark shiny substance. Then, to Llewellyn's horror, he realised that it was blood. Leaning over her was a man in a white coat which was also splattered with crimson stains. As Llewellyn entered the chamber the man glanced up in surprise, his eyes wide and manic. It was a moment that was forever etched on David's mind. Like a scar, that image was to stay with him for life; it was seared into his consciousness ready to feed his nightmares and catch him unawares during unsuspecting waking moments. It was as though a fierce flashbulb had exploded, the harsh, vibrant light freezing the scene as vile photograph.

The creature seemed unconcerned that he had been disturbed in his activity. The lower half of his face was dripping with blood and something seemed to be trailing from his mouth, glistening and moist. As Llewellyn took a step nearer, he realised to his disgust that it was a piece of pink meat. Instinctively, his gaze moved to the mutilated body of the naked girl and then the truth hit him like a mighty blow to the solar plexus. This fiend was eating her flesh.

TWO

1944

After the death of my girlfriend Max... after her brutal murder... I spiralled down into an undignified state of self-pity. I tried to escape reality through booze and sleep, failing to function either as a detective or even a human being. I rejected the ministerings and comfort offered by those close to me: Peter, my sort-of adopted son, Benny, the little Jewish café owner who treated me like family, and my old mate Detective Inspector David Llewellyn. In their various ways they all tried to shake me out of my depressive malaise, but failed. It was not their fault. Perversely, I didn't want to be shaken. I wanted to wallow. Ironically, as I think back to that period now, I can see that being deeply miserable was in a strange way the only thing that was keeping me sane.

As an orphan, I had never seen much affection in my life and then to meet the beautiful Max and receive it from her in spades was miraculous and wonderful. My innate cynicism forged out of a life of disappointments should have warned me that it wouldn't last, but nothing or no one could have prepared me for the savage and dramatic way in which she would be taken from me. What increased my pain was the sense of guilt I felt for her death. She was killed by a crazed maniac as a means of wreaking revenge on me.* She was an innocent who had wandered into my dirty little world and because of me she had lost her life. It was my fault that she ended up with a bullet in her head.

My fault.

The image of my dead love with her wide staring eyes and the spidery tendrils of blood spilling down her face haunted me in those months and days that followed. And, indeed, haunt me still.

What dragged me back to reality and, in truth, saved my sanity was one of the strangest and most challenging episodes of my life. It was late March and winter's grip on the country was still in evidence. It might have been spring on the calendar, but the elements were not acknowledging the fact. The daffodils and crocus may have reluctantly raised their heads about the stiff frost-bound earth, but the fierce gales continued to blow and sleet showers doused the city. It was on such a foul morning when the wind rattled the window panes and the rain sloshed against the glass that I was sitting huddled by the electric fire, clasping a cup of hot coffee while trying to raise some enthusiasm for facing the day. I realised that I had to go back to work and soon. I had been scrounging on my savings such as they were for the last few months and as a result they had dwindled drastically and

* See **The Darkness of Death**, the fifth Johnny One Eye novel, for full details

were now in danger of disappearing altogether. I had turned down a couple of mundane cases simply because I couldn't face the prospect of returning to my old routine, pretending that everything was normal again. 'Pull yourself together man', would be the sentiment. 'What the hell, life goes on y'know!' Sorry, but I just couldn't accept that resilient and unfeeling philosophy.

However, as I sat in my cramped sitting room, staring at the small twisted orange wires of the electric fire gently vibrating with feeble warmth I came to accept that even mundane cases pay and I needed money. Even if I was just going to spend it on booze. I knew that it really was time to try and get back in the saddle as that stupid phrase has it. I could hear Benny's voice in my head: 'Work is the best antidote to sorrow, my boy.' Well, perhaps the old boy was right.

With some effort, I dragged myself down the hall to the bathroom. I gazed at myself in the mirror over the sink. It was probably the first time I really had looked at myself properly since before Max died. I was shocked by what I saw. Here was a stranger. A grey, hollow-cheeked ghost of a man, wearing a haggard parody of my face, was staring back at me. My vivid impersonation of a consumptive tramp was enhanced by the several days' growth of beard.

Suddenly I heard another voice inside my head. This time it was my own and surprisingly, shockingly, it came up with a new thought – something that had not crossed my mind until the image of the dissipated wreck in the mirror had prompted it. What would Max think? I asked myself. Would she be happy at the way you are behaving? Of course not. She wouldn't want you this way, would she? Not her Johnny. By turning into a self-pitying drunk I was letting her down. This realisation struck me hard. What a stupid bastard I was!

With some effort, I held back a sob and rooted in my toilet bag for my razor. 'Let's get rid of the fuzz for a start' I muttered to myself through gritted teeth.

Thirty minutes later, I was back in my sitting room fully dressed with a clean white shirt on and a smooth chin and combed hair. I still looked like death warmed up, but a much tidier version than before. As I checked myself out in the mirror I even afforded myself a smile. It was a stranger to my face and it had difficulty settling there but I persevered and made it stay for a few seconds before it slipped away into the ether. Perhaps I was only pretending to myself that I could do this but, I reckoned, if I stuck to the pretence maybe that would become its own reality. I'd just got to try.

As a reward for all my efforts, I sank in my armchair and lit a cigarette. Watching the bluish smoke spiral gently away from the amber tip, I made plans for my day.

My first port of call was St Saviour's Church, the little Catholic church situated in one of the thoroughfares off the Edgware Road. It was here where Max was buried. I managed to buy a limp bunch of daffodils to place on her grave. The rain had stopped, but dark clouds loured over me and the wind stabbed me and pinched my nose as I stood in the graveyard and had a brief conversation with my dead love. 'I'm back,' I said. 'Back as me. Back as you knew me. Well, almost. I still don't have that spring in my step but I'm going to try, my love. I'm going to try for you. Be the old Johnny Hawke I used to be. I'll never quite manage that, but... I'll try to make you proud of me.' I grinned and dabbed my moist eye.

As I turned to go I was conscious of someone standing close to me. It was Father Sanderson, the priest who had conducted Max's funeral and had been so kind and understanding towards me.

'Hello, Johnny,' he said, his blue eyes twinkling. 'How are you?'

I gave a gentle shrug. 'I think I'm on the mend.'

'That's good to hear. The pain of loss never quite goes away, nor should it, but it does become easier to bear. It's early days yet.'

I nodded.

'I wonder if I could have a word with you. I have a little problem you may be able to help me with.'

'Well, yes, of course, if you think I can be of any use.'

'How about a cup of tea and a digestive biscuit in my office? That should help warm you up. I must admit you look like a frozen ghost.'

I grinned. 'I'm anybody's for a cuppa and a biscuit.'

* * *

21

Father Sanderson's office was a cramped little chamber just beyond the vestry. It smelled of damp, dust and altar candles. Various tomes were piled up along the walls and there were a couple of bentwood chairs and a bench which also held books as well as a gas ring, kettle and other tea-making equipment. Alongside these were several goblets and a bottle of what I assumed was communion wine standing on an old newspaper. Around the base of the bottle, the paper was spotted with dried splashes of the wine, creating a delicate pattern in varying hues of red.

'Sit yourself down, Johnny, and I'll brew up.'

I did as he asked, wrapping my overcoat around me. For my money it was colder in here that it was outside in the graveyard. A few minutes later I was sipping a cup of scalding hot tea and nibbling on a damp digestive.

'Sorry to bother you, but I'm in a bit of a quandary, really,' said the old cleric as he seated himself opposite me. He had a kind, heavily wrinkled face framed by a thatch of thick white hair. I guessed that he was in his seventies, but he could have been younger: it was just that his desiccated skin and stooped shoulders suggested otherwise.

'I know you are a kind of detective, Johnny, and I thought you might be able to offer me some advice,' he began hesitantly. It was obvious that he felt awkward about having to approach me in this way.

'If I can,' I said. 'What's the problem?'

'It's one of my parishioners, Annie Salter. She's a widow. A lady in her fifties. Lost a son at Dunkirk. Been a regular at St Saviour's for many a year. A few weeks ago I found her in the church. She was praying in one of the pews near the altar and seemed upset. She was muttering something. I could not hear the words but it was quite clear that she was asking for help – for divine assistance. I stood in the shadows not wanting to interrupt her private moment. From time to time she would pause in order to stifle a sob and then she would begin again. My heart went out to the poor soul. Whatever afflicted her, it was tearing her apart.

'I waited at the back of the church while she had finished and then as she made to leave I approached her. I could see clearly that she'd been crying – and I thought I might be able to help her. Offer comfort, at least.'

'What is troubling you, my dear?' I asked, taking her hands in mine.

She tried to shrug off her distress with a faint smile. 'I'm all right, really. Just feeling a little low. Came in to ask Jesus for some help. It's the war, isn't it? Sometimes it gets you down a bit.'

I knew that she was not telling me the truth. Not the full story, at least. I told her that I was there to listen, to help. I was one of Jesus's helpers. Perhaps I could come to her aid. My offer of help seemed to upset her more than ever.

'At the moment, I don't think anyone can help me,' she told me as her eyes moistened again. Then she pulled her hands from mine and hurried away without further words or a backward glance.

'That was the last time I saw her.'

I said nothing. I knew that there was more to come. There had to be.

'The following Sunday, Annie did not turn up for the Sunday service. I had not known her to miss in three years, apart from one occasion when she was struck down with influenza. The following morning, I went round to her house to see if she was ill and needed some help. There was no reply when I knocked on the door. I knocked hard, I can tell you, Johnny.' He smiled. 'A priest always does. Sometimes the householder will hide behind the door hoping I'll go away. If you bang loud enough, eventually guilt makes them open up.' His smile broadened and then faded quickly. 'But on this occasion there was no reply. I was just about to leave when the lady next door popped her head over her threshold. 'I've not seen her since Friday. I reckon she might have gone away,' she said. 'Where to?' I asked and received a puzzled shrug in response.

'Annie's behaviour in church and her absence prayed on my mind. I was worried about her – so much so that I visited the house again the following Thursday. Still there was no reply. My concern grew. I thought it was time to take further action so I went down to the local bobby shop on Frampton Street. They know me down there and took my concerns seriously. Sergeant Harmsworth came back to the house with me and after the rigmarole of knocking and waiting, waiting but no response, he applied his weight to the door and forced it open. 'It'll be up to you, Father, to pay for any repairs,' he said trying to lighten the mood of the operation. We stood on the threshold and he called out Annie's name. His voice echoed through the innards of the house but no one answered. I feared the worst. And so did Sergeant Harmsworth if his grim features were anything to go by. We moved into the tiny hallway and then into the kitchen. All was neat and tidy. All perfectly normal, I suppose. And then we came into the living room. It was terrible, Johnny. Simply terrible. There she was dangling from one of the beams, her mouth agape, tongue sticking out, her eyes… her eyes… well, it was terrible.'

'She'd hung herself.'

Father Sanderson shot me a glance. 'Well, that's what it looked like. There was a dressing gown cord tied around her neck and a stool on its side under her. And there was a note on the mantelpiece.'

'What did it say?'

'I can tell you exactly what it said. Just five words only. 'I just couldn't go on.'

'A fairly traditional sentiment for a suicide.'

'Mmm. Exactly. Traditional. Cliché even. Oh, the police are quite convinced that poor Annie committed suicide.' He paused and flashed me a piercing glance.

'But you're not,' I said.

'No, I'm not. It's not her way. She was far more stoical than that. She's not a quitter. And another thing… that note. It's not her writing.'

'You told the police this.'

'Of course I did. They just said that when a person is in a disturbed phase of mind their handwriting goes haywire. They can't control their movements or some such notion. But I know, Johnny, I know that Annie did not write that note. Apart from the writing, it was too brief and trite for Annie.'

'What are you saying?' I asked, fairly certain I knew the answer anyway.

Father Sanderson looked me in the eye and said sternly, 'I am saying that she was murdered.'

THREE

Dr Francis Sexton sat in his car and stared through the windscreen at the forbidding building before him. Even on a bright day in March when the sky was making every effort to shrug off the greyness of winter and allow little patches of blue to appear, Newfield House looked bleak and gloomy. To Sexton the building, stark against the bright sky with drab stonework marked with the strands of long-dead ivy, and the strange acute angles of the gables, along with the blank shuttered windows, made the place look like an illustration from a work by Edgar Allan Poe – *The Fall of the House of Usher* – maybe. The house, an early Victorian monstrosity, stood in isolation in its own grounds, now uncared for and neglected, like the inmates within.

Sexton shifted his gaze to the paint-peeling notice erected near the main door:

Newfield House

Psychiatric Hospital

No Unauthorised Admittance

Home Office Property

Newfield House, once the house of some rich industrialist, had been converted to a lunatic asylum for the criminally insane as an overflow of Broadmoor and had only been renamed within the last ten years. The name may have changed but the purpose and régime remained more or less as it always had. There was little psychiatry practised there. It was just a matter of keeping the inmates contained and sedated. The state had seen fit not to hang them, so instead they must rot in a drug-induced state in this God forsaken place near the Essex marshes. Sexton could understand and to some extent sympathise with these sentiments. The twenty inmates had all committed horrendous crimes while 'the balance of their mind was affected.' Madmen, then. But as Sexton knew, madmen could also be rational and reasonable for most of the time. It should be possible to rehabilitate these creatures so they could return to society. They did not ask to be mad – just as a man who is deaf or blind or a fellow with a lisp did not ask for these disabilities. Madness was a disability. It was Fate or God who allowed it. It was up to man to help, not to condemn. That, at least, was the litany that Dr Francis Sexton preached and that is why the authorities with great reluctance allowed him to attend one of the inmates at Newfield for 'research purposes'. Sexton was writing a book on the human psyche with particular attention to the diseased criminal brain. That is what the authorities believed and that is why they permitted Dr Francis Sexton to visit Newfield the third Thursday in every month to spend time with one of its notorious inmates: Ralph Northcote.

* * *

The said inmate Dr Ralph Northcote waited for his visitor in a small, featureless room that had become his home for the last eight years. His cell, in fact. It consisted of a bed – clamped to the floor so that it could not be moved – a chair, a washbasin, and a small bookshelf crammed with medical volumes he had managed to retain from his old life and a barred window which was too high for him to peer out of, even if he stood on the chair, which he had no inclination to do. Northcote was no longer the lithe, clean-shaven charmer of his younger days. Not being able to shave unless under strict supervision, he had grown a straggly beard while boredom had led him to consume as much of the foul institutionalised food as he could. He was now a rotund, heavily bearded, blotchy-faced parody of his former self, looking much older than his forty-eight years. He certainly no longer resembled the man who had stood in the dock accused of a series of horrendous crimes. The man the press named as 'The Ghoul'.

Northcote was particularly excited about today's visit from his new friend, Francis. His monthly visits had become the highlight of his life in this dreary place. They thought him mad and that's why they had dumped him in this hellhole, to be forgotten, to rot until death. He wished they had hanged him. That, at least, would have been the end of it. He was not mad. He had known what he was doing. He would do it again – given half the chance. His passion for raw flesh may seem strange to the outside world, but to him it was no different from stuffing your face with bits of dead cow, pig or chicken. He was convinced that it was because of this fact that the judge hadn't dared to pass the death sentence. The old fool knew he was not mad but couldn't condemn him for his unusual appetite.

At first he had resented Francis Sexton's visits. He only agreed to them because they would bring some kind of novelty to his drab routine. But he didn't want to be scrutinised, analysed, compartmentalised and patronised. However, he soon realised that Francis would do none of these things. He had come in a spirit of friendship. Of course, he asked questions – wanted to know things about him, his history, his thoughts, what made him tick. But friends did that. And they had become friends. He knew that Francis grew to value these visits as much as he did. Northcote believed that a bond had grown between them and that was because Francis really understood him and his predilection.

Francis was the only one who had really listened to him, listened and understood his passion. He felt at ease with this man and was able to tell him things he had never confided to anyone else. Things about his childhood and his first encounter with uncooked flesh and the revelations that this had brought about. Francis never condemned or criticised him. Indeed, he began to smuggle in little treats: a piece of liver, a small cut of beef, and some pork. All uncooked and red with blood. It was their little secret. A secret that bonded them even closer.

And then the plan had developed. An idle remark. A casual aside. But it had created a spark with gradually ignited and the plan flickered into life.

And today was the day to put it into operation.

Through an innate ability to master his emotions, and a learned facility developed from being shut away in this Godforsaken dump, Northcote was able to maintain a cool and collected outlook even when exciting and dangerous things were about to happen. As he sat in his cell patiently waiting for the arrival of his visitor, the observer would have noticed nothing about his appearance to suggest a mood of suppressed anticipation and excitement. Except perhaps for the gentle – ever so gentle – movement of Northcote's thumbs. While all other parts of his body remain statue-like still, his thumbs circled each outer in a lazy moribund fashion. It was the one chink in his armour, his one expression of inner excitement. Meanwhile the eyes were dead, glacial and dead, and the body remained rigid with the feet splayed flat on the floor. You could hardly tell the man was breathing.

But the thumbs continued to move like comatose butterflies.

* * *

As was his usual practice, Dr Francis Sexton kept on his hat, scarf and coat once he was inside the building. He was such a regular visitor to Newfield that he only had to flash his authorisation in a casual fashion to the guard on reception before he was allowed to pass through the locked section into the hospital.

'You here again?' asked the guard in a cheery fashion, hardly looking up from his library book, a western with the title 'Me, Outlaw'.

Sexton nodded.

'Hardly seems five minutes since the last visit.' The man chuckled. 'Time flies when you're having fun.' He chuckled again at his own sarcasm and returned to the dust of Arizona.

Sexton made his way to E block where Northcote's cell was situated. It was a cold, gloomy building with the smell of damp and decay always in the air. The décor was a mixture of the faded and neglected original Victorian furnishings and the utilitarian touches institutionalised grimness. He passed a few staff on his way but no one took much notice of him or gave him a greeting.

Eventually he reached E block and passed through swing doors which led him down a short tiled corridor at the end of which was Northcote's cell: E 2. A young man in a white coat sat outside the room. It looked to Sexton as though he had dropped off to sleep – and who could blame him, sitting on guard outside a madman's room just in case he became unruly, agitated, violent. To Sexton's knowledge, Northcote had exhibited none of these symptoms since he had been admitted eight years ago. The sound of Sexton's shoes clipping sharply on the tiled floor seemed to rouse the young man from his doze. He glanced up and observed the approaching visitor. Before the doctor was upon him, he recognised that grey overcoat and the black fedora. He rose to his feet and taking a key from the pocket of his white coat he slipped it into the door.

'A glutton for punishment, I reckon that's what you are,' grinned the young man sleepily.

Sexton emitted a non-committal grunt.

The door swung open and he entered the cell. No sooner had he done so than the door clanged to behind him.

Northcote rose from his chair and the two men stood facing each other, neither of them opening their mouths, but their eyes spoke volumes. Gradually Northcote raised his right arm, and extended it towards his visitor. Sexton took it and the two men shook hands.

'Dr Sexton, it is so good to see you,' said Northcote in his strange gravelly voice, which had developed since his incarceration. He spoke little, hardly a few sentences a day, and it was as though his vocal chords had become rusty and were in danger of seizing up.

'And you too, Ralph,' he said with a ghost of a smile, as he placed his briefcase on the floor.

Northcote's eyes darted in its direction, wide with anticipation. 'You have perhaps brought me some treats.'

'Later. For now, it is time to get rid of that beard.'

Opening the briefcase he extracted a small cardboard box and handed it to Northcote. It contained a pair of scissors, a shaving brush and a piece of shaving soap. 'Put the débris in the box,' said Sexton.

Moving to the little sink with a piece of aluminium which acted as a mirror, he began chopping away at his unruly growth. Sexton, took off his hat, coat and scarf and sat on the bed to watch. Ten minutes later, Northcote had completed his task. Scratching his chin, he turned to his visitor. 'Well, what do you think?'

'Well, you look like the ghost of Christmas Past, but at least you don't look like you did.'

'Feels strange,' Northcote said, rubbing his chin. 'But that's good. Anything which has a touch of novelty is good in this place. Now, can I have my little treats?'

Sexton nodded and retrieved a small damp brown bag from his briefcase. 'A little liver,' he said. 'Fresh meat is very hard to come by at this time,'

'The war, you mean?'

'Yes, the war.'

Northcote shook his head. 'I know nothing of the war in this shabby cocoon.' He tore open the bag and his eyes flickered with glee at the sight of the slimy red offal. There were two pieces each about the size of a child's hand. He snatched one up and slapped it to his mouth and chewing on it noisily for a few seconds, sucking the blood from it, before he bit into it. He gave a gurgle of delight as he chomped on a ragged fragment. Sexton watched with fascination as with the serious deliberation of an animal Northcote devoured the liver, slowly but with enthusiastic relish. When he had finished his lips and cheeks were smeared red. He looked like a crazy clown.

'You'd better clean your face,' said Sexton with a half smile.

'A little water clears us of this deed,' replied Northcote moving to the sink where he ran the tap and swilled the blood away. He stared as blood, now pink diluted by the water, spiralled away down the plughole.

'Thank you,' he said. 'That was most tasty. I get nothing like that in here. Everything is incinerated before it reaches a plate.'

Sexton ignored the remark. He had heard many similar ones before. It was Northcote's usual and predictable mantra after consuming his meaty titbit.

'Are you ready? Are you prepared?'

Northcote nodded. 'I am.'

* * *

The young man was interrupted from his day dream – a languorous affair that featured one of his favourite film stars in a state of undress – by a tapping on the door of cell E 2.

'My session is over. I'm ready to leave now. Thank you,' said a voice.

It was exactly the same set of words Dr Sexton used on every occasion he visited.

The young man roused himself and unlocked the cell.

'Thank you,' said Sexton gruffly, pulling down his hat and then hurrying off along the corridor.

Some minutes later, he passed the guard on reception with a brief wave and was soon out into the growing dusk, breathing the free fresh air for the first time in eight years.

* * *

The evening meal, if such a grand term could be used for the lukewarm slop that was usually served up for the inmates of Newfield, was dished up at around six in the evening. And so it was on this occasion. The young man, still on duty, was presented with a tray by one of the kitchen staff. It contained a plate of mashed potatoes and some greyish meat substitute and piece of bread and a glass of water.

'For his lordship,' said the skivvy with a sneer.

The young man grinned and unlocked the cell door.

'Grub up,' he called as he entered. What met his eyes caused him to drop the tray. It clattered noisily on the tiled floor, the food spilling widely, some of it onto the trousers of the prone figure which was slumped face downwards by the bed.

The young man bent down and turned him over. The sight that met his eyes caused him to emit a strange strangled cry.

The unconscious face belonged to Dr Francis Sexton. He had a deep cut to his forehead which was seeping blood down his face.

'My God!' cried the young man. 'Christ!' he added for good measure.

For a moment these exclamations were all he felt capable of. He was shocked and stunned into inaction by this weird turn of events.

Gradually, his brain began to function and the situation before him came into focus. He rose to his feet and rushed into the corridor to press the alarm bell.

Out in the darkened car park, the man in Dr Francis Sexton's coat and hat unlocked the boot of his car and clambered inside.

FOUR

I sat staring at the pint of beer before me, watching the minute bubbles that were clinging to the rim of the glass disappear one by one. Fascinating though this vision was, my thoughts were elsewhere. I was running my interview with Father Sanderson over again in my mind. It was now lunchtime and I had sought shelter and sustenance – a pint and a cheese sandwich – in a small pub near the church.

The conversation – the one about the hanged woman whom Sanderson thought had been murdered – intrigued me as a detective. He was so convinced that the police had got it wrong, read the signs incorrectly and/or were happy to tidy up yet another death into the solved drawer. Well, it wouldn't be the first time this had happened. I was a copper before the war and I knew how desperate some officers were to wrap up an investigation as soon as possible and in a self imposed, blinkered fashion, accepting the probable as the truth rather than consider other options.

'I'd rather like you to investigate the matter, Johnny. Something is rotten in the state of Denmark, I'm afraid.'

'I'm not sure I'm the man to do the job,' I said, my feet already getting cold. I wasn't confident that I was up to this investigation and besides…

'Oh, I expect this to be a professional arrangement. I will pay you, of course.'

I shook my head vigorously. 'I couldn't accept money from you…'

'Because I'm a priest? A man of the cloth?'

My expression must have told him that he was correct in his

assumption. How could I charge this impoverished old cleric for my services? And yet how could I afford the time and expenses to carry out an investigation for him? I was impoverished too.

'But I'm your client,' he responded with some warmth, his cheeks flushing. 'I have a little money put away for a rainy day and I reckon this is it. I was very fond of Annie. I wish to engage your services. This is not a favour I'm asking: I want to see justice done.'

Reluctantly I agreed, but I had little needles of guilt pricking me at the idea of taking money from the old fellow.

So that was it. My first case in the new year. My first case since the death of Max. I raised my glass of the now rather flat beer in a toast to the beginning of the rehabilitation of John Hawke.

While I was in the vicinity, I visited the police station on Frampton Street and as luck would have it, Sergeant Harmsworth was on desk duty. I explained who I was and Father Sanderson's concerns. Harmsworth grinned. He seemed an affable, comfortable chap, easy going if a little bovine. Unlike some coppers, he did not seem at all concerned that I was a private detective meddling in their affairs.

'Oh, I know all about the Father's theory that the old bird was murdered. I suppose being a man of God, he likes a little mystery. But I can tell you, there was nothing mysterious about Annie Salter's death. She hung herself. Plain and simple. There was not a scrap of evidence that a second party was involved. She even left a note.'

I nodded sympathetically to create the impression that I agreed with him fully and that Father Sanderson's notions were groundless.

'Could I see the note?' I asked.

'If we've still got it. Hang on. I'll have a look in the back office.'

He shifted his ample frame off his stool and disappeared into the far reaches of the station, returning a few minutes later holding a piece of paper.

'Here you are, Mr Hawke,' he grinned again, passing me the note. It was written in pencil on a scrap of paper torn from a cheap note book. There were the words as I had been told: 'I just can't go on any longer.' The handwriting was shaky and clumsy – whether this was as a result of emotion was a matter of contention.

'Father Sanderson says that this is not Annie Salter's handwriting,' I said casually.

Harmsworth shrugged. 'We'd nothing to judge it against, but as far as we could tell old Sanderson didn't have much familiarity with her writing in any case. And besides, if you are going to top yourself, the last thing you're gonna do is write in your best handwriting, are you? The hand'll be shaking too much for your actual copperplate.' He chuckled at his own conceit.

I turned the note over. The paper was blank but there was a little stain in the bottom corner.

'You can keep it if you like,' said Harmsworth, hoisting himself back on his stool. 'We've no use for it now.'

'Thank you,' I said graciously, slipping the note in my pocket. I reckoned I had seen more in that scrap of paper than the ample sergeant and his colleagues had.

My first real task was to find out more about Annie Salter: her history and her circumstances. Father Sanderson had been able to jot down the address of her cousin, a Mrs Frances Coulson, the only blood relative to attend the funeral. She lived in Chelmsford and her rather bijou semi-detached house was to be my first port of call.

If anything the day had grown more miserable by the time I had travelled to Chelmsford and found my way to Worthington Avenue. The sky had coagulated into a uniform dark grey and the wind had sharpened, piercing the folds of my overcoat causing me to shiver involuntarily.

Father Sanderson had told me that Frances Coulson was a woman in her mid-forties. She was a widow. Her husband had been something important in one of the city banks and had left her reasonably well provided for. That was all. I got the impression that he would have liked to tell me more about the woman, but he held back. No doubt he did not want to colour my impression of the lady. He thought I should make up my own mind about her. I was the detective after all. However, his reticence in this matter suggested to me that there was something he didn't quite like about Mrs Frances Coulson.

The Coulson dwelling was a very neat affair indeed: neat privet hedge, neat rectangular lawn, and neat shiny knocker on a neat green front door. I knocked, straightened my tie and waited.

I heard a voice somewhere in the house calling out, 'Coming.'

And indeed in less than a minute she came. Frances Coulson opened the door bringing with her a strong whiff of pungent perfume. When she saw me, the broad crimson grin disappeared almost immediately from her lips and her eyebrows lowered with disdain. I was either a great disappointment to her or she had been expecting someone else. I decided it was both.

'You're not selling anything, are you?' she said, managing to inject a sneer into the query.

I raised my hat and proffered my card. 'I'd like to have a little chat with you about Annie Salter,' I said gently with a polite smile.

She studied my card for a moment. 'Some detective you are,' she observed sourly, the sneer still in place. 'Haven't you heard? Annie Salter's dead.'

I nodded. 'Yes, I know. That's why I wanted a little chat with you.'

'What's this all about?'

'Well, if we can have that chat, I can explain.'

Indecision clouded her features for a moment and then she sighed. 'Very well, you'd better come in – but only for five minutes mind. I am expecting a visitor.'

That explained the crimson smile then.

Mrs Coulson was an attractive woman, full bodied, veering towards the stout with a smooth complexion which she attempted to hide with too much face powder. She wore a pin-striped pencil skirt and a tight angora sweater which emphasised her curves, which were substantial. At a little over five foot she was too short for my liking, but I can imagine many a middle-aged gent taking a fancy to the sweet-smelling and curvy Mrs C.

She lead me into the lounge, which like her was attractive, if a little over the top. Vibrant cushions, shiny trinkets and a garish rug clamoured for attention with the rather nauseous patterned wallpaper. There was a wedding photograph in a silver frame on the sideboard. It showed a younger but similarly over-dressed version of Mrs C with her husband outside a registrar office. She was in large checked suit with fox furs and a ridiculous hat; he, a weedy incongruous fellow, was draped in a pin striped suit that seemed two sizes two big for him and had a grin which suggested he couldn't believe how lucky he was to have this lovely creature on his arm and, indeed, in his bed.

The gramophone in the corner was playing a dance tune when we entered the room but, with quick staccato movements, Mrs C stopped it, replacing the lid with a sharp snap.

She didn't ask me to sit down or offer me a drink. She really did mean five minutes.

'What's all this about, then?' she snapped, standing with her back to the fireplace and giving me a gorgon stare.

'There is some concern… some doubt as to the manner of Annie's death and so…'

'Nonsense. She committed suicide. Didn't they find her hanging from her own ceiling? And she left a note.'

'The authenticity of the note has been called into question.'

'Authenticity? You mean whether she wrote it.'

I nodded. 'The handwriting…'

'She was distressed. She was just about to top herself. Her handwriting would have been all over the place…' She paused her eyes widening with feline ferocity. 'What are you suggesting?'

'It's possible that she didn't kill herself.'

She looked shocked at this suggestion. Whether she was acting, I couldn't tell. If she was, it was a good performance.

'You mean that she was… that someone killed her?'

I said nothing.

'That's ridiculous,' she said, reaching for a cigarette box on the mantelpiece. 'Who'd want to kill her? For what reason?'

'Sometimes there doesn't have to be a reason.'

There came that stare again. It almost came with a cat-like hiss this time.

'You're not with the police, are you?'

'No. My client is not satisfied with the suicide verdict. He's asked me to investigate.'

'Who is this lunatic, your client?'

'I'm not at liberty to say. It's a confidential matter, you understand.'

Frances Coulson rolled her eyes. 'Oh, I understand. Okay then, Dick Tracy, what do you want to know?'

'Anything you can tell me about Annie. You were cousins.'

'We were cousins, yes, but in our case blood wasn't thicker than water. I knew her best when I was a kid and I didn't care much for her then. She was twelve years older than me and she used to look after me when mother went out.'

'Why didn't you like her?'

'She was too prim and proper. A real goody two shoes. She was no fun. And she remained no fun all her life. Hanging herself just about summed her up.'

'What do you know of her marriage? Her son?'

Suddenly Frances Coulson emitted a strange laugh. I guessed it was one of amusement but it was chilling in its sharpness and ferocity.

'What's so funny?' I ventured.

'That was when Madam Goody Two Shoes fell by the wayside. There was no marriage. The lady was no widow. She just got herself pregnant with the first man who showed any interest in her. And as soon as he'd got her into bed, he disappeared from sight and who could blame him. She invented the phantom hubby for the sake of respectability. Once the baby was born, she turned to religion and never let another man near her.'

'What about her son?'

'Malcolm? Don't know much about him. I only met him a couple of times. He could twist his mother round his little finger, though. Still, mustn't speak ill of the dead. Poor bugger copped it at Dunkirk. He was only nineteen.'

'When was the last time you saw Annie?'

'Oh, God, that was years ago... no, hang on a minute, I tell a lie. I bumped into her by accident a few months back when I was up in town. I was meeting a friend to go to the pictures and I'd just popped into Woolworth's down Oxford Street and when I came out I ran into

Annie.'

'How did she seem?'

Frances Coulson shrugged. 'Much the same as always: dowdy and a bit miserable. No, actually she was more than a bit miserable. She seemed quite distracted. She didn't really want to talk, which was fine by me because we have… had… nothing in common. I mean blood ties stand for nothing, do they? There's more fallings out between families… Just because you're related doesn't mean you have to get on, have to like one another, does it? Anyway, I must admit I did feel a bit sorry for the poor old cow that last time. She seemed so down and …old. She'd aged quite a bit. I suppose looking back, I can now see that she was probably depressed. Obviously she got worse and couldn't face going on anymore. And so…'

'Did she give any clues as to why she was depressed?'

'No. I asked her how life was treating her and she said something about God helping her to carry on.'

'What about friends? Do you know if she had any?'

'If she did, she never mentioned them to me. There might have been some sad soul at her church that she cottoned on to but somehow I doubt it. She was always a lonely woman, solitary, and when Malcolm died she shifted right back into her shell.' With a dramatic gesture she stubbed out her cigarette. 'If you want my advice, Mr Detective Man, I should abandon this wild goose chase. It's clear to me that Annie Salter committed suicide because she saw no reason to go on living. The idea of someone murdering her is plain daft. Why on earth would anyone want to? For what reason? How would her death benefit anyone? Forget it.'

She moved to the door and swung it open to indicate that the interview was over. That was OK by me. It was clear that I wouldn't be squeezing any more juice out of this particular orange. However, I was convinced she had told me all she wanted me to hear. That there was more to the story was certain, but I wouldn't get it from her.

'Thanks,' I said, heading through the hall to the outer door. 'You've been a great help.'

I could manipulate the truth also.

To be fair, the chat with the sparky Mrs Coulson hadn't been a complete waste of time. It did help me start to build up a picture, albeit one-sided at the moment, of the dead woman.

As I walked down the street, I passed a smart wiry fellow who seemed in a great hurry. He was the sort of chap one saw at the dog track: tweed jacket, bright yellow waistcoat, extremely shiny brogues and a trilby perched precariously on one side of his head. He had marked aquiline features but shifty with it. I suppose he was quite good looking if you go for that sort of thing. I reckoned Mrs Coulson did for I turned and watched his progress and saw that he moved swiftly up her garden path and rang the bell with alacrity. So, he was the reason I had only the five minutes.

* * *

On my way back into town, to my neck of the woods, I selected the information I thought was relevant and useful from my conversation with the prickly Mrs Coulson and filed it for further use. I reckoned that now I needed a more in depth chat with my client, Father Sanderson. At the moment he seemed to be the only person who could give me more unbiased details about Annie Salter's character and circumstances. Unbiased? Well, maybe I was being naïve.

Something the delectable Mrs Coulson had said was very pertinent to my investigation: 'How would her death benefit anyone?' The answer to that was the key to the whole matter. It usually boils down to motive. Why had Annie been killed? What purpose did her death serve? And to whom? That is what I had to discover. It was a challenge, but I had been faced with such challenges before and succeeded.

One thing I had realised in making my brief excursion to Chelmsford was that I had begun to feel a little bit like my old self again. It was good to be on the scent once more and exercising my detective skills, however modest. In fact I even managed a smile, a genuine one this time.

With this lightening of my mood, I decided that it was time to repair a few fences. It wasn't that I had fallen out with Benny, my old friend the café owner who had mother-henned me for years, it was that I had shunned him in recent months. I couldn't put up with his kindness and solace. I was hurting too much. I didn't want kind words and pots of tea. I was selfish, I suppose: I wanted to wallow unsolicited in my own grief.

It was growing dark when I reached his café. It was nearing closing time and there were just a couple of customers, each huddled over a cup of tea staring into space. Benny was at the counter reading a newspaper. He looked up as I entered, his face registering a mixture of emotions. It was clear that he didn't know whether he ought to be pleased or dismayed at my appearance.

'Any chance of tea and toast?' I said cheerily.

For a few moments Benny still remained uncertain how to react, so I broadened my grin. 'Today would be good.'

Benny's face suddenly lit up with pleasure. 'Today it is. Grab a seat and I'll have it with you in a trice.' With a little chuckle, he hurried off to the kitchen.

Five minutes later I was munching toast lavishly smothered with margarine and strawberry jam while Benny sat opposite me, an indulgent grin wreathing his features.

'So… how have you been?' he asked gently, testing the water.

'Miserable. Feeling sorry for myself, but I think I'm starting to crawl out of that particular hole.'

'That's good. That's what we all want: the old Johnny back.'

'I'm not so sure you'll get that, but I'll try not to be a pain in the backside.'

Benny rolled his eyes. 'The old Johnny was always a pain in the backside.'

I nodded wearily. I reckoned that Benny was right.

Suddenly his features darkened. 'You should see Peter. He's been missing you. He comes in here twice a week and mopes. He's deliberately stayed away from you because he feels you don't want to see him…'

I shook my head with dismay. 'That's not true. It's just… it's just…'

Benny touched my arm. 'I know. But he's very young still. A tender shrub. Despite his height and long trousers, he's still just a kid and kids need love and affection.'

'What about the girlfriend? How's that going?'

'Oh, well, I think there has been some cooling off there.' He grinned. 'The flames of passion have waned a little. As I say he's still just a kid. He needs some mature advice.'

'I'm not sure I'm qualified to offer it. Look at the mess my life is in.'

'Hey, I thought we had stopped feeling sorry for ourself. Count your blessings, Mr Hawke. There are many folk in this town in a far worse state than you. You lost a loved one. Yes. But there are thousands out there in that same big boat. Remember with fondness and grieve for them but get on with your life. Grieve for them – not for yourself.'

As always, Benny was the source of sound advice.

FIVE

Gingerly Dr Sexton touched the bandages that covered the wounds on the back of his head.

'I reckon you'll have a stinker of a headache for quite a few days, sir' observed Inspector Horace Wisden gravely. He was a big man with a face like a rumpled pillow which housed a pair of kindly brown eyes.

'Yes. But I suppose I should be grateful that the brute didn't kill me.'

'Too true,' replied the inspector in a distracted fashion as he turned over the pages of his notebook.

They were sitting in a small office in Newfield House. It was here that Sexton had been bandaged by one of the medical orderlies after it had been established that he had suffered only surface wounds. He had then been interviewed by Wisden who had arrived on the scene with a body of men shortly after the alarm was given of Northcote's escape. The officers were searching the grounds while Sexton gave his statement.

'Well, I think we've got all the information that you can give us at the moment. It may be that we will call on you again, of course.'

'Does that mean I can go?'

'Well, yes, but are you sure you're safe to drive? I mean …a blow to the head.'

'Oh, I'm perfectly fine apart from the headache. I'm not likely to keel over at the wheel and I can see perfectly well. No double vision.'

Wisden seemed unconvinced. 'If you're sure.'

Sexton nodded gently. 'I'm sure.' He rose eagerly and made his way to the door but Wisden took hold of his sleeve and held him back. Sexton's heart skipped a beat.

'There was just one thing, sir.'

'Yes.' Sexton's voice was dry and tense.

'Well, I reckon you probably know this Northcote as well as anyone. The workings of his brain, I mean.'

Sexton gazed at the police inspector non-committally and said nothing.

'In your opinion, what is the fellow likely to do now that's he's out, escaped? Where do you think he will go? What will he do?'

'I am sorry but I can't really help you there. You see there's no logic in a mind like his. A mind without reason is unfathomable. We can sometimes discover what stimulates such violent and antisocial behaviour but one cannot predict what such a creature will do. It's a cliché, Inspector, but I'm afraid your guess is as good as mine.'

'Do you think he will try to kill again?'

Sexton gave a bleak smile. 'Oh, yes. I am quite sure of that.'

* * *

Dr Sexton stood on the steps by the main door of Newfield House and breathed in the cold night air. Already the frost was forming on the bushes and exposed rooftops of the outbuildings and his breath escaped in little white clouds. A number of police officers, their torches like mini-searchlights, were roaming the grounds in search of the fugitive.

It was a futile task.

Sexton made his way to his car. On reaching it, he tapped three times on the boot lid, paused and tapped three times again. After a brief pause, he heard the same set of taps repeated by the resident within the boot. Sexton beamed and swung himself into the driver's seat. Within minutes he had passed through the gates of the institution and was out on the open road.

* * *

Just over an hour later, he pulled into the drive of his detached house. Unlocking the garage, he drove the car inside and then closed the doors before pulling open the boot of the car. The occupant within, who had been hunched into a ball slowly unfurled himself with a groan. With the help of Sexton he managed to clamber out of the boot. With a further groan, he stood erect. For some moments neither man spoke.

Northcote eventually stretched, his arms reaching above his head and grinned. 'That feels good,' he said at length, almost to himself.

'Let's go into the house and get you settled in your quarters,' said Sexton with some eagerness. He was anxious to have the fugitive out of sight.

'Lead on,' replied Northcote easily. He was enjoying himself.

Once inside the house, Sexton drew the curtains in the sitting room before switching on the lights. Northcote slumped down in an arm chair, his feet splaying out before him. 'This is grand,' he said, still grinning. 'After what I've been used to it's like the Ritz.'

'A cup of tea or something stronger?'

'Tea will do just fine for now. I reckon I need to find my sea legs before I get onto the liquor with not having had a drop for eight years.'

'O.K. I won't be a moment. Then we can talk.' Sexton bustled off into the kitchen.

Left alone Northcote sat back, closed his eyes and relaxed. He couldn't remember the last time he felt so contented. He could hear the rattling of tea cups and the gush of water into the kettle and the popping of the gas ring in the kitchen – ordinary domestic noises that were music to his ears. He had almost fallen asleep by the time Sexton returned with a tea tray.

The tea was dark brown and strong. Northcote gulped it down. 'Not your normal brew, is it?'

'Earl Grey. Very refreshing. Would you care for another cup?'

'Yes, I think I will.'

Sexton poured him another cup. He himself had settled for a gin and tonic.

'Smooth as a baby's bottom, eh?' said Northcote as he sipped his second cup of tea, his voice heavy and tired.

Sexton nodded. Automatically his fingers reached for his bandaged scalp. As he pressed gently, he felt a small twinge of pain. 'You certainly gave me a bit of a headache,' he observed drily. There was no humour in his voice.

Northcote gave a lazy grin. 'Sorry about that but we needed some authenticity.'

He stumbled over the word 'authenticity' and shook his head slowly as if to dislodge the overpowering sensation of tiredness that was creeping over him. It was as if all the life in his body was being drained from him.

'Authenticity,' he repeated in the same clumsy manner before allowing the cup and saucer to fall from his grasp. His eyes widened momentarily in dreamy surprise as the room swirled about him, he slumped backwards unconscious in the chair.

'Sweet dreams,' said Sexton, smiling at last. 'Time to escort you to your new home.'

* * *

When Ralph Northcote regained consciousness, he found that he was lying on a camp bed in a darkened chamber, illuminated by one dim electric light bulb dangling above his head. As the clouds of the drug slowly dissolved and his vision and mind stumbled back into focus, gradually he was able to take stock of his new surroundings. He saw that he was in a vaulted cellar, the limed walls of which were grubby and blemished with patches of green mould at irregular intervals. Confused as to where he was and why he was here, he tried to drag his body into a sitting position but had great difficulty in doing so. In fact he failed. Something was preventing him. It took his hazy mind a few seconds to realise why. His left hand was handcuffed to the metal bed head.

He was a prisoner.

Again.

He could not move from the confines of the bed.

Panic and distress overwhelmed him in an instant and he screamed. His utterance was loud and inarticulate, like a wounded animal caught in a trap – which in essence he was. Strangely he found some comfort and solace in screaming, so he continued. With his eyes screwed tight and his fingers clenched, he bellowed at the top of his voice.

Suddenly a door at the end of the dank chamber opened and a figure in a white coat entered. Northcote ceased yelling and, opening his eyes, he stared at the figure in disbelief as it approached the bed.

It was Francis Sexton.

'Ah, you've returned to the land of the living, eh?' he said smoothly, moving towards the bed, a self-satisfied grin touching his shadowy features. 'Strong stuff that tea.'

Northcote shook his head in a desperate attempt to dislodge this hallucination from his sight. This mad vision. Was he dreaming? Was this really happening? Or was he going crazy?

'What... what the hell is going on?' he asked, his voice tired from all his screaming, now reduced to a hoarse whisper.

'Welcome to your new home.' Sexton threw his arms out in a theatrical gesture to encompass the gloom.

Northcote shook his head miserably. 'I don't understand.'

'There's not a lot to understand. Simply, you're my prisoner now.'

'Prisoner? Why?' Northcote tugged on the handcuff. 'Why have you done this?'

'Because it suits my purposes, my plans.'

'What plans?'

'Oh, I don't think you need concern yourself with those for the moment. They do not require your active participation. Let us just say that you are simply my insurance, my alibi.'

Northcote felt a wave of despair crash over him. He didn't know what Sexton meant but he knew that he was in deep trouble. 'You can't do this to me,' he wailed. 'You and I were going to be partners...'

'Were we? In your dreams, my dear fellow. Why should I associate myself with an insane murderer?'

'You know I'm not insane.'

Sexton gave a little shrug as a wry smile touched his features briefly. 'Maybe I do, but that's not what the authorities think and will continue to think once I set to work.'

Northcote shook his head in confusion. The effects of the drug were still fogging his mind. 'What are you going to do?'

Sexton chuckled. 'Couldn't possibly tell you. Don't you know careless talk costs lives?' His laugh grew louder, echoing loudly inside Northcote's brain.

'Sweet dreams,' added Sexton softly as he made to leave. 'Don't let the bed bugs bite.' He switched out the light and closed the door. In the pitch darkness, Northcote could hear the key turning in the lock.

SIX

The vicarage of St Saviour's was a run down affair. The crumbling Victorian edifice had been an impressive adjunct to the church in its day but now it was in serious need of repair with damp and mould making a major invasion both inside and out. Father James Sanderson used only a few of the rooms, the rest were closed up and left for the insidious decay to take possession. It crossed my mind that it would almost be a blessing if the building received a direct hit on a Nazi bombing raid – providing no one was hurt – so that the place could be put out of its misery.

When I called that evening, Father Sanderson was just washing up a few dishes from his evening meal. He bade me take a seat by the meagre fire and offered me a cup of tea. Soon I would be awash with the stuff.

'I didn't expect to see you so soon,' he said, sitting opposite me. 'Don't tell me that you've made some progress already.'

'I won't tell you, because I haven't, but I realise that I need to know more about Annie Salter so I can start building up some theories. It's all a bit vague at the moment.'

This was a soft start to the questioning. I had decided to bide my time for the moment.

Sanderson shrugged his shoulders. 'I don't think I'm going to be much help to you. I doubt if I can tell you any more that I have already. I didn't know the woman's background all that well.'

'Who did?'

He shrugged again. 'I'm not sure.'

'What about neighbours?'

'Well, Annie was a very private person, she kept herself to herself but I believe she was quite friendly with the chap next door. Archie Dawson. He's an artist, cartoonist. He does a strip in one of the kids' comic cuts. He's at number 14. I got the impression from what she said that he kept a kindly eye on her.'

'Anyone else?'

'Not that I know of.'

'What about Annie's son?'

Sanderson screwed up his face as though he were in pain. 'He was a little devil. Got himself into trouble with the law before the war. I reckon if he hadn't gone into the army, he'd be back in gaol now.'

'Did he have any friends locally?'

'Malcolm made enemies not friends. You're not thinking that there's someone who might have a grudge against Malcolm who'd take it out on his mother?'

It was my turn to shrug. 'Not really. It would be a little convoluted and as the boy is dead there'd be little point. But, I suppose, stranger things have happened. I'm not ruling anything out yet.'

'You know best. You're the detective.'

These words did not cheer me. They just reminded me of the burden I was carrying. I remembered that earlier in the day I had regarded this case as a challenge. In a few short hours it had become a burden. Oh dear!

'What regiment was Malcolm assigned to?'

'The London Regiment, I think.'

'And there was no other member of the congregation that Annie was friendly with?'

Father Sanderson thought for a moment. 'Well, she shared the flower rota for the church with Mrs Dewhurst, Rita Dewhurst. I don't think the two women had much in common but they did sort of work together.'

Father Sanderson gave me her address and I made notes of all these names in my little notebook, although this procedure did not fill me with much hope. All they promised were a series of bland conversations à la Mrs Coulson. I reckoned it was time to grasp the nettle. If I was to get anywhere with this case, there was no room for holding back or pussy-footing around.

'Well,' I said, rising from my chair, 'thanks for your help, but no thanks for your hindrance.'

To my great satisfaction Sanderson's jaw dropped. 'I'm sorry,' he said, his voice full of uncertainty.

'And so am I. To be honest Father, I am puzzled. Do you really want me to find the murderer of Annie Salter?'

'Why bless you, of course I do.'

'Then I must ask you to stop prevaricating. You know more than you've told me. You have given me only half a tale and expect me to work with that. If Annie Salter was murdered, you know why. She has been distressed for some time. There was no one closer to her than you. She must have unburdened herself to you. But, for some reason, you and God were unable to help her. It was your guilt that led you to engage me, wasn't it?'

The priest turned from me, his body shaking with emotion. He muttered something but I did not catch what he said.

'Tell me,' I said, my voice rising in frustration. 'Help me.'

'I cannot,' he muttered, swinging around in the chair to face me once more, his eyes moist with tears.

'She told you something, didn't she? In confessional? That's what the box is for, after all, isn't it? For people to tell you their horrid truths. I reckon that she told you something that made you aware that she was in great danger. Greater than you realised.'

Father Sanderson said nothing but I could see from his expression and the haunted look in his damp eyes that I was on the right track.

'So when you found her hanging there, murdered, you wrote a suicide note in a strange hand to help convince the police that it was murder. But, unfortunately for you, they weren't having any of it.'

'You are a clever detective, after all,' said Father Sanderson, allowing himself a slight smile. 'How do you know?'

'Because you are not such a clever deceiver.' I fished the suicide note out of my pocket. 'This paper was torn out of a notebook. It is the identical kind of notepaper, in fact, on which you wrote Mrs Frances Coulson's address for me.' With a flourish I now produced this sheet and matched the two together.

'Careless, but not conclusive,' I continued. 'However, although you tried to disguise your handwriting in the note, you could not quite eradicate some of your own stylistics. The squashed 'e' and the little flourish on top of the 'o', for example. There is much personality in an individual's handwriting and like certain facial features, they are difficult to disguise. To be fair, you did quite well, but not well enough. On top of all that there was a small red stain in the bottom left corner. Communion wine, I suspect'.

Father Sanderson ran a bony hand through his thick crop of grey hair. 'I can see that I seriously underestimated you, Johnny.'

'It's easily done. Usually with just cause – but not in this instant. Anyway, now it's time to come clean and tell me all. Why was Annie Salter murdered? What was her dangerous secret?

'I cannot tell you what she told me in the confessional. You know that. It is against the strict laws of my calling. It is between her and God.'

'So where do you fit into this relationship? As an errant

eavesdropper? I am sure God would approve of you helping me catch a murderer.'

Father Sanderson shook his head and placed his hand on his heart. 'I would like to, my son, but I just cannot.'

With a great effort – and it was a great effort – I contained my anger for the moment. My instinct was to grab the old cleric and shake him violently until he spilled the beans, but what stopped me was my respect for a man of the church and, more particularly, the belief that even if I shook the fellow until his teeth fell out, he still wouldn't tell me.

'You are right,' he said slowly. 'I was the first to find Annie and I did write the note before I went round to see the police. I thought that if I convinced them that the note was written by someone else, they'd believe it was a murder and investigate. In this way I wasn't betraying any of Annie's confidences.'

'Isn't it a sin to let the murderer go free?'

'I don't know who the murderer is, Johnny. Please believe me. I just knew that Annie was fearful of something from her past.'

She had good reason to be, I thought. 'There are things you know that are vital to this case. You must help me.'

Sanderson simply shook his head gently in reply.

I don't know whether it was tiredness combined with a mixture of the remaining fragments of my own grief and blind frustration, but I exploded with anger. A fierce fury took hold of me, rippling through my body like an alien possession. All my previous restraint shot out of the window. I jumped up, grabbed hold of the cleric's shoulders and gripped them tightly, dragging him to his feet. 'Tell me,' I roared. 'Tell me what you know, you stupid old fool.' I bellowed the words as though I was reciting someone else's script. It wasn't me who had turned into this ranting bully: I had become another person who was inhabiting my skin. For a few fleeting moments Sanderson looked terrified and then a kind of strange serenity settled on his features. He offered no resistance to my violence and made no attempt to wrench himself from my grasp.

'I can't, Johnny,' he said, his voice a frail whisper. 'I can't.' His lips trembled with emotion. As he gazed at me with his sad and serene eyes, my anger subsided. It went as quickly as it had arrived. I could feel the heat and tension leaving my body. I felt weak and ashamed. With a sigh, I released Father Sanderson from my grip and he slumped back down in a chair, while I stood before him, disheartened and embarrassed.

Neither of us spoke for quite some time and then slowly Sanderson moved to a cupboard by the door and retrieved an item from within.

'There is something I can give you that may help.' In his hand he held a key. 'It is Annie's house key,' he said. 'She gave me a spare when she had that attack of influenza some years back. She was frightened that she might be trapped in the house too ill to move... Her house is empty now and will be for a few weeks. Maybe you could go there and investigate. There may be a clue, something to help...' His words trailed away and he held out the key to me.

'Maybe...' I said quietly. I took the key and left. There were no further words to say. Only I wish I had said them. I wish I had apologised for my threatening behaviour. But I didn't know that would be the last time I saw Father Sanderson alive.

SEVEN

Patience was a virtue. Francis Sexton knew that. It was one of those clichés that actually had a basis in truth. Indeed, he was well aware that it was not only a virtue, but in his case, it was essential. However tempted he was to begin his operations, he must not give way to such desires. Oh, yes, he longed to be out there in the darkness seeking victims, seeking to satiate his appetite for blood.

But he must wait.

He had waited this long. A few more nights would not hurt. His plan, carefully plotted and executed, had taken months to reach fruition: to spoil it all now with rash and ill-prepared actions would be foolish and possibly ruinous.

Two more nights and then the feasting could begin.

EIGHT

The cleaner found Father Sanderson the next morning. His body lay sprawled on his back on the kitchen floor amidst a scattered array of broken crockery. His eyes were wide open, bulging from their sockets and his tongue lolled out of the side of his mouth.

He had been strangled.

The cleaner did not know this was the cause of death. It was the police pathologist who established this fact and informed Detective Inspector David Llewellyn who in turn informed me.

'Why are you telling me?' I asked casually as I lit a cigarette, just managing to conceal the shock I felt at learning that my client had been brutally murdered. I was immediately reminded of my unreasonable treatment of the old priest the previous evening. How I had shouted at him and shook him. An icy wave of remorse surged through my body, but I fought hard to retain my poise. I knew all too well that in situations like this guilt and regret were futile emotions.

It was round ten o'clock in the morning and I had been slow to get my act together that day. I'd had a restless night and then as dawn began to break, I slipped into a deep sleep, only surfacing well after my usual get-up time. I had only just shaved and breakfasted – a grand phrase for coffee and the stale doughnut I had snared creeping out of the larder cupboard – when my old copper buddy came a calling.

I knew this would not be a purely social call. It never was with David. Hence my question.

David raised an eyebrow in a whimsical fashion at my query and smirked.

I smirked back. 'You don't usually call in and give me the low-down on your latest investigation – the new corpse in view – without an ulterior motive.'

'You know the victim.'

I nodded. 'Yes, he conducted Max's funeral. You were there. You saw him.'

'You know him better than that.'

I frowned. 'I'm sorry. Am I missing something?'

'Your name and telephone number were on a piece of paper found in the dead man's pocket.'

'So...'

'So, indeed. Tell me about it.'

I ran my fingers through my hair and sighed. I knew this was no time for subterfuge. 'I was doing a little job for him,' I admitted reluctantly.

David sat in a chair opposite me, his trilby nestling neatly in his lap. 'I think you're going to have to be a bit more explicit, boyo.'

'I was afraid of that.'

David grinned. 'A cup of tea is a fine accompaniment to a good yarn. You still got a kettle or do you suck the tea leaves through your teeth?' He chuckled at his own joke.

I brewed up a tarry cuppa for us both and told him my story.

'So,' said David slowly, when I had finished, drawing out the preposition to infinity, 'he was killed because he knew something. He was silenced. Whoever murdered him was worried that the old priest's conscience would override his religious convictions and that he would blab.'

I could not fault David's logic and I confirmed this with a nod.

'Any ideas?' he asked.

'At this moment, no.'

'But you will have?'

Possibly.'

'Probably – in fact knowing you, definitely.'

'You have more faith in me that I have.'

'I know you, Johnny Hawke. You are a terrier. Tenacious and impudent. You'll worry at this until something happens. You don't like to be beaten. Unfortunately, you also like to play the solitary game, but that is something you cannot do in this case. It may have started out as a private investigation, but now the Yard is involved it is a police matter with all the ramifications that phrase holds. Murder. Police matter. Understand, Johnny? Any information relevant to this investigation that you dig up or stumble over must be passed on to me.'

I saluted. 'Sir.'

'Yes, very funny. But I mean it. We're pals. Let's stay that way.'

'Of course,' I said, slipping my right hand out of view beneath my desk where I crossed my fingers. 'I'll share everything with you.'

David drained his mug of tea and slapping his trilby back on his head, sighed heavily in such a way that clearly indicated that he thought he was wasting his time with me.

'I'll be seeing you,' he said as made for the door.

'Of course, you will,' I grinned.

* * *

Within ten minutes of David's departure, I was leaving my office also. I had a house to search.

Annie Salter's terrace cottage was in a row up a narrow pathway at right angles to the main road. Her tiny garden which had obviously been tended with care was showing signs of neglect. The new growths of spring, bulbs and daffodils were in contention with weeds and hay grass. When entering a property illegally, one should always do so with confidence as though what you are doing is natural and official. Never skulk or look around nervously. Those are my rules, anyway.

As it happened on this bright March day, the coast was apparently clear: there wasn't a soul in sight.

Passing through the front door one was immediately in a small hallway and before you knew it, you found yourself in the parlour. It was tidy but cramped and smelt of damp. There was an ancient three piece suite, a mahogany sideboard bulky radio. A large mirror hung over the fireplace which caught my reflection and for a split second sent my blood racing because I thought I had company. I indulged in a quick rummage through the drawers of the sideboard but there didn't seem anything there of relevance to the case. Of course, I was searching blind. I really didn't know what I was looking for and as a consequence I had not an inkling what would be useful. I just hoped that something would jump out at me.

Annie had a secret, a secret that someone was prepared to kill for. Two people had died in order for the secret to remain. Would it be something obvious, if one knew where to look or would it be hidden – this mysterious something?

I moved into the kitchen. It was dark with only one small window by the sink to give illumination. There was a rough wooden table and two chairs. One still lay turned on its side. The one used in her hanging. I shuddered at the thought. How had he done it? (I assume it was a man). How had he persuaded Annie – or forced her up onto the chair and put the noose around her neck? Was the poor woman too terrified to resist or was she resigned to her fate? Seeing the scene of her demise brought the horror of the situation with great force. Surely there was some sign that there was another presence in the room, in the house? I examined every dusty surface, every drawer in the room but it seemed a fruitless task. And then I found something under the sink. An empty cigarette packet. Ten Capstan Full Strength. It may be nothing, but I seemed to remember that Father Sanderson saying that Annie neither drank nor smoked. And, besides, Capstan Full Strength was very much a man's fag.

I went up the stairs and found an even more exciting discovery. There were two small bedrooms and a bathroom. The main bedroom was a tidy affair with various religious artefacts adorning the walls, but the other room, a tiny cramped chamber, contained a zed bed which had recently been occupied. And by the side of it was a saucer that had been used as an ashtray containing several stubs of cigarettes – Capstan Full Strength. It seems that Annie had a lodger. Someone had stayed with her one night at least. Now who would that be? Well, whoever it was, he'd long gone. There were no clothes or other personal possessions. No suitcase and no other signs of his occupation. Or so I thought at first, but then I noticed something sticking out from under the mattress; a little flap of paper. Pulling the mattress back, I revealed a crumpled old newspaper: the *Evening*

Standard. Three weeks old to be precise. It was folded over at the accommodation section and there was a portion torn off. This little discovery brought a smile to my weary face.

I returned to Annie's bedroom and gave that further scrutiny. There was nothing of any real significance but I discovered a photograph album at the back of the wardrobe which I decided to take with me for further study.

I reckoned my job here was done. I'd hardly made giant strides in the investigation but it was clear that things were not as cut and dried as the police had believed them to be. Annie had had a man staying in the house and he may have been responsible for her death and even if he wasn't, he must know something about it. And maybe, the *Evening Standard* may help me track this fellow down.

* * *

I was just locking the front door when a lanky fellow with a wild bush of grey hair came up the neighbouring garden path. He was dressed in a smart oatmeal coloured overcoat with a garish painted tie at his neck. He grinned at me and gave a friendly wave.

'Are you going to be my new neighbour?' he said in a breezy fashion. This I assumed was the artist Archie Dawson.

I shook my head. 'No. I've just been doing an inventory of Mrs Salter's effects.' The lie came easily and smoothly. I've had years of practice at the art of dissembling.

'Oh, yes, very sad business,' he said, his features darkening. 'Lovely woman.'

'You knew her well?'

'Not really. Just to pass the time of day with really, but she often did me little kindnesses, like looking after my cat when I had to go away and letting me borrow some milk or tea when I forgot to stock up. I'm awfully absent minded.' The smile returned. 'A very Christian soul.'

I nodded sympathetically and then I tested the waters. 'She had someone staying with her just before... just before she died...'

'Yes. A friend of her son's I gather. He died you know, her son.'

'What was this friend's name?'

'Frank, I think. He was only here a short time. He'd been gone a week before Annie met her sad end.'

'What did he look like? You're an artist, aren't you? Could you draw him?'

Archie Dawson pursed his lips and furrowed his brow. 'Well, I could I suppose. But why? What's your interest in him?'

Good question, chum, I thought.

'It's a legal matter concerning Annie's estate. We may need to talk to this fellow.'

Mr Dawson did not seem convinced. I could tell he was about to refuse.

'It would be a great help,' I said. 'I could pay you for your efforts.'

His eyes flickered brightly at this news. 'Oh, very well, but it will only be a sketch.'

'That's fine,' I grinned.

'You better come in then,' he said, producing his front door key

Half an hour later I was ten bob poorer, but in possession of a nicely detailed drawing of Annie Salter's mysterious lodger.

NINE

He looked down at the street through the grimy window. The outside world carried on in its mundane fashion while he watched on with envy. People passed by, muffled against the chill wind, the odd motorcar purred past and even stray dogs roamed freely. He groaned softly as though suffering from some grinding abdominal pain. But the agony was in his mind rather than a physical ache. He was going crazy cooped up in the attic room like a bloody prisoner. Part of him wished that Marshall would find him and the whole business was over. In essence, he was living on borrowed time as it was. He was dead really. To die again – properly this time – might be for the best. It couldn't be worse than hiding away indoors during the daylight hours, frightened of noises, shadows, men in black felt hats. This was no life.

He'd even thought about giving himself up to the authorities, but he knew that Marshall could still get to him, even in police custody. The devil had ways and means, contacts and favours and his tentacles were long and deadly. He knew Marshall would not rest until he was six feet under.

Perhaps if he got away from London. Into the country somewhere. He'd need money though, more than he had now. Instinctively his hand strayed to his wallet. He knew exactly how much money he had in there. Not much and the rent was already overdue. He'd have to do another flit. It had better be tonight.

Of course, he had plenty of money. But he didn't want to touch it. Not just yet. He was too frightened to. He reckoned as soon as he got his hands on it, Marshall would turn up like a bad smell.

He sighed heavily, left the window and dropped on his back onto the bed. The rusty springs groaned at the pressure he put them under. He didn't even have a fag to ease his nerves. What he wouldn't give for a drag on a Capstan Full Strength. He stared at the cracked ceiling, eyeing the brown damp stains in a mindless fashion, waiting for the darkness of night to arrive.

* * *

The door of Inspector David Llewellyn's office opened silently and the visitor, who had not knocked, entered. David glanced up from his paperwork, an irritated frown creasing his forehead. He hadn't wanted to be interrupted, especially by some ignoramus who hadn't the courtesy to knock before entering.

He was about to express these thoughts when he observed that his visitor was Deputy Commissioner Bradshaw.

'Sorry to interrupt, David,' he said with great charm, sitting in the chair opposite his desk.

'That's all right, sir,' said David, shuffling the papers on his desk in a nervous fashion. A visit from such a senior officer like Bradshaw was a rarity and more than a little daunting. It usually indicated that some form of telling off was imminent. Suddenly, David felt like a naughty schoolboy facing his headmaster.

'I won't keep you,' said Bradshaw, eyeing David's nervous hands twitching with the sheets of paper. He was well aware what effect his presence was having on the inspector. Such reactions came automatically with the post. He was used to it and often turned it to his benefit. But he liked Llewellyn and had no need or desire perturb him more than necessary.

'I have some disturbing news, I'm afraid,' he said, getting to the point. 'Ralph Northcote. He's escaped.'

At the mention of the name, David Llewellyn's stomach churned. Ralph Northcote. Those two words brought back so many dark memories: the cellar, the blood, the poor mutilated girl and that mad face with the raw flesh dangling from its grinning mouth. The stuff of his nightmares.

He ran his fingers through his hair. 'How? I thought that place was supposed to be secure,' he found himself saying, while his mind refused to eliminate those dreadful images.

'He's been playing a long game, it seems. Over the last few months he's been visited by a psychiatrist who is writing a book on the criminal mind. A fellow called Sexton, Dr Francis Sexton. All seemed quite innocent enough but a few days ago, Northcote attacked this Sexton in his cell and slipped on his hat and coat as a disguise and managed to do a bunk.'

David shook his head in disbelief. 'What bloody incompetence,' he snapped.

Bradshaw nodded. 'I have to agree with you there. It's easy to understand how complacency takes root in these madhouses, but there is no excuse for such slackness. Anyway, it's no good crying over spilt milk. The devil is out and on the loose. Because of your close connection with the case, I thought you ought to know.'

Close connection? I should bloody well say so, thought David, bitterly. I was the one who trapped the bastard, brought him to justice and got him locked away for life. Except he isn't locked away now, so all my efforts have been in vain. And some poor girl will pay the price, sure as eggs is eggs – powdered or not. With a grimace, he allowed these thoughts to simmer but remain unspoken.

'Have we any notion where he went? Have his old haunts been checked?'

'Of course; checked and double checked. Nothing. For the moment it seems he has gone to ground – biding his time. But leopards do not change their spots, I'm afraid. I do not think it will be long before he will be on the hunt again.'

David nodded in agreement. 'We should have hung the bugger.'

'Spilt milk, Inspector.'

'Please, sir, do keep me informed. If he does kill again, I want to be in on the investigation. I must be.'

'Of course. Your previous experience with him would be invaluable. In the meantime, we keep searching and…'

'Holding our breath?'

Bradshaw gave David a bleak smile. 'Yes, I'm afraid so.'

The Deputy Commissioner rose from his chair and made for the door.

'Thank you, sir. I appreciate the visit,' said David.

Bradshaw gave the inspector a brief tight smile and left.

David slumped back in his chair and swore softly. Whatever wind had been in his sails, on this brisk spring day, had been removed. In his career, the case which he had been most proud of, the arrest that had given him the greatest satisfaction had just been screwed up and dumped in the rubbish bin. It was enough to make a copper throw in the towel. He wouldn't, of course. That wasn't his style. Like Johnny Hawke, he was a terrier and would worry at a problem until it was dealt with. But, nevertheless, the news had stabbed him through the heart and he was infused with a mood of desolation.

After a few moments, he turned his attention once more to the papers on his desk. The top sheets formed the statement of the cleaner who discovered the dead body of Father Sanderson at St Saviour's Church. This matter seemed small beer compared with the escape of the madman Northcote. 'Come on, boyo,' he muttered to himself, 'focus.' But his self-chiding was to no avail: his mind was filled with the vision of Ralph Northcote's horrible bloodstained face.

TEN

I read a lot as a youth, especially at the orphanage. Books were my escape from the unpleasant day-to-day reality. Indiscriminately, I gobbled them up: Dickens, Sapper, Conan Doyle, Rider Haggard, Trollope and Edgar Wallace. Other lives, other worlds, other adventures provided a welcome escape route from my dreary institutionalised life. I continued reading avidly until the outbreak of war when events seemed to rob me of my appetite for fiction. And losing an eye did not help. But in my late teens and early twenties I was a habitué of the Marylebone Library, snatching books off their shelves at least once a week. It felt strange, like a sentimental homecoming, to step back through the portals of this building again after a gap of three or four years.

It still smelt the same, that aroma of old damp books and polish assailed my nostrils as of old. I stood in the entrance lobby, breathed in deeply and let the nostalgia engage my senses and entrance me for a while. Briefly I allowed it to take my back to a time when the world was kinder and my life less damaged. With a sigh, I shook off my melancholy and made my way to the reference section. Low and behold, the little stout lady with the straw-coloured hair wrapped in a tight bun who used to serve me was still on duty behind the counter. She looked exactly the same, her large tortoiseshell glasses perched precariously on her nose and her brow puckered in a permanent state of concentration. I was tempted to greet her like an old friend with a cheery smile and a warm handshake, but I knew she wouldn't remember me. Nevertheless her presence behind the desk was somehow comforting and reassuring. In these dreadful changing times, there were some things that stayed the same.

'How can I help you?' she said, the voice was brisk and efficient but tinged with friendliness.

I pulled the copy of the *Evening Standard* from my pocket. 'Have you got this edition in your files?'

Pushing her spectacles up her nose, she examined the paper and then nodded. 'We should have. It's quite recent. Just a moment.' She disappeared through a frosted glass-fronted door which bore the word PRIVATE in green lettering. While I waited, I gazed around the room, at the desks, some which were occupied by static silhouettes pouring over various volumes and periodicals. They were like figures in a still life that was beginning to fade with age.

In less than five minutes, Miss Tight Bun returned bearing a large cardboard box which she placed on the counter between us.

'This contains the last six weeks' editions of the *Standard*. You'll have to search for it, but the one you require should be there,' she announced and allowed herself the briefest of smile.

I thanked her and took the box away to one of the desks, becoming another static figure in the landscape.

It did not take me long to find the issue of the *Standard* I was after and to hone in on the page I needed: the page that had been disfigured by Annie's mysterious lodger. I could see now that the missing portion from the Accommodation Available section contained details of a bed and breakfast establishment at Aldbridge Street off the Old Kent Road: 'Reasonable Rates. Discounts for ex-servicemen. Mrs Booth, Windsor House'.

Cheap lodgings, in other words.

I grinned. Rarely had the following up of a clue resulted in such a perfect result. Perhaps I was a fairly good detective after all.

I made a note of the address and returned the box to Miss Tight Bun.

'Did you find what you were after?' she asked, stroking the box as though it was some beloved pet.

'I did. Thank you.'

This seemed to please her greatly. Reluctantly, I bid her farewell. A figure from my past, my more settled times. I suspected that I would never see her again. It was a sad parting.

* * *

The Old Kent Road runs parallel with the Thames on the borders of Bermondsey and Rotherhithe. I made my way on foot across Tower Bridge and down this dusty and shabby part of London. It was shabby before the bombing, but now the rubble and shattered structures added further distress to its features. Travelling east, I encountered Aldbridge Street running off to the right. It was a narrow thorough-fare of down at heel houses with small overgrown gardens. It was a ghost street: there wasn't a soul in sight, not even an errant child playing out in the gutter or a stray dog or cat loping around. The place was dead and now I was haunting it.

Windsor House was about halfway along. It stood out from the rest because the door was clean and was not caked in grime and the steps appeared to have been swept. I knocked heartily using the great black knocker in the shape of some unidentifiable animal. I could hear the results of my efforts booming inside the building. I had not long to wait before the door opened and I found myself facing a pretty woman, dressed in a Fairisle sweater and slacks. She wore a turban but wisps of hair escaped the tight wrapping giving the effect of an auburn halo. She was short, not much over five feet, but her stance and demeanour suggested she was a bright and lively soul. She greeted me with a smile.

'Hello. Can I help you?'

I raised my hat and returned the smile. It was the only polite thing to do.

'Miss…?' I saw the ring and remembered the 'Mrs' bit in the ad, but a spot of flattery never goes amiss.

'Mrs. Mrs Booth. Cora Booth. Are you after a room?'

'Actually I'm looking for someone and I believe he may be one of your guests.'

'Oh?' The smile had faded now and she looked at me warily. 'Why are you looking for this person? Are you from the police?'

This was a situation I found myself in many times: the 'who the hell are you?' query. I was never quite sure what was the best way to respond. Admitting that I was a private detective often caused suspicion or fear or resentment – or all three. On the other hand, if I made up some cock-and-bull story about being a relative or an insurance agent with good news to impart, I was often asked questions that I couldn't answer and my cover story would be blown apart. In this instance I didn't even know the name of the person I was looking for. Taking a chance, I avoided replying to the lady's question. Instead I pulled out the sketch Archie Dawson had drawn for me of Annie's mysterious lodger.

'It's this fellow,' I said.

There was no mistaking the sense of recognition that passed over the woman's features on seeing the drawing.

'Mr Bristow,' she said. It was an unguarded, automatic response.

I nodded. 'So he is staying here.'

Mrs Booth could hardly deny it, but she didn't admit to it either. 'What do you want with the gentleman?'

'It's a private matter concerning his poor brother,' I said softly, adopting what I hoped was a mournful expression 'He passed away quite recently in rather sad circumstances.'

'I see.'

'It was all rather upsetting. I wanted to pass on the news to him quietly.' I was virtually mouthing the words now in a soft unctuous whisper. They seemed to have their desired effect. Mrs Booth nodded sympathetically.

'Well, yes, Mr Bristow is one of my paying guests. How awful for him.'

'Yes,' I agreed. 'Is he at home now?'

'I believe he is. He rarely goes out during the day.'

'Well if I might see him, I can pass on the sad tidings and give him some comfort.'

'Yes, yes, of course.'

My performance had completely won over Mrs Booth who seemed as upset at the bereavement of Mr Bristow's phantom brother as though he were her own.

'Come in, Mr...?'

'Hawke. John Hawke.' I saw no reason to give a false name.

'He's on the top floor.'

It was a very tidy house which smelt of polish and disinfectant. Mrs Booth led me up three flights of stairs to the top of the building.

'This is Mr Bristow's room,' she announced in hushed tones and then tapped gently on the door. 'Mr Bristow,' she called. 'Mr Bristow, you have a visitor.'

There was no response. Mrs Booth threw me a puzzled glance. 'I felt sure he was in. I certainly haven't seen him go out today.

She knocked again – louder this time. Still there was no answer.

'Do you think he'll be all right?' I said. 'Perhaps he's ill?'

'Mr Bristow,' she called loudly, 'It's about your brother.'

Silence.

I stepped forward and tried the door. It was locked. This action did not please Mrs Booth.

'Mr Hawke,' she snapped. 'I'll remind you that this is my establishment. I can't have you rattling my guest's doors carte blanche.'

I looked suitably chastised. 'I'm sorry. Do you have a key? I mean the poor man may be laid out in there, too ill to respond.'

I could see that Mrs Booth considered my idea as arrant nonsense, but none the less she pulled out a bunch of keys from her trouser pocket and applied one to the lock of Bristow's room. She turned the handle and opened the door a few inches and called out her lodger's name once again. And once again there was silence.

Gingerly, she entered the room and I followed directly behind her.

The room was occupied.

A man stood by the far wall in the shadows. I couldn't see his face properly, but I did observe that he was holding a gun.

'Oh, Mr Bristow,' said Mrs Booth, seeing the shadowy figure and then added, 'Oh, Mr Bristow,' an octave higher when she saw the gun.

'Get away from the door,' he snapped, taking a step forward.

We did as he asked.

'You're not going to use that, are you, Mr Bristow?' asked Mrs Booth.

'As long as you don't interfere with me. Now get right over there. I'm leaving.' So saying he moved swiftly towards the door. I wasn't about to let this fellow slip though my grasp so easily, gun or no gun. I stuck my leg out and he stumbled. I was on him in an instant. I jumped on his back and had my arms around his neck as he staggered forward, carrying me piggy-back style on to the landing.

With a gruff cry, he reversed with great force, ramming me against the wall, smashing my right elbow into the plaster. An electric shock of pain ran up my arm and I released my grip sufficiently for Bristow to pull away.

He now swung round and beat me on the head with the gun. Luckily, I had kept my hat on which softened the blow a little, but nevertheless I did see stars and my legs wobbled and gave way. With a grim reluctance I slumped down to the floor.

He swung back his leg with the intention of booting me in the face, but I managed to grab hold of the speeding limb as it approached me and yanked it upwards, causing his owner to lose his balance. With a yell of surprise, Bristow flew backwards, towards the edge of the staircase where he tottered briefly at the top of the landing before crashing down the flight of stairs to the floor below.

I pulled myself to my feet and peered over the banister. Bristow looked dazed and dishevelled, but was already pulling himself to his feet. On seeing me gaze down upon him, he aimed the pistol in my direction and fired two shots. I dodged down and heard the fierce missiles whiz past me and lodge in the plaster behind me. At this point, Mrs Booth, who had been strangely silent through the shenanigans, began to whimper and shake.

Bristow let off two more shots, keeping me well away from the top of the stairs and then there was silence apart from the bleatings emanating from the distressed landlady.

At length, I peered down to the floor below but, as I suspected, there was no sign of my quarry. He had bolted. I ran down the stairs, along the hallway and out into the street, but there was no sign of Bristow in either direction. He had carried out a very effective disappearing act.

* * *

Twenty minutes later I was sitting in Mrs Booth's parlour, administering a large glass of brandy to the shaken lady. She had stopped whimpering and the tears had ceased, but she still shivered as though she were sitting on a block of ice.

'You are from the police, aren't you?' were the first coherent words she spoke since entering the room.

'Not quite,' I said, lighting a cigarette in an attempt to calm my nerves. Despite my occupation, I wasn't used to being shot at in the afternoon in a respectable boarding house.

'What does 'not quite' mean?'

'I am a private detective.'

'Why didn't you tell me? Why didn't you warn me?'

'To be honest, I didn't realise there was anything to warn you about. I didn't realise this chap would be violent – that he had a gun.'

'Who is he?'

I shrugged my shoulders. 'I don't know. Yet. He's involved in a mysterious death I'm investigating, but at the moment I don't know how he's involved.'

'Well, he was certainly determined you weren't going to catch up with him.'

I nodded. 'I reckon he was more frightened than aggressive. He didn't use his gun until the last moment.'

Mrs Booth gave me one of her whimpers. 'But he did use it. In my house. My respectable house.' The tears began again and I placed my hand on her shoulder in a feeble attempt to comfort her. I felt guilty at having put the poor creature through this ordeal, for having placed her in danger. I never thought my visit would turn out in such a dramatic fashion, but perhaps I should have considered the possibility.

'Shouldn't we call the police?'

'I don't think that would be wise. It might get your place a bad reputation: harbouring gunmen and such...'

Her look told me she needed little persuading in this matter.

'You don't think he'll come back, do you?'

I gave her a grim smile. 'That's the last thing he will do. He's off to pastures new – wherever they may be.'

This seemed to reassure her and she took another swig of brandy. 'And he owed me back rent,' she said softly as though she was speaking to herself.

So my friend Bristow – if that was his real name, which I doubted – was short of the readies.

'If you don't mind, I'd like to pop back up to his room and have a look around. See if I can find any clues as to where he'll go next.'

'I suppose so. It'll be a while before I have the courage to go back up there myself.' She reached over and poured herself another measure of brandy.

* * *

It was a bleak room. Being the attic, the outer wall sloped down almost to the floor with a dormer window fixed at its centre, through which the occupant had a fine view of the street below. I noticed an ashtray by the bed containing a stack of tab ends – Capstan Full Strength. Apart from these scorched souvenirs, the mysterious lodger, Mr Bristow, had left behind very few possessions, most of which were scrunched up in a small brown case: underwear, a few shirts, socks and similar items. There was however a small envelope secreted in the lid containing a couple of photographs. One was of Mr Bristow himself in army uniform with another chap, tall, saturnine and decidedly shifty. The other was a studio shot of a lady I recognised. It was Annie Salter. Glancing on the back of the snapshot of Bristow, I saw in neat pencil the words Private Malcolm Salter and Lance Corporal Marshall. Looking at the pictures again I could see the similarity of features shared by Bristow and Annie. For it was clear that Bristow was indeed Annie's son. And lo and behold, he was alive and kicking, returned from the dead. That was part of Annie's terrible secret. Her ne'er-do-well son had not been killed at Dunkirk. Now he was on the run, but there was something about his behaviour that told me that he was terribly frightened of someone or something. Involuntarily, I shivered, as I realised that I was wading into deeper and darker waters.

ELEVEN

He tingled with a strange mixture of excitement and confidence. It had been a long process and now he was about to realise his ambition. He had waited in the wings for so long and now he was about to step out into the spotlight – a very dark spotlight. It was his due. He had endured months of waiting patiently while he built up his relationship with Ralph Northcote, cultivating the man's intimate friendship, slowly and gently persuading him that there was a fully active killing-and-eating life waiting for him outside the drab walls of his prison. 'Drab walls of his prison' – this last phrase made him smile. Northcote had a far worse prison now, enduring a mere existence rather than a life. But that was his own fault: he hadn't been clever or perceptive enough to be suspicious of the all too accommodating Sexton. Greed and self interest alone had governed his actions and blinded him from the truth.

Well, thought Sexton with a sardonic grin, tonight I am going to enhance your bloody and notorious reputation. Tonight I will kill and feast in your name. He waited in the shadows, in a shop doorway near the municipal hall. It was late but he could still hear the strains of the small band playing inside. A jolly dance to cheer up the tired and jaded natives of old war-ravaged London Town. Sexton imagined the scene inside. A group of geriatric musicians in tired and shiny dinner suits on stage churning out a series of old tunes in three-quarter time, the room misted with cigarette smoke and a motley crew of dancers shuffling around the floor, trying desperately to forget the war, the blackout, the bombing, the deaths and their deprived miserable lives. There would be a few servicemen on leave on the hunt for a goodnight kiss and a fumble afterwards; a few grannies and grandads showing off, dancing with annoying panache; and guilty wives having a quick waltz with a stranger while their hubby was away fighting for King and country overseas. Sexton smoked several cigarettes while he waited, waited patiently, enjoying the taste of the tobacco as it mingled with the cold night air. Eventually the music stopped and the dancers began to leave, stepping out into the dark spring night, their voices bright and chatty, carrying some of the pleasure of the evening with them.

A group of four girls bustled by him, giggling and humming one of the dance tunes. Individually, each was ideal for his purposes, but bunched together as they were there was no chance to select just one of them. Others left the hall in dribs and drabs. A couple seemed to be having an argument on the hall steps. He was a loutish youth with greasy hair, wearing a pin-striped suit that was too big for him. She was a plump girl with an explosion of frizzy blonde hair and a stupid face. He was pulling her arm, trying to persuade her to go one way, while she was of a mind to go in the other. Sexton couldn't hear what they were saying, but the boy was particularly angry, his voice lowered to a vicious staccato rasp. She started to cry and with a snarl he pushed her away from him and turned to go. Now she seemed undecided and took a step in his direction but he had walked off at such speed that he had disappeared into the night.

For a moment, the girl stood unsure what to do, apart from stifle her sobs with a handkerchief. And then with a dejected sigh, she set off in the opposite direction from the boy, moving along the pavement towards where Sexton was hiding. His pulse quickened. She could be the one if he was lucky. He had picked the spot carefully. Two hundred yards further down the road there was a small park where he had planned to could carry out his work undisturbed.

The street was now empty and quiet apart from the click clack of the girl's heels on the damp pavement. When she had passed by him, Sexton untangled himself from the shadows and began following her at a discreet distance. Caught up with her own emotions the girl had no sense of the dark shape that was slowly but inexorably bearing down on her.

'Excuse me, Miss,' he called softly as they reached the open park area.

Instinctively, the girl turned around to observe the silhouette of a tall man carrying a suitcase.

'Excuse me,' he said again, as he stepped forward, close to her, so close that she could see his face in the moonlight which filtered through the straggly night clouds. It was pale and strained and the eyes looming behind large spectacles were strange and somehow hypnotic.

'I wonder if you can help me,' he said, placing his suitcase at his feet.

The girl did not know how to respond to his request. She just stared at the stranger blankly. He gave her an odd smile and then, before she knew what was happening, he had his gloved hands around her throat. It happened so swiftly that she hadn't time to cry out. Her eyes widened in terror and her body rippled in panic, briefly as she began to struggle, but his grip on her throat was too strong and she quickly lost consciousness, slumping like a large rag doll against her assailant.

Quickly he dragged her into the bushes and found a space big enough to lay her down. He then retrieved his suitcase. In the cover of the bushes he began to undress the girl. Slowly and methodically he removed all her clothing in order to reveal her naked form. Taking off his gloves, he ran his fingers over her skin, his head buzzing with excitement, his sexual juices flowing. Then he slipped off his overcoat and placed it neatly on the ground some distance away from the body. Underneath he was wearing a protective white smock. With nervous fingers he opened the suitcase, withdrew the instruments and with precise deliberation began the butchering process.

Some fifteen minutes later, the smock now spattered liberally with blood, he had removed the organs and limbs he required and wrapped them in muslin and newspaper which he carefully stowed away with the instruments in the case. He gazed down with satisfaction at the girl's mutilated body which glistened in the pale light. He dipped his fingers in one of her wounds and then sucked them dry. A little appetiser before the feast that would follow.

As some far away clock chimed the midnight hour, he stepped from the bushes with his suitcase and its grisly contents and with calm deliberation headed for home.

TWELVE

I spent the night at the cinema with Peter. I had befriended this runaway orphan in the early part of the war* and through various incidents and adventures, I seemed to have become his unofficial guardian. He was now looked after by two spinster sisters, Edith and Martha Horner, but I kept a fatherly eye upon him and tried to provide him with the care and guidance I'd lacked as a child. However, I had neglected my duty somewhat in recent weeks, indulging in my grief over the loss of Max. But now I was determined to make amends.

I picked him up early from the Horners' neat little villa and treated him to fish and chips – a slap up meal, he called it – followed by the best seats at the Odeon, Leicester Square. I knew that apart from my neglect, the lad needed cheering up. His first big romance had crashed into the buffers and the experience had hit him hard. Poor sod. Although he had no biological connection with me, he seemed to have inherited by some weird kind of osmosis a very tender shell where affairs of the heart were concerned. Well, the greasy fish and chips followed by Abbott and Costello's antics as they 'Hit the Ice' along with a tub of ice cream cheered him up considerably and he was a lot chirpier on the way out of the cinema than he had been on his way in.

We found a little café open in Beak Street, and concluded the evening with a cup of tea. As usual Peter was eager to hear about my latest case, but I directed the conversation away from this particular topic. If his romance had hit the buffers, so, it seemed, had my investigations into Annie Salter's death. It had been a revelation to discover that her son was still alive and had been dossing down with her for a while and that now it seemed he was in hiding. Well, he was officially dead, so the authorities would not take too kindly to him still breathing the civilian air of London when he should be in the army. Circumstances suggested that he may well have killed his mother, but something told me otherwise. I'm no Sherlock Holmes: this wasn't a

---

* see the first Johnny One Eye novel, **Forests of the Night**

deduction – just an instinct. But carrying a shooter – and, indeed using it – clearly indicated that Master Salter was a bit of a villain. A nice fact to establish, but unfortunately the blighter had slipped through my fingers and was somewhere out there in this vast city impersonating a needle in a hay stack. The sudden recollection of this sad fact must have found its way onto my features.

'What's up? You look miserable,' Peter observed, gazing at me over the lip of his mug of tea.

I shrugged. 'Nothing important,' I replied, glancing at my watch. 'Hey, it's time I was taking you home. It's school tomorrow.'

Peter frowned. 'Hey, don't treat me like a kid. I'm fourteen you know and mature with it.'

I grinned. 'I'm not. I've got a little problem with trying to find someone. It's niggling me. That's all.'

'Tell me about it. I might be able to help. Remember, when I'm fully grown up, I'm going into the detective business too.'

I was about to say, 'over my dead body', but thought better of it. I didn't want to tempt fate. 'O.K. And then we get you in a taxi and home.'

Peter nodded with enthusiasm.

I gave him an abbreviated version of events while over dramatising the tussle I'd had with Malcolm Salter alias Mr Bristow on the top floor of Windsor House in order to disguise my incompetence at allowing him to escape.

Peter listened eagerly and narrowed his eyes in a sage-like fashion when I had finished. 'So,' he said, 'your problem now is to find out where this Bristow/Salter character has gone to ground.'

'That's one of them.'

'What does he look like?'

I reached inside my pocket for the sketch but changed my mind. Instead, I slipped out the photograph of Malcolm Salter I'd taken from his room in Windsor House. 'That's the chappie,' I said. 'Innocent looking cove, isn't he?'

Peter's eyes widened. 'Who is the other man?'

I shook my head. 'A mate of his from the army, I suppose. The name on the back of the snap says he's Lance Corporal Marshall – no first name.'

'I've seen that face before. I am sure of it.'

'Really? Are you sure?'

Peter nodded emphatically. 'Yes,' he said, drawing the word out as he narrowed his eyes. 'Of course... He's in my scrapbook.'

'Your scrapbook?'

'Yes, my crime scrapbook.'

'Explain, young master.'

'I keep a scrapbook of newspaper cuttings connected with big crimes. I follow the progress of their investigation – or lack of it – and make notes. It's good training for when I start as a detective.'

'I'm sure it is,' I said without much conviction. 'So who is this chap,' I pointed at the Lance Corporal.

'I think he was mixed up with an armed robbery in Chelmsford a couple of months ago. Can't really remember properly – but it's in my files.'

'In your scrapbook.'

Peter's eyes flashed brightly and nodded. 'Yes.'

'I think you'd better let me have a look at this scrapbook of yours.'

* * *

Later that night, I sat in my office, a small glass of Johnnie Walker in my mitt and Peter's scrapbook on my desk. I was reading an account of an armed robbery at the Benson Road branch of the Midland Bank in Chelmsford. Two men had entered the small branch just as it was about to close one Wednesday in late February. Once inside, they shut the doors and revealed they were carrying weapons. One had a shotgun, the other a pistol – recognised as an army pistol by the only teller on duty, a Mr Percy Crabtree. Both men wore handkerchiefs across the lower part of their faces to hide their features. The robber who appeared to be the leader – the one that did most of the talking – wore a dark blue felt fedora. There were only three customers in the bank at the time and these were made to stand facing the wall by the thief with the pistol while the other forced the teller to open the safe.

Being Wednesday the safe contained the cash for wages of two local factories and the thieves managed to bag over two thousand pounds.

As they were leaving, one of the customers made a grab for the robber. He was a young lad who was just about to join the army and had a fit of the heroics. He managed to knock Mr Fedora down and snatch the handkerchief from his face. In panic, the other robber shot him, wounding him badly in the thigh. Following this dramatic incident, both men fled with their haul.

The newspaper account was accompanied by an artist's impression of the unmasked felon. It was to my way of thinking, as it had been young Peter's, that the villain was none other than Lance Corporal Marshall. Blimey, I thought, the power of the artist's pencil had certainly been working in my favour today. So Lance Corporal Marshall was a nasty piece of work and no doubt his accomplice was Mr Bristow alias Malcolm Salter. So that's why he was hiding out. But where was Marshall and where was the loot? Salter certainly hadn't got it. He certainly hadn't been painting the town. Mrs Booth assured me he was hard up, owing her rent.

Well, in some ways the situation was a little clearer now but the solution was still as far away as ever. With this dismal thought, I headed for bed.

THIRTEEN

'She was discovered by an ARP Warden on his way home. He usually takes a short cut across the park and found the body lying on the pathway. Apparently she had been killed in the bushes...'

'But the murderer dragged the body out here so that she'd be discovered very soon,' said David Llewellyn finishing the uniformed sergeant's sentence for him. He'd been called out of bed early that morning by a telephone call from Deputy Commissioner Bradshaw. 'It looks like our friend has started his work again, Llewellyn. I reckon you'd better take charge of the business from the start. Get yourself down there pronto.'

And pronto, with the aid of a police driver, he had got himself down to Camden and the little park where the poor girl, Doreen Maberley, had been found.

'I still don't understand why he dumped the body out here where anyone could find her?' the sergeant was musing.

'To show off his handiwork, I suppose.'

'Handiwork is right. Poor girl: it looks like Jack the Ripper got at her. All her insides have been interfered with,' said the sergeant, having great difficulty in keeping his breakfast down.

'You've searched the area, I presume.'

'With a fine tooth comb, sir. I got two of my lads on it as soon as it was light. They've been over the ground half a dozen times. Nothing. Not even any shoe imprints. He's left the murder scene as clean as a whistle.'

Llewellyn knelt down by the corpse and examined it closely. 'He's taken the heart, liver and cut out her tongue.'

'What sort of man would do such a thing? He must be raving mad.'

'Mad, certainly. But not raving. He has a cunning intelligence with nerves of steel.'

'Blimey, sounds as though you know the blighter'.

Llewellyn sighed but said nothing.

Leaving the body in the capable hands of the pathologist from the Yard, the inspector departed the scene, taking in lungfuls of fresh air as he left the park. He couldn't remember feeling as depressed as he did now. The bastard he'd nailed all those years ago, the bastard he hoped would feel the hangman's noose around his neck, was free and had killed again. Killed? Well, it wasn't quite as simple as that. He had ripped and torn the flesh of a young girl to satisfy his appetite for flesh and blood. This wasn't just murder, it was mutilation and, God forbid, cannibalism. He shuddered at the thought of it.

And now his task was to find him, and find him fast before he was able to carry out another of his gruesome crimes. How on earth was he going to do that? He paused and lit a cigarette before climbing into the police car.

'Where to, sir?' enquired the driver, revving the engine. 'To the Yard, is it?'

'No,' said Llewellyn wearily. 'Priors Court, off the Tottenham Court Road.'

* * *

He felt good. He had hunted, killed and now he had dined on his spoils. He washed down the last of his bloody titbits with a glass of water – nothing stronger than water so as not to interfere with the taste – and sat back with a sigh of great satisfaction. He wiped his mouth and grinned. The whole experience had been as wonderful as he had anticipated. All that was left was to read an account in the press of his glorious escapade. Maybe in the evening edition. Certainly in the next day's nationals.

He lit a cigarette and puffed contentedly. It would be good to show the newspaper reports to Northcote: another twist of the knife, aggravating the wound. Idly, he thought of his prisoner as he blew smoke rings on the air. There he was in that dark chamber below, lying on his rank bed unable to do anything but sleep and regret. In the few days he had been incarcerated in the cellar, he had regressed into a child-like moronic state. Sexton was convinced this was the result of the shock he had suffered by having his dream of freedom so brutally snatched away from him and being tethered like an animal in a dank cell. Well, in reality, Northcote had fulfilled his usefulness. There was no real point in keeping the beast alive for much longer. He would only become a nuisance, like an ill pet one had to attend to on a daily basis.

As soon as Sexton was able to have the final pleasure of showing Northcote the newspaper story about the girl he'd killed and boast how tasty she had been, as soon as he was able to witness the wild rash emotions that this would raise within his captive, he would have done with the fellow.

And then he would snack off him.

FOURTEEN

It was just before noon when I arrived back at my office following my morning labours and found a note pushed under my door. It was from David Llewellyn. It read: 'Would really appreciate a chat. Can you make The Guardsman at one o'clock? DL'

The Guardsman was a pub not far from Scotland Yard where David and I often met up to sup a few pints and moan about our respective investigations. I was intrigued and indeed thirsty, so I did a quick about face and headed off in the direction of that particular watering hole.

As I pounded the dusty streets of the capital, I thought over what I had learned that morning. I had taken myself down to the War Office and made contact with an ex-client of mine, Bobby Driscol, a good-looking lad with a club foot who had been wrongly accused of being involved in a dog doping scam at White City greyhound track a few years back. I had managed to prove his innocence and as a result he'd been grateful ever since and always eager to do me a favour. He was only too happy to dig out some details for me concerning Private Malcolm Salter and his oppo Lance Corporal Marshall. In a sense, most of what I learned only confirmed what I had surmised, but it was reassuring to know I was on the right track. The two men had served with the London Regiment – but had not served for too long. The two had gone AWOL shortly after enlisting. They had joined that invisible platoon of deserters that somehow had blended back into civilian life without a trace. It always puzzled me how these men could manage to do that so effortlessly and, indeed, without conscience. They were selfishly turning their back on their country and its plight when they were needed most. I was sure that in the main it wasn't just a matter of cowardice; these blighters wanted to be free of the regimented restraints that the life in the forces brought.

Anyway, we now knew for certain that Annie's son did not die in battle. This was a lie; this was her secret, which she no doubt manufactured for respectability's sake. It would hurt her too much to admit that her son was a deserter. And, it would seem that the prodigal had returned home and was kipping down in her spare room. I was convinced that this secret was tied up with her murder. However, I found it hard to contemplate that her son was responsible for her death, but I couldn't discount it completely for I had encountered stranger and crueller things in my career.

I had never known The Guardsman be less than buzzing with business at lunchtime and today was no exception. As I opened the door to the saloon bar, I was met with a barrage of noise and raucous conversation from the crowd within: office workers snatching a quick dinner break, old folk whiling away their time, waiting for the war to end, soldiers, sailors and airmen on leave, along with some uniformed Yanks and various shady looking types, all enveloped in a fine mist of cigarette smoke and a web of chatter. And one other: a burly blonde-haired Welsh police inspector hunched on his usual stool at the end of the bar.

I was early for our one o'clock appointment, so he must have been much earlier. His stiff posture and sour expression indicated that he was not a happy man. Squeezing my way through the throng, I slipped onto the stool beside him and gave him a cheery grin.

'At last,' he said grumpily.

'I'm early.'

'Two more pints, Arthur,' he called the barman, who was in the middle of serving two plump ladies. Arthur nodded.' Wait yer turn,' he called with a grin.

'So,' I said, 'you wanted to see me. I can tell by your expression it's not to tell me you've come up on the pools.'

'Too bloody true. It's bloody Ralph Northcote.'

The name rang a tiny bell in my memory, but not loud enough to bring the fellow to mind. My expression obviously conveyed my lack of comprehension.

'It was my first big case back in '35. He'd been killing girls, this Northcote. Killing them and then eating their flesh.'

I shuddered. Now the bell rang louder. I remembered the case. It was before I'd joined the force, before I'd lost an eye and before I knew

David, but it was very big in the papers.

'What about him – this Northcote?'

'He's escaped and murdered again.'

'Crikey. Escaped?'

'From the nut house.' David ruffled his hair in frustration. 'The bastard should have been strung up and then this wouldn't have happened. All that work I did to get his conviction and then the bloody powers that be deemed he wasn't of sound mind. Course he wasn't of sound mind: he was a bloody murderer who ate his victims.'

The pints arrived and I paid for them. 'Have a gulp of this and try to calm down.'

David did as he was told. He devoured half the glass almost in one go. 'I had to talk to someone about it and I knew you'd understand more than any other,' he said, at length, wiping the froth away from his upper lip with the back of his hand.

'I'm flattered.'

David gave me a weary smile.

'Go on,' I said, 'give me the whole sad story.'

And he did – from Northcote's capture, arrest and conviction up to that very morning when he'd been examining the mutilated body of a young girl who had been savaged in exactly the same way as Northcote's other victims.

'It's his work all right. The devil's resumed where he left off.'

'Was the girl's handbag or purse missing?' I asked.

David shook his head, 'Untouched.'

'So he must be OK for money. Where's he getting it from? Someone must be hiding him. Providing him with cash, food and shelter.'

David curled his lip unpleasantly. 'He caters for himself where food is concerned. But you have a point.'

'Were there any other associates from his past who are likely to sympathise with him – even share his predilections…?'

'Not that I know of. He was a lone wolf.'

'Mmm. I see a brick wall looming ahead.'

'So do I. Why do you think I'm in here drowning my sorrows?'

'It seems to me your best bet is to have a long in-depth conversation with this Dr Sexton chap. If he's been visiting Northcote on a regular basis, surely he would have learned something that would help. Some indication, some clue as to where he is and what his plans are.'

'I reckon I can guess what his plans are: to kill again and have a fleshy banquet. But, you are right. Sexton seems to be my only hope for the moment.'

'And where there is hope, there is a chink of light.'

David gave me a tight grin. 'I knew chatting to you would be good for me. Just telling you about it and expressing my frustration helps. It's a bit like a confessional.'

'Bless you, my son.'

David laughed briefly and then he added seriously, 'I don't think my colleagues would fully understand what this Northcote business meant to me.'

I understood. In this respect David and I were alike. Rightly or wrongly, we became personally involved in our cases and cared greatly that we achieved justice and closure. David thought he'd had both with the Northcote affair but that particular rug had been well and truly dragged out from under him.

David ordered another round. I settled for a half this time. I wasn't in the mood for boozing. Alcohol sometimes helped me not only to relax, but also enabled my brain to see possibilities and scenarios concerning my investigations that the sober mind couldn't – but somehow today I just didn't fancy it. I wanted to keep a clear head.

'So, how are you getting on with your little murders: the Annie Salter and Father Sanderson business,' said David, looking and sounding more relaxed now that he'd unburdened himself to me and downed a couple of pints. 'I'm off the case now; the Northcote business has taken priority. So come on, spill the beans.'

Now it was my turn in the confessional. I told him all I knew so far. I saw no reason not to. I wasn't going very far with things at the moment. Maybe he could throw me a morsel of hope too.

When I had finished, my companion gave me a gloomy nod. 'Difficult,' he said slowly. 'That Chelmsford bank job. I know a bit about that. Old Percy Herbert's been assigned to the case. We know who the leader of the gang is.'

'Well it's Lance Corporal Marshall.'

'Yeah, but that's not his real name. Some of the boys at the Yard recognised him from that artist's impression in the paper. It's Bruce Horsefield. He did time before the war.'

I dragged out the photograph from my wallet with Salter and his mate. 'Is this him?' I asked.

'That's the boy. He worked himself up from street mugging to robbing a jeweller's shop in '36. Got four years for that. Then he disappeared. Obviously he changed his name but not the colour of his spots. I reckon he's a real wrong 'un.'

'And is Inspector Herbert anywhere near catching him?'

David grinned. 'Is he heck. Old Herbert has trouble catching a cold. I reckon Horsefield could run rings around him.'

'I suppose he's tried Horsefield's old haunts.'

'I suppose so. I don't really know. I only pick up bits of info in the canteen but I do know that Percy ain't making any progress.'

'Somehow that does not cheer me.'

David chewed his lip. 'I suppose I could let you have a copy of Horsefield's file. You might see something in there that Percy hasn't.'

'It might help.'

'I shouldn't, of course. It's strictly against the rules, you understand.'

'I understand.'

He gave me a quick wink. 'I'll get a copy to you by tonight.'

No more was said on the matter and we sat for a while in silence, two weary detectives with unpleasant loads on our shoulders, deep in our separate tunnels with no light flickering at the end. Just darkness.

'Well,' David said at length, draining his glass, 'I either have another and fall down sozzled or get back to the office and bang my head against the wall.' He slipped off his stool. 'See you soon, Johnny boy. Good hunting.' With a brief smile he turned and squeezed his way towards the door.

I lingered over the dregs of my drink for some time mulling over the case in general and what I had learned in particular. I sketched out in my mind a rough plan of action – a very rough plan – and then I too headed for the exit and some fresh air.

I spent the afternoon visiting another client: a simple marital job that I knew I could clear up within a week. I hated these jobs but they were my main means of earning a living – exposing some poor sod's infidelity.

As it was growing dusk, I found myself in Benny's café with a mug of tea and a salt beef sandwich. We chatted for a while in a desultory fashion, but I could see the old boy was tired, so I left him to lock up and made my way home. The lunchtime beer was still sloshing unpleasantly about in my stomach and I had no desire for more.

Arriving back at Hawke Towers, I found a brown envelope on the mat. David had been as good as his word – not that I doubted he wouldn't be. Inside the envelope were the file notes on Bruce Horsefield aka Lance Corporal Marshall. Here then was my bedtime reading.

FIFTEEN

Mrs Frances Coulson had only just bid one of her gentleman callers adieu and was enjoying a cigarette and a small glass of sherry, when her mellifluous doorbell rang. A frown manifested itself on her carefully made up face. She wasn't expecting anyone – she had no more appointments that day – and so this could only be some sort of inconvenience. As she made her way to the front door, she hoped it wasn't that detective fellow with the eye patch. He was too inquisitive and too sharp for comfort.

She could see a bulky shadow through the frosted glass. So it was a man.

With some trepidation she opened the door and on seeing her visitor, her mouth dropped open.

'Hello Auntie,' said the man. 'Aren't you going to invite me in?'

SIXTEEN

'So what do we know about this Sexton bloke, sir?' Sergeant Sunderland eased the car into third gear as he posed this query.

'Not a lot,' said David Llewellyn, glumly. 'He used to be a GP but now practises as some sort of psychiatrist. I suppose there's more money in doling pills out to the nervous and depressed. And he is supposed to be writing a book about the criminal mind.'

'I could give him a few pointers on that subject,' grinned Sunderland.

'I'm sure you could, Sergeant, but I reckon the good doctor is more concerned with the causes of criminal behaviour rather than how to spot a snout at a hundred paces.'

'You may be right.'

'But Sexton spent a lot of time interviewing Northcote at Newfield House. He must have got to know him very well. God help us, he should be able to give us some inkling of where the bastard is now and what his plans are.'

'You would hope so,' said Sunderland without much conviction.

* * *

Dr Francis Sexton's surgery was in Bedford Row, a smart thoroughfare situated between High Holborn and Theobalds Road. As Sunderland pulled the car up outside, he asked, 'Do you want me to stay out here, sir?'

David shook his head, 'No, come in with me. Four ears and two brains, eh? What one of us might miss, the other should pick up. At least we can dissect things afterwards.'

A rather matronly secretary showed the two policemen into Dr Sexton's consulting room. He rose magisterially from behind his desk and shook Llewellyn's hand.

'I take it you've not caught him, then?' he said easily as he gestured that the two men should take the seats opposite the desk.

He was a tall man, somewhere in his late forties with a prominent nose and grizzled hair, shot with silver strands. He was, thought David, someone who was used to being in command and at complete ease with himself. He was dressed in a well-cut grey double breasted suit and had a relaxed and confident manner. The inspector gazed down at his own old baggy suit and scuffed shoes and immediately felt awkward.

'No, we haven't caught him – but I'm afraid that he has already committed murder.'

Sexton pursed his lips and nodded. 'Sadly, that does not surprise me. The man has an inner compulsion to kill…'

'And then eat his victims.'

'Yes. In hospital, drugs can sublimate the condition, keep it in check to some extent, but now he is away from any kind of control or restraint his desires will be… unfettered.'

'Why does he do it?' asked Sunderland.

'That is the big question I was trying to answer by talking to him. Cannibalism – the eating of human flesh – has been with us since the dawn of time, but it is mostly a cultural phenomenon. It was often based on the belief that by eating one's enemy you inherit his power. Humans have also indulged in the practice as a means of self preservation. In many non-European countries, it was not regarded as a sin or a crime to consume human flesh. For example in the Aztec or Mayan culture cannibalism was reserved for royalty. After a ritual human sacrifice to their Gods, they would feast upon their victims. However, in Ralph Northcote's case, he kills purely for pleasure and celebrates his act by devouring part of the flesh of his victim.'

'For pleasure?' said David.

'Yes.'

'Then the fellow is mad.'

'From our perspective, yes.'

'But ours is the sane one.'

Sexton gave the inspector an indulgent smile. 'But who's to say that our perspective is the correct one – the only acceptable one? Northcote just views the world from a different hilltop. As a psychiatrist I have to take the position that the mind controls the man – not morals, laws or customs, which in essence are all artificial codes imposed on us by exterior forces, created by society. I was trying to unlock the door in order to find out why his view of the world differed from the majority.'

'It sounds as you feel sorry for him.'

'In a way, I do. Imagine yourself trapped within a psyche that was vastly different from the accepted norm and there was nothing you could do about it. It is so much easier to give in to our natural urges than fight them. We do it all the time.'

'Natural urges.' David scowled.

'To Northcote they are natural. Do you smoke, Inspector?'

'Yes.'

'It's bad for the health, you know.'

'I know.'

'Have you tried to give up?'

'From time to time.'

'But you haven't succeeded.'

'No.'

'No doubt the temptation to light up was too strong. You gave way to your natural urges despite the fact that you knew you'd be better off not smoking. The pleasure you receive from tobacco is greater than the concerns you have for your health. The principle is the same. Northcote has given up all attempts to stifle his appetite for murder and blood.'

'I think perhaps we are wandering a little way from the purpose of this visit. Whatever weird psychological processes control Ralph Northcote, I represent the mainstream law and order of this country. In my eyes he is a violent murderer and it's my task to find him and stop him before he takes any more lives.'

Sexton nodded urbanely. 'I understand. And you think I can help.'

'Well, I hope so. You have spent quite a lot of time with him. I would have thought that he must have given you some inkling about his plans. You got inside his head... knew how he thought.'

'I was beginning to understand some of his rationale, but I'm not able to think like him, if that is what you are suggesting.'

'If not think like him – guess what he might do next. Guess what his plans are.'

'I doubt it. He is a very cunning man. I must admit that he had me completely fooled. I thought he trusted me – saw in me someone who at least could understand and sympathise with his mania.'

'Sympathise?' David could not keep the shock out of his voice.

'In the scientific sense, of course. It is true that in order to gain his trust I did pretend to empathise with his cravings. In this way he felt safe to confide in me his innermost thoughts.'

'And…?' There was a note of irritation in Llewellyn's voice. He was getting a little tired of Sexton's mumbo jumbo sophistry. It was as though all this psycho-jargon was a smokescreen. This fellow knew something. Llewellyn had no idea what but he was determined to find out.

'Well, I learned a fair bit about Northcote's biography and his early encounters with the tasting of flesh. I began to fathom what triggered off the overwhelming urge to kill and feast.'

David groaned inwardly. The phrase 'to kill and feast': it was a conscious, flashy, overly-clever construct which glamorised the subject describing it in a facile way. No doubt, he thought, Sexton will use it as the title for his book.

'And what was that? What was this trigger?'

'I believe it was connected with sexual arousal. Instead of the need for sexual intercourse and the physical and mental release that this brings, Northcote transferred this natural desire to…'

'An urge to kill and feast,' added David pointedly.

'Yes.'

'To learn all this, Northcote must have trusted you.'

'Yes… to some extent. Not enough to reveal any plans to escape, if that's what you're hinting at. Well, that would have been foolish. After all I was his means to freedom. I was certainly kept in the dark about that.'

'But he must have talked about his desire to get out of that place.' It was Sunderland who made this observation.

'Not really. He seemed resigned to his fate. I suppose that fact alone should have alerted me to the notion that he was planning something.'

'Could you explain what you mean?' asked David, unable to keep the irritation out of his voice.

'Incarceration, drugs, therapy can never fully quell the innate cravings of a patient like Northcote. The desire is forever there, lurking in the shadows. It may be sedated for a time but it is never eradicated. The fact that Northcote appeared placid and in a state of acceptance should have warned me that he was keeping something back from me.'

'And you've only realised this now?'

'Since I was coshed on the head in Newfield House, yes.'

David sighed heavily. This was going nowhere and certainly Sexton was making no real effort to help. He was wrapped up in his own esoteric psychobabble world and the practical realities of catching a vicious murderer did not seem to concern him in the slightest. He decided to try a different tack with this obtuse medic.

'Dr Sexton, if you were me, a policeman trying to trace Ralph Northcote, what would you do?'

Sexton seemed amused by the question and stared into space for some seconds before responding. 'Do you know, inspector, I really have no idea. As I say, he is a cunning fellow. Do not mistake his mania for overall madness. He has a cool, clever rational mind and he would have no difficulty in becoming invisible in this city. Actually that is something that is quite easy to do these days what with the blackout and so many damaged properties where a fugitive could easily hang out without being detected.'

'In the course of your chats, did Northcote mention any old colleagues, friends – even enemies?'

The psychiatrist shook his head. 'His past life was a closed book to him. I don't suppose he could have made his way to his old house, could he?'

'It no longer exists. It was pulled down. There's nothing there now.'

Sexton gave an elegant shrug of his well-tailored shoulders. 'I'm sorry. I have nothing else to suggest. Northcote is now both the hunter and the hunted: there is no template for such a role. Certainly not one that I could fathom. I am sorry.'

* * *

'That man is an arrogant, supercilious, irritating, pompous smug twit,' growled Inspector David Llewellyn as he slumped into the passenger seat. 'No, I take that back. He's not a twit. He had no intention of helping us and he made that patently obvious.'

'Why do you think that is, sir?' said Sergeant Sunderland turning the key in the ignition and revving the engine.

'I don't know. Perhaps he didn't want to get his hands dirty with police work. Perhaps his sympathies for Northcote were genuine and he's pleased the bugger's escaped.'

'Really!'

'Well, no not really, I suppose. But during all those visits Northcote must have said something – something however innocent or trivial that could give us some sort of clue as to where he's hiding out. One thing is for certain, I don't go along with Sexton's notion that he's hiding in some bombed out building. He's found somewhere much smarter than that. I'm sure of it.'

'How do you make that out?'

'When he killed that girl, he didn't touch her purse – he left her money alone which suggests that he has sufficient for his needs. If that is the case, where has the dosh come from? He has secured a supply from somewhere.'

'Maybe a secret stash that he hid before he was captured.'

'That's a bit far fetched. He's been locked away for eight years. That kind of perspicacity would be remarkable. And then there's the murder itself. It's obvious that Northcote used proper medical equipment to cut up and dissect the body. Where'd he get them from?'

'I could check if there have been any thefts of such stuff from hospitals or surgeries in the last few days.'

'Yeah, you do that, but I reckon you'll get a nil result. My hunch is that our friend Northcote is being harboured, given refuge by some twisted sod who sympathises with him.'

'Sympathises?' Sunderland's voice rose an octave.

'Yes,' said David thoughtfully, lighting a cigarette. 'Sympathises. There's that word again.'

* * *

Back in his office, Francis Sexton was also smoking and idly watching the smoke spiral fade while his mind lingered over the interview he'd just had with Inspector Llewellyn and his lackey. In retrospect Sexton believed that he had handled it badly. He had been too smooth, too unhelpful. He'd certainly been in control and had effectively deflected each of the policeman's questions, giving absolutely nothing away but in doing so he had obviously irritated him. That, Sexton knew, had been a foolish thing to do. He really should have thrown Llewellyn a titbit to chew on to send him off on a wild goose chase; a false clue that indicated that he was trying to help the police instead of being apparently indifferent to their investigation.

Now the policemen had gone away, frustrated and annoyed with him. He cursed softly. He had been so pleased with his smooth performance at the time that he had been unaware of the damage he was doing. Had he, by his mannered performance, aroused their suspicions? Surely not. But the thought lingered like a dark cloud.

SEVENTEEN

Before turning in for the night, I'd sat up in bed and read through the file on Bruce Horsefield, the true identity of Lance Corporal Marshall but had learned nothing of any significance. Well, nothing that could give me a lead. It was a familiar scenario: unruly kid developed into a teenage hoodlum, petty crimes and then in 1936 he'd tried his hand at holding up a jewellers' shop. It was an amateurish attempt, albeit with a shooter, and he was chased down the street and caught. He was gaoled for five years but released early in order to join the army to fight for his country. Within months he had deserted and disappeared. He was an only child, brought up by his widowed mother. She was still alive, but claims not to have seen him since he went in the army. Her house had been searched and initially a watch had been put on it to no avail. End of story.

With a heavy sigh, I switched out the lights and then just as my head hit the pillow, a thought came to me. It was nothing to do with Horsefield – well not directly – but it amazed me why I hadn't thought of it before. I lay in the dark smiling for some time before I slipped into a dreamless sleep.

The next morning I was up bright and early and out on the streets before nine. I had my revolver with me, weighing down the pocket of my raincoat. It is rare that I carry a weapon. I'm not keen on the beasts, especially after what one malfunctioning rifle did to my eye, but in this instance it was a case of forewarned being forearmed. I had worked out in my little brain that Malcolm Salter was not only on the run from the police but also from his partner in crime, Bruce Horsefield. For some reason they had split up, probably some argument over the spoils of the bank robbery and he was desperately trying to lie low so neither Horsefield could find him nor the coppers could feel his collar. He'd kipped out at his mother's place until her death – that was still a bit of a mystery to me. Then he'd holed up at Mrs Booth's boarding house, until I turned up on the doorstep and he turned nasty with a pistol. Where might he go next?

Well, I had an idea.

I knocked once more on the shiny knocker of Mrs Frances Coulson's bijou bungalow. As I did so, the door partially swung open and there was no one on the other side. A little warning voice in my brain went, 'Oh-oh!' I knew what it meant. Experience has taught me that when you go to a door you anticipate will be locked but it isn't, you usually can expect trouble.

I stepped over the threshold and pulled out my gun. 'Hello,' I called down the hallway.

There was no reply.

Something was up. Something was very up.

And then I heard it. A faint sound, rather like a groan. There it was again. It was a groan – and it was coming from the sitting room.

Cautiously, I entered the room. The tidy little parlour was in a state of disarray. One of the chairs had been overturned and many of the ornaments were lying haphazardly on the floor. It was obvious that there had been some sort of struggle in here. This deduction was further strengthened when I observed Mrs Frances Coulson stretched out on the couch, her left arm hanging limply to the floor while she clutched a wound to her forehead with her right. Blood veined its way down her pale face making her resemble some kind of bizarre clown. At first she wasn't aware of my presence. I knelt down beside her and touched her shoulder gently.

'Mrs Coulson,' I said softly.

Her eyes rolled open and with a sharp grimace she turned her head in my direction.

'Who... are you?'

'It's Johnny Hawke... the private detective.'

Her eyelids fluttered and then closed. 'Oh. You.'

'What happened?'

'I was attacked. He... came for Malcolm.'

Here voice was raspy and lazy like that of a drunk.

'Malcolm Salter. He's been here.'

'His last refuge. But ... he found him. He came for him.'

'Who?'

'The man. The man that did this to me.'

'Which man?'

Mrs Coulson's brow creased with irritation and her eyes flickered open again. 'Horsefield. He came for the money.'

The money. Like a rusty machine that had just been serviced and well-oiled, suddenly all the cogs slipped into place and began whirring with increased efficiency. Now it all became clear to me. Or most of it, at least.

'I told him Malcolm wasn't here, but he didn't believe me,' Mrs Coulson rambled on. 'So, he hit me. Broke my skull.'

'You'll be all right,' I said without any knowledge or conviction that this would be the case. At least I knew her skull wasn't broken. She had a bad cut and her dignity had been bruised. 'Let me get you a glass of water.'

'A glass of water… yes. Put some gin in it too, would you?'

I reckon she'd survive.

I got her the water – without the gin. I didn't want to waste precious time searching for booze in the kitchen.

'Where have Malcolm and Horsefield gone now?' I asked after helping to prop Mrs Coulson up into a sitting position on the sofa and handing her the glass of water, which she clasped unsteadily with both hands.

She took a gulp from the glass and then turned a puzzled face to me. 'What did you say?'

'Malcolm and Horsefield – the man who attacked you – where have they gone?'

At the mention of the attack, Mrs Coulson's fingers wandered towards the wound again. 'They've gone to get the money, of course.'

'Where?' I tried to keep the frustration and eagerness out of my voice, but I feel I failed.

Mrs Coulson looked at me crossly as though I was an idiot. 'To Victoria Station. Malcolm said that he'd put the money in a left luggage locker for safe keeping.'

'How long ago did they leave?'

'How the hell do I know? I've been attacked. I don't know how long I've been lying here, suffering.' She took another drink. 'Hey,' she said, 'there's no gin in this.'

As I hurried for the door, I noticed the clock that had been on the mantelpiece lying on the tiled hearth, no doubt where it had fallen during the struggle. The glass face was cracked and the hands had stopped at ten to ten. I glanced at my watch. That was twenty minutes ago. Crikey, I had only just missed them. I reckon they had about a fifteen-minute lead on me.

In a trice I was out of the house and racing up the road in search of a taxi. I felt no guilt in leaving the wounded Mrs Coulson to her own devices. She was a tough old bird and I'm sure that she'd summon up enough strength to get to the gin bottle and comfort herself that way.

Despite the coolness of the morning, I had worked up quite a sweat before I managed to secure a taxi. They were thin on the ground in suburbia.

'Victoria Station,' I yelled as I jumped inside.' As fast as you can. It's a matter of life and death,' I added for dramatic effort.

The cabbie gave a brief smile. 'Yeah, it always is mate,' he muttered and slammed his foot down hard on the accelerator causing the cab to leap forward and for me to be thrown with some force back into my seat. The fellow had taken me at my word.

As we travelled, I tried to assemble my thoughts and build a clear scenario of this troubled affair. I was making some assumptions certainly, but they were all based on things I knew for certain. Here's how I read the riddle at that time. Malcolm Salter and Bruce Horsefield – i.e. Lance Corporal Marshall – had absconded from the army and formed a criminal partnership. Horsefield had experience in breaking the law, albeit a fairly unsuccessful one, and probably gave Salter a crash course in the mechanics of stealing. No doubt they carried out a few small robberies and then went for the big time with the bank job in Chelmsford. It seemed to me that it was at this time that Malcolm got greedy and somehow absconded with the loot. Big mistake. Horsefield had form for being a violent beggar and certainly would not take this lightly.

I reckoned that Salter had turned up at his mother's place intending to hide out there while the heat died down. But Horsefield had tracked him down and he only managed to get away before his old partner came to call, finding the cupboard bare, as it were. Horsefield took it out on the old woman, hanging the poor old soul. Probably it was done partly as revenge and partly as a warning to Salter. He made it look like suicide so the police wouldn't be suspicious of her death, but he knew Malcolm would know the truth.

Salter went on the run and that's where I came in, tracking him down to Mrs Booth's lodging house. Actually, I did him a favour for in giving me the slip, he did the same to Horsefield who was no doubt hot on his heels. As a last resort he went to Auntie Susan for shelter. I didn't know to what extent she was party to all this, but she certainly wasn't a whited sepulchre. Now Horsefield's got him and is dragging him to where he secreted the loot – a left-luggage locker at Victoria Station. I had no doubt that when Horsefield had got his hands on the cash, he would have no compunctions about killing his traitorous partner.

Unless I could get there in time.

And getting there in time was proving a problem.

In the good old days – i.e. before the war – travelling around London was fairly easy. Of course, there were the usual snarl ups on the road at busy spots but, in general, journeys went rather smoothly without any serious delay. And then came the Luftwaffe causing all kinds of havoc: bombed buildings spilling across the thoroughfares, water and gas mains destroyed, rubble and debris blocking roads, craters causing diversions, a whole catalogue of obstructions which hindered the swift and easy passage from place to place.

While my cabbie was driving as fast as he could we did not seem to be making much progress. Once in the city, there were so many detours, down this back street, up that road, to just get a little bit further on the direct route. The only consolation was that Horsefield and Salter would have suffered the same problems. I assumed they had gone by road. If they had taken the underground, the odds on me getting there at the same time or even before them shortened. There were several changes on route and tube trains ran infrequently during the day between rush-hour times.

We jerked to a halt and the cabbie suddenly peeped his horn ferociously. We had got stuck behind a horse and cart, the driver of which seemed oblivious of other road users.

'Deaf bastard!' snarled the cabbie and leaned out of his window. 'Shift your arse, mate,' he yelled.

The driver of the cart was indeed deaf or impervious to such urging and maintained his snail-like pace.

With a grunt of anger, the cabbie wrenched the wheel to the right and mounted the pavement, while at the same time stabbing his hand down firmly on the horn to produce a loud and continuous blare of warning. Pedestrians scattered, but the cart trotted on calmly. With an extra surge of speed, the cab rocketed past the cart and we shuddered back down onto the road and continued our journey at speed.

The cabbie said nothing to me, but I could hear him chuckling to himself.

Soon the great edifice of Victoria Station hove into view. What, I wondered, would I find inside.

EIGHTEEN

He was used to pain. He could handle pain. In many ways pain was pleasurable. And in this instance it was necessary. He tugged even harder but forced himself not to wince, despite the fierce sharp electric shock waves that shot up his arm. The flesh was scraping off now. Shredding like thin slices of uncooked beef.

He tugged again and this time, he could not suppress a cry and a curse. But as he cursed, he tugged even harder, the blood welling over the cold metal of the handcuff.

Now he was wracked with pain and wanted to curl up in a ball and sob. But he knew he couldn't. He had gone this far. He had to go all the way. All the excruciating way. Before making another almighty effort, he gazed down at his damaged hand. It was almost down to the bone by the knuckles and the rest was raw flesh which glistened in the shadowy light.

Taking a deep breath, he bellowed loudly, bellowed until his lungs hurt, hoping the noise and the discomfort would help to mask the pain of one more violent effort. Contracting his fingers as much as he could, he wrenched his damaged hand further through the metal hoop of the handcuff. Without waiting for the full extent of the agony this caused to register in his brain, he did it again. Flames shot up before his eyes, bright red and yellow and his whole body rippled with agony.

But he was free.

He was free.

He looked down at the bloody mess that was his hand and tied to flex his fingers. Reluctantly they obeyed. Ralph Northcote smiled and then fell back on the bed in a dead faint.

When he awoke some twenty minutes later, he first became conscious of the throbbing ache in his right hand. Memory of his actions seem to aid the pain and as he sat up, it grew in intensity. Strangely, he smiled, his dry lips pulling back across his teeth in a feral grin. He could cope. The pain would lessen in time. The main thing was that he had not damaged the function of the hand – and that he was free. He swung his legs over the side of the bed and tried to stand up. He did so for a few moments and then collapsed back down again. He was very weak and a little light headed due to a lack of sustenance. After a few moments, he tried again and remained upright this time. His first tasks were to bandage his hand and obtain some food and water. Then he could prepare to make good his escape.

Haltingly at first, he walked to the cellar door and with his good hand, he managed to pull it open. He sneered. Sexton had been so confident that his prisoner could not escape he hadn't even bothered to lock the door.

Slowly in a shambling manner he made his way upstairs into the main body of the house and located the kitchen. In the larder he found a pork pie and a few sausages. He devoured them savagely, washed down with water. Then he attended to his hand, running it gently under the tap before using a tea towel as a makeshift bandage. In the sitting room, he found Sexton's cigarette case on the mantelpiece, the initials F S engraved on the top. Extracting a cigarette, he sat in one of the armchairs and enjoyed a smoke. As he stubbed the tab end out on the arm of the chair, he smiled again. From now on things were going to go his way.

For hours, while he had lain on that filthy bed in the cellar, he had planned in meticulous detail what he would do when he got free and now he set about doing it. Only the strange geography of the house hindered him slightly. Upstairs, in the bathroom, he found a medicine cabinet and he treated his wound, dabbing Dettol onto it, and crying out in pain as he did so, and then dressing it with a crèpe bandage. The cabinet also offered up a treasure: a small neat case containing a set of surgical instruments. He opened the case and admired the bright metal tools of his trade and his hobby. They glistened pleasingly in the natural light.

'Excellent,' murmured Northcote, stroking the leather case. 'That eliminates one of my perceived hurdles.'

This lucky find seemed to increase his energy levels. With enthusiasm, he washed, combed his hair and shaved using Sexton's razor, an act that gave him great pleasure.

Moving into the main bedroom, he raided the wardrobe, taking a smart brown suit and a cream shirt and tie. Then came the shoes. He chose a nice pair of sturdy brogues. Sexton had small feet, but cramped toes were small inconvenience compared with the throbbing discomfort of his injured hand. Every time he thought of it, he moved his fingers to reassure himself that they were still working. He also found a small stash of notes and coins in the bedside drawer – around fifteen pounds. Northcote scooped it up and slipped it in his pocket.

He selected a smart overcoat, something dark and discreet, and checked himself out in the wardrobe mirror. He looked almost human. The face was ghostly white and haggard, the eyes bloodshot and the posture a little hunched, but he reckoned he would pass unnoticed in a crowd.

He was prepared to face the world once more, but before he did, there was just one more thing he had to do.

He moved back into the sitting room and picked up the cigarette case and slipped it into his pocket.

Now he was ready.

Within minutes, he was walking down the street, away from Sexton's house and towards freedom and the city of London.

NINETEEN

I paid off the cabbie with a healthy tip. His kerb-mounting routine was beyond the call of duty, and without his ingenuity and bravado, I would, no doubt, be still stuck behind that crawling horse and cart.

I entered the portals of Victoria Station, not really knowing what was going to happen to me here. A wave of noise washed over me: a multitude of echoey voices floating round the great domed structure, built like some great industrial cathedral. The place was crowded, passengers of all sizes, shapes and ages criss-crossed and interwove with each other like a moving canvas of drab colours.

I knew where the left luggage lockers were situated, down the side of Platform One, and headed in that direction. I moved as quickly as I could, fighting against a tide of folk rolling the other way. The whole of London seemed to be squeezing their way past me. At last I reached Platform One, my hand clasped firmly on my revolver. I peered down towards the lockers and the various individuals hovering around them like expectant bees around the proverbial honey pot. I'd come face to face with Salter in the flesh, so I thought that I would recognise him, but Horsefield was only a face on an old sepia photograph. There was, of course, his hat, the large grey felt fedora.

And there it was! Large as life, bobbing towards me.

My heart began to race. I knew now that a confrontation was inevitable and certainly one of us would get hurt. I just had to make sure that it was not me. I pushed forward towards the hat, while at the same time trying to see if Malcolm Salter was accompanying it. It did not seem so.

The jostling crowd seemed to coagulate as I neared that distinctive titfer and then suddenly there was a gap into which I was propelled and faced the owner of the hat. It wasn't him. It wasn't Horsefield. It was a gentle-faced fellow well into his seventies who was having great trouble hauling a large brown case along the platform. Under normal circumstances I would have stopped and offered assistance, but these were not normal circumstances.

I squeezed past the old fellow and moved further down the platform, feeling that now I was on a fool's errand. The row of green metal lockers stretched for about twelve feet and about half a dozen passengers were installing or extracting luggage or parcels when I arrived. None of them was Salter or Horsefield. It looked like I was too late and my hopes of bringing this investigation to a swift conclusion were well and truly dashed. With sloping shoulders of defeat, I loitered by the lockers for a few minutes and turned to make my way back up the platform.

And then I saw it again. That hat! But it wasn't the same one. Not unless the old chap with the big case had turned around and was making his way up the platform now. But no, this hat certainly belonged to Horsefield for there was his thin sallow face beneath the brim and at his side was my old sparring partner, Malcolm Salter who looked as cheerful as a fat turkey on Christmas Eve. He was almost being dragged along by Felt Hat Horsefield, whose face was set in a ferocious scowl, his hand thrust deep in his raincoat pocket. Unless I was mistaken that unpleasant bulge indicated there was a gun in there, a sinister little persuader.

As soon as I'd clocked them, I turned around to hide my face and moved to the side of the platform by the Gentlemen's lavatories, and waited until they had passed me. Then I turned and followed them.

On reaching the lockers, I could see Horsefield snapping instructions to Salter, who very slowly retrieved a key from his wallet and passed it to his companion. Horsefield refused to take it and made Salter open the locker himself. Obviously he was taking no chances for Salter to do a bunk. Slowly, he opened the locker door and withdrew a dark maroon holdall. Horsefield snatched it from him and uttered some instructions and the two of them turned and began to retrace their steps. I turned sideways and appeared to be reading one of the railway notices on the wall as they went by me. They turned and disappeared into the gents' lavatories. I reckoned that Horsefield was just going to check that the money was indeed in the maroon holdall. And then what? It seemed to me there was only one likely outcome. He would shoot Salter.

* * *

Taking a deep breath, I entered the lavatories a few moments later. At first sight, it was empty. There was no one there at all. It was as though the two men had disappeared into thin air. Had I been tricked? Had it all been a performance for my benefit? But no. I head a rustling noise from one of the cubicles and bending down I could see two sets of feet visible below the door. I pressed the door gently; it was locked. Without hesitation, I stood back and lifting up my leg I rammed it hard with my size nines. It sprang open and there were cries from within and to my horror the sound of a gun shot.

Horsefield spilled out, clasping the holdall to his chest with one hand and holding the smoking gun with the other. Behind him I could see the body of Malcolm Salter. He was slumped on the lavatory, his head down on his chest.

On seeing me, Horsefield thrust the gun in my direction. I could tell from his distracted glances that things had evolved too fast for him to realise exactly what was happening. He had no idea who I was or what I wanted. For all he knew, I could be a chap in desperate need of a lavatory cubicle. I took advantage of his hesitation. With the gun still in my raincoat pocket, I shot him in the leg. He went down immediately with a cry. For some reason, I glanced down at my coat and saw the awful hole and scorch-marks that disfigured it. Damn!

I should not have been so lax. A bullet whistled past my ear and I stumbled backward in surprise. Horsefield had staggered to his feet and was edging his way to the exit. His leg was bleeding through his trousers, but I reckoned he was not badly hurt. Probably the bullet had skimmed the flesh causing only a slight wound. Well, I hadn't exactly been in a position to aim with any great accuracy. He paused in his flight and I could see that he was ready to fire again. I knew that this time he wouldn't miss. With a speed I didn't know I possessed, I dived into the cubicle, almost landing on Malcolm Salter's lap. He sighed and his body shifted sideways. He wasn't dead then, I thought. And neither was I.

I waited a moment before I and my gun appeared around the edge of the cubicle. There was no reaction. Horsefield had gone.

I ran out onto the platform, glancing both ways. A wild array of jostling passengers met my gaze both ways. But again, the hat caught my eye. There he was. There was Horsefield. I spied him some hundred yards ahead of me, racing – well, hobbling – in a speedy fashion down towards the end of the platform, away from the main concourse. I set out after him.

TWENTY

Peter should have been at school and he did feel a slight pang of guilt about playing truant, but he reckoned that his bunking off was in a good cause. At least, he had convinced himself this was the case. He was determined to follow in Johnny's footsteps and become a detective when he started work and his plan today was in a sense a trial excursion to see how successful he would be in this pursuit. With a bit of luck he may well help Johnny to bring his case to a close. That would be a real feather in his cap and convince Johnny of his talents as an investigator. Well, it was worth a try anyway.

And he had dressed for the part. He had adapted his school clothes – ditching the cap and tie and slipping on his scruffy playing out trousers – while messing his hair and smearing a little dirt on his face so that he looked like a scruffy urchin of whom no one would take any notice. A scruffy urchin of the type, he assumed, would be roaming around the streets of Houndsditch. So successful was his 'disguise' that the conductor wouldn't let him board the bus until he had provided evidence of his ability to pay. He was not in the least bit embarrassed by this challenge as the 'real' Peter would have been.

Peter had never been to Houndsditch before, but as a student of crime he knew that it wasn't very far from Whitechapel, the scene of the Jack the Ripper murders and the violent Sydney Street Siege in 1911. It was a scruffy down at heel district, but most places in London were these days: the dust and débris of war invaded all areas of the city. Peter was well aware that this was a bit of a wild goose chase but he reasoned even wild geese get caught sometimes. He had studied the picture of Bruce Horsefield from the paper and his description. He knew from Johnny that this fellow was in the habit of wearing a grey felt hat, almost like the cowboys wore in the films. Houndsditch was his home territory. Of course it had been reported in the papers that the police had visited his mother and she claimed that she hadn't seen 'neither hide nor hair of the blighter since he joined up.' They had searched her house and, of course, found nothing; but that was not to say that Marshall hadn't been waiting until the police went away. Of course, Peter realised that they would probably have put a man on to watch the house, but a clever criminal should be able to enter and leave his old home without being seen. But what brought Peter to Houndsditch was not just this thin possibility but his belief that if Horsefield was in hiding, what better place to do it than in his old manor. There would be cronies here who would help him, shelter him and keep the rozzers off his back.

Peter's plan was to patrol the streets hoping to pick up a clue or, better still, catch sight of Horsefield.

But first he had to indulge in a little dramatic interlude.

He made his way to 25 Napier Grove. The home of Mrs Horsefield.

Old Mother Riley opened the door. Or so it seemed to Peter. Standing on the threshold was a bony old woman with high cheekbones, a prominent nose and fierce eyes which were fixed permanently in the accusative mode. This vision before him was the epitome of the music hall character he'd seen in a few films and had a two-page spread in one of his favourite comics. Her arms from the elbow down were bare and flapped like a trapped seagull in true Mother Riley fashion. The impression that this harridan was indeed the famous comic washerwoman was completed by the tartan shawl draped around her shoulders.

'Yes?' she bleated without ceremony.

'I'm sorry to trouble you, Mrs, but could you let me have a glass of water? I've sort of come over a bit faint. I... er... didn't have no breakfast. Sort of dizzy.' He rocked backwards and forwards on his heels as if to demonstrate his 'dizzy' state.

The woman peered over his shoulder into the street beyond as though she expected to see others there all wanting a glass of water – or perhaps something more sinister.

'You're not from round here?' she croaked.

'No, Mrs, I'm on my way to visit my grandad. Just a glass of water, please.' He rocked on his feet once more and rolled his eyes to add further icing to his little dramatic cake. He had carefully rehearsed this performance the night before.

'Don't you go passing out on my doorstep,' the old crone said.

'I'll try not to,' he replied faintly and gave an extra roll of the eyes.

'All right. A glass of water. Then you get off to your grandad's.'

'Thank you.' He made a move to step inside, but a bony hand on his chest held him back.

'You wait here. I'll bring a glass out to you.'

Peter hadn't expected this. He had thought that he would be invited in to the kitchen. He wanted to case the joint. The plan was failing. The woman, who Peter assumed was Mrs Horsefield, retreated down the hall and disappeared. He took a few steps into the house and gazed down the hallway, hoping some clue would leap out at him. There was a coat rack at the far end with several items of clothing hanging from it. Sadly they all appeared to be those worn by ladies. There was no grey felt hat dangling from one of the hooks.

'Hey, I told you to stay where you were.'

Old Mother Riley had appeared again carrying a glass of water.

'Sorry.' Peter retreated on to the top step.

'Get this down you and then be off with you. I ain't no bleedin' hospital.' She thrust the glass at Peter, spilling some of the contents down his jacket.

Without a word, he drank the water. It was cold and salty.

'Thank you,' he said, as the bony hand snatched the glass from him. Then the door slammed in his face.

Wiping away the drips of water from around his mouth with his sleeve, Peter walked away from 25 Napier Grove hugely disappointed. His dramatic ploy had produced nothing at all – no evidence that Bruce Horsefield was hiding out at home or, indeed, any clue as to where he might be. The plan, for which he had such high hopes, had been a failure.

Thoroughly despondent, he walked a little while up the street and then sat on a low wall to ponder what to do next. He had been so sure that he would be invited in to Widow Horsefield's kitchen where he would spot some clue that indicated that her son Bruce was hiding out there – two places set at the kitchen table, a pair of men's shoes in the hearth, a jacket draped on the back of a chair or even the grey felt hat hung behind the door – but nothing. This failure was completely unexpected and he had not thought beyond it.

After wallowing in his disappointment for ten minutes or so, he shrugged his shoulders, realising that as a detective one must overcome setbacks all the time. Johnny would certainly not be beaten by such an outcome. He would have to persevere.

Houndsditch was Horsefield's stamping ground and it seemed to Peter that a man on the run, like a wounded animal, would return to his own lair. If not his family home, some gaff in the vicinity. So, he would pound the streets, pound the scruffy streets of Houndsditch, in the hope of… something.

And so hauling himself to his feet, Peter began his trek. It was now mid-morning and the streets were fairly empty: those who had jobs were at work, night shift fellows were in bed and housewives were inside doing what housewives do. In one of the streets there were a few kids who like Peter were bunking off school and were involved in an impromptu game of cricket. He hung around and watched and waited and after retrieving the ball from the gutter a couple of times, managed to get himself involved in the game. This led to idle chatter which at length he was able to swing his way. Eventually, he felt comfortable to ask if they knew the local villain who had been in the papers for robbing a bank. A geezer called Horsefield. The query met with blank stares. Even when he described Horsefield, including the detail of his felt cowboy hat, the stares remained blank. Another dead end. Realising that there was nothing to be gained from this particular cricket match, he quickly dropped out and began to mooch his way along another street.

At lunchtime he called in a café for a mug of tea and a piece of cake. He gazed around at the customers, mostly folk on their own, pale-faced and lost in thought. They all looked respectable and sad. No sign of a felt hat anywhere.

The afternoon was spent drearily tramping around streets of the area once more. He passed the Horsefield house again and even scouted around the lane at the back to no avail. Tired and fed up, Peter reckoned he'd better go home. It was nearly five o'clock and he needed to be back for tea or the Horner sisters would get worried. And anyway, it had been a futile mission. Nothing was going to present itself to him now.

But he was wrong.

TWENTY-ONE

When Horsefield reached the end of the platform, he dropped over the edge and began to cross the railway tracks. I was tempted to shoot at him, but I knew that I was no Wyatt-Earp type sharp shooter and I was probably too far away from the target to be successful. However, unlike my quarry, I was an able-bodied fellow – no wound to hinder me – and I reckoned I could soon catch up with him.

In copycat fashion, I slipped over the edge of the platform too and began picking my way across the tracks. By now Horsefield had progressed past the end of the next platform and further out, beyond the confines of the canopy of the station. In turning to see how far I was behind him, he stumbled and fell full length with a sharp cry. Now was my chance. But it was foiled by the appearance of a goods train that seemed to loom out of thin air and shudder slowly past me on the line between Horsefield and myself. The clanking, thundering monster rattled by at a snail's pace while I stood impotently immobile, unable to move or indeed see my man.

When the train had passed in a cloud of gritty smoke, I peered ahead. There was no sign of Horsefield. 'Damn,' I cried out loud and set off across the tracks again in the direction my quarry had been heading. Every so often I saw a splash of red on the iron or the sleepers: blood from his wound. I stopped for a moment and gazed around me. I suddenly realised how bizarre this situation was. Here I was standing in the middle of a tracery of railway lines searching for a wounded man who was escaping with a fortune in stolen notes. I had a vision of myself as viewed from above – a solitary human figure staggering across a series of interconnecting silver rails like some vision created by Salvador Dali or some other crazy surrealist painter.

My reverie was interrupted by the sound of a shot. On instinct I dropped to my knees. One shot, the bullet pinging onto the rails some yards ahead of me. I scanned the scene before me: signals, static rolling stock and those hypnotic silver rails sliding off into the distance – but there was no sign of Horsefield. Where had the shot come from?

And then I spied him. Or rather his legs. I saw a movement behind one of the goods trucks some hundred yards away to my right. In the gap between the wagon and the ground, I saw two legs shifting slightly.

Adopting a low crouch which that fellow from Notre Dame would have been proud of, I made my way as quickly as I could towards the wagon while keeping my eyes focused on those legs. As I grew nearer, I saw Horsefield move to the corner of the truck and peer around the corner. On seeing the loping figure bearing down on him, he fired again. As he did so, I threw myself sideways. Just in time, as it happened, for the bullet thudded into the sleeper where seconds earlier I had been crouching.

Now the legs disappeared altogether. Maybe the devil was climbing up the side in order to get onto the roof for a better view. Certainly, I'd be a much easier target from up there.

I ran the rest of the distance and on reaching the goods wagon I pressed my body to its side. I listened carefully for any sound which may give me a clue as to Horsefield's actual whereabouts. Had he clambered on to the roof or was he just around the other side clinging on? I could hear nothing, but as I moved stealthily towards the right corner of the truck, I heard the sounds of raised voices. I turned quickly and saw in the distance behind me, three men racing in my direction. One was a uniformed policeman, and the other two appeared to be railway officials, guards or something like that. They were raising their hands in the air and shouting loudly. I couldn't hear what they were saying, but I caught the word 'Stop!' It was clear they were some kind of posse and by their demeanour, it seemed I was their quarry.

I had stared at them too long for suddenly I was conscious of a shadow and then a presence near me. I turned quickly but too late. I saw Horsefield. I saw Horsefield with his arm raised high. I saw Horsefield bring the butt of the gun down towards me. I saw blackness.

* * *

When I awoke, I found myself lying on a small utility bed with screens around me. As I tried to sit up, a hand grenade went off in my head. I groaned. The screens parted and a young woman in a nurse's outfit appeared and smiled gently.

'So you have returned to the land of the living, eh?'

It was a pleasant voice, low in register and with an accent. Middle European. I guessed that, but I had no idea where I was.

'Where am I?' My voice escaped like a tired mole into the daylight.

'You are in the First Aid room at Victoria Station. You have been hit on the head.' The explanation was succinct and explanatory and was accompanied by a warm smile.

'I can feel it. Where… where is the other man? The one who hit me?'

She shrugged. 'I don't know. Would you like a cup of tea?'

'No, no. I must be going.'

'You'll be going nowhere.' This injunction came from a second figure who appeared beside the nurse. It was a police sergeant: a robust red-faced fellow with a comfortable girth.

'You've got a lot of explaining to do, my lad,' he said as though he was admonishing a youngster for breaking a window with his cricket ball.

'Horsefield – did he escape?'

'If you mean the bloke what dinted your skull; yes, he legged it.'

'He's a killer.'

'Is he now? And was it him that did for the bloke in the lavatories?'

Salter. I had forgotten about him. 'Oh, he's dead, then.'

'As a doornail.'

'The man that I was chasing, a fellow called Horsefield, was the dead man's accomplice in a bank robbery… I'm a private detective.'

The sergeant held up his hand. 'Whoa. Save your breath, son. You can tell it all to Inspector Sullivan. He's on his way here now.'

'In the meantime,' said the nurse, 'how about that cup of tea and a couple of aspirins?'

I nodded in acceptance and another hand grenade exploded in my skull.

The sergeant disappeared, but the nurse sat with me as I drank my tea. She told me her name was Ivana and she was Russian. She was originally from Stalingrad but had left the city at the outbreak of the war and made her way to England. Her family had perished in the terrible battle for the city in 1942 and now she was alone in the world. She seemed to gain some comfort telling me her story – a stranger whom she would never see again. A stranger whom she expected to be carted off to prison any moment now.

Her eyes misted as she spoke of her parents and the terrible atrocities that the Nazis had wrought in Stalingrad. She had a strong face, mannish almost, but a lovely smile and deep expressive brown eyes.

I liked her.

Suddenly there was a rustle behind the screens and then Inspector Bernard Sullivan appeared.

'Oh, it's you,' he said.

* * *

Sullivan knew me from my days as a serving policeman. He was a copper of the old school: fair, scrupulous and down to earth.

'I'd heard you'd gone private. A ladies detective. Spying through

109

keyholes on naughty husbands. So how come you get mixed up in a murder and a nasty affray in a railway station?'

'Just luck,' I said and he laughed.

'O.K. Johnny. Give me the low-down,' he said pulling up a stool.

As succinctly as I could I filled him in him on the scenario involving Malcolm Salter and Bruce Horsefield. Sullivan listened intently, his eyes twitching all the while, a sign I knew that he was making a mental note of all that I was telling him. He was that kind of copper.

After I'd finished, he rubbed his chin sagely. 'A bit of a mess all round. You O.K.?'

I touched my head where Horsefield's gun had landed and found to my surprise that it was bandaged. 'I'll live,' I said.

'A good night's kip and a stiff brandy, as my old granny used to say.'

'So Salter's dead.'

'The bloke in the lav. Yes. He hung on for a while but he didn't make it.'

'And the money.'

'Well Sergeant Morris found a bag but it was empty. That'd be the one, I reckon.'

'Yes. It had two thousand pounds in it.'

Sullivan whistled. 'Nice little horde. So it looks like your mate Horsefield got away with it after all.'

'Yes,' I said disconsolately. 'It looks like it.'

Sullivan gave a wry chuckle. 'Not your finest hour, then; eh, Johnny? Perhaps you'd better get back to one of those keyholes, watching those naughty married people.'

'Ha ha,' I replied, for want of a wittier or more acerbic response. 'Does that mean I can go?'

'Well, I reckon so. We know where to pick up you up if needed. You say it's Herbert whose handling the Chelmsford robbery?'

'Yes.'

Sullivan beamed. 'Well, it will be my pleasure to dump this little lot in his lap. You may find him on your doorstep in the morning. The grin converted into a chuckle. He rose from the stool. Before he disappeared behind the screens he turned back and gave me a friendly nod. 'Look after yourself, lad,' he said.

TWENTY-TWO

Tired, disheartened and hungry, Peter dragged his weary bones towards the bus stop. It was time for him to return home. His search had been fruitless. His bright hopes had been dashed. Perhaps detective work wasn't as satisfying as he thought it would be. It was a little devil of a thought and he quelled it. You need perseverance and determination to succeed as a private investigator, he told himself firmly. You don't give up if at first you don't succeed. He knew this was true but it was hard to accept when his feet hurt and his tummy rumbled.

'Perseverance and determination,' he muttered, almost as a mantra. 'Perseverance and determination. And luck,' he added as an afterthought. Yes, luck was what he had lacked today. 'If only I'd had a bit of luck…'

And then he did. It came out of nowhere and pinned him to the spot. He froze like a statue as he observed a tall thin man turn the corner, walking in a slow awkward fashion towards him. Peter could not see his face clearly because it was shielded by a large grey felt hat.

His heart almost stopped at the excitement of this encounter. Surely, here was the man himself. The one that he'd been searching for. He rubbed his eyes to make sure this wasn't an hallucination. It wasn't. Here was Bruce Horsefield. In the flesh. He was sure of it. He stared at him as he walked past and noticed that there was a dark stain on one of his trouser legs below the knee – the leg that seemed to be giving him some discomfort.

The man was injured – that explained his rather clumsy gait.

Horsefield took no notice of Peter as he slipped past him, making slow but steady progress along the pavement. Peter waited only a few seconds before turning and following the man.

After some ten minutes when Horsefield had led Peter into the maze of small streets lying behind Middlesex Road, he reached a row of down at heel terrace houses. Here Horsefield paused and gazed around him as though he was checking he hadn't been followed. Peter had the presence of mind to push his body into the tangle of an overgrown privet hedge, some of the prickly branches getting up his nose.

Believing himself safe from shadows, Horsefield mounted the steps of one house and disappeared inside.

Peter gazed at the gaunt shabby building, its mildewed façade and blank windows darkened by the blackout shutters which were still in place, and smiled. The villain's hideout, he thought. He had found it. All on his own.

He must inform Johnny and how proud he would be in doing so. He remembered passing a telephone box a few streets away and sprinting he retraced his way there. Frustratingly, it was occupied by a young woman with a brightly coloured turban and large dangly earrings. She was in full flow. He could hear her voice in high-pitched moaning mode as her left hand fluttered wildly like a trapped bat. He couldn't catch her words but one didn't have to in order to know she was expressing some grievance in a grumpy tirade.

'Come on, come on,' murmured Peter in frustration, glancing at his watch. He was well aware that it was quite possible that Horsefield would only stay in the house a short time before moving on. The woman in the box sensing his presence and his impatience glowered at him and then turned her back without a pause in her diatribe.

Seconds ticked by into minutes. Then to his great dismay, he saw the woman put more coins into the slot. God, she was going to tell all the world about her grievance.

Peter was joined by a tall smartly dressed man outside the box. A queue was forming.

'Has she been in long?' he asked.

'Forever,' said Peter.

The man leaned forward and tapped on the glass of the telephone box. The woman turned abruptly, scowled and mouthed some obscenity at him.

'Charming,' he said.

At last, the woman put the phone down, but made no real effort to leave the box.

The man pulled the door open. 'Have you done?'

'Yeah, yeah,' she returned scowling. 'This is private in here. You should wait.'

'I have been waiting. I have an important call to make.'

With a belligerent shove, she brushed past him. 'It's all yours,' she said.

The man turned to Peter. 'It is rather important, sonny. I hope you don't mind if I go before you.'

Peter's nerves along with his temper were somewhat frayed by now and he wasn't going to have this. He had waited his turn and his turn it was.

'Yes, I bloody do mind,' he found himself saying, swearing out loud in front of a grown up for the first time in his life. Without waiting for a reaction, he yanked the door from the man's grasp and entered the box.

As his nervous fingers pressed the coins into the slot, he prayed that Johnny would be in his office. It was teatime. Surely, whatever he'd been dong all day, he'd be back for a cuppa and his usual makeshift evening meal.

But the phone kept on ringing.

In his mind's eye, Peter saw the lonely instrument on Johnny's desk, the dim shadows of evening falling softly onto it as it vibrated gently in the gloom, but there was no arm there to reach out and pick up the receiver. Eventually, he gave up and pressed button B.

With a sigh, he dialled another number. This time the call was answered.

'Hello,' said a voice in a tone that intimated that the caller had interrupted something of vital importance.

'Benny. It's Peter.'

'Oh, Peter, hello, my boy. What a pleasure to hear from you.' The voice was sweeter, friendlier now, rich in warmth.

'Benny, is Johnny there at the café?'

'Not unless he's the invisible man. He doesn't come here as often as he used to… not since…' The voice trailed away.

'Do you know where he is?'

'How should I? Trailing some hoodlum maybe or taking a drink at the Velvet Cage. Your guess is as good as mine.'

Peter ruffled his hair with his free hand. 'Look, Benny, it's important I get a message to him. It's about his latest case.'

'What message?'

'I've tracked Horsefield to his lair. It's 23 Commercial Street, Houndsditch.'

'Let me write this down. Hey, wait a minute, what do you mean you tracked this horseperson to his lair. Are you in danger? What's going on?'

'No, no, I'm safe but I don't know how long Horsefield will stay there. Johnny needs to get here fast.'

'Are you sure you're safe? You shouldn't be involving yourself in such activities.'

'I'm fine, Benny; don't worry about me.'

'Of course I worry. No more funerals do I want to go to this year.'

'Look this is urgent. Please try and get in touch with Johnny. I've rung his office but he's not there. Maybe you could try the Velvet Cage.'

'Very well.'

'Oh, and could you ring Aunt Edith and Aunt Martha with some excuse of why I won't be home for tea. I don't want them to worry.'

'A web of lies.'

'Just a little fib. I'd better go I don't want to leave Horsefield for too long.'

'Be careful, my boy. Be very careful.'

Peter replaced the receiver quickly and exited the phone box. The man waiting outside glared at him, but Peter had other things on his mind and did not notice. Breaking into a sprint, he headed back to 23 Commercial Street.

TWENTY-THREE

Even before Frances Sexton entered his house, he knew that there was something wrong. It was instinct rather than evidence at first. As he walked up the path, he experienced a strange, irrational sensation as though a shadow had fallen over him and he shivered. When he discovered the front door was unlocked, it was no longer instinct. His heart constricted and a desperate inner panic took hold of him. Flinging down his case in the hall he raced to the cellar, his terror growing with every step. Before he got there, he knew what he would find – the unlocked front door had told him that much. Nevertheless, when he entered the gloomy chamber and saw the empty bed, and the blood-smeared handcuff, his legs grew weak and his body shook with horror. Within seconds of entering the cellar, he found himself leaning against the wall while his stomach retched, attempting to propel his midday meal on to the floor. With Herculean effort, Sexton controlled this powerful reaction, groaning with despair as he did so.

The repercussions of this nightmare situation that the empty room presented were so frightening and impenetrable that at first Sexton's mind could not cope with them. He just slithered to the floor and placed his head in his hands and groaned again, while rocking to and fro on his haunches.

Northcote had escaped. Northcote was free. Now Northcote could destroy him.

And he had no idea what to do.

He sat there for some fifteen minutes or so, his mind fixated on that one and only fact: Northcote had escaped. The bastard was free!

Eventually, he dragged himself to his feet and, like a sleepwalker, made his way back upstairs and to the drinks cabinet where he poured himself an enormous brandy.

He took a large gulp before slumping down in an armchair, clasping the glass tightly between his two hands.

He had no idea what he was going to do – or what he could do. His tired, ragged brain revealed to him that there were no options. He certainly couldn't go to the police. He had no idea what Northcote would do next or where he would go and so there was no hope of recapturing him. And, of course, his dream of using him as a scapegoat was in tatters.

Or was it?

Oh, God, he didn't know. He just couldn't think straight.

More brandy might help. He reached out for the bottle.

* * *

In the shady environs of Cartwright Gardens, Dr Ralph Northcote waited for the dark. He had found himself cheap lodgings in the King's Cross area and was now ready – more than ready after years of incarceration – to kill. There would be an extra frisson to the act tonight, not just because it would be the first time in years, although this fact was mightily significant to him, but also because he would fatally wound that traitorous swine, Sexton. Sitting on a bench in the shadow of a large plane tree, he watched the moon as it grew brighter while the blue of the evening sky deepened. Soon it was an eerily yellow orb hanging against an indigo setting. A hunter's moon and he was a very eager hunter indeed.

* * *

There was one stretch of the Caledonian Road, about half a mile from King's Cross Station, that to Sally Hopkins's mind was darker than the rest. She knew that the blackout was the blackout, but somehow this section seemed to have an added layer of inky darkness. There was a line of tall, blank featureless commercial buildings which towered above the road, standing like grim sentries which seemed to her vivid imagination, as though they were waiting to pounce on an unsuspecting pedestrian. Every night when she walked home after her stint as a barmaid in one of the public houses up by the station, her pace quickened when she reached this part of her route. She knew she was being illogical, but she couldn't help her feelings. And tonight strangely she felt more frightened than usual.

She had good reason.

Suddenly a dark shape stepped out in front of her, causing her to collide with it. Sally Hopkins gave out a little scream but her attention was immediately taken by the sudden pain in her abdomen. She pulled away from the figure, the pain increasing, but the man – she now recognised the shape as a man – came towards her again and thrust something towards her stomach. She moaned with pain and sank to the floor. Feeling dizzy and faint, she gazed up at her assailant and saw that he was holding what appeared to be a knife. As consciousness faded, she became aware of the wetness that was seeping through the material of her coat.

Blood.

The man knelt down beside her and without a word, stabbed her again, this time twisting the knife in the wound. She hadn't the energy to cry out. Her mouth opened, spittle dripped down her chin and then her head fell back on the pavement.

Within seconds Sally Hopkins was dead.

With a satisfied murmur, Ralph Northcote dragged the body down a narrow opening between two buildings, to a small area hidden from the road where the dustbins were kept. Here, he lit a candle, placed it on one of the dustbin lids and then undressed the girl. In the pale shimmering light, he extracted the instruments he needed from the bag he had left there and began work.

* * *

Half an hour later, he had completed his task, having removed the heart, liver and a section of the left thigh and wrapped them in newspaper before stowing them in his case. For a moment he gazed down at the girl's face, now gently laced with blood, the eyes and mouth still wide with shock and horror. He felt nothing for her. No emotion touched his heart or mind. She was just dead meat to him.

He was ready to go, but he still had one task to perform. Taking Francis Sexton's silver cigarette case from his pocket, he placed it on the ground near the body. This action did prompt a reaction: a gentle, unstable giggle.

TWENTY-FOUR

When Inspector Bernard Sullivan had departed, I intended to do the same. I reckoned I needed a drink and some thinking time. And, boy, did I have something to think about. However, when I swung my legs around on the camp bed and attempted to stand up, the room began to bend and sway. With a groan, I slumped back staring at the ceiling waiting for it to settle down. Then into my field of vision appeared the face of nurse Ivana.

'You are a naughty man,' she said in her rich Russian voice, making it sound like an invitation to an orgy. 'You cannot move just yet. You must rest for a couple of hours at least. Your system has had a very big shock. You lie back. I will bring you a cup of sweet tea.'

'You couldn't make that a double whisky, could you?' I grinned, in spite of my discomfort.

She returned my smile. 'You really are a naughty man.'

'No ice,' I added with a chuckle as she disappeared around the screen. She returned a few minutes later with a mug of hot, sweet tea.

'Just as you ordered: no ice,' she beamed, as she handed it to me. 'Now drink that and rest for a while.'

'Yes, ma'am.'

The tea was good despite the sweetness and I did feel as though it revived me a little, but I still hadn't the energy or the sureness of foot to get up and leave and so I obeyed nurse's orders and lay back and stared at the gently shimmering ceiling. In the distance I could hear station noises, the echoing hiss of steam, speaker announcements, the shrill screech of a guard's whistle and the muted cacophony of the sea of travellers as they ebbed and flowed up and down the concourse and the various platforms. So many lives, so many journeys. It seemed that despite the drama I was involved in, the world was getting on with its mundane business.

I closed my eyes and ran through the events of the day. It struck me that I'd been lucky. I could be lying on a slab in the morgue now instead of a fairly comfy camp bed being nursed by a very pleasant Russian girl. The mystery surrounding Annie Salter's death had been cleared up once and for all, but unfortunately the real villain of the piece, her murderer, had escaped. Strangely I felt sorry for Malcolm Salter. I knew he had been a deserter and an armed robber, (past tense) but I didn't think he deserved to die in such a manner. Some leopards can change their spots and I'm a strong believer in giving a chap a chance at reforming himself. Well, there was no chance for Malcolm now.

I suppose my part in the case was effectively over. I had carried out Father Sanderson's wishes and discovered the truth of poor old Annie's death. However, I knew I couldn't let it rest there. I had to find Horsefield and bring him to justice. If only in revenge for the gargantuan headache he'd given me. And besides, surely it is what the old priest would have expected me to do. Well, I was going to do it. Or at least try.

Mind you, I had no idea how I was going to do it. I reckoned that I would have a go at formulating some sort of plan after a good night's sleep when I hoped the blitzkrieg in my head had ceased.

I gave a shrug, closed my eyes and, before I knew it, I had fallen into a gentle sleep.

I was woken sometime later by my Russian nightingale. She had her raincoat on and seemed to be ready to go somewhere.

'I've just come to say goodbye,' she said with a smile. 'My shift is over and Nurse Kerry is taking over.'

I glanced at my watch. It was just after six in the evening: I had been asleep for over three hours.

'You can stay here until you feel fit enough to leave.'

'Oh, that's now,' I said, pulling myself up more quickly than I should. My head throbbed as though a small road drill were digging deep into the convolutions of cerebral cortex but my vision, though not perfect, was much better. Everything seemed to have a fine double edge.

Ivana caught my arm. 'Whoa,' she said, with a half smile. 'Are you sure you're ready for this?'

Certainly am,' I said with more confidence than I felt, as I pulled myself to my feet. Thankfully the room stayed where it was, but the drills were still pounding away. 'Perhaps you could walk with me a while, just until I get my sea legs, as it were.'

Nurse Kerry, whose rosy red features had been peering around the screen, gave me an old-fashioned look.

'I suppose so,' said Ivana.

Breathing deeply, I stepped forward and took her arm. I needed it for my legs were still weak and unsure of themselves. We left the first aid room with me clinging to Ivana like some over attentive boyfriend. She seemed to take this strange perambulation in her own confident stride. Once outside the confines of the station, I began to breathe in the cool night air. It filled my lungs and began to clear away the cobwebs in my brain. Like some magic rejuvenating elixir, it coursed through my body giving me strength. After we had gone a hundred yards or so, I was walking normally again and my vision was clear, but I was reluctant to release my grip on Ivana's arm. It was good to be close to a woman again.

'I don't suppose you'd allow me to buy you a drink?' I said as casually as I could.

'Now why do you suppose that? I'd love a drink.'

I grinned back sheepishly. 'I know just the place.'

* * *

It was around seven o'clock by the time we arrived at The Velvet Cage, my favourite watering hole. We had walked part of the way and then taken a taxi. It was quiet in the club, with very few customers and the musicians were only just setting up for their first set that evening.

We sat in a booth. Ivana asked for a sweet sherry – I grimaced at this but ordered the drink all the same while I settled for a whisky. For some time we sat in awkward silence. We seemed to have run out of conversation. We had chatted merrily on our journey, she telling me that she shared a small flat in Earl's Court with another nurse called Mildred and how she liked to read in her spare time 'the great British writers like Charles Dickens and Emily Brontë.' I had told her about my accident when I lost an eye and why I was a detective. 'So you get beaten up a lot,' she had observed wryly.

'I try not to be,' I said.

But now we seemed to have run out of steam. My supply of small talk was very limited at the best of times but now it seemed as though it had disappeared altogether.

Suddenly she turned to me and placed her hand on mine. 'You seem sad. I know you joke and smile, but I think you are a sad man. Why is that?'

I gave a non-committal smile.

'You perhaps have lost someone?'

'In this war, hasn't everyone? You, your parents.'

'Yes, that's true. But I hide my pain. I see yours in your face.'

'Look lady, I've just been bopped very hard on the head. No wonder you see pain in my face. Ouch!'

She grinned. 'Yes, you cover it up with a joke. Let me see your hands – your right hand.'

I held it up and wiggled my fingers. She took it gently and laid it palm upwards on the table and stared intently at it.

'Well,' she said, 'you will be pleased to know that you have a very healthy life line. You should live into an old age.'

'Goodness, you're not going to read my palm?'

'Of course. All my family have the gift. The God-given lines on your hands tell many secrets about your character and your life. See, your heart line is strong and straight.'

'What does that mean?'

'You are idealistic and sometimes you let your heart rule your head.'

I took a drink of whisky. Can't argue with that, I thought, but said nothing.

'You are complex man, Johnny. Some of your lines do the oddest things.'

'Do they tell you whether I'm going to capture the fellow who tried to break my skull?'

She smiled and shook her head. 'I'm afraid not.'

I was about to make some flippant remark when I was conscious of a shadow falling over us and the heavy wheezing breathing of its owner.

I looked up and saw Benny, his face shiny with sweat and his eyes bulging from the exertions he had obviously just undergone. He mopped his brow with a handkerchief before he spoke. 'Johnny, thank heavens I've found you.'

'What is it, Benny? You look done in.'

'That's because I am. I ran most of the way. I'm so relieved you're here. Peter said you might be.'

'Peter? What about him?'

Benny shook his head. 'Such a foolish boy. Apparently, he's been trailing one of your villains – the bank robber.'

'Horsefield!'

Benny nodded. 'I think that was his name. Well, Peter's traced him to an address in Houndsditch'. He paused to drag a scrap of paper from his pocket. '23 Commercial Street. He said he'd wait for you there, somewhere outside in the street.'

'The idiot. How long ago was this?'

'About twenty minute… half an hour ago.'

I turned abruptly to Ivana. 'I'm sorry, I have to go.'

'Of course.' She squeezed my hand. 'Be careful.'

'I'll try,' I said giving her a quick kiss on the cheek.

Without another word, I left the two of them staring after me as I dashed for the exit.

* * *

After a rather hectic and bumpy taxi ride, I arrived in Houndsditch. I asked the cabbie to drop me a few blocks away from Commercial Street. On the journey my mind had been trying to work out how Peter had ended up trailing Horsefield. He'd studied those bloody newspaper reports he'd shown me, hadn't he? No doubt on a hunch he'd gone down to Houndsditch and somehow by some fluke found where the fellow was hiding. I doubted if he realised how dangerous Horsefield was – especially now he was wounded and had managed to retrieve the cash from the bank robbery.

I suppose it was my fault that Peter fancied himself as a super sleuth, trying to impress me, and if he got hurt or worse, it would be on my conscience for life and possibly longer.

It was now quite dark as I turned into Commercial Street. The place was quiet and empty. There were no pedestrians and no traffic. An eerie silence seemed to inhabit the place. Casually, I lit a cigarette and strolled along the pavement noting the house numbers as I did so. Eventually I came to number 23. It was cloaked in total darkness which, of course, was not unusual in these days of the blackout. I looked around for Peter. There was no sign of the scamp.

Where the hell was he? What was he up to now? I called out his name, hoping that he would emerge from the shadows and greet me. But he didn't.

My heart sank.

What was I going to do now?

TWENTY-FIVE

David Llewellyn was cleaning his teeth prior to donning his pyjamas for an early night when the telephone rang.

'You'd better get that,' his wife Sylvia called from the bedroom. 'It's bound to be for you.'

She was right of course. He knew as he lifted the receiver that he could wave goodbye to the early appointment with his pillow.

'Sunderland, here, sir,' announced the tinny voice at the other end. 'There's been another murder. A young woman. Cut about something shocking. Looks like it's Northcote's work all right. She was found on Copenhagen Street, just off the Caledonian Road down by King's Cross. One of the local tarts stumbled over the body.'

Llewellyn gave a little groan as he felt the chill hand of fear grip him. It was happening all over again. The same nightmare, but this time somehow it was worse. The killer had turned into a phantom of the night. He had no idea where he was or where and when he would strike next.

'Give me the exact details and I'll be down there within the hour,' he said sourly.

* * *

The remains of Sally Hopkins were covered with a large grey blanket and part of the road had been cordoned off. Llewellyn stepped forward and raised the blanket, allowing the thin beam of his torch travel over the grisly corpse.

'Very nasty, eh, sir?' said Sunderland, standing close to him.

Llewellyn grunted a reply. 'Do we know what's been taken? The organs?'

'The pathologist says that her heart and liver have gone and part of the thigh. He says he'll have a better idea when he examines the body back at the Yard.'

Llewellyn dropped the blanket. 'Well, get her back there, then. There's little use her being here.'

'Right, sir.'

Llewellyn was about to turn away when something caught his attention. The beam of his torch fell on something that glittered in the gloom at the far side of the blanket, in the shadows over by the wall. He stepped forward, bent down and picked it up. Holding it close to his face, he saw that it was a silver cigarette case.'

'Very interesting,' he said slowly, his eyes widening with surprise.

'Do you think it was dropped by the killer, sir?' asked Sunderland.

'I'm not sure, but what makes it interesting – fascinating even – is that it has a name engraved on it.'

'Not Northcote?'

'No. Not Northcote. The name is Francis Sexton.'

* * *

While Inspector David Llewellyn was examining the cigarette case of Dr Francis Sexton, the man himself was preparing for his great vanishing act. After wallowing sometime in despair, following the discovery that his prisoner Northcote had escaped, the section in his brain that dealt with self preservation and survival had suddenly kicked in. He realised that his only course of action now was to disappear. Go somewhere in the country – maybe Devon where he had spent many childhood holidays. He had to become someone else in an out-of-the-way place, where neither the authorities nor Northcote could find him. With this vague and desperate plan in mind, he was quickly packing a bag with essentials, including a few small valuable items which he could sell to help him get by, along with the fifty pounds he had taken from his wall safe.

With a great strength of will, he was not allowing his mind to dwell on his old life which he now had to leave behind. If he was to survive – and indeed it was a matter of survival – he realised that he must forget all that and accept the new and unpleasant, drastic circumstances in which he found himself.

Clutching his case, he headed for the hallway and retrieved his hat and coat. Once he had donned these, he couldn't resist stepping back into the living room to cast a final eye over his home.

It was then that it struck him. He just couldn't depart like this. Walk out and leave all this behind intact. It wasn't just the fact that he was turning his back on the comfort and security of his home but, in a more practical sense, he couldn't leave the house like the Marie Celeste, like a ghost home, still keeping the signs of recent habitation: discarded newspapers, crumpled sheets, half empty gin bottles. And more importantly he couldn't leave the cellar: the room where Northcote had been kept prisoner for prying eyes and expert analysts. That would really give the game away. That canny Welsh policeman would very quickly put two and two together and make a sparkling four.

Although he was aware that he was tired, his brain frayed at the edges and his thinking processes ragged and shaky, he also knew that the idea that came to him now was the right one.

He would torch the house.

Burn it to the ground.

The flames would expunge, purge any evidence useful to the police. With a smile he realised that the added bonus of this idea would be that they might think that he had perished in the flames. It would be a sound assumption to make. Then he really would be off the hook. They might search for a body, but he knew that the war had taught the police to cut corners. There were too many burnt out buildings and missing corpses to cope with efficiently. Whatever, setting fire to the place would certainly buy him time.

Inspired by this notion, he dropped his case and headed outside to the garage where he kept a spare can of petrol. That would ensure the flames would be all-devouring.

He chuckled to himself as he unlocked the garage door and swung it open. So focussed was he in his task, that he failed to see a bulky shadow by the gate. Dragging a metal canister from a shelf at the rear of the garage, Sexton returned to the house, followed at a distance by the shadow.

Once back inside the house, Sexton went down into the cellar, unscrewed the top of the canister and began sloshing the petrol around in a liberal fashion before returning to the sitting room. Here he repeated the process, dousing the carpet, the sofa and the curtains. He smiled broadly. He felt there was something satisfying about being an agent of destruction.

Soon the canister was empty and he flung it down and then stood for a moment breathing in the fumes. The aroma was intoxicating and pleasing. Then he heard a slight movement behind him and turning swiftly he saw a figure standing in the doorway. His heart juddered with shock.

It was Ralph Northcote.

'Trying to destroy the evidence?' he said quietly.

The sight of Northcote immediately ignited Sexton's anger. He gave no thought as to how or why the devil came to be standing in his sitting room. Rage exploded within him. He roared with fury and like an automaton moved stiffly towards him, his arms outstretched.

Northcote stayed put. He simply lifted his right arm which held a long sharp knife.

'Stay,' he snapped, as one would to a dog. 'Stay, or I will gouge your eyes out.'

Sexton faltered and then did as he was told.

'I know it is melodramatic,' Northcote said quietly, without any emotion, 'but I have returned for my revenge.' He gazed about him. 'And it seems as though you have helped me in my preparations.'

Sexton took a step forward, but Northcote thrust the knife towards him. 'It would be foolish to come any closer. I cannot tell you how much pleasure it would be for me to cut you up, to hear you cry in agony – the man that tried to deceive me. The man that imprisoned me and treated me like an animal.'

Sexton's mind sought in vain for some course of action. He knew he could not reason with Northcote. He knew he could not tackle him: one false move and he would feel the blade of that vicious knife on his face. Could he perhaps run? But where to? Northcote was blocking the only viable exit to the outside. If he turned and ran into the kitchen, he knew that the exterior door was locked. By the time he had retrieved the key, the fiend would be upon him. The situation seemed hopeless.

'Not only will you die tonight,' Northcote was saying, 'but your secret will be exposed. The police will know all about you.'

Sexton shook his head. He didn't know what the fellow was talking about and besides he was only half listening while his eyes darted around the room in search of something he could snatch up and use as a weapon against Northcote. His eyes lit upon a large glass ashtray on the coffee table to his left, just a few feet beyond his reach. He knew he would have to risk it. It was his only chance.

Slowly he stepped backwards and then in a desperate sideways motion he reached out for the ashtray, but Northcote had sensed what was happening and attacked. He lunged forward thrusting the knife at Sexton, who had moved so quickly that the blade only caught him in the arm. With a cry of pain, Sexton stumbled sideways on to the edge of the sofa, where he lost his balance and crashed to the floor.

Northcote stood over him, legs astride like a maniacal colossus and raised the knife, ready for the fatal blow. In wild desperation, Sexton lashed out with his legs, catching Northcote violently in the crotch. With a moan, Northcote doubled up, the knife spinning from his hand. Scrabbling across the floor from his assailant, Sexton reached out for the ashtray once more and brought it crashing down on

Northcote's head. With a muted grunt, Northcote slithered forward onto his face in an apparent faint.

The light of unstable triumph illuminated Sexton's eyes as he rose unsteadily to his feet and stood panting over the inert frame of his enemy, the throbbing pain in his shoulder almost forgotten. He was inclined to bring the ashtray down once more on the man's skull, but he resisted the temptation. The flames would finish the job off more satisfactorily.

He felt in his jacket pocket for his cigarette lighter, wincing as he did so, the pain of his wounded arm reasserting itself. Taking an old newspaper from the magazine rack, he twisted it round into a makeshift torch and lit one end with the lighter. It blossomed into a bright yellow flame. With a satisfied grin, he flung the burning paper onto the petrol soaked hearth rug. It spluttered awhile and for a moment Sexton thought that it would go out, but then with a gentle woomf, tendrils of flame shot across the rug and rose upwards. Within seconds, the hungry fire, with the help of the petrol, reached out beyond the rug to touch the carpet and other items of furniture with its fiery contagion.

Sexton was surprised and pleased at the speed with which the fire was spreading. Already he could feel the searing heat on his face and he knew that he had little time to lose before he left the building. But as he turned to go, he stumbled. Something had caught hold of his ankle.

Someone.

Northcote.

The fiend had roused himself. Sexton tried to wrench himself free of his firm grip but failed. He dropped to the floor, kicking his leg as violently as he could in an attempt to shake his assailant off. All the while the flames were multiplying, growing hungrier and more fierce.

'Let go, or we'll both be killed,' screamed Sexton.

Surprisingly Northcote released his hold, while at the same time, jumping to his feet and scooping up the knife which lay inches away from the devouring flames. Sexton could only see him now as a dark silhouette against the yellow wall of fire.

For a second time Northcote loured over him but Sexton was too slow to react on this occasion. With a snarl of anger, Northcote brought the knife down, straight into Sexton's right eye and piercing his brain. Sexton opened his mouth to cry out but no sound emerged. His body jiggled for a few seconds like a man on a gibbet and then lay still, a trickle of blood smearing his cheek.

Fixing that pleasing image in his mind, Northcote ran from the burning building out into the enveloping darkness.

TWENTY-SIX

I made my way up the overgrown path of number 23 Commercial Street. It seemed to me that the house had not been occupied for some time. The door was boarded up as were the downstairs windows. However, on closer inspection, I noticed that one of the boards across the window at the left-hand side of the door seemed to be hanging loose. So it proved to be. With just a gentle movement I was able to swing the board to one side, creating a gap big enough for me to gain entry to the house, a feat managed easily as the window pane behind the planking was missing. It lay in shattered shards on the floor inside.

In a trice I was standing in a dark, damp and rank smelling chamber. I lit a match and the decaying room sprang into flickering relief. This had been the sitting room, I guessed, noting the broken down horsehair sofa and a decrepit armchair, the seat of which seemed now to be the home for a family of mice. As the match dimmed, prior to going out, I heard a movement somewhere in the room and then as darkness returned, a bright light shone in my face.

'Johnny!' a voice called. It was Peter. I felt a mixture of relief and annoyance.

'Take that torch out of my eyes, will you?' I snapped.

'Sorry,' he said, lowering the beam.

'What the hell are you doing here?'

'I followed Horsefield. I saw him enter the house but now he's disappeared.'

'What do you mean disappeared?'

'I watched him climb through the gap in the boarded up window and come in here just before it got dark but he didn't come out again, so I came in after him.'

'You little fool, don't you know the man is very dangerous? He's a murderer. He wouldn't think twice of putting a bullet in you.'

'I was careful.'

I rolled my eyes in angry derision but, of course, in the darkness Peter could not see disdain.

'Anyway, I've been around the house and looked in all the rooms and he's not here,' he continued. 'He must have left another way, probably out of the back.'

'Are you sure he's gone?'

'Positive.'

'That's very odd. What made him come here in the first place if it wasn't to hide out.'

'He might come back.'

'I suppose so, but I reckon that's unlikely. When you saw him was he limping?'

'Yes. His left leg, I think.'

'That's my handiwork. I wounded the fellow today.'

'Really!' In his excitement at this revelation, Peter's voice rose an octave. 'How?'

As briefly and succinctly as I could, I gave Peter a recital of my adventures at Victoria Station.'

'Wow, a real shoot out. That's terrific.'

'Not all that terrific. The man got away and with the money after killing his greedy partner and giving me a whopping headache.'

'So, what's our plan of action?'

A good question. I pushed my hat back on my head and scratched my forehead. I was puzzled and no ideas were coming to my rescue.

'Well,' I said at length. 'There's nothing we can do here tonight. Let's get you home.'

'Ah, Johnny, we can't give up now.'

'Oh, yes we can, partner. We have no leads and even if I had, I certainly wouldn't be involving you in following them up.'

'Why not? I found Horsefield, didn't I?'

I couldn't argue with that point. Then an idea struck me. 'When you saw Horsefield, was he carrying a bag, like a small holdall?'

Peter thought for a moment. 'Yes, I reckon he was. He sort of clutched something to his chest as if he was holding a baby. I suppose it could have been a holdall.'

I grinned. 'Holding a baby, eh? His bonny baby: two thousand smackeroos in crisp bank notes. So that's why he came here.'

Peter shook his head in puzzlement. 'What do you mean?'

'To stash away the money. A nice little hiding place while the heat is on. This is his neck of the woods. He'd know about this old house. An ideal location to secrete the stolen cash. Safe as old houses.'

'So it's here somewhere,'

'Somewhere. Yes, I reckon it is.'

'So we'd better search for it.' Peter was getting really excited now.

'Whoa,' I cried. 'You've heard the phrase 'needle in a haystack', well that's the situation we have here. Old house full of various nooks and crannies. Pitch black and a small torch. How on earth are we going to be able to search for a small bag containing some stolen loot?'

Peter gave a heavy sigh. 'I see what you mean.'

'I need to contact Inspector Sullivan about this – get him to send a body of men to keep an eye on the house and when it's daylight give it a thorough search.'

'And what about Horsefield? Where do you think he'll be now? What if he comes back tonight?'

'I don't think he'll do that. He needs to rest up... to...' My mouth stopped working mid-sentence as my brain took over and an idea formed slowly in my mind.

'What is it, Johnny?' Peter asked after a brief pause.

'He'll need medical treatment – for his leg. The wound needs cleaning and bandaging. He can't go to a hospital. They'd ask too many questions. So would a doctor. Where would he go for help and a bit of simple nursing?'

'His mother. He'd go to his mother.'

'Indeed, he would. She lives in the neighbourhood.'

'I went there this morning. To her house.'

'What!'

'I pretended I wanted a glass of water. I tried to spy out to see if Horsefield was there – but I got nowhere. She gave me the glass of water but I didn't get past the front door.'

'Well our man certainly wasn't there this morning – he had other fish to fry then… at Victoria Station – but I reckon there's a strong chance that he'll be there now.'

'Ok, let's go.'

'Not on your life, Peter. I'm not risking taking you with me. As I've told you Horsefield is a very dangerous man. Even more so now that he's got his loot.'

'Oh, come on, Johnny. Look, I can help you, I know. All we need to do is establish that Horsefield is at his mother's and then we can call in the police.' He reached out his hand squeezed my arm. 'Come on, Johnny, we can do that together, can't we?'

TWENTY-SEVEN

In the distance David Llewellyn could see a bright crimson smear illuminating the sky as they turned down the road where Francis Sexton lived.

'There's been no bombing tonight, has there, sir?' asked Sergeant Sunderland as he manoeuvred the car slowly towards the fiery glow.

'No,' David replied slowly, as he peered ahead of him and caught sight of a fire engine and the darting silhouettes of firemen. 'But it looks like our suspect's house is blazing away nicely.'

Sunderland parked the car some hundred yards from the conflagration and the two men walked slowly towards the burning house. Even from this distance, they could feel the heat of the conflagration blowing towards them in waves. However, the flames were beginning to surrender to the force of the water and a mixture of steam and smoke were beginning to envelope the damaged building like a surreal bank of fog. Llewellyn made his way through a small knot of onlookers and approached one of the firemen who seemed to be in charge.

'What's happened here?' he asked.

The man turned abruptly, his sweaty face tinged red from the reflection of the flames.' Stand well back, sir. It's not safe for you.'

'I'm a police officer,' said Llewellyn drawing out his warrant card. 'I need to know.'

'Oh,' responded the fireman, a little nonplussed. 'Well, I can't tell you much. A neighbour called us when she saw the flames. We think there's a body in there but we couldn't reach it. The heat was too intense by the time we arrived. We've got it under control now, but there won't be much left of the house when it's over. Now if you'll excuse me.' He moved forward and began issuing orders to a group of men wielding one of the hoses.

Llewellyn passed a knowing glance at his colleague. 'This is a funny business. If there is a body in there, I'd like to know whose it is.'

'Well, if it's Sexton, that saves us a lot of work.'

'Indeed. That might be too convenient though.' He gave a harsh laugh. 'Still, I'm a cynical old bastard.'

Slapping Sunderland on the back, he turned to go. 'Come on. We can't do anything here for the moment. I have an appointment with a pillow.'

The two men began walking back to the car. They were oblivious of a tall, bulky man standing amid the throng of onlookers who studied their every movement.

It was Dr Ralph Northcote, who had stayed behind to watch the resulting finale of his handiwork. He had been shocked to see Llewellyn turn up on the scene. David Llewellyn, the man responsible for his foul years of imprisonment in Newfield House. He had forgotten about him. Something in his psyche had blanked this cursed policeman from his consciousness. He had not thought of Llewellyn for years. But now, seeing him again, suddenly all his anger and hatred for the man welled up inside him once more. If ever anyone in his life deserved to die, Llewellyn did. He had been the one that had done for him. Had exposed him. Had consigned him to a life of ignominy and imprisonment.

Northcote had to control himself from rushing forward then and there and grabbing the bastard by the neck, throttling the life out of him. He could feel his fingers sink into the soft flesh of the policeman's throat. He saw the eyes bulge in terror as he tightened his grip. He could hear that strange thin reedy death whistle as Llewellyn's lungs gave up the ghost. He felt the body slump against him, the dead mouth damp with spittle...

But Northcote didn't move. Some instinct of self-preservation stopped him. It can wait, a voice told him. *He* can wait. The anticipation would add further pleasure to the deed. But Northcote knew that the death of David Llewellyn was to be his next project.

* * *

Northcote waited until the two policemen had returned to their car and driven away before he moved. Giving one more glance to the glowing ruins of Sexton's house, he turned and walked with slow deliberation back down the road, away from the blaze that he had started, the furnace in which lay the blackened remains of the man whom he had thought was his saviour but who turned out to be his cruellest enemy. Now he just regretted that he didn't have the time and opportunity to take a piece of Sexton's flesh as a tasty souvenir. But this was not a time for regrets or for dwelling on the past. He was free – the shackles of Newfield House and Sexton's cellar had been severed. He really was free now – and he had a new passion to make his pulses race. The destruction of Detective Inspector David Llewellyn.

* * *

Sheila Llewellyn heard her husband climb the stairs and sigh heavily as he reached the landing. She glanced at the phosphorescent numbers on the alarm clock on her tiny bedside table. It was nearly three in the morning. David's shadowy figure appeared in the bedroom.

'Are you all right?' she murmured.

'I'm fine,' came the weary unconvincing response from the darkness.

'Do you want a cup of tea or anything?'

'No, love. You don't disturb yourself. Get back to sleep.'

'Aren't you coming to bed?'

'In a while. I need to calm down a bit.'

'Bad night?'

He did not reply but bent over the bed and gave her a kiss on the cheek. 'Nothing for you to worry about, love. You get your beauty sleep.'

Sheila knew it was David's way. When he was really depressed about a case, he would keep it all to himself. He would not bother her with his troubles. It was part of his chivalrous nature. She had learned to live with it. Matters would not be improved if she started to probe. From very early on in their relationship she had realised that he compartmentalised his police work, never letting the detail of it spill over into his private life. It was his way of protecting her from the darkness in his life.

'If you're sure,' she murmured sleepily.

He kissed her again. 'I'm sure, my lovely.'

'O.K.' Within minutes Sheila Llewellyn was fast asleep again, while her husband sat in his favourite armchair downstairs, with only a small table lamp for illumination, puffing discontentedly on a series of cigarettes.

TWENTY-EIGHT

Peter and I stood in the shadows on the opposite side of the road from Bruce Horsefield's mother's house. Like all other dwellings in the road it seemed to be in total darkness. This was a result of the blackout curtains or shutters which not only deceived the Hun, but a weary private detective and his eager young assistant also. The problem was how to ascertain whether Horsefield was inside the building, resting his wounded leg and receiving succour from his mother without alerting the occupants of the place – whoever they may be.

'I could go and listen by the front room window and at the kitchen round the back,' said Peter. 'I might be able to hear voices.'

'You might hear voices, but it's unlikely you'll hear what's being said and whether Horsefield is one of the speakers or not.'

Peter shrugged in response. 'Well, have you a better idea?' he said with an air of petulance.

He had me there. In truth, I really didn't want Peter with me. He was too young – and to be frank – too inexperienced to be involved in such a job. He was more likely to be an encumbrance than a help and I was concerned for his safety. But I was stuck with him.

'Let's make our way around to the back of the house and see if there is anyway of getting inside without being detected.

Peter's eyes lit up. 'Great,' he said.

To approach the rear of the building we had to make our way down a narrow track which cut between the row of houses three doors down. This gave us access to the lane that ran behind all the dwellings along that stretch.

Once we had reached the rear of the Horsefield dwelling, I pulled Peter to me and whispered harshly in his ear: 'You are to stay here on guard…' I held up my hand and placed it over his mouth before he could protest. 'No ifs or buts, my boy. This is important. Listen! I am going to try and gain entry and see if I can locate Mr Horsefield. You are to stay here and wait. If I am not out of there within fifteen minutes, you must go for the police. Do not, I repeat, do not attempt to come in after me. Do you understand?'

In the dim starlight, I could see the disappointed look on Peter's face deepen. He wanted adventure and excitement; standing guard outside did not quite fit in with his concept of thrilling detective work.

'Don't let me down. It's very important that you do as I ask. Understood?'

He gave me a reluctant mute nod.

I had to trust him – but I knew that he could be reckless and impulsive.

'Now hand over that little torch of yours. I reckon that'll be very useful.'

He did so without a word.

Good lad,' I said. 'Fifteen minutes,' I repeated, as I slipped over the garden wall and made my way to the back door.

With the small pencil torch, I examined the lock. It was old and rusty. And easily dealt with. Within a minute, I had manipulated the fragile workings with my nail file and gained entry. The beam of the torch informed me that I was in some kind of laundry room. The finger of feeble light picked out a large sink, a tub and posser, and a mangle, while a drying cradle laden with damp greying garments hung menacingly over my head like some giant surreal spider waiting to pounce. I stood in the darkness and listened. A muffled sound from some far room came to my ears. It sounded like a radio playing.

Pulling my gun from my coat pocket – my fingers clasping the cold handle was a real comfort to me – I opened the inner door and quietly moved into a darkened corridor at the end of which was the room where the radio was playing. The door of the room was slightly ajar and a thin yellow strip of light fell onto the dusty linoleum on the floor. As I stood and listened, I could clearly hear the voice of Jack Warner. The occupant or occupants were obviously listening to *Garrison Theatre*. At that moment I wished I were at home in front of my own hearth doing the same thing.

Stealthily I moved down the corridor towards the lighted room. On my left was the staircase leading upstairs. I heard the laughter of the radio audience supplemented by a hoarse chuckle which I deduced must belong to Bruce Horsefield. Or at least I hoped so. At this thought, my heartbeat quickened.

With gritted teeth, I swung the door open gently and surveyed the interior. It was a shabby but nonetheless cosy sitting room. Bruce Horsefield was sitting by an electric fire with his injured leg up on a stool and a glass of beer in his hand smirking away at the radio banter. So enamoured was he by the radio show that he did not at first realise another person had entered the room. Then some sixth sense made him twitch and he turned awkwardly and saw me. I held my gun clearly in view.

'Don't do anything foolish, Bruce. I want to deliver you breathing in one piece to our friends at Scotland Yard.'

Horsefield was shocked by my sudden appearance and he dropped his glass of beer, the liquid spilling on to the hearth rug. However, he soon recovered his equilibrium and shifted his wounded leg off the stool as if he intended to rise from the chair.

'Stay put,' I barked.

His eyes flamed and for a moment I thought he was going to ignore my order and that I was going to have to use my gun. My stomach juddered. I didn't want to shoot him. I didn't want to shoot any man. It's not my way.

But then strangely, he relaxed and I could almost swear that a ghost of a smile touched his lips. The odd flickering of his eyes, as though he were watching something over my shoulder, should have warned me that there was danger but it all happened so quickly that I really had no time to react.

There was a sudden violent cry worthy of a weird horror film harpy and then someone jumped on my back and clamped their scrawny arms around my neck. It did not take me long to realise that this was Mrs Horsefield – the mother.

She screamed obscenities as I swung myself round in a desperate attempt to dislodge this creature who like some fearsome piggy-backing child clung on tenaciously. Meanwhile Horsefield had risen from his chair and was advancing on me. I raised the gun.

'Stop now or I will shoot,' I cried. But as I did so, the screeching gargoyle on my back, released one of her arms and brought it down hard on my wrist. The gun spun from my grip and clattered to the floor by the hearth.

Horsefield dived for it. Within seconds the tables had turned. Now I was the one who could easily end up in the morgue.

With a grin worthy of the Cheshire cat, Horsefield rose to his feet, the gun in his hand, pointing in my direction. I could see from the cold glint in his eyes that he meant to pull the trigger. In essence, I had only seconds to live.

With a concerted effort, I swung my whole body round, heaving my shoulders upwards as far as I could push them in one enormous shrug. This violent revolution caused Mrs Horsefield to billow out, her legs swinging free. As I spun round like a whirling Dervish, her body collided heavily with her son's, knocking him to the floor. The collision caused my passenger to give a great whoop of horror. Her confusion made her release her grip and thus dislodged, she ricocheted into her son, landing on top of him.

While Bruce still held the gun, he was now flat on his back with his spindly mother spread-eagled across his frame. It was a slapstick routine worthy of Abbott and Costello. Quickly regaining my composure after my bizarre fairground ride, I stepped forward and stamped on Horsefield's wrist. He gave a yelp of pain and his fingers uncurled from around the handle of my gun.

I snatched it up and pointed it at Horsefield's head. I fired but aimed to miss. The gunshot reverberated round the room like a clap of thunder, the bullet lodging in the skirting board. My little demonstration had its desired effect. Both mother and son stopped moving and lay still, staring with apprehension at me and more particularly at the weapon I held in my hand.

'Now if either of you wish to live long enough to have another breakfast, albeit in a cell at Scotland Yard, I suggest you do exactly what I say. Understood?'

Mute nods came slowly in response.

'Right, sit together on the sofa and please, no funny business, eh? Bullets cost money, you know.'

They did as I asked like chastened children.

I knew that I would not have long to wait. I was certain that the gunshot would assure me of that.

Indeed, a couple of minutes later, I heard a frantic muffled voice calling my name and seconds later Peter burst into the room.

'Johnny,' he cried, 'are you all right. I heard a gunshot.'

'Yes, I'm fine. Just a little target practice'.

Then he saw the two characters on the sofa and grinned. 'You got him!' he cried, his face breaking into a broad grin.

'Now that you've answered my summons...' I held up the gun. 'Off you go to that phone box and call the police. 'Tell them, we've got a thief and a murderer for them.'

'You bastard,' sneered Mrs Horsefield.

I shrugged. 'Everyone's a critic.'

* * *

I got to bed very late that night, but as I lay my head on my pillow, I had a smile on my lips. Horsefield and his mother were in custody at Scotland Yard. Inspector Sullivan had organised a search of the derelict house for the morning and I had deposited the grinning Peter back at home with the Horner sisters who had been reasonably forgiving about his late arrival. A successful conclusion to my case. I hoped Father Sanderson approved.

Strangely, sleep did not come easily that night. In the darkness, my mood of gentle euphoria faded quite quickly to be replaced with an unnerving sense of disquiet. I felt as though some dark cloud was louring over me. Tired as I was, I lay awake for some time wondering why I felt so apprehensive.

TWENTY-NINE

Sheila Llewellyn played idly with her toast. She really didn't want it, but out of habit she had grilled two slices of bread and smeared them with a thin coating of margarine. Now, as she sat alone at the kitchen table, she had no desire to eat them. Her mind was far from food. She was thinking about her husband. Worrying about her husband. Well, it was part of her 'job' she supposed. When you are married to a policeman, you cannot expect to have an easy life. There were the terrible hours and the danger. The job was like a third person in the relationship. And she could read David like a barometer. He rarely discussed his work, his investigations, but she could tell by his demeanour, however much he tried to disguise it, whether things were going well or not. If the smiles were not quite as frequent and the charming worry lines on his forehead deepened, she knew David was dealing with a real stinker. When these came along, she worried all the more, as she was doing this morning.

For the last few days, David had been really low. He had hardly made any real attempt to hide it. For him that was rare, if not unique. At the thought of his tired and worried face, Sheila felt a dark cloud descend upon her. Absent-mindedly she picked up one of the slices of toast, held it for a moment and then dropped it back on the plate.

'Come on,' she said softly, chiding herself. 'This will not do.' She knew she had to be strong for the man she loved. If she showed that she was down in the dumps too, that would be an extra burden for him to carry. No, she must remain bright, cheerful and supportive whatever she was feeling inside. Surely, whatever was bringing David down would pass and he would return to his usual cheerful self. Surely?

Scooping up the pieces of toast, she dropped then into the waste bin under the sink and set about washing up. While she was drying the few items, left by herself and those much earlier by David before he had set off at dawn for the Yard, the door bell rang.

With a little puzzled frown, she dried her hands and went through to the hall to answer the door. Through the pane of frosted glass she saw the dark frame of a tall man. As she undid the latch, she wondered if it was one of David's colleagues. At this thought, a slight tremor of fear ran through her. She hoped to God that it wasn't bad news.

As soon as she opened the door she knew two things. It wasn't one of David's colleagues and she should not have opened the door.

The man who stood before her was unkempt, his shoulders hunched in a strange menacing fashion, but what was really unnerving was his rather twisted grin and the fierce malevolence in his eyes.

'Mrs Llewellyn,' he said, his voice gruff but polite.

'Yes,' she replied hesitantly.

'That's good,' he grinned, the eyes widening in pleasure and he stepped forward as if to enter the house.

Instinctively Sheila made a move to close the door on him, but she was not quick or strong enough. He forced the door back and pushed her inside.

Her instinct was to scream, but she knew that this would achieve nothing. There was no one near to come to her rescue. She did not know who this creature was or what he wanted, but she knew he was dangerous and a threat. She turned to run, but he caught her by the throat and held her.

'Please don't struggle, Mrs Llewellyn. I really don't want to hurt you. Not yet, anyway. It would be best for you and your husband if you did as I tell you.'

'My husband,' she croaked. 'What about my husband?'

'He and I have a little unfinished business to conduct.'

'What do you want with him?'

The man giggled obscenely. 'All in good time. Now if I release my grip, I want your promise not to try anything silly like trying to run away. You can't run away and if you try I shall get mad and that means I'll probably hurt you.'

The sentiments were expressed in such a matter of fact way that they filled Sheila with all-consuming dread.

'Now, are you going to be a good girl?'

'Yes,' she said.

''That's very sensible,' he grinned, releasing his grip on her throat. 'Now I've got my car outside and we're going for a little ride.'

He took her arm and pulled her towards the door. 'Now, no funny business. OK?'

She nodded, her mind whirling with desperate thoughts.

Outside, was an old Vauxhall which he'd driven up the drive right to the front door. With swift deft movements, he opened the boot. 'Step inside, my dear.'

Sheila Llewellyn looked at him with incredulity.

'Do as you're told, if you know what's good for you.' He squeezed her arm until it hurt.

Sheila was tempted to try to break free and make a bolt for it down the drive, but some instinct stopped her, told her that she wouldn't make it and then, who knows what the brute might do to her. With a sinking heart she clambered into the boot of the car.

'Lie down and curl up,' he snapped.

She did as he ordered and then darkness enveloped her as he slammed the boot lid down.

Moments later as the engine revved into life and began to judder forward, Sheila Llewellyn curled her hands into tight fists so that the nails dug into her palms and very quietly she began to cry.

* * *

'I've had word from the fire officer in charge of last night's blaze,' said Sergeant Sunderland as he wandered over to David Llewellyn's desk. His boss was staring at a pile of papers, but not really seeing them. His mind was elsewhere.

'Oh, yes,' he looked up distractedly. 'What's he got to say?'

Sunderland perched on the edge of the desk. 'Apparently they did find a body in the shell of the house this morning. Or to be more precise the remains of a body. It's too far gone to be any use to us. Apparently they can't even tell if it's a man or a woman.'

'Great.'

'Just some bones and ash.'

'So we don't know if it's Sexton or not,'

'Well, it was his house.'

Llewellyn shook his head. 'That proves nothing. There's something fishy about this affair. Look at the facts. Sexton visits Northcote on a regular basis in the loony bin on the premise of writing a book about criminal madness or some such. Suddenly Northcote escapes – very easily it seems – and disappears. And strangely Sexton seems unable to explain Northcote's behaviour or to help us in anyway. In fact, his lack of assistance was in essence a hindrance.'

'Then the murders begin,' added Sunderland.

'Yes... in the same manner as before. And then we find Sexton's cigarette case at the scene of the most recent atrocity. You know what I wonder, Sunderland, don't you?'

Sunderland threw his boss a quizzical look. 'Not sure.'

'I wonder if these two were in cahoots. I mean it's a fairly unhealthy pursuit to keep visiting a cannibal murderer, isn't it? Perhaps Sexton developed a curiosity about the killings... about the ritual of eating flesh. Maybe he wanted to try them out for himself.'

Sunderland grimaced. 'It's enough to turn your stomach.'

'Your stomach, yes, 'cause you're a straight forward pie and chips man, but to some twisted minds like Northcote ... and maybe Sexton... it's lovely grub.'

Sunderland grimaced again. 'You're putting me right off my lunch.'

Llewellyn afforded himself a little smile at his sergeant's discomfort. 'Well, whether they were working together or not, we are still no nearer catching either of them. And, I hate to admit this, but I've no idea what we're going to do next. We seem to be up that creek without a bleedin' paddle.'

With this dark admission, both men fell silent. At length, Sunderland roused himself. 'Shall I make us both a cuppa?'

'Why not?' sighed Llewellyn. 'It might help invigorate the brain cells.'

Sunderland had only just left the office when the telephone rang. David casually lifted the receiver, 'Llewellyn,' he said.

There was a pause before the caller spoke. 'Good morning, Inspector. This is Dr Ralph Northcote.'

David's body stiffened and a little electric charge seem to run up his backbone. He sat bolt upright in his chair, gripping the phone hard enough to snap the receiver in two.

'Oh, yes...' he found himself saying, his words escaping somewhat muffled from a dry mouth.

'Oh, I assure you I am Ralph Northcote. This is not a hoax call. Surely you remember my voice... from before.'

David thought he did. 'What can I do for you?' he said as casually as he could.

Northcote chuckled. 'It's more a case of what I can do for you. You see I have your wife... but I really don't want your wife, I want you.'

'Sheila...' stuttered Llewellyn, fear and apprehension fogging his brain.

'Yes, little Sheila. Blonde-haired Sheila. I have her.'

David shook his head in disbelief. Was this maniac telling the truth or was it some cruel, wild bluff?

'I called on her this morning and persuaded her to come away with me. She was not too keen at first, but you know I have my little ways of persuasion.'

'Bastard.'

'Of course. That goes without saying.'

'If you have hurt her...'

'Oh, please, don't trot out the impotent threats. If I have hurt her... there is nothing you can do about it, Inspector. However, I have not hurt her. Really, I have no interest in hurting her, although I am sure her flesh is quite tasty...'

David's stomach lurched and he wanted to bellow a stream of obscenities down the phone at his tormentor, but his wiser nature told him that not only would it not help the situation but it might make it worse.

'What do you want?'

'I want you. I want to do a swap. You for your wife.'

'Very well.'

'I thought you would agree. But you must obey my instructions to the letter or I will slit dear Sheila's throat and prepare myself a very tasty snack. Is that understood?'

For a brief moment, David wondered if this were really happening. Was it just a bad dream? A cruel nightmare from which he would wake any second. But as he stared unseeingly at the black telephone he knew in his heart that it was real. Very real.

'What do you want me to do?'

'You tell no one – no one about this call. Your colleagues must not know. You are in this on your own. Is that clear?

'Yes.'

'At six o'clock this evening, you will be on the corner of Horseferry

Road and Millbank by the Lambeth Bridge down by the river. There is a telephone box there. I will ring you and give you further instructions. I cannot emphasise enough that no one must know of this arrangement and you must come alone. Failure to comply with these instructions and… well, it's goodbye Sheila. Is that understood?'

'Yes.'

'Do as you are told and your wife lives. Act foolishly and… well you know the consequences.'

The line went dead.

For some moments David Llewellyn sat like a frozen statue, his hand still gripping the telephone receiver in his hand, his heart thumping in his chest. Suddenly he became conscious of a trickle of sweat travelling down his cheek from his temple. He slammed the receiver down savagely and grabbed a handkerchief from his trouser pocket and mopped his face.

'Tea up,' cried Sergeant Sunderland, breezing into the room carrying two mugs and plonking one down on David's desk.

Automatically, he picked up the mug and took a sip of the hot tea.

'So, what do we do next, sir?' said Sunderland, returning to his usual perch on the end of the desk.

David desperately tried to force his scrambled brain into functioning normally. When he eventually spoke, he found that his voice emerged in a strange mechanical fashion reminiscent of a speak your weight machine.

'I'm… I'm not sure. Things… are a bit … desperate. Look, Sunderland, why don't you take a trip to Sexton's surgery and… have a snoop round his office… his files. See if you can come up with something.'

Sunderland looked at his boss with some concern. He seemed odd somehow. His face was white and damp with sweat and he was talking in an weird way.

'Are you all right, sir?'

'I feel a bit queasy. Probably a dodgy sausage I had for… breakfast. Anyway, you get off and see what you can sniff out at Sexton's surgery, eh?'

'I can finish my tea first, can't I?'

Llewellyn forced a smile. It almost hurt him. 'Of course. As for me, I've got a little lead I'd like to follow up.' Without a further word, he snatched his hat and coat from the rack and left the room.

Sunderland gazed at the full mug of tea, untouched, on his boss's desk and raised his brow in surprise.

'Now what's got into him?'

* * *

Twenty minutes later, David Llewellyn was in the bathroom at home, his head over the toilet bowl. He had just relieved himself of his breakfast, including the supposedly dodgy sausage. His stomach was now empty, but he was still retching, his ashen face bathed in sweat.

On leaving the Yard, he had telephoned home, hoping against hope that Sheila would pick up the receiver at the other end. But it just rang and rang. And rang. He had then driven like the devil back to his house trying but failing to block out all the dark and despondent thoughts which were desperate to crowd in and taunt him.

On arriving home and finding the door ajar, his worst nightmare was confirmed. He carried out a cursory search of the house but knew he would find nothing. Northcote had been telling the truth. He had Sheila in his bloody clutches. It was then that the overpowering sense of nausea overcame him and he rushed to the lavatory to be sick.

After a while, he rose from his crouching posture and washed his face and swilled his mouth out with cold water. As he gazed at his haunted face in the bathroom mirror, one question above all pounded in his mind, thundered repeatedly in his brain like the stroke of a blacksmith's hammer. What was he going to do? What was he going to do?

THIRTY

I was in business again! The following morning after my adventures with the Horsefield family, I was visited by a new client. Time was when such a small, rather sordid case of suspected adultery would have seemed small beer and depressed me, but after the several empty 'feeling sorry for myself' months, to get a regular client seemed wonderful. Normality seemed to be rearing its head again. It was a remarkable feeling and I am sure Max would have been pleased for me. I blew a kiss to her picture on my desk.

I was just lighting a celebratory cigarette when the telephone rang. Wow, I thought, not another client? I was wrong.

It was David Llewellyn.

* * *

I met him in The Guardsman at noon and we secured one of the little private booths at the rear of the saloon bar. Here, away from the noise and the smoke we were afforded a little privacy. My friend looked terrible. His face was grey as though all the blood had been drained from it and his skin had a damp sheen to it. His eyes blinked nervously as he raised his pint glass to his lips.

I knew something was wrong – very wrong. I had deduced that from the tone of his voice and his strange manner during the telephone call. He had told me nothing, only that he needed to see me urgently. David never asked to see me urgently.

'What's this all about?' I asked casually, eager to get the ball rolling.

David ran his hand over his face. 'It's this Northcote case.'

'Northcote. Mr Cannibal?'

David nodded. 'He's got Sheila.'

'What do you...?'

'What the hell do you think I mean? He's got Sheila. He's abducted her.'

'My God!' I said, my mind filling up with questions, only to ask the one that I shouldn't.

148

'Are you sure?'

'Of course I'm bloody sure!' His eyes widened in anger and his hand shook so much, the beer slopped over the side of the glass.

I touched the sleeve of his coat with what I hoped was a reassuring gesture. 'Tell me about it.'

David took a large gulp of beer before responding. 'He came to the house this morning after I'd gone to work and… took her. Then he rang me at the Yard. He said he'll let her go in exchange for me.'

'Exchange. A kind of swap?'

'He wants revenge. I was the copper who nabbed him in the first place. I'm the one responsible for getting him locked away for life. Now he intends to get his own back. I'm supposed to be in a phone box down by Lambeth Bridge on the Millbank side at six this evening and he'll give me more instructions. Where to go. Where to meet him. Once he's got me, he'll let Sheila go.'

Like hell he will, I thought but knew now was not the time to air such an opinion. Instead, I said nothing.

'The problem is,' he continued after another gulp of beer, 'there has to be no police involvement. I've got to do this on my own or else… or else he'll slit Sheila's throat.'

'But you can't do this without a surveillance team to help.'

'I can't risk it, Johnny. If he gets a whiff of a police presence… I just can't risk it. I've got to do it on his terms… for Sheila's sake'. There was a catch in his voice and he turned his head away momentarily while he brought his emotions in check.

I wanted to say all kinds of sympathetic, reassuring and encouraging words but I was well aware this is not what David wanted to hear just now. Besides, I knew I would struggle to make them sound convincing. In truth, my old friend was in a no-win situation. How can you take the word of a mad killer as gospel? This Northcote creature may well have killed Sheila already; if not, he wasn't going to release her when he'd got his hands on David. What fun he could have torturing Sheila while David was forced to watch. Or *vice versa*. My heart sank at the thought of this impossible situation. I knew that David was an experienced and intelligent enough policeman to be fully aware, as I was, of the drastic implications of this terrible scenario. His face clearly indicated that this knowledge was tearing him apart. And there was nothing I could say that would alter the situation.

'I need your help', he said quietly but forcefully.

I did not have to think about a reply.

'Of course. Whatever I can do.'

'I need you as my shadow tonight. Even if the bastard gets me, perhaps you'll be able to get him.'

* * *

Later that afternoon, I sat hunched over my desk, staring into space, both hands grasping a mug of coffee. I was miserable and I could not believe it. I had started the day with a brightening of the spirit. After the dark months after Max's death, I felt I was reaching for the light again – normality at least. I had completed the case for Father Sanderson and I'd got myself back on the detective treadmill. Things were looking up. And then came the hammer blow. I had just lost the love of my life and now one of my friends, a man who has been so good to me, was in great danger of losing his.

Whoever was in charge of our Fate up there needed a good kick in the crotch.

I broke my reverie to glance at my watch. It was only three thirty. Time goes so slowly when you are waiting. I had great forebodings about that evening's venture. I did not know how it could end happily. I chided myself for being so negative but the feeling of dark apprehension would not go away.

On leaving David at lunchtime, I had gone along to Barry Forshaw's garage to hire a motor for the evening. If I was going to follow David, I needed my own set of wheels. Certainly shank's pony would not do and equally the situation was far too dangerous and uncertain for me to rely on the services of a taxi driver. Barry was an old client of mine. I had extricated him from a forged number plate business when he'd gone in too far. With my help, we exposed the gang and I managed to get Barry a reduced sentence for helping with the arrests and turning

King's evidence. He's been grateful ever since.

'I have a nice little roadster, you can have,' he said, leading me into the compound at the back of the garage. The motor certainly looked smart and nippy, but just a little too individual and therefore too noticeable. I needed something that would blend in with the stream of traffic and not catch anyone's eye. An ordinary motor.

'What about the Wolseley?' I asked, moving over to a shabby-looking vehicle.

'That old thing. It's been around the block a few times, I can tell you.'

'Just the kind of crock I'm after. It is roadworthy, I suppose.'

Barry grinned at my impertinence. 'Certainly,' he said, with feigned irritation. 'I don't deal in any other kind of motor car.'

'Good. Then I'll take it. How much?'

'Bring it back in the morning without a scratch on it and a full tank of petrol. How about that?'

'You got a deal.' We shook hands.

The car was a bit clunky, but so am I as a driver. I'm in control of a car so infrequently that I remain as rusty at the steering wheel as the mudguards on this old jalopy. I hoped that I was up to my duties for this evening. I drove around for about an hour getting used to the controls and feel of the vehicle before heading home. It certainly was a sturdy drive. Driving this for a month would certainly develop one's arm muscles.

I drained my coffee mug, lit a cigarette, and glanced at my watch again. The hands had hardly moved.

Would this evening ever come?

Suddenly the rumbling of my tummy alerted me to the fact that I hadn't eaten anything since breakfast and that consisted of a cup of tea, a scrappy piece of toast and a fag. I needed some grub to help sustain me through the ordeal tonight. I decided to pop down to Benny's and treat myself to one of his specials. I smiled at the thought. Knowing Benny's cooking it would hardly be a treat and it certainly wouldn't be special, but at least it would be warm and I'd have a chance to see the old boy. I felt sure that his banter would help lighten my mood temporarily before setting out off on my evening adventure.

As I pulled up in the Wolseley outside Benny's café, I saw him peering through the window and he caught sight of me as I got out of the car.

'Up the world we've come, Mr Rolls Royce!' was his greeting as I entered.

'It's an old Wolseley and it's on loan for the night. It goes back in the morning.'

'A Cinderella motorist, eh? You got a special date with that lovely Russian girl.'

I grinned. I knew Benny would cheer me up.

'You could say that,' I lied. I certainly didn't want to tell Benny the real reason for hiring the motor.

I ordered the special of the day and a pot of tea and took a seat by the window. Five minutes later Benny delivered the goods – a plate of liver and onions accompanied by a greyish splodge of mashed potato.

'I must say that you are looking a little more like your old self, Johnny. But you still need feeding up.'

'You said I needed feeding up when you first met me five years ago.'

Benny chuckled. 'Yes I did.'

'I'm fine, Benny. I'm back in the saddle and I've almost stopped feeling sorry for myself. When you get a blow like I did – losing Max so suddenly in such a terrible way – you think you're the only one going through hell. It numbs you to other's pain. So many people are suffering in this bloody war...' I paused, my knife and fork motionless over the food, the image of David Llewellyn's drained and tortured face shimmered before me. Suddenly I didn't feel hungry any more.

'Loss is always with you, Johnny. A day doesn't go by when I don't think about my Daisy, but you learn, you learn to cope with it. And you get on with your life. It's what they would have wanted.'

I prayed that this wasn't a lesson that David would have to learn.

THIRTY-ONE

In her dark tomb, Sheila Llewellyn had lost track of time. She had no idea how long she had been incarcerated in the boot of this maniac's vehicle. Initially, she had curled up foetal-like – like a frightened child, but gradually her fear had subsided and a kind of numbness of mind came to her, almost an anaesthetic, removing the pain of reality. At one point, when the vehicle had parked, she had actually fallen asleep.

The car was on the move once more, and it swayed and shook violently as though it was being driven at great speed. And recklessly. Suddenly a thought struck Sheila, Perhaps he never intended to let her out ever again. She was meant to die here, to lose consciousness through lack of food and water and then rot. She would be found months later – a rotting corpse. She shuddered at the thought but somehow she was glad to have considered such an outcome. Facing the worst in some strange way gave her courage and hope.

The vehicle slowed and ground to a halt. After a moment, she heard the driver's door slam and then the key in the lock of the boot. Seconds later, the boot lid was raised slowly. Sheila screwed up her eyes as the blinding daylight flooded in.

And then a shadow fell over her.

'The circular tour is over,' her captor observed. 'Time to leave'. He reached into the boot and grabbed Sheila's arm. 'Come on,' he said gruffly.

Her body was stiff and awkward and her limbs failed to obey her. He dragged her over the edge of the boot and she fell forward, her hands hitting the harsh gravel. With some effort, she pulled herself forward until her legs flopped to the ground also. She lay there like a landed fish on a riverbank.

'Welcome home,' sneered Northcote, once more clamping his hand around Sheila's right arm and hauling her to her feet. Her vision blurred, she felt nauseous for some moments and then gradually her surroundings came into focus. Her mouth opened in shock. Sheila couldn't believe it. She was back home. She was in her own drive. The car was almost in the same position it had been when she had been bundled into it those long hours ago. Was this some kind of cruel hoax?

Her eyes and expression must have clearly mirrored her thoughts and Northcote laughed at her confusion.

'I've brought you back home, to wait for hubby to return. We're going to have a cosy evening together.'

'What the hell are you talking about?' Sheila was surprised at the ferocity and the volume of her retort. Frustration, confusion and desperation had commingled to make her very angry. So angry in fact that she lashed out with her foot, kicking Northcote in the leg.

He gave a cry of surprise and staggered back. Sheila was tempted to kick him again and this time aim at somewhere more vulnerable, but instead she turned and ran. Passing down the edge of the car, she headed down the drive for the gate.

She hadn't been prepared for the awkwardness of her body. Cooped up in virtually one position for many hours, it was learning to function again. Her limbs were stiff and did not automatically obey her. She ran like someone who has severe arthritis travelling over a bed of hot coals.

Within seconds, Northcote was upon her and brought her to the ground. She crashed onto the hard gravel.

'Naughty, naughty,' he gasped. 'I see that I shall have to watch you. Now get up.'

Reluctantly she did so.

'That's a good girl,' he said, and marched her back down the drive. After retrieving a small case from the back seat of the car he dragged Sheila into the house.

'Can I have a drink of water, please?' she asked.

'Another trick?'

'No, no. I am very thirsty.'

Northcote pulled a knife from his pocket. He held the shiny bright blade in front of Sheila's face. 'I don't want to cut you just yet, Mrs Llewellyn, but if I have any more trouble from you, I'm afraid I will have to slit your throat. Is that understood?'

Sheila shivered with fear and nodded vigorously, words failing her at this moment.

Northcote took her into the kitchen where she filled a glass of water from the tap and gulped it down eagerly.

'Now it's time to secure you for the evening. We must have you ready and nicely trussed for when hubby comes home.'

'What... what are you going to do?'

'Oh, that's a surprise. You like surprises, don't you?'

At knife point, he took her upstairs. When he led her into the bedroom, she feared the worst. She determined that if he was going to try and sexually molest her she would kick, scream and bite like a demon. She would rather be knifed to death than succumb to his advances. He would not violate her without a damn struggle.

But it seemed that Northcote had other ideas.

Opening his case, he took out several lengths of rope and a reel of strong tape.

'Time to truss up the turkey,' he observed with a grin.

Sheila actually felt a sense of relief when she realised that this maniac only intended to tie her up rather than rape her. She offered no resistance as he bound her feet and tied her hands behind her back. Then he rolled off a strip of tape, cut it with his knife and placed it across her mouth. As he did this she tried to scream but the tape prevented the sound escaping.

'You'll have to breathe through your nose for a while, my dear.' Northcote chuckled to himself. He was really enjoying this grotesque charade. 'And now a final touch,' he added as he thrust her onto the bed. Snatching up a pillowcase, he detached the pillow and slipped the empty case over Sheila's head.

'That should keep you nice and quiet until your hubby arrives,' he said, standing back and admiring his handiwork.

Sheila lay on the bed, engulfed in darkness and began to sob softly.

Northcote left her to her misery. Locking the bedroom door he went down stairs and checked his watch. It was almost time to set off. His features broke into a broad smile. He was going to enjoy this evening. Who was it who said revenge was a dish best served cold?

THIRTY-TWO

David Llewellyn arrived at Lambeth Bridge early. He was terrified that if he did not obey Northcote's instructions to the letter, he would be placing Sheila's life in jeopardy. Or, as he grimly reconsidered, more jeopardy than it already was – if that were possible. His mind was all over the place and his stomach was spinning like a top. He was sure that he was going to be sick at any moment.

The day was on the brink of evening and a stiff breeze blew off the river. Instinctively, he pulled his overcoat around him, although he was fully aware that it wasn't the cool air that was making him shiver. It was fear. Fear that whatever he did this evening, the outcome would be tragic.

At a quarter to six, he approached the telephone box, which was on the opposite side of the road to the bridge. As he did so, he gazed around him as casually as he was able in order to see if he could spot Johnny anywhere.

He couldn't.

This did not dismay him too much. He that knew Johnny wouldn't let him down. Would he? No, of course not. He prayed that he wouldn't anyway.

The phone box was occupied. A large woman with a shopping bag was in full flow. David checked his watch. Still ten minutes to go. That was all right. As long as this woman finished soon.

For a moment, he had a vision of him swinging open the door of the box and hauling her out mid-sentence, so that he could receive his call on time.

Crazy thought. He mopped his brow. He hoped it was a crazy thought. God, he could do with a drink, but that was the last thing on earth he should have now. He knew that he needed a clear head to deal with the unknown events ahead of him; at least as clear as he could make it. Alcohol would only slow his reactions, muffle his thinking and take the edge off his reactions.

He mopped his brow again and stared into the box as the woman oblivious of his presence rattled on. Once again he gazed around him as casually and as nonchalantly as he could, hoping to catch a glimpse of Johnny. He still couldn't. In his fraught state he didn't know whether this was a good thing or bad. If Johnny was performing a brilliant chameleon trick, that was fine. He just hoped that he was actually out there watching, for without his aid, he was a goner and indeed so was Sheila. At the thought of his wife, David's stomach lurched once more.

He was just about to reach inside his jacket for a cigarette, when the large lady emerged from the phone box. She passed him without a glance and crossed the road and headed for the bridge.

David hauled open the door and squeezed himself inside. It was like being in an acrid smelling womb... or coffin. Now he just had to wait. Just had to wait for the next move in this deadly game. He stared at the black bakelite telephone crouching there like a wary spider. How long would it be before it rang?

God, a thought struck him. What if it didn't ring? What if this were some cruel hoax? What if Northcote had set this up, just to buy himself some time? What if he'd already murdered Sheila and was now miles away from London?

What a fool he'd been.

He felt faint and began to sweat profusely. The walls of the telephone box seemed to press in on him and felt claustrophobic.

'Ring,' he croaked addressing the telephone. 'For God's sake ring.'

But the phone remained silent.

The minutes ticked by and David's anxiety grew. At one point he lifted the receiver to see if it was actually working. The reverberating burr that emerged from the earpiece told him that it was.

He dropped the receiver back in the cradle as though it had caught fire. He didn't want the telephone to register an engaged tone and miss the call.

But the call did not come.

He checked his watch. The minute hand was crawling up towards ten past six.

'Oh, my god, it is a trick' he cried softly. 'A bloody cruel joke.'

And then suddenly the door of the telephone box swung open and someone forced their way inside.

'Good evening, Inspector,' said Ralph Northcote, a nasty grin plastered on his face. He held up a knife so that David could see it. 'One silly move and you get this right between the ribs. Is that understood?'

'Where's Sheila?'

'Oh, she's quite safe for the moment. And will remain so, as long as you do exactly what I tell you to do. Is that understood?'

David nodded, the sweat now running profusely down his face and he felt faint. What, he wondered, had this mad man got in mind – what nasty plan had he got up his sleeve?

'I trust that you have brought no weapon with you. Nothing concealed somewhere?'

'No.'

Northcote patted his jacket, coat pockets and felt down the legs of his trousers. 'Mmm,' he said, 'you seem to be telling the truth.'

'I am, I swear.'

'Good man. Now when we step out of this box, we shall turn right and round into Thorne Street. You'll see a Vauxhall car there. We shall stand behind it and I will open the boot and we'll look inside as though inspecting something in there. When the coast is clear, you'll climb inside.

'But...'

Northcote pressed the knife against David's ribs. 'No questions, Mr Policeman. Do as I say or else...'

Northcote pushed his weight against the door of the telephone box and with an eerie creak it swung open. 'You walk before me and, please, don't try anything heroic. Remember, I have the knife and I know where your wife is.'

David stepped ahead of Northcote onto the pavement and walked slowly in the direction that he had been instructed to take. As he did so, he gazed around him as inconspicuously as he could in the desperate hope of seeing Johnny. There was no sign of him whatsoever,

They turned into Thorne Street and he saw Northcote's car.

Northcote moved bedside him and opened the boot.

'Lean forward and inspect the interior,' he said.

David did as he was told.

Northcote gazed around the quiet street. Dusk was falling and there were no pedestrians or traffic. The time was ripe.

'Right, get into the boot,' he snapped

David climbed over the edge of the boot and hunched his body in order to fit in the confined space.

Suddenly darkness fell as the boot lid came down. He was trapped in an airless dark bubble. And he was helpless.

Outside, he could hear the dark satanic laughter of his captor.

THIRTY-THREE

I left Benny's café just as he was about to shut up shop for the day. He came on to the pavement with me to inspect the motor car. He pulled a face on seeing the vehicle close up.

'Beggars can't be choosers, I suppose,' he said. 'But this old crock is like me: it's seen better days.'

'It gets me from A to B,' I said with a smile.

'But what if you want to go further?'

It was a good question. One that I could not answer.

I clambered into the cab, wound down the window, gave a quick wave and turned the ignition to start up the engine. It resisted my first attempt and indeed my second, but with further coaxing and a little extra choke, it spluttered into life on the third go.

'I think it's time you gave it back to the circus,' said Benny, as I pulled away in a manner far more stately than I had hoped.

I glanced at my watch. It was twenty past five. I reckoned it would take me about twenty minutes to get to Lambeth Bridge. I would be in plenty of time to witness David's telephone call.

Or so I thought.

It soon became obvious that the car thought otherwise. I was just passing down Redcliffe Gardens on my way to the Embankment when a strange gurgling and hissing noise emanated from the bonnet. This was quickly followed by a violent jerking motion before the car juddered to a silent halt. I turned the ignition desperately, but the engine did not respond. 'What the hell!' I thought, as I jumped out onto the pavement and gazed impotently at the dead animal. What on earth was I going to do? My knowledge of the internal combustion engine was less than nil. I didn't even know how to raise the damned bonnet. Out of frustration, I kicked the front wheel. This action was not only of no practical use but it didn't make me feel any better either.

'A spot of bother?'

I turned to face the owner of the voice who stood a few feet behind me. He was a tall, distinguished looking gentleman in a smart dark overcoat and a bowler hat. He had well chiselled aristocratic features, bright blue eyes and a well trimmed jaunty moustache which was now white with age.

'The thing has died on me.'

'Did it splutter, steam and then shudder to a stop?'

I raised my eyebrows in surprise. 'That's about the size of it.'

His pale face split into a smile.

'The old ones often do. These Wolseleys are nice little runners in their youth, but I'm afraid time does wither them and spoil their infinite reliability. But fear not. It will be dirt in the carburettor. It always is. As they get older and worn, these motors let in all sorts of alien smut. I should know; I had one of these for nearly eight years. I was sorry to see it go. Open her up. We'll soon sort the old girl out'.

I shook my head. 'I'm sorry, I've no idea how to do that. Open up the bonnet, I mean.'

'My, you are a novice. Are you sure you're fit to drive this beauty.'

On the evidence so far, I didn't think I was. But then again, she was hardly a beauty either.

The old gentleman led me round to the driver's side, opened the door and reached inside. 'See, here, there's a lever,' he said in the manner of a friendly school teacher. 'This releases the catch on the bonnet.' He gave the lever a sharp tug and the bonnet responded with a gentle snap.

My mentor lifted up the bonnet and leaned over, peering beneath the canopy. He hummed a little as he inspected the interior and then dipped his hands inside. Heaven knows what he was doing, but he seemed to be doing it with supreme confidence.

'Just as I thought,' he said at last. 'Dirty carburettor. Well, dirty and decrepit, if the truth be known. It really needs renewing. It's on its last legs. Have you an old rag?'

'I'm not sure,' I mumbled and inspected the inside of the car for such an item without success. I dug into my pocket and pulled out my handkerchief. 'Will this do?'

The old gentleman gave a sad shake of the head. It was clear that he thought I wasn't fit to be in charge of this motor car – a man who has no idea how to open the bonnet and does not even possess an old piece of rag to wipe up spills and smears.

'You'll not be able to use this handkerchief again,' he said, returning to the task of doing something under the bonnet.

As he did so, I gazed at my watch. It was five forty-five. Time was running out, but I could hardly tell the old fellow to hurry up. He was doing me a great favour after all. A favour to an incompetent ignoramus of a motorist.

After a few moments, he stood clear of the car. 'That should do it', he said, handing me my handkerchief back. It was now thick with soot and grease. I threw it on the floor of the car.

'Give the engine a try,' he said cheerily. For a moment I thought he was about to add, 'You do know how to do that, don't you?' and although I suspect he was tempted, he restrained himself. I sat in the driver's seat and turned the ignition. The car whirred and whined for a moment and then remarkably coughed its way into life.

The old gentleman beamed and he slapped down the bonnet. 'There you are,' he said. 'They only need a little care and attention and they'll serve you well. I recommend that you have her serviced pronto and get the garage to replace the carburettor. That done, it'll keep going for a few years yet.'

'I don't know how to thank you,' I said, reaching for my wallet.

Spotting this gesture, he held up his hand. 'No, no. I don't need thanks. It was a pleasure for me to get my hands on one of these old machines again. I don't get a chance these days. It's shank's pony for me now. It was my pleasure.' He patted the bonnet affectionately. 'Goodbye, sir, and happy motoring.'

Without another word he walked off stiffly down the street with a jaunty gait.

I did not wait until my mechanical good Samaritan had disappeared into the throng of pedestrians, before revving up my old jalopy and driving off at speed. My watch informed me that I had less than ten minutes to reach Lambeth Bridge.

I could hear the sonorous tones of Big Ben striking the hour as I raced down Horseferry Road, my heart beating like a rumba band and a fine sheen of sweat on my brow. At the junction with Millbank, I pulled in at the kerb and jumped out. I soon clocked the telephone box across the road and there was someone inside. From where I was standing I could not make out whether it was David or not. With as much nonchalance as I could muster, I crossed the road and made my way towards the box. As I sauntered past, I saw, to my relief, that the occupant was indeed David. I hadn't missed him. I sent up another prayer of thanks to my mechanical good Samaritan.

I returned to my car and sat inside watching the box.

Time moved on, but David remained where he was. Was it a very long call or no call at all? Was the whole thing a trick? Only time would bring the answers; all I could do was sit and wait.

And then at about ten past six, a heavily built man approached the telephone box and entered. His actions were so deliberate and calculated, that it was clear to me that he knew that David was in there. My God, I thought, it's Northcote. He's come in person for David. There was to be no phone call. My mind was a whirl. What was I to do? Attempting to rescue David from this situation would bring its own problems. Northcote still had Sheila somewhere and we had to find out where.

After a while the door of the telephone box opened and David and Northcote emerged. They walked slowly across the road towards the bridge and then stopped at the rear of a car. Northcote opened the boot, said something to David who then appeared to be inspecting inside it. He leaned forward so that half his body disappeared from view. Then to my horror, I saw that he clambered inside the boot and Northcote with a triumphant gesture slammed the lid down imprisoning my friend.

Gazing around him briefly to see if he had been observed, he got in the car. Immediately, I switched on my engine and revved up. I must not lose this monster: two people's lives depended on me.

As Northcote pulled away from the curb into the thin stream of traffic, I shot forward at some speed so that by the time we were across the bridge I was only one car away from him.

Luckily for me, Northcote did not seem to be in a hurry and he drove at a moderate speed. This was reassuring for it meant that he had no idea that he was being followed.

We passed the Oval cricket ground and headed in the direction of Kennington and the maze of domestic avenues in this area. Northcote had just turned down one of these streets when it happened. Or to be more precise: it happened again. The strange gurgling and hissing sound under the bonnet returned with even greater ferocity than before. This then was followed by the strange juddering motion of the whole vehicle. Suddenly, I was driving a bucking bronco. These gyrations were a brief precursor to the whole machine gasping to a full stop. Obviously, my mechanical good Samaritan had only managed a temporary repair.

I pulled the little lever to release the bonnet and peered inside. There was no way I was going to be able to repair the fault this time. I could not even identify the carburettor.

I swore. Northcote's car had disappeared from sight. I had lost him. And I had lost any chance of saving David and his wife from fates that were unimaginable.

THIRTY-FOUR

David lay in the back of the swaying vehicle in a cramped foetal position. He had never felt as helpless in his life. He had no idea where he was being taken or what fate was in store for him. He was fairly sure that Johnny was not on his tail. There had been no sign of him when he and Northcote had left the phone box. Only a bloody miracle could save him and Sheila now and as he wasn't the least bit religious, he didn't believe in miracles.

After about fifteen minutes, Northcote's car came to a stop. David could hear the scrunch of tyres on gravel as it did so. He waited in tense anticipation for the boot lid to rise, for the evening light to flood in and for Northcote to release him from his cramped prison. But nothing happened.

He banged on the boot lid but there was no response.

There was no response, because Northcote had gone into the house. He wanted to check on his prisoner inside first, to be certain that everything was as he had left it. He opened the bedroom door and saw that Sheila was lying on the floor. She obviously had made some desperate attempt to free herself of her bonds and in doing so had toppled off the bed. He found this amusing and chuckled in response.

Sheila, still hooded with the pillow case aware of a presence in the room wriggled and made a gagging sound but because of the tape across her mouth the words were indistinguishable.

Northcote pulled the pillow away from her head and lifted Sheila back onto the bed. Her eyes were wide with fear and wet from crying. This also pleased Northcote. Inducing fear was always a delight to him. He smiled as he ran the back of his hand down her cheek.

'Not long now,' he said softly.

Sheila gave a croak of fear.

'Now you stay there like a good girl and then I'll give you a big surprise. One I'm sure you'll like.'

His smile broadened as he left the room. He was pleased with himself. This was all going rather well, he thought. He couldn't remember when he had felt so happy, so fulfilled. And soon, he was sure, he would feel even happier when he was cutting up the flesh of Mr and Mrs Llewellyn.

* * *

In the sitting room, he poured himself a drink and lit a cigarette. With a sigh of pleasure, he slumped in an armchair. A moment's relaxation, contemplation before the fun of the evening. But he was too excited to relax fully. He stubbed the cigarette out before it was half-smoked and he abandoned the drink after only a few sips. He really wanted to get on with the show.

It was quite dark out now. The moon was hidden by clouds and there were few stars visible; it was only the lights from the house that dimly illuminated the drive way and the car. Knife in hand, Northcote raised the lid of the boot. The sight that met his eyes made him gasp and almost drop his weapon.

The boot was empty.

* * *

After the car had been standing still for some minutes, David called out. At the top of his voice, he bellowed out the word, 'Help!' several times. The word reverberated dully in the airless confined space. There was no response. No rescue. But then again there was no attempt to silence him. Northcote must have left him for some reason – abandoned him.

That was good news.

Somehow David knew he had to take advantage of this hiatus. He reckoned that Northcote would not leave him there for long and so he had to do something quickly. David swivelled his body round in the cramped space so that he had his back against the inside of the boot lid and his feet were pressing on the partition between the boot and the rear seats. With as much force and as much leverage as he could muster he began kicking this partition with both feet. Surely, he thought, it cannot be that secure. At first his blows met with strong resistance, but he persisted, aiming at different portions of the partition to gauge which was likely to be the weakest. Then at last he heard a slick crack, a kind of tearing sound.

Bingo!

In the darkness, he grinned and renewed his efforts.

Slowly but with a pleasing surety, the partition began to give way.

The more he was able to drive it forward, the greater the force he was able to use to break down this barrier. Finally, with a satisfying crack, David's particular wall of Jericho came tumbling down. The seat fell forward providing a jagged aperture through to the rear of the car.

He swivelled his body round, and like a burrowing mole, pushed his way through. Within seconds he had clambered over into the front seat and was out of the car.

He stood briefly to catch his breath and fill his lungs with the cool evening air. And then, as he gazed around, he was amazed to find himself in his own driveway. He was back home. What the hell? For a moment, he thought he was having an hallucination, but a movement inside the house brought him rapidly to his senses. It was probably Northcote coming for him. He dodged to the side of the door of the house out of sight and waited.

* * *

The boot was empty. Northcote leaned forward and saw the gaping, damaged partition – his prisoner's escape route.

'You won't find me in there,' said a voice behind him.

THIRTY-FIVE

I swore again and to ease my frustration further I kicked the bumper of the accursed car. Both actions did not really help my sense of despair – and I hurt my foot in the process. Foolishly, in desperation, I looked under the bonnet once more. It was pointless. I certainly couldn't work the conjuring trick that the bowler-hatted gentleman had performed so niftily and effectively. Clean the carburettor or whatever he'd done. Perhaps I should have watched him carefully and then I could try to mimic his actions. I should have taken Barry Forshaw's advice and taken the little sporty number. I bet that little thing wouldn't have let me down, like this old crate. For a few seconds my mind whirled around such stupid thoughts while my heart thumped desperately within my breast. A little confused, I may have been, but I was fully aware how desperate and apparently hopeless my situation was. What on earth was I going to do?

The road was quiet. There was no traffic. No motorist chugging by whom I could flag down and persuade to give me a lift. Give me a lift? Where on earth to?

I had no idea.

Then my eyes fell upon the road name plate on the wall opposite. Sycamore Rise.

They lingered on it for a while and then a certain dim recognition came to me. Sycamore Rise.

Sycamore Rise!

The name reverberated in the cobwebbed passages of my memory. I knew that name. Somehow. I had heard it before. Where? How?

I was aware of the phrase 'to cudgel your brains' before but I'd never really known what it meant – or the real effect of it until that moment. Here I was on a dark spring evening staring at a road sign, repeating it over and over again, cudgelling my tired brains in an attempt to remember…

Sycamore Rise.

It was a misnomer as the road did not 'rise' perceptively and certainly from where I was standing there were no sycamores in view. This was an observation that I'd had before. Sycamore Rise – silly name, I'd thought.

Of course!

The cudgelling had worked. It came back to me. I had been down this road before. And, yes, suddenly I knew that it led into Chestnut Avenue from which one could reach Oak Road and from thence one could turn down Larch Close.

And Larch Close was where Detective Inspector David Llewellyn lived! I could see it now in my mind's eye: a very smart modern villa situated down a long tree-lined drive. I knew because I had visited him on a couple of occasions in the early days of the war just after setting up as a private detective.

Then the terrible implication struck me. My God, I thought, the fiend was taking David home. He must be holding Sheila prisoner there. As this notion came to me as frighteningly fast and violent as a lightning flash, I felt both excited and horrified in equal measure.

It was then that my natural instincts took over from my brain and within seconds I found myself running – running as if all the devils in hell were on my trail. The neat suburban houses of Sycamore Rise swept past me in a blur as I raced along the pavement heading for Chestnut Avenue, my feet pounding hard on the flagstones. Inconsequently, I chided myself for being so unfit. Fags and booze had certainly taken a toll on my fitness. Nevertheless, I increased my speed, sweat drenching my shirt and my heart fighting to burst free of my chest. I ran that evening as I have never run in my life before.

At least now I knew where I was going. What I would find when I got there I did not know, but the thought filled me with dread.

THIRTY-SIX

The boot was empty. Northcote leaned forward and saw the gaping, damaged partition – his prisoner's escape route.

'You won't find me in there,' said a voice behind him.

David had not expected Northcote to react with such speed and violence. He had thought that the shock of finding the boot empty would have confused his captor and therefore slowed his reactions.

But this was not the case.

Swiftly and with a nimbleness that belied his size, Northcote swung round on the balls of his feet with great alacrity and lunged at David with the knife. To his dismay, David was the one who was caught by surprise and although he pulled back swiftly and dodged sideways in an attempt to avoid the sharp blade, he was not quick enough to go beyond Northcote's reach. The knife pierced his shoulder, the blade going in deep. David felt a searing hot pain and he dropped to his knees, his vision blurring. Suddenly he was aware that his mouth was filled with vomit and before he could expel it, he collapsed unconscious on the gravel drive.

Northcote stood over him, legs apart like a grisly colossus and laughed.

* * *

When David recovered consciousness, the first thing that he became aware of was the searing pain in his shoulder. Gradually as his vision and memory asserted themselves, he became aware that he was in his own kitchen. He was sitting facing the table on which lay the body of his wife, Sheila. She was dressed only in her brassière and knickers and had tape across her mouth. She wasn't moving but it was clear from the rise of her chest that she was alive.

David made to go to her. It was only then he realised that he was bound tightly to the chair.

'Just sit where you are. Don't try to move, Inspector. I've had enough trouble with you already.'

The voice came from behind him. It was Northcote.

'I've arranged a ringside seat for you, Inspector,' said Northcote, moving round to face him.

'You swine, let me go.' David knew that his words were impotent. The man was cruel and he was mad. Nothing but a bullet through the heart would stop him now.

'Let me explain what I intend to do so that the anticipation of the event will bring you as much anguish, discomfort and pain as possible. Almost as much as the event itself. But I can assure you that it will be spectacularly upsetting. You see, I really want to make you suffer, really suffer. It is because of you I festered away in a little white cell for eight years – eight long years. Have you any concept what that is like? To wake up each morning knowing that you will be staring at the same blank four walls for the rest of the day. There will be no one

169

to talk to or be with. The same – day after day after day. That is your life, if you can call it life. There is no one to talk with. No one to share things with. There is just nothing. The brain atrophies and the bitterness grows. It festers, Inspector and becomes focused. It focused on you – because it was you who gave me that fate and indeed nothing I can do to you can possibly make up for the pain and distress I suffered. They say that revenge is a dish best served up cold. Well, Inspector, this one is going to be particularly icy.'

Northcote chuckled at his own conceit and walked over to a kitchen cabinet near the sink. Here rested an instrument case which he opened and extracted a long shiny scalpel. He ran it gently across face of his thumb causing fine line of scarlet to appear. He sucked it noisily.

He grinned. 'Nice and sharp. A very efficient slicing tool.'

'What are you going to do?' David could hardly make his mouth work and these words emerged almost as a hoarse whisper.

'I am so glad you asked me that. Fear not, it is my intention to explain everything to you in great detail.'

Holding the scalpel aloft, he moved to the kitchen table and stood over the inert form of Sheila Llewellyn. For a moment he looked down at her, lost in dark thoughts his eyes lit with a wild fire and then after a moment he broke his gaze and turned to David.

'Lovely smooth arms your wife has got, Inspector. And that is where I intend to start.'

David's stomach lurched and he groaned. 'Please, I beg you, leave her be. Use me, cut me instead. I'm the one you hate. She hasn't done you any harm. Please leave her alone.'

'Oh, yes, you are the one I hate and indeed I will come to you in due course, Inspector. But here's the beauty of all this. In cutting up your wife, I manage to hurt you twice. As she suffers, so will you. As she screams, so will you. A wonderful chorus of pain and despair, And I haven't even started on you yet. There's a beautiful symmetry about it all.'

David's head slumped down in abject despair.

'Come, come, Inspector. You have a ringside seat. I expect you to watch. You see I will begin slowly by taking a pleasing slice of flesh from the upper arm – not too deep, not as deep as the bone, but deep enough to provide a tasty piece of meat about the size of a rump steak. A little appetiser before the main feast. Internal organs are the best for that particular course.'

David swore loudly and with all his might he tried to move, to break free of his bonds, but it was to no avail. The more he tugged and wriggled, the tighter his bonds appeared to grow.

'Once I have secured our lovely slice of arm, so welcome in these days of meat rationing, I do not intend to be selfish. I will devour half and allow you to snack on the rest. Oh, do not look so revolted. I shall insist that you share the tasty morsel. Refusal to do so will mean more pain for your wife. So you see in a way by tasting her flesh you will be doing her a favour.'

'You bastard!' David bellowed at the top of his voice, the words echoing dully around the kitchen.

Northcote just beamed. 'Indubitably, I am a bastard. Oh, yes. But a clever one. You've got to give me that. A clever bastard who has the upper hand. Now, I think it is time I begin.'

He leaned over Sheila Llewellyn and with a steady motion brought the scalpel down towards her bare arm.

THIRTY-SEVEN

By the time I reached Larch Close, my lungs were on the verge of bursting. I imagined them, barrage balloon-like inflating beyond their accepted capacity inside my aching chest surging up towards my mouth. Surely they would burst at any time? But until they did, I kept on running. Two people's lives could depend on me. I just hoped that fate would be kind and allow me to arrive in time to prevent the terrible scenario my mind had conjured up.

At last I reached David's house. I skidded as I turned down past the gateway and moderated my speed. I spied the car that Northcote had been driving parked by the side of the neat villa at the end of the tree-lined drive. There were lights on in the downstairs rooms and I discovered that the front door was unlocked.

It had been two or three years since I had been in the house so that my memory of its geography was a little hazy. I stood in the hallway and listened. I was still breathing heavily from my exertions and my own breath, for a time, masked any other noises in the house. Desperately, I tried to control my breathing and as I succeeded, I heard voices or to be precise one voice. It was muffled and indistinct. There was no way that I could identify it or tell what it was saying. However I could deduce that it was male.

I opened the door of the sitting room. It was empty, but I could now detect that the noise I could hear was coming from the kitchen beyond, the door of which was closed. I crossed the room at speed. I knew that this wasn't the time to eavesdrop. Seconds were precious, especially when there was a madman involved. I also thought that a surreptitious opening of the door would be more dangerous than slamming it open. This way, whatever was going on in that room would for a few moments stop, freeze, as it were, and all attention would be on me.

Clasping my gun in one hand, I placed my other on the door handle. As I did so, a high pitched scream rent the air. I slammed the door open and rushed into the room. As quickly as I could in that moment of startled silence I tried to take in the scene before me. To my right, I saw David, pale and drawn, bound to a heavy dining chair, his eyes wide with panic. In the centre of the room, on a kitchen table lay the body of a barely clad woman whom I dimly recognised as Sheila Llewellyn. Standing over her with what looked like a small vicious knife was Dr Ralph Northcote. He had just made a cut in Sheila's arm, a thin trickle of blood ran down onto the table top.

On seeing me, the madman glared at me with wild animal ferocity and with a roar of rage took a step in my direction. I fired my gun. I did not have time to aim accurately and the bullet whizzed past the devil. He lunged at me. I fired again. This time my aim was surer. It caught him in his right arm. He gave a cry of pain but this did not stop him. Before I knew it, he was on me.

172

We crashed to the floor, the gun slipped from my grasp. The power and weight of my assailant pinned me down to the ground. He growled and slobbered like a giant bear over me. I couldn't reach my gun so I punched him as hard as I could in the face but that did not deter the devil either. He seemed to be functioning on some kind of obsessive energy that ignored pain. He raised the knife high above his head ready to plunge it in me. I struggled to break free but failed to extricate myself completely. As I slithered sideways, he stabbed me in the shoulder. In an instant, despite the excruciating pain my hands sought out his throat and squeezed hard against the thick flesh. Still the monster was not deterred. He raised the knife again.

Then there was a shot. It sounded like a thunderclap in my ear.

Northcote grimaced and his body froze. The blade only inches away from my face – from my good eye!

As he faltered, I pulled myself from under him and rolled aside on the floor out of his range. Then I saw blood suddenly fountain from his throat. It frothed and bubbled around his Adam's apple. He had been shot in the back of the neck. With an obscene gurgle, he fell face downwards on the floor where seconds earlier I had been lying.

I gazed up and saw Sheila Llewellyn. Her face was ashen and haunted, her eyes wide and blank as though she were in some kind of hypnotic trance. She was standing by the kitchen table, one arm resting on it for support. In the other hand she held my gun. Fine tendrils of smoke were still emerging from its muzzle.

THIRTY-EIGHT

'Well, boyo, this is a turn up for the book,' observed my friend David Llewellyn without a trace of irony. 'I never expected to wind up in a hospital bed next to you. And we're both suffering from the same complaint: a wound to the shoulder.'

'Life is funny that way,' I mused.

It was the morning following the night before. The horrendous night before when I had tackled Ralph Northcote and Sheila Llewellyn had shot the demon in the back of the neck, killing him. In the end, apart from being terribly shaken and no doubt the inheritor of ghastly nightmares for some months to come, Sheila was the least physically damaged of the three of us. Luckily, Northcote had only just begun his butchering work and the scalpel had only broken the skin. She had just a nasty little cut on her upper arm. However, David and I had both been badly wounded in the shoulder by Northcote's scalpel: almost an identical twin branding, as though we were initiates into a very brutal and bloody secret society.

After the police had arrived and taken Northcote's corpse off to the morgue at Scotland Yard, we had been scooped up by ambulance and taken to Charing Cross Hospital for treatment and an overnight stay. The injuries were not life threatening, just painful and inconvenient. At least we were alive, as David had reminded me on more that one occasion. He had revived both in energy and outlook with remarkable resilience and as the morning light streamed through the windows of the small ward in which we were incarcerated, he seemed to have metamorphosed back into his old cheerful self. I suppose the fact that Sheila was alive and no longer in danger and that Northcote was on a slab in the police morgue had a lot to do with his revived demeanour. His nightmare had evaporated. I was delighted for him.

The door opened and a pretty nurse entered carrying a tray with two mugs of tea and two plates of biscuits.'

'Our elevenses, eh, nurse? I could get used to this pampering,' said David brightly.

The girl smiled. 'I don't think you're going to get a chance. Once the doctor's has a look at you, I reckon he'll be sending you home. You'll just need to take it easy for a few weeks and you'll both be as right as ninepence."

'That's a shame. I was counting on a long stay in here,' grinned David.

After the nurse departed, we drank our tea in silence. I could not get the images of the events of the previous night from my mind: my race along the darkening streets; my dramatic entrance into the kitchen and the dreadful sight that greeted me; my desperate tussle with Northcote; the shot and the terrible frothing wound at his throat. I shuddered as these dramatic pictures flickered before me as though they were projected on a screen. I looked across at David and could see from his furrowed brow and staring eyes that he too was experiencing his own private horror show. At least his loved-one was safe and sound. If only I could have done the same for my sweet Max. If only I could have saved her. With a determined effort I shut down that avenue of thought. That way madness lies.

The door opened again and three individuals bustled in. We had visitors: Sheila, Benny and Peter.

'We've come to see the heroes,' chimed Benny.

'Survivors more like,' grinned David as Sheila embraced him and then planted a large kiss on his cheek.

'I'd hug you, my darling, but I'm afraid my arm isn't up to it yet,' she said.

'I can wait,' said David, returning the kiss.

She stroked her husband's face affectionately. Although her face was pale and she looked tired, Sheila seemed remarkably robust for a lady who had undergone such a terrible ordeal less than twenty-four hours earlier.

'In the wars again, eh, Johnny,' said Benny, pulling up a chair by my bed.

'I'll do anything for a cup of tea in bed and being fussed over by a pretty nurse.'

'You know, one of these days, I'll be coming to the morgue to identify your body, Johnny Hawke.'

'More than likely.'

'You need more protection,' piped up Peter. 'An assistant to help you. To watch your back.'

'An assistant like you, you mean.'

Peter's eyes brightened. 'Exactly. I could leave school this summer and come and work for you.'

'I don't make enough money to keep myself from teetering towards the breadline, let alone support an assistant.'

'But with the two of us, we could double the business.'

'You wouldn't let him, would you Johnny? He's too young to be involved in your nasty line of work.'

'I'm already involved,' asserted Peter. 'I helped Johnny catch Bruce Horsefield. He couldn't have done it without me.'

'It's madness,' moaned Benny.

I agreed with him, but I also knew of Peter's one-track determination. I wasn't sure whether it would be wise to take him in under my umbrella rather than risk him doing something foolish and trying out on his own. He was headstrong enough to do that. Whatever, now was not the time or place to consider such possibilities.

Thankfully, Benny read my mind and changed the subject. 'When will you be going home?'

'Today, I hope.'

'Today! But you are seriously injured.'

I grinned. 'I've got a very nasty cut, that's all. It's deep and painful but no damage has been done, although I'll never play the violin again.'

'Really... I never knew... Ah, a joke.' He smiled with that strange disapproving grin that was peculiar to him.

* * *

Some hours later, I was standing in the room alone. We, the fellow members of the damaged shoulder club had both been discharged with appointments in the outpatients in seven days' time. David had been whisked off by Sheila, who had given me a gentle hug, while whispering the words, 'Thank you,' in my ear.

My arm was in a neat sling and the nurse had very kindly draped my jacket and overcoat over my shoulders like a cloak before hurrying off for more important duties. Well, there was a war on.

I needed a smoke. Some stimulation before I faced the outside world once more. A smoke was such a normal comforting thing. But now it wasn't going to be easy to organise. I sat on the bed and with great difficulty extracted a cigarette from my jacket pocket and slipped it in my mouth. Now, I thought, how on earth am I going to light the beggar, when a match flared near me and was held close to the end of my cigarette.

I looked up at my helpmate and gazed into the face of Ivana. She smiled.

'Light it quickly, or I'll get my fingers burned.'

I obeyed, inhaling the smoke with gusto.

'Benny told me you were here. You have a habit of ending up on hospital beds.'

'It's my only opportunity to meet pretty women.'

Her eyes twinkled with amusement and then darkened suddenly. 'You don't mind me coming here, do you?' she said hesitantly.

'Mind! Of course not. You are a gorgeous sight for this sore eye.' I leaned forward and kissed her on the cheek.

'In that case, Mr Hawke, I suggest that I take you home and cook you a very nice meal to help build up your strength. What do you say?'

Ellipsis

Nikki Dudley

Nikki Dudley

Nikki is managing editor of *streetcake* magazine and also runs the *streetcake* writing prize and MumWrite. She has a chapbook and collection with KFS. She is the winner of the Virginia Prize 2020 for her second novel, *Volta*.

"The boy stood on the burning deck..."

Felicia Dorothea Hemans

ellipsis (Gk 'leaving out')

Cuddon J. A., (1999), *Dictionary of Literary Terms & Literary Theory*, Penguin Books, London

Dedications

For my Mum and Dad. Thanks for being my best PR and for the inspiration.

And to Joe, for helping me believe in myself and for thinking up the most exciting plots for everyday life.

Acknowledgements

A big thanks to the following: my whole family, who have made me stronger and helped me to achieve; Pip and Martin, for their backing and for some amazing adventures; Sam and Megan for their friendship and critiques; my good friends for keeping me smiling; Parliament Hill School, for providing me with a good grounding as a reader and a writer; all the students and lecturers on the Creative Writing BA and MA courses at Roehampton University, who helped me develop as a writer (in particular Louise Tondeur and Leone Ross for 'growing' my fiction); the members of authonomy.com, who provided valuable feedback; Andy Sweetman (DNA Graphic Design) for helping me realise my front cover; and lastly the team at Sparkling Books for supporting me and my novel.

1 Red Snake

I chose him because of the red scarf.

My palms sweat. Dirt from the walls is smudged across them and slithers in the folds. There is a faint smell of kebab in the air and an excited murmur moving down the platform like Chinese whispers. I wonder how distorted the message will be by the time it reaches my end.

Can you hear it too, Mum? Do you think they're whispering about me?

There are other scarves too, red and white combined and I guess that a football game must have taken place. Yet, his scarf is different. It is pure red, the red people affix to the badge of fiery passion, the badge of cold-blooded murder, without the interludes of white to dull its beauty.

He is unique. I've watched him for weeks now and the time has finally arrived. The clock says 15:32 as casually as ever but it secretly signals to me: this is the correct time. It is not destiny; it is careful planning and the instinctual knowledge inside

Mum, this is the moment.

Now, my breath barely disturbs the stillness of the cavern the swarm of strangers are gathered in, all awaiting the rush of wind that will open up the arteries, revive us. Everybody appears lost, shuffling on their feet, staring at the same grotesquely large posters until they become less overpowering, fiddling with buttons, holding their phones and longing for reception. Anything to avoid eye contact.

My favourite moment is the shared objective, the upraised eyes facing the same direction, the temporary and forced community as the wind invites the dusty air to dance, flings the litter in celebration. All I can do to keep calm is count the seconds down in my head. Even when I think of you, you are bouncing in my mind.

The only details I know about him have been gathered through observation from afar. This is actually the closest I have been to him in three weeks. From here, I can smell his sweat weaving with his aftershave. I can also see how he has missed a belt loop and a tiny bald patch in the back of his hair, perhaps where he has a birthmark.

Are you excited too, Mum? I know you've been thinking about him when we've been trying to sleep. Now, we're so close…

He is reading one of those trashy papers that have stormed the city. The wires of his iPod headphones are coming out of his ears and snaking down his chest to his jacket pocket. If he knew what is about to happen, would he change the song he is listening to, faintly nodding his head, and not struggling to remember the throwaway words? Would he fling down that paper and rush off to buy his favourite book?

It is the scarf that ensnared me. I had been wandering the streets three weeks before, in another dimension of thought or nowhere at all. Then, it flashed at me, like a camera suspending a moment in time. It is a snake that has coiled around my attention and shot its venom into my blood. I latched onto the scarf and followed it all the way home. The rain tried to bully my eyes closed but I stood firm, keeping them set on the scarf weaving through the grey world. When he reached his house, I stood outside for another half an hour, smiling, pouring with gratitude.

Since then, he has been my daily plot. Today, he has thrown his scarf on haphazardly, perhaps being late or not wearing it for warmth but simply out of habit. I can only guess who bought it for him. His girlfriend? His mother? An old friend or relative who put no thought into a present for him? Or perhaps he chose it himself and red is also his favourite colour.

Despite following him, I recall very little about his appearance and when I try to remember three days later, I won't have a clue. I can guess that he has black hair but then I can also guess it is blond. I can say he's short or maybe tall. I can say he is black, white or Asian. Yet the fact is; I haven't paid attention. When the photo appears in the paper, I will look on it as fresh-eyed as everybody else.

What I remember most is a sense of him, a presence. He is like a positive image in a photograph where the rest has been inverted. Even more peculiar is the sense that he is aware. Sometimes I have caught him pausing in the street, as though to let me catch up. Another time, when he was trying on clothes, he seemed to single me out in the mirror and mentally ask my opinion.

The countdown begins to flash: **STAND BACK TRAIN APPROACHING**. My chest implodes and the rest of my body springs alive. All I hear is a harmony of sounds: beating inside and the roar of the train.

Step forward.

Peer into dark.

Wind hisses at hot skin.

Folding newspapers.

Roar gallops in heart.

Eyes of light emerge.

Monster creeps closer.

A unison of feet.

Red scarf flutters.

Spring forward.

Head slightly turns.

Outstretched arms connect.

Eyes of train wide.

Mouths silent words.

Falling.

Newspaper flailing.

Reach out.

Touch the scarf.

Train screeches.

Screaming.

Monster engulfs.

Faces press up to windows.

Scarf a ball in fist.

I breathe. Stop. Think: *Right on time*. As he fell, his lips moved in the shape of these words: *Right on time. Right on time. Right. On. Time.*

Mum, did you see?

2 The Phone Call

At 15:32 a day later, Thom Mansen stops. He drops his pen as though it has stung him. He pushes away from the desk and stretches his legs. He doesn't pick up the phone even though it cries out. He stops and cannot find a place to start again.

He wonders what his boss would say if he went to his office and said, "I've stopped and I can't begin again." Would he himself be able to explain this? He doubts it. He doesn't feel hungry yet, he doesn't need to piss, and life is unusually 'fine'. In fact, his boss even suggested a promotion might be in the works and he hasn't argued with his girlfriend in months.

So he is lost.

Perhaps he has some rotting disease that works its way to the surface inside out and that's why he feels strange. Perhaps his heart has stopped and he has unknowingly passed into death at his desk whilst helping Mrs Rayder understand that her policy does not cover the death of her beloved tomcat, Bubbles.

He laughs into the air. "Shit," he mumbles, knowing it's entirely possible for this to be the case. Yet, hearing his own voice reassures him that he is still in a physical realm of existence, not in a twisted form of limbo where everything is similar to the life he has been leading up to this point.

The pen lies on the pile of paperwork. He stares, narrows his eyes, screams at his hand to move forward a few inches and clutch it. But his hand ignores him. His eyes begin to ache and tire in their sockets. He closes them for a few moments and reopens them.

Yet, he still doesn't move. He begins to panic and thinks he's having a stroke or an unworldly force is possessing him. But he knows he has to meet Emma later at the restaurant. Will he make it? Will his body simply imprison him here throughout the night? He would much rather be with Emma, having sex, talking about nothing.

He sees the light of the phone glaring at him. There are incoming calls on four lines. He is sure one of them is the old man who phones every day, pretending to ask questions about his housing policy, but in reality just wanting to connect with another human being. Apart from that, it could be any one of the thousands of customers, waiting to chew an ear off.

"Come on Thom, get yourself together!" He shakes out his shoulders. He smiles at his progress and prepares to get back to his day. However, he now finds he has no desire to pick up the pen, to continue signing the rejections on policies, to hear another customer saying "of course I read the fine print" when they haven't, to continue in any way at all.

He goes through every part of his job specification in his mind and cannot put a tick by any of the duties. He watches the other people walking by his office through the glass, like a helpless goldfish not functioning at the same level or speed. They are all busy – moving papers, picking up phones, and chatting about who's shagging who this week. What is stopping him from doing the same?

He imagines if any of them cared enough to notice him, what they would see. A man, who is clean-shaven, has straight and recently cut brown hair (which curls at the sides if he doesn't monitor it), a straight tie, a dribble of ink trailing from his lip that he doesn't know about. Thom complies with every rule about uniform in the employee's handbook; he is the physical representation of company policy. Would they know he hasn't moved for five minutes? Would they assume he has been working up until the moment they happened to glance in?

Although his body is functioning again, Thom's mind is suddenly heavy. His head drops into his chest like his neck has dissolved. A depression pulses through him, makes his chest rise and fall in a pitiful sigh, makes his body sprawl out on the desk like a person who has just suffered a heart attack. He watches his breath make a mist on the wooden face of the desk.

Abruptly, the phone stops wailing. Then ten seconds later, it rings again.

He grabs hold of the receiver. He balances it on his face which is still flat against the desk and awkwardly muffles, "Hello. Thomas Mansen."

"Thom. It's Richard."

Thom shoots up as though someone has electrocuted him. "Rich, what's going on?" It's the voice... He can tell from the first syllable, the downward direction of the tone.

Richard delays, his breathing heavy for a moment. "Thom... it's about Daniel." Thom is sure Richard is crying, or perhaps he has a cold. "He's dead." Crying, then.

"What?" Thom stutters, then again, "*what?*"

"He fell under a train. Yesterday." Richard's words are so direct, poisoned darts that keep hitting him. Thom's chest starts to tighten; his bones are shrinking like clothes washed at the wrong temperature. "I'm sorry I didn't call earlier. Aunty didn't take it well, *obviously*... I had to call the doctor," Richard adds, making Thom feel like he has been squeezed out of his body and now lingers somewhere above the desk, not knowing the way back in. *He needs to get to Aunty Val.*

"Oh," is all Thom says.

And then he listens to Richard, talking about the funeral, an inquest, the reading of the will and asking can he come and can he bring Emma, and Aunty Val would've called herself but she is still crying, and she needs him there. Tonight.

3 The Note

Highbury and Islington station. 15:30 Sunday.
It is Daniel's handwriting. Thom recognises the way Daniel crosses his Ts with slanted lines, the way the top of his zeros never quite meet. *Not meet,* met. Daniel won't be in the present tense anymore.

At this, the note in Thom's hand starts to shake and he buckles onto the bed.

Thom supposes he should know better than to snoop in Daniel's things. Looking in Daniel's possessions is similar to how it had been trying to relate to him in life. Thom feels like he is swimming against the current and he has found a small piece of flotsam, but it instantly falls apart. This note could be written in Chinese, for all the sense it made.

There are so many drawers in Daniel's room, small ones for tiny secrets, large ones with small compartments inside; large ones ordered in such a way that no one would dare touch a thing. Thom can smell Daniel's authority. Invisible foot soldiers are standing guard around the room, willing to die in order to protect his classified information.

Yet here Thom is, having been compelled by the only drawer half open, like a partly opened wound. He shouldn't be in here anyway, as Aunty Val and Richard haven't even managed to open the door a crack. He is trespassing because he knows Daniel won't be able to stop him. He wants to see the magician's secrets that have bemused him for so long. He has poked around in this drawer and his hand has seemingly come out dripping with blood and sticky with pus, and all he wants to do is stuff everything back inside and close it up.

He refocuses on the note.

This is the time and place he died.

Thom shivers and tosses the note away at the thought. Yet moments later, he slowly leans closer to it and re-reads it at least ten times. He is a mouse tiptoeing around a mousetrap.

What do these words mean? Was Daniel meeting someone? And were they involved with his death? Was it suicide even? Or is this merely a coincidence that he wrote down *this* time and place, when they just so happened to denote almost to the minute, his death?

Thom feels his stomach groaning in part shock and part confusion. He rushes to the toilet and vomits. This has happened before, only a few times in his life – well, the worst times if he is honest. However, although he has clearly vomited up most of his breakfast, the questions remain inside Thom, like ulcers, nagging and ugly. He washes out his mouth with cold water and makes his way back to Daniel's room.

The note is still there. Thom doesn't know why the note shouldn't be there still, but perhaps he would prefer it to disappear; leave him alone to be sad about Daniel. The last thing he needs is more questions. Whenever somebody dies, there are enough questions anyway. All he can think about is the last time he'd been in the hold of this endless interrogation, when he'd just turned twelve, and both his parents hadn't come home. He'd vomited then too. A few times in fact.

Oddly enough, this room is where Thom was transported that night. He vaguely recalls Aunty Val kissing him goodnight whilst Daniel watched from the doorway, having been evicted for the night to the sofa. Thom felt unsettled then by the clatter of the railway that ran behind the house, but over the course of his adolescence it became as natural as birdsong.

In this moment however, the sound of the railway makes him feel nauseous. Although thankfully, he has nothing left to eject. He looks down at his suit and, seeing a vomit stain on his left cuff, rubs at it anxiously. If he turns up at Daniel's funeral covered in vomit, surely he may as well smear it over the coffin. After all, they were more than just cousins, yet not quite brothers.

Now that Thom thinks properly, he wishes he had known Daniel as well as he did Richard. Although, he and Daniel were the same age and even shared the same birthday, it seems these things merely gave them more reason *not* to bond. Instead, as soon as Thom arrived after his parents' deaths, he and Richard, who was two years older, fell into a closer friendship.

Thom tried with Daniel, yet Daniel didn't seem interested. Whenever Thom pictures their shared birthday parties, Daniel is set back in some way, a step further from the table where everyone was singing 'happy birthday' or at Christmas, Daniel waited until everyone else had torn at their presents frantically and only then, he carefully chose one to begin with.

And what is the last thing he had said to Daniel? He searches through his memory and can only come up with a brief conversation at Richard's last birthday party. Daniel was standing by the front door. They exchanged pleasantries about general health and jobs. And what is it that Thom said to him? His last proper words to his cousin; face to face?

"Daniel, do you know where Aunty Val is?"

"In the kitchen." He nods towards the house. His smile

acknowledges what they both feel; a need to find an exit as fast as possible, a sad knowledge that they will never linger with each other.

"Thanks. Speak later."

Yet Thom didn't speak to him later. And he never would again.

Thom wishes now he had tried harder. If not to be closer to him in life but for this moment, in order to understand this note, to understand why Daniel had written it so precisely and had left it in the only half-open drawer in the room, as if he knew...

4 Lips Stick

He isn't wearing the scarf in the photo.

When I first see the photo in the paper, I only glance at it and feel my body collapse inwards. Tears gather at the corners of my eyes at the absence of it. I instantly pull the scarf towards me and hold it up to my face, kiss it; smell his aftershave and his sweat, to pretend I am still following him. I have thought of him at 15:32 each day and probably always will.

After hours of comforting myself with the scarf, I allow myself to examine the photo. Before this, I have enjoyed merely remembering his presence and I think seeing his photograph, probably some false one from his graduation or a family holiday, will spoil the essence of him that I can feel if I close my eyes. Concentrate.

When I finally set the page in front of me, I scrutinize it. Apparently, he was twenty-four years old. Apparently, he had short brown hair that threatened to curl at the sides. Apparently, he had a scar on his left cheek about three inches long. Apparently, they are appealing for witnesses.

I am wrong though; in guessing it would be a cheesy family photo. Part of his face is covered in shadow as though he is a nocturnal animal peeking out at the daylight and there is no smile, only a faint fizzing up of a smile hiding behind his pursed lips. His eyes are dark brown and, for a moment, my heart accelerates, so convinced he is actually looking at me. In the same moment, I see his eyes as he hung in the air. Yet this is all invention because of the photo. The photo has brought him back to life.

Now, I see the only detail that is clear to me: those lips, speaking to me, pronouncing each word. He had been so precise, inserting them into my memory like he'd penetrated me and caused an embryo to grow inside and begin to kick.

Right on time.

I thought perhaps I misunderstood or imagined them but underneath the doubt, I feel certain. He wanted me to know. Perhaps the only thing I misinterpreted is why he seemed aware, not because he stood out, but because he knew who I was, my intentions, and my actions. Even before I knew? Perhaps my crazy notions that he slowed down and waited for me and looked at me in that mirror weren't so 'crazy'.

I close the paper and look at the walls. Yet all I see are his lips, curling and sneering. His menacing face is projected onto every surface, daring me. The only place I can't see him is in the television, which instead reflects my image. So I sit cross-legged on the plastic wooden floor and look into the tiny screen.

There isn't much choice about where to go here. It is a bedsit with only a small bedroom, and a kitchen along one wall sectioned off by a stained curtain. The toilet and shower are a few doors down, shared with three others. It's so small in there, every time I get out of the shower, I nearly stand in the toilet.

They tell me this place will be good for me, to get me back on my own feet, to get away from the place where it happened. Nobody asked my opinion and my estranged brother has gone ahead and sold the house, refusing to give me my share of the money until I feel 'more balanced' as he puts it.

How can he decide that for us, Mum? How can he take away our home?

So, here I am, in this place that is not only the definition of scum, but also a place where things come to die. I have several potted plants, all of them refusing to live, no matter how much I water them and ask them what else I can do. There is a dead rat in the corner and dead insects that were feasting on the rat's carcass, before they, too, died. I don't move any of it. I look at the rat and the insects sometimes, feel the dead leaves between my fingers and remember I am alive and feel superior.

Oh, what would they say if they knew their ploy to put me on 'the road to normality' has landed me here, in the house where everything is dying or already dead?

However, the worst thing isn't the death rate. The worst thing is the landlord. He smells like road-kill and every so often tries to have a 'chat'. He knocks clumsily on the door and says, "Hi sweet cheeks," exhaling a bottle of whiskey over me. He always manages to talk his way in, pretending he has some issues about rent or the building to discuss, and as there is nowhere else to sit, we always end up on the bed. He then says things like "I love your soft hair" and runs his hand through it, making my curls moist with sweat and "that's a very... very... *nice* top" when he's really looking at my cleavage. When he tries to grope me, I always throw him out. I'm a tough girl so I don't mind.

I have to cope with these things because you can't protect me now, Mum.

Although, if he does it again, I may have to kill him.

5 The Dead, Silence

Thom is surprised during the funeral. No one seems to have known Daniel. Thom himself spends the whole funeral in a daze, thinking about adjectives for Daniel, only realising it's over when Emma squeezes his hand. She looks great in her black dress. If it weren't so inappropriate, he would take her to the car and distract himself with a good dose of indecent exposure.

By the time they watch the curtain devour his coffin, Thom has thought of only useless adjectives for Daniel. He was mysterious, elusive, and witty. He always seemed like he knew more than everybody and he probably had. That's what drove a wedge between Daniel and everybody else. That's why during the funeral there are few tears. The entire room is suffocated with only one feeling: guilt.

The wake is at Aunty Val's house. Thom feels the pieces of furniture he grew up with are stabilisers. He can't help but think he has missed seeing it more than he has missed seeing Daniel over the last few months. The tired grey sofa in the living room is so old and so used that you can see the mould of people's arses. His is the one in the middle. Aunty Val doesn't care much for decoration as she always tells him people are more important than houses. Therefore, she doesn't care (especially today) that the wallpaper in the living room has started to peel at the seams and that a stain has grown on the ceiling, the colour of tea, from when Richard always spills his bathwater. The mourners walk mud into the living room and nobody complains.

During the wake, Thom drifts between everybody, trying to catch snippets of conversation about Daniel. Yet, everybody seems to be discussing the food: "These sausage rolls are tasty," or the weather: "It's warmer than I expected it to be," or where they bought the clothes for the funeral: "It was a bargain, especially as I'm only going to wear it once..." Worst of all are the people who are saying nothing at all. The only bit of shocking information is that Mrs Launder's dress, which looks like shit, apparently cost her one hundred pounds. She has clearly been robbed.

Thom slumps onto the nearest thing for the second time that day and rests his head in his hands. Emma appears a few minutes later, kissing him on the ear. She sits across from him, pushing a cup of tea in his direction. He gives a faint smile and takes a sip, then pushes it aside.

"How are you?" she asks, reaching across the table to touch his hand. He is conscious of the dried sick on his sleeve but hopes she won't notice it.

"Fine," he says automatically.

"No. How are you *really*?"

"I'm *really* fine," Thom pauses and adds, "I've just been thinking about how little I knew him."

"Don't people always think that when someone isn't around anymore?" Emma counters, thinking this isn't serious. He hasn't told her about the note, which has crackled in his pocket throughout the day, so loud at points that Thom wonders why someone hasn't heard it.

"This is different."

"How?" She is leaning forward.

"I'm not sure." He shrugs, chickening out. Sometimes, he is worried that he finds it hard without a script for every eventuality, a line to satisfy people when they want clarification. Emma lets him get away with it for now. She doesn't say anything else. She just pulls him closer and kisses him on the lips, deliberately, hard. She holds his face an inch from hers for a moment, saying she is here for him; she will wait, until he understands himself.

6 Red Pen

Nobody notices when I slip upstairs during the wake and go into his room. I tag onto the group again when they arrive back from the funeral and mill amongst the people who knew him. I wonder about the connections in this group. Who loved him? Who has come out of guilt? Who is tagging along like me? What would these people say if they knew his murderer is here?

I check all the rooms on the second floor and decide which one is his. The first one obviously belongs to a woman, judging by the lacy bras. The second has a letter in it addressed to Richard Mansen. The third is a guest room or a storage room, where old furniture that will probably never be used again is waiting, hopefully. The other room is a bathroom so it only leaves the last door, which doesn't look any different from the others, but the wood is pulsing when I press my hand against it. There is a secret message written along the wood that only I can read.

His room is plain. The walls are white, the carpet a dull brown. There are several sets of drawers, all light MDF wood. One of the drawers is slightly open but not enough to see inside. A large antique looking wardrobe sits behind the door. His bedspread is white with only one black line near the top, showing where the head should be. The spread is creased and one corner is folded back like an eyelid permanently open.

I sit on the bed, clutching the scarf in my fist and try to imagine him sitting beside me. I imagine the speed and heaviness of his breath in the silence, the size and presence of his body, the depth the bed would sink under his weight. Would he say something to me? Would he whisper or speak in a loud deep voice? Would he pronounce the Ts in his words?

The only thing I am certain about him is that he made me kill him.

I had believed it started with me but the chain began somewhere before that, and I have to find out where and when. This is why I am here in this room, listening to the clattering of the train and the murmuring mass of people below. I am a trespasser, the murderer transforming into an investigator. I'm going back to the start of the flow chart to discover the direction and force behind each move.

The open drawer seems the nearest place to begin. It is one of six drawers, all about 5cm by 5cm, in a set beside his bed. I edge towards it, feeling like it's a landmine waiting for me to add stress and unknowingly kill myself. Yet I still stick my hand in, with my eyes closed.

Nothing. I feel nothing. I think my hand must have gone numb. I peer inside. The drawer is empty. I tug open all the other drawers in the set and find the same. They are all empty. I jump to my feet and begin flinging open all the drawers in the room, the wardrobe, checking under the bed, opening the cupboards above the wardrobe, even pulling back the bedspread in the hope of finding something.

Yet I find everything is empty. There is nothing in this room. He was never here. The only discovery I make in the room is a small red pen mark on his bed sheets and the only object in the room is the angry bedside radio, which is screaming red numbers at me and they happen to be, 15:32…

I wilt onto the floor. The carpet smells new. And I notice, belatedly, the faint smell of paint. He has completely erased himself from this house. He has pressed backspace on the keyboard and removed his life. And this all seems to add to his words as he fell.

He planned it. He chose me. He moulded me.

Mum, how did this happen?

15:32 hadn't been instinctual. It had been as set as the train tracks onto which I pushed him.

7 Aunty Val

After the wake is over, Thom agrees to stay the night. Emma leaves because she has to go back to work the next day. He says goodbye to her at the door and, as her car pulls away, he has to grasp onto the door handle to stop himself from waving to her.

Inside the house, the lock sounds like a bullet. This is followed by soft crying from upstairs and the clatter of plates that can be heard from the kitchen. He decides Aunty Val is the priority of the two.

He tiptoes upstairs, wincing at the creaks he should have remembered were there. It is instilled in him that death is quiet; something the living shouldn't flaunt themselves in the face of.

Aunty Val's door is open. He stands outside for a moment and peers in, instantly smelling the sorrow, hanging in the air like smoke clouds. The walls seem to be quivering in disgust, the paint flaking like dead skin.

"Hello," he whispers through the crack in the door and slowly moves his head through.

Aunty Val gasps. A fresh tear is rolling down her face, an afterthought, because now she has turned white as paper. She is breathing hollowly, holding herself up with her arms. Then after a few minutes of looking at him, proofreading his features, she gulps in air and starts to cry again.

It's only now that he springs into action and rushes to her side, taking her in his arms. She is crying words into his body, something like "your voice" and "Daniel." Thom doesn't want to think about what she is saying though, feeling his heart begin to shiver behind his rib cage, so he presses her into him until her words are too muffled to hear. It isn't the first time someone has mistaken his voice for Daniel's but this is the only time when it scares him.

Yet, almost thankfully, she is too concerned with crying to continue moving her mouth, and her lips forget. She sobs onto his neck and he remembers sobbing onto hers for a week after he'd first moved here. He knows from those times to let her finish, let her run out of water, and let her moans grow muted, disappear.

When these things happen, she looks up at him shyly. Thom tries a smile but even his mouth knows it's stupid. She leans her head on his shoulder. He thinks her eyes are washed out, as if somebody has diluted them. They used to be a much stronger green. He knows it's to be expected but when he thinks back to a month ago, when he last came to visit, he'd noticed it then too. She has let her hair go grey, when usually she keeps it coloured a medium blond.

Aunty Val always keeps herself well dressed and maintained. He always thinks of her saying, "You've got to keep up the hard work if you want to look good." She is fifty-two and looks good for it, although she is always embarrassed when a man shows interest in her.

So did this neglect start a month ago? Or even longer? He hasn't visited as much as he should have. And if this neglect had been occurring before Daniel's death, then why? Had she been worried about Daniel? Perhaps this supported the theory that he committed suicide. But would he have? Thom guesses they are questions he can ask later (and some which he cannot) but now he has no right to bother her.

"He's really dead," is how she breaks the silence. It seems obvious but Thom feels like it stabs him in the ribs then. She is right, he can't argue. He can only nod, trying to breathe.

"Did you like the song we chose?" she asks.

"It was good. Did Daniel like it?" he blushes.

"It was one of his favourites," she confirms, and he feels himself smile, glad that at least one person feels certain regarding Daniel. She is the kind of person who always takes notes and stores them in a mental filing cabinet, in order to refer to them later. Thom on the other hand keeps forgetting people's birthdays and buying Emma gold jewellery when she only likes silver.

"I'm sorry." He throws in a worthless phrase to secretly apologise for not knowing Daniel and now it's too late.

"I'm too young to be losing kids," she says, adding, "like *you* were too young."

"Let's not talk about that," he dismisses, and kisses her forehead.

"But I want to," she croaks, wiping her nose on her sleeve. He can't help but find this uncomfortable, especially as she has always been so strong for him, more so than with her own children. She faces him and holds onto his arms at the elbows, pressing down, needing to make her point. "I know it's different but I thought you would be the best..." Her lips rebel against her, muffle her words. "I thought you would understand *this*..."

"Okay," he interrupts.

"No Thom, please," she begs, "I *know* you hate talking about it."

"It's not the same," he tells her, wriggling in her hold.

"But it was wrong too." She is staring at him, searching. "Your parents shouldn't have died then and Daniel..." she falters again, "shouldn't have..."

"What do you want me to say?" He cuts over her, unable to go back, even for her. He has never been able to discuss it properly. The week he cried himself to sleep is the closest she ever got to it. The closest anybody has got in fact. Even he struggles to get near to his feelings about it all. Perhaps back then, he asked somebody why or what happened or some question that didn't matter like what happened to the car but he hadn't opened a showroom to let everyone examine his feelings. Perhaps, this is his problem. Perhaps that is why he has a job where he always knows what to say because there is a handbook.

"I don't know what I want you to say," Aunty Val eventually admits. He moves and puts his arm around her, pressing her shoulder against his.

He thinks about work, about the people who phone about a loved one's life insurance, how they've lost that person and to really rub it in, they have to argue with him about the clauses in the contract. And so he says what he says to them (because he isn't a bastard), "I'm sorry. I'm *so* sorry. I'll do all I can."

8 The Reading

Thom is only beginning to recover from the funeral when the reading of the will pops up like an uninvited relative. He doesn't even remember he has to attend until Aunty Val shakes him awake in his old bed, three days after the funeral, where he has been having nightmares for most of the night. She says they're leaving in an hour.

He turns on his side and stares at the wall. He sees the faint remains of the treasure map he and Richard drew on the wall the first summer he'd been here. Daniel insisted it was too simplistic and went to draw his own, more complicated and realistic map. Two hours after they finished their hunt, Daniel appeared with a five-page map, complete with cryptic clues. He and Richard could make no sense of it and resorted to mocking him instead.

This is how Thom feels now. Like he is standing in a map, an infinite number of pages long, trying to find somewhere familiar, somewhere he can start from. He can't help thinking he has lost the solution page to the puzzle that had been Daniel. But as soon as he returns from the solicitors, he is determined to find at least an impression in the wet sand, however small, that will lead him somewhere.

The solicitor is a well-spoken man and all Thom can remember about him is his twitching moustache that nods along to his every word. A desire to laugh jabs at the back of his mouth throughout the reading. Yet Thom is sure that laughing will be inappropriate and it is so quiet in the office that the clock could be arrested for excessive noise. Its only competition is the shuffling of papers on the solicitor's monster of a desk for five minutes, and the formalities of death, voiced softly by moustache man.

The solicitor, Thom, Richard, Aunty Val and a shrunken prune of a woman, who has yet to identify herself, occupy the room. Aunty Val's husband left when Richard was two and Daniel not even born, and no one cared to find him. In this room were the people that Daniel wanted to share himself with, or share his possessions with, which were probably just as estranged from him as most of them felt.

After reading the obligatory paragraph, the moustache moves on to awarding prizes, for knowing Daniel, for loving Daniel, for caring he is dead. Yet Thom misses most of the information. He drifts away until he realises the moustache is addressing him.

"And to Mr Thomas Mansen, I leave *this* key." The moustache slides a key across the desk, as though he is passing him a bribe. "I hope he finds his gift as thoughtful as I hoped it would be."

Thom takes the key, weightless in his hand, contradicting his heavy frown lines. Why did the comment about his *gift* seem loaded? After all, what twenty-four-year-old has a will anyway?

Aunty Val and Richard have passed by, without event. Then focus turns to the prune woman. Her face is a fruit gone bad, folding and collapsing into itself. Her skin is a landscape of rough ground filled with ditches. She stares at the moustache throughout, squinting, holding a handkerchief. Thom doesn't remember seeing her at the funeral.

"I leave Mrs Mary Tray, the sum of two-hundred pounds, to spend as she pleases." The moustache has concluded, abruptly. The woman, Mrs Tray, doesn't flinch or express any emotion. She continues to sit for a further ten seconds, Thom counts, then excuses herself with a graceful wave and hobbles out of the room. The rest of them watch, on the edge of words, silenced by the resolve of the door.

"Thank you for attending the reading," the moustache says,

dismissing them. The three of them, a small fabricated family, help each other up.

The reading of the will means more questions. Thom has a desire to put his hand up, like a schoolchild, and wait for somebody to ask him what he wants. Perhaps that way, someone will have to answer him and he won't need to think anymore.

9 Postbox

I have been watching them for twelve days. After the emptiness I encountered in Daniel's room, I have latched onto them, not knowing where to go or what to do anymore. They fill up the emptiness with their sorrow, their quiet desperation, and their connection with the dead.

I stand outside their door every day from about 8am to 9pm, following each of them separately or together when they leave the house, learning about their habits and lives. I hate when I have to go home and try to sleep, when all I can think about is where they might go and what I might miss. Sometimes I do follow them until the early hours of the morning and survive on only a few hours sleep before running through the streets, excited and breathless, to see them again.

The woman constantly has a stringy tissue creeping out of her hand and down her wrist, like a bandage she hasn't been able to remove since it happened. She looks like she has been on a drinking binge. Her hair is a tangled mass of wires; her lips are the colour of pale ham, her body a faltering argument that she used to be winning. She often goes shopping and usually returns with two or three bags from Sainsbury's. She has twice visited another woman, about the same age, in a house around the corner. She and this woman appear to drink tea together and watch Bargain Hunt. She has several times broken down in the street and had to be collected by one of the men living in the house. She is Daniel's mother.

The first man is called Richard. He doesn't look like Daniel. He has darker hair and a slightly chubby face. His eyes seem to be smiling constantly, despite anything else. He usually wears jeans and t-shirts and often has a screwdriver or some other tool on his person. I presume he is an engineer or a mechanic. He often stays in at night and only a few times walks past me, holding hands with a blonde-haired girl who wears short skirts. He sometimes smokes on a bench on the corner of the street and stares up at the sky.

Richard is the one who spoke at the funeral. I watched him from the shadows at the back of the church, watching the sorrow unfold, watching the tissues gathering like flags of surrender. He hadn't said as much as I expected him to, he hadn't filled out Daniel's personality, he hadn't seemed anything but extremely sad that he couldn't perform better.

It was nothing like your funeral, Mum.

There were more than three people at this one for starters. At yours, there were no pictures, no eulogies, and no communion in the face of death. Perhaps it had been this way because of the circumstances; perhaps because people didn't know how to face me when there were two people from the hospital waiting outside to take me back when it finished.

I miss you.

The second man is the one I am interested in. He didn't speak at the funeral. And from what I have observed, he doesn't speak much generally. He has walked beside the mother almost every time she has left the house; if only to drop her off and leave, then return to pick her up. He has sat in the living room of the house staring at the wall and I have watched him, wondering if all he sees in the paint is Daniel's face also. He has stood in the front garden three times, separating his m & m's into colours and eating them in order: brown, blue, red, green and yellow. I don't know what this means yet.

He looks uncannily like Daniel. The same dark menace haunts his eyes, although he doesn't seem to be relishing in it like Daniel, as the photo in the paper seems to portray. They have the same coloured hair and over the last few weeks, the curls threatening Daniel in the photo, have crept up on this look-alike, along with fuzzy lazy stubble. Yet, this man doesn't have the same presence as Daniel and I think he would hate it if he did. When he walks down the street, he bows his head and avoids eye contact with everybody. He keeps his right hand in his back pocket when he isn't using it. He makes me want to shake him awake, punch him in the nose until he realises he's bleeding; tell him Daniel is dead and not him. I feel like I have committed two murders.

It takes almost two weeks of watching for him to finally take action. The key he has been randomly slipping out of his pocket and examining, so intently that I'm sure he could identify it in a line-up, finally springs him into action, a delayed mechanism.

He rushes past me so fast that I have to completely turn my back and pretend I am reading the notes about delivery times on the postbox. This has been my way of hiding whenever one of them passes by. Sometimes I am so transfixed by the postbox that I cannot leave. I stroke the smooth chipped paint, press my fingerprints into these chips, and think about you. I often think about hugging it but somebody always interrupts and pushes their unimportant letter into its mouth and I wish I could get inside there, so easily hide in the darkness and feel the red body encompass me, a new womb for the one that I have lost.

10 Storage Lock Up Number 11

Shit.

The lock up is filled from floor to ceiling with huge bookshelves. The bookshelves are arranged like a labyrinth so when Thom turns around the first corner, he fears he will never find the way out. He begins to wonder if he should have told Aunty Val where he was going. The fluorescent lights in the ceiling are partly blocked by the shelves and the light is scattered awkwardly, as though the light is coming through unevenly spaced floorboards and he is trapped beneath.

The thought of floorboards reminds Thom of the numbers on the door. 11. They are like two exclamation marks with a dash on the top left. When he arrived at the door, he pressed his two fingers against them but felt nothing. Why did he feel drawn to these numbers, these simple shapes?

The woman on the desk told him the lock up had only been acquired three months before. Yet, there is a smell of rotting food, especially the strong stench of banana. Thom wonders if he will stumble upon a disgruntled monkey who has been unable to find the way out, who will promptly kill him. Although would it be the worst thing?

Along with the banana, there is a dusty air that can be seen swirling around him whenever he passes a slot of light. The light also reveals some of the contents of the bookshelves that, apart from the expected books, are clearly full of numerous unrelated items. To name a few of them, there are empty cardboard boxes, cracked ornaments, ripped pieces of paper and notebooks, old car parts, rotting food, pots of ink, perfume bottles and these are just the things Thom can make out initially.

Thom thinks about the moustached man's words: "I hope he finds his gift as thoughtful as I hoped it would be." If Daniel's thoughtfulness created this dark labyrinth which smells foul and looks like a rubbish tip – *why?* What did he want Thom to get from this? Or is it possible that somebody else had come in here and sabotaged the contents?

Thom reasons that it's not impossible that somebody broke in here and sabotaged it, but it is unlikely. Although if the note is a clue that Daniel had been in some kind of trouble, it is a justified suspicion. Overall however, Thom thinks perhaps he is reading too much into the note, the key, *everything*. The only thing he needs to do is find something in this lock up that makes sense, between everything that doesn't.

He decides to start at the end, that way he is working his way towards the exit and not working his way inside, deeper into the labyrinth. He has no concept of how big the lock up is because he cannot see the walls. Every space is occupied with a shelf, a path is marked out with other shelves jutting out in various places. He is suspicious that the shelves are leading him somewhere he shouldn't be going.

Each bookshelf has ten large shelves. They are made from quality wood and each detail like this makes Thom feel increasingly uneasy. Why did Daniel pay so much to have all these shelves put in? Was it just for his benefit? Thom lets the question float around in his brain but drowns it with his present task. He kneels on the floor, his jeans instantly browned with dirt, and rifles around on the first shelf.

His hands come back blackened, full of scratches from unexpected items hiding underneath others and smelling of filth. He came in a well-dressed and clean man and he will leave smelling and looking as dirty as a man who has been homeless for several months. He imagines the look on his boss' face if he'd gone to work in this state, and it brings a smile to his face. Although, his smile quickly sours into a frown. Can he ever really go back there?

There is nothing of interest on the first shelf, or not that he can tell. He moves onto the second and the next and the next, plucking out the objects that he thinks mean something, whilst in his head the mantra repeats: *you could be wrong you could be wrong you could be wrong you could be wrong you could be*

11 Red Slippers

I am stupid. Whenever I think about how I lost you, guilt punches me in the stomach and I have to tell myself to breathe again, just breathe. It happens every day; sometimes once, sometimes repetitively like a song on constant repeat, niggling at my nerves. At times, I can convince myself it is our neighbour's fault, for interfering, for believing I am crazy.

Our neighbour is a middle-aged man, who 'worked' from home, which actually means he watched his precious street like a child he couldn't allow to grow up. He knocks on our door to find out why the rubbish bin hasn't been taken in for five weeks. When I open the door a crack, my eyes are squinting because they aren't used to the sunlight. I haven't been out since it happened. I have cooked meals for two, and one is always left uneaten. We are steadily running out of food but I'm not concerned. Every day is an ordeal, a bloodying battle from morning to night; a dam rebuilt and knocked down.

I don't see his nose twitching. I don't realise that the smell, from both of us, might be suspicious. Myself, smelling unwashed and neglected. You, smelling cold, removed. I am unaware. My senses have become trapped in little boxes inside and they have been jumbled up. I smell objects. I touch the aromas and emotions around me. Right then, I can touch my neighbour's confusion. It is blue, a spotted cluster that bangs against the door, trying to see what is hidden.

I tell him I've been ill and slam the door.

I hear him shout, "Are you crazy?" It is a question I will hear many times and a question I will ask myself when I am alone in that minimal room without personality, afraid to give me anything, for fear I will somehow use it to injure or kill.

Inside the house, the air is filled with brown flakes that constantly cry from the ceiling and swirl around me. As soon as I wake up, they begin, and gather on the floor until each step is like trudging through mud. The sadness is an algae corrupting our house, the place where you are ingrained on each floorboard, each blemish on the paintwork, each smudge on the window. I go around and touch everything, feeling your presence throbbing, seeing the beat physically making the surfaces and objects rise and fall.

You are in the bedroom. I visit you every hour. You are always cold, never reply to my questions, and don't even look toward the chair in which I sit. Yet I won't leave you, I know you'll be back to your old self soon. I know your skin will redden, wrinkle, contract and slacken with expressions, in time.

If only you would eat again. Each night I call up that dinner is on the table, but you never appear. Sometimes I leave the food on your bedside table but when I return, you haven't touched it. I get angry and tell you I won't bother making you food if you're just going to waste it. Although I know tomorrow, I'll make it again. And I know soon you *will* eat it.

It's been just the two of us for six years now. Michael left for university when he was eighteen and never returned. I went to the local university and stayed at home. You and I always got on so well and I didn't want you to be lonely. And this is my home. I'm not ready to leave. Screw Michael anyway, he hardly visits and he hasn't been able to look me in the face for months.

You've been brilliant recently. I've been depressed. I've been afraid to go out, afraid to look in the mirror. Every time I stop for a moment, all I see are those angry muscles pressing me down, Harry's eyes asking for forgiveness yet determined, violent words thrusting into me, my defences pricked and flooded.

I don't know how to live without you. You've been nursing me for the last three months and now I am nursing you. We don't need anybody else around. I didn't even think of taking you to the hospital.

It was five weeks before, when I opened the door and found you lying with one side of your face squashed against the floor, a line of blood neatly dried on your chin. When I moved closer I noticed your neck was bruised, the skin flaccid like a sock that had fallen down, your skin chalky. You were sprawled out like a star, legs pointing towards the door. Your fluffy hair dashed over your eyes. I thought you must have been unconscious and hoped you weren't concussed. One of your red slippers had somehow travelled several feet away and the other was beneath you. I collected them and put them back on.

I carried you upstairs and put you to bed, pulling the covers right up. I kissed you on the head and told you you'd feel better in the morning. You didn't say anything.

In the night, I woke up and thought I saw your slippers underneath my door. You often check on me in the night and I always catch you just as the door closes, your red slippers flashing in the crack under the door, before I turn over and go back to sleep. That night, I strained to hear the soft bump of your bedroom door against the door-frame but there was nothing. I crept across the landing and listened outside your door and there was nothing. Only silence. I told myself I must be going crazy and went back to my room.

Two days after the neighbour knocked, I lost you.

12 Objects

Thom sits in the dark with his eyes fastened. He knows he can open them if he tells his brain to send a message to the muscles and nerves surrounding his eyes, yet he doesn't. He lets his facial muscles lie comatose, like caterpillars inert but full of potential.

He feels an object with his shaky fingers. He has spent two days looking over the objects collectively and hours scrutinising each object's every feature. With this brush it's the plastic body with rubber welts that has embedded the pattern into his palm, the stubbly beard that has pressed into his pores until they sting and remind him of his own unkempt face, the curled lip of its head like a sneer. He has devoted hours to using all his senses to analyse this object and now he has spent half an hour holding it in his hands, expecting the lights to suddenly blind him.

It is several minutes later, when he begins to wonder, why the hell is he holding this washing up brush? Why out of all the contents of that lock up, did he deem this specific object important? Was it instinct that drew him to this object or untold desperation?

Questions again. And where have all the answers gone? Thom wonders if he should place a missing 'answers' report. They seem to have camouflaged themselves in the scenery, the people, the words all around him, and he can no longer distinguish them. The answers he once recognised so easily in life have grown and their adult forms are so matured, he cannot pick them out in a line up.

He drops the brush onto the floor and it thuds against the collection of other items gathered there. The train grumbles outside the window as though it's hankering for food. Thom jumps to his feet and yanks the window wide open. He screams.

It's a loud high-pitched scream. An animal gnawed apart by a metal trap, or a hedgehog disorientated and screeching for rescue.

The train doesn't respond. The train continues to clunk onwards, on its set path, unaffected by this one man's pain from a window beside the tracks. The passengers inside the train probably don't notice his cry and if they do, they probably imagine it's a rowdy schoolchild playing with another nearby. Or if they're listening to music, they probably think it's part of the music that they've failed to notice before. If they see him even, they presume he is merely shouting to somebody he knows or he is insane and they turn away, back into the safety of isolation.

Thom wonders if he should talk to somebody. He has barely communicated with anybody since the day he heard the news. The news of Daniel's death seems like the last thing he heard clearly. The normal sounds of everyday life seem duller like he is submerged in water. The world is an art gallery where he walks amongst the pieces yet he is not a part of them.

There is a random series of knocks on the door and Richard pops his head in. Thom is relieved that he is no longer alone with the pile of objects, as though they have been bullying him and he is glad he now has someone to fight with him. Although as Richard settles himself on the bed, Thom kicks the pile beneath the bed as he pretends to rearrange himself.

Richard is a mixture of two extremes and he displays them within the first thirty seconds of sitting down beside him. He fidgets with his hands and his lip twitches, a lizard bouncing on legs like mattress springs. Then, he throws his head back and gives a long extended yawn, gulping in air like an addict.

"How you going, Thom?" Richard asks and pulls at his ear lobes. He pulls at them every few minutes. Thom has never figured out why. Perhaps it is nervousness. Perhaps it is merely an unfounded habit. Perhaps he just likes how the skin of his ear lobe is so soft. Thom has no idea of the reason or the cause, yet he knows Richard will do it, as he knows the sun will rise tomorrow.

"I'm okay. You?" Thom isn't looking at Richard. In fact, to an outsider, he looks disinterested. Similarly, Richard is tracing the lines of the pattern on the duvet.

"Yeah," he says slowly, not sure how to answer even a simple question. Perhaps he is merely lying like Thom is. Neither of them probes any further though. They leave it at the words they use to fend off queries, to keep people from digging underneath the pretence worn like clothes every day.

"Rich..." Thom begins, scratching his stubble, "do you think he jumped?" The words claw out of his throat, each letter stabbing him, breeding in size as he tries to arrange them in order and make sense.

"What?" Richard frowns. His head suddenly filled with ditches reminds Thom of Mrs Tray and he remembers he must find out more about her.

"What do you think?" Thom persists. Richard looks down at his lap. Thom loves Richard. He can't imagine how he would've survived his teens without him. Yet, Richard has one major fault, which is his need to believe that life is as it seems.

"I don't know." Richard shrugs. Thom feels like he has snatched a treasured toy from a child. Richard tugs his ear lobe a few times in a row.

"So you haven't thought about it?"

"I guess I haven't..." Richard mutters, glancing at the door, which is still slightly ajar. "I haven't thought much about... you know..." He slaps his hands against his knees and a moment later, adds: "*trains.*" It is a whisper that could be misinterpreted as 'chains' or 'lanes' or anything else that rhymes with it. Only Thom knows because he has the context. This is the first time he has felt superior with the knowledge he has. *Small victories.*

"Was Daniel okay before it happened?" Thom ventures, a feeble attempt, as he knows he should've asked much earlier. Richard closes his eyes, thinking.

"It's hard to tell. I mean, we both know how strange he could be." Richard rubs his head as though he is massaging a bruise.

Thom hates to see Richard massaging that invisible bruise so he

211

shakes his head. "Don't worry mate. Let's leave it, *for now*." He can't drag Richard into turmoil too; it wouldn't be fair. Not now, anyway. He needs to find out more.

Richard looks at him like he has been given a reprieve and stands up. For a moment, Thom thinks he is going to leave the room but he walks over to the window and heaves it open without flexing a muscle. He reaches into his pocket and pinches his packet of cigarettes out, flipping it open and sucking one out between his lips. He turns round and raises an eyebrow.

"Want one?"

Thom doesn't smoke. Yet, a moment later he finds himself cautiously watching a flame move towards his face, making his eyes cross. He sucks on it tenderly and instantly exhales, as Richard taught him when he was fourteen and they first tried smoking at the back of the garden.

"I know it's a stupid thing to say but I *do* miss him," Richard says, glancing at Thom. "But the worst thing is I can't remember the little things he did." Richard grimaces at the window panes.

"Don't feel bad," Thom tries to comfort him. Yet there is no reason behind the words, no weight for Richard to grab onto.

"I haven't cried you know… since it happened."

"I vomited," Thom volunteers, sheepishly. They both chuckle but the chuckle is dry and brief. Thom moves towards the window and tries to flick ash through the gap but he misses, and it falls onto his jeans.

"You're a shitty smoker." Richard grins. Thom starts to protest but eventually shrugs, trying to brush the ash away. "Sometimes when I'm smoking," Richard starts, watching Thom closely, "I imagine I'm being watched." Richard rolls the cigarette between his fingers and flicks his eyes towards Thom, squinting as if Thom's judgement will scald him.

"What?"

"I just mean, like in films, when the guy's sitting on some bench somewhere and it's just him and his cigarette…" Richard gives his a long kiss, moving his eyes along a train snaking past outside. "It's like one of those moments, when they're thinking about everything that's happened over the course of the film and the audience are either really happy for them or thinking *God, they're fucked*."

Thom thinks about this for a moment and wonders what the audience would think of him, a pathetic smoker with jeans he's been wearing for five days that are now smudged with ash.

"So, *which* are we?" Thom asks, hopefully. Richard pulls at his ear and leaves a temporary red blotch there, like the spark of his cigarette, slowly fading.

"I can't decide yet," Richard answers, disappointing them both.

13 Blood

She can't ruin everything.

I won't let her come swooping down on my new life, my new friends and take me back to that room where the walls won't even talk to me. The only person who talks is her: about *her* thoughts and feelings, *her* family life, *her* next delightful holiday from work with all the trimmings. When she should have been asking me about something, *anything* and not smearing her perfect life all over my room like shit, to taunt me by having to smell it every day that the lock turned in the door.

I guess at least her self-fascination got me out of there. And seeing her again now, smoothing her hair in the murky mirror in the hallway leading to my bedsit, I know nothing has changed. She sucks the end of her pen desperately, like a baby controlling a dummy, then pauses to check if she has any ink on her lips and being satisfied, stuffs it in again. Doctor bitch Rosey.

After our first meeting, I decided she must've changed her name to *Rosey* because it is so fitting. It can't be a coincidence. Or perhaps her name coerced her into being such a deluded, ignorant donkey. She is the literal translation of rose-tinted glasses.

I watch her from the bottom of the stairs, her nagging pen harassing the clipboard and paper she carries with her. I'm sure she is making some official note about me not answering her calls and failing to be present for a follow-up appointment. If I could, I would push her in front of a train. And perhaps I will… I can't let her disturb me, now I have a new family to look out for, now that they need me to help them cope with Daniel's death, now that I need to find out how he managed it.

I am just beginning to tiptoe away like a mime artist when the landlord's door opens.

"Thanks so much," a voice says. I halt. His face immediately floats into my head. I think: *run!* Yet, my knees seize up like cogs unable to turn. For a moment, I imagine he won't see me, like when we used to hide under the kitchen table and giggle, pretending we were invisible until you grabbed our legs and pulled us out. I am six again and he can't see me either.

Yet he does. I have my face turned towards him, my legs and body still facing the door. He backs out of the landlord's flat, clearly knocked back by the stench of sweat, his breath and the collection of half-dead fish swimming in shit. I recognise his nose that is exactly like mine, slightly bent on the bridge and pointed up a millimetre or two at the end. I notice the stubble he has left to fester and stray, his hair creeping over the top of his ears like ivy.

I see my brother.

"Michael," I say. It's not a question. It's not the start of a sentence. It is nothing at all. It is as though he is a familiar object I am trying to articulate in a new language.

His eyes are wide, blood shot. He grabs onto the banister, a lost child doing the sensible thing and waiting for somebody to find him, and he plants his feet firmly on the ground. The landlord burps and closes his door.

It is only us now, two animals afraid to start a fight, too afraid to find out who is the fittest, who can survive. I think I love him still. I think I still love.

Mum, your kids are together again.

He is looking at the door behind me. It is a black hole that will swallow me up and he will not be able to find me in that darkness. I wonder if he can ever detach himself from what he thinks is right and cry with me for the loss. He never talked to me about you; all he did was dress up like a fraud and act his way through the funeral and every conversation we've shared since.

"Hi," he croaks and coughs, trying to regain his power. The noise causes the dust in the air to pirouette around us. I am entranced for a moment but shake myself awake when I see him staring at me. I wish he would hide with me again. I glance over at the small table by the door and realise it's far too small for the both of us. I just want to share stories with him and pretend we're on a submarine looking at all the fish on the seabed, pretending every time your legs pass, you are an enemy submarine that we have to fight with.

But Michael doesn't play anymore. He takes people away from their home they've always lived in, he tells his children their Aunty is mad, he works at a bank and owns a red BMW, he stands in hallways and doesn't know what he should say to keep me there.

"You're going bald," I say and watch his lip tremble, like a fishing line bobbing as a fish takes the bait. He lifts his head upwards, his pointy nose keeping face.

"How are you?"

"Wonderful. And you?" I smile like the Joker from Batman, manic and sad. Perhaps I am bipolar, insane?

"You can tell me how you are…" Michael pauses, for effect, "truthfully?" He always does this. He loves to separate his sentences to really emphasise his point, to pretend he is a diplomat. I wish I could scream in his face just to make him turn white and scare that smug undertone out of his words. At the same time, I wish I could fall into his arms and ask him to tell me why I pushed that man.

"Why are you here?" He doesn't think fast and the silence wraps around us like anaesthetic numbing bodily function. We are speaking quietly, secretly and, so far, the evil Doctor hasn't heard our reunion. In fact, I think she is in my bedsit, poking around in my things, trying to understand me for the second time.

"I'm here. That's what matters," Michael says, taking a step towards me. He strokes the banister tenderly as though he is comforting me. Yet my skin only feels cold.

"That's a poor way of not answering the question." I stare through him. Although trying to keep such a flat expression only makes me want to laugh.

"The doctor asked me to come," Michael finally explains. Yet his words are no surprise and I wonder why he even bothered to verbalise them.

"Do you miss her, Michael?"

"Who?" He bows his head.

What a traitor, Mum!

I want to kick him in the teeth and watch each tooth swim in blood and slide away from his gums. I want to watch his lips inflame with hardened skin and struggle to form words that he uses to create scrawny excuses and reasons. I can't think of a way to express these thoughts without actually carrying them out so I don't speak. Instead I turn towards the small table that has innocently witnessed our meeting and I grab it by its top. With my arms straightened to their fullest, I watch him watching me and I think *the tables have turned.* Then I smash the table into the wall.

One of the table legs breaks and I let it fall to the floor. I only wish it could be his face, his identical nose smashing irreversibly. I'm not sure who looks sadder – him or the table. Then in the next moment I hear the Doctor shouting from the top of the stairs and Michael lifts his face like a soldier following orders.

I run. The door opens up and swallows me. Michael chases me into the darkness, calling my name, weaving through people, calling my name and getting stuck between the cars. Michael shouts my name and I cry because he is calling me and I want to go back and ask him what he wants.

Michael, Michael, do *you* need me?

14 The Notebook

Thom opens the notebook. The first page is blank and he is on the edge of relief, feeling like he is peeping into his girlfriend's diary. It has taken him two days to even get this far but it's time, after his complete failure with the other objects he chose from the lock up. Thom reasons he shouldn't feel bad about looking at this notebook though. After all, Daniel left him the lock up and its contents. So, this notebook is his property and he has the right to read every scribble and word it contains.

The second page is full of writing. The handwriting is an angry scrawl, not like Daniel's usual composed hand. In this notebook another side of him seems to have taken over or he was too excited to put on a charade, even for himself. He notices the rest of the notebook is full from quickly flicking through the pages. He begins to read:

I am wandering around without belonging, without stable identity or a true family who love me. From the outside, I'm sure I appear just like anyone else. I'm sure I look like a clean pane of glass but the glass is hiding what's really there: a stormy sea that is swallowing me up. Sometimes, I can't even breathe and have to really concentrate on normal everyday actions.

I'm afraid of myself. I don't trust my body or my mind anymore. I have begun to hate people. It's because I'm different, that's all. I keep losing people and I wonder whether it's all my fault.

Perhaps I was born to live alone. Although I have no one I can really ask this question, no one listens to me anymore. My family say they love me but I know they secretly wonder about me, whether there's something wrong with me.

I have no idea what to do anymore. I spend hours sitting alone and planning ways to escape. Then I change my mind and go back to living like I have been. I wish someone would help me.

The bottom of the page has blotches of ink on it and Thom guesses Daniel's pen broke. Thom feels weighed down by the words, weighed down by guilt for not helping Daniel more when he had the chance.

But would Daniel have accepted his help?

Thom doesn't understand how Daniel could've felt this way. Why did he feel so alienated from his family? Why did he feel like he was losing his mind? If anything, this notebook supports the idea that Daniel had actually thrown himself in front of that train. Perhaps the note Thom found is an indirect admission from Daniel that he committed suicide.

Thom wonders how he will even begin to tell Richard and Aunty Val.

Thom flips through the notebook, catching glimpses of the same angry scrawl continuing throughout and sometimes, just pages filled with scribbles or others completely heavy with biro covering every inch. Then Thom sees something that makes him freeze. He has reached the last page and written in much clearer ink are the words: *property of Thomas Downing.*

First, Thom throws the notebook at the house and it slams against the ground.

Second, he sobs into his ink stained hands.

Third, he looks at his hands and wonders when his hands and his brain disconnected and wrote these hopeless words...

15 The Woman

Ten minutes later and Thom is no closer to understanding the notebook and how his name, his *real* name appears in there. Is it possible that Daniel merely took a notebook belonging to Thom and wrote in it himself? Or had Daniel written it and for some reason, put Thom's name in there on purpose? Otherwise the only other possibility is what he feared: that he wrote it himself.

He thinks about the words in the notebook like *belonging* and *losing people* and *alone* and they swarm around his head. The words were a shock to read and Thom realises it isn't so much because Daniel may have written them but because they sum up many of his feelings about his own life.

Thom *does* feel alone, even when he is surrounded by others. Since Daniel's death, he has taken his solitude to extremes and it has been easy to do so, because most people in his life barely notice him or can be bothered to hear how he really feels. And there have been times when he has wondered about Aunty Val, Richard and Daniel, and whether he is an unwanted extra. Other times, he has been sure they all love him.

It dawns on Thom then, that he can think of a perfect time when he could have written these words. Immediately after his parents died, he suffered from complete shock and distress, not sleeping properly and often finding himself doing things without realising it. He lost grip on life for a while and slowly, Aunty Val and Richard mainly, recovered him. But what if during the time when he'd been so confused, effectively 'losing his mind', he wrote this? But it all sounded so adult, so informed – could his young self really have written this?

It is possible, Thom decides. This would explain his name being written as *Thomas Downing*, his name given to him by his parents. He took Mansen after their death, when Aunty Val adopted him and as far as he knew, had tried to use it as soon as it was confirmed. The period between him losing his parents and the adoption wasn't that long, as the authorities had deemed it necessary. It had been perhaps six months to a year at most. So that is the only period where Thom could have written those things, although his confusion and anger remained with him like an ulcer, obvious and sore, for much longer.

Thom realises, the more he turns it round in his mind, it is possible he still thinks these things even now, he has diluted feelings to the same effect at times. He shouldn't feel sorry for Daniel at all, he should feel sorry for himself.

Thinking again of Daniel, Thom wonders if Daniel read this. Did he leave it in the lock up so that Thom would find out how he felt and perhaps to let him know he'd been depressed too? Is this another link to the suicide theory? Or did Daniel just want to upset Thom for some unknown reason?

Thom wants to believe Daniel's intentions were good. He can't quite fathom the other possibility, it makes his head become groggy and makes vomit rise in his throat, like the day he found the note. He wonders whether he should've saved the vomiting, as he can't think of a suitable way to respond to the notebook now. His only option seems to be to amputate a limb in disgust.

In that moment, as Thom is grimacing about the prospect, he sees the arm peeping out from the side of the house. He wonders if Aunty Val or Richard are hiding there and are too ashamed to come out, having witnessed him crying. He gets to his feet quietly and tiptoes towards the side of the house. Yet as he gets a few yards away, the hand whips out of sight and Thom guesses the owner of it has begun to run.

Thom chases past the house and into the front garden. He sees his target, a woman with dark curly hair and a skirt dragging behind her, fiddling with the gate. Thom dives towards her and grabs her around the stomach, pulling her to the floor. They make a collective groan as they tumble onto the grass that hasn't been mowed since the funeral and has grown wild, tickling their bare skin. A piece of grass prods up Thom's nostril, and he sneezes.

The woman is limp underneath him and he wonders for a panicked moment if he has knocked her unconscious. Yet when Thom looks down, he sees her blue eyes watching him with unwavering interest and not the fear or guilt he expects. He moves away, scratching his stubble as he separates himself from the woman, suddenly conscious of it. She eases herself up casually, as though she is sunbathing on the beach, not having just tried to escape him.

He is about to speak when she yanks at her elbow and frowns at a small cut that is slowly oozing blood. She makes a noise of disapproval and looks up at him. For a moment, he feels like a boyfriend who has forgotten to buy her an anniversary present and then remembers; she is the one that owes him an explanation.

As Thom looks down he notices her skirt has ridden up around her legs and he sees her smooth thigh and above that, the edge of the red knickers she is wearing. Thom gulps on air and looks away again, pretending to check his knee for damage.

"Thom," he says after a moment, involuntarily, like a hiccup.

She is quiet for a moment and then replies, "Sarah." Thom thinks there is something strange about the way she says it, almost as if she has plucked it out of the air or it is a name she has always loved and has now chosen it for herself.

Thom manages to smile at her, despite the awkwardness and the lack of explanation. They have only managed two words but Thom feels better. After about thirty seconds of more silence, she smiles back. The gesture has clearly been thoroughly considered, something she doesn't want to give away easily. Therefore, Thom appreciates it.

"Hello Sarah," Thom says, checking to see if she flinches at the name. She does nothing, just continues to stare at him as though he is an alien object that has landed in her path. When he moves his hand towards her, she jumps back. Thom points at her elbow and she understands and offers it to him. His sleeve soaks up a little of her blood and he moves it away, thinking about how much they have already shared in such a short space of time.

"Why were you crying?" Sarah asks, surprising Thom. He had no idea anyone saw him in the garden and he wonders what she must think of him. He hesitates for a moment, his gut spinning like a Catherine wheel, shooting off in all directions.

"My cousin died," he tells her, feeling his tongue struggling with the words. His saliva has turned to wallpaper paste.

"I'm sorry," she says automatically, emptily. Thom almost laughs; her voice is like a glacier splitting his body in half. Even stranger than her tone is that he likes it. He is sick of people cooing him like a baby. Sarah is bashing him over the head with a rock instead.

"Please come in. We can wash that." He gestures to her elbow.

Flicking her curls out of her eyes, she nods and Thom pulls her up.

16 Red Mug

"How did he die?" I ask as Thom places a mug of tea in front of me. The mug is red and I am instantly intrigued by it. Thom pauses for a second in front of me, unsure what to do with his body, unable to let go of the mug handle. I reach over to lift the mug into my hold, desperate to feel the colour pulse into me but I miss and touch his hand instead. He looks up, almost blushing and then throws himself backwards onto the sofa. I grit my teeth. After all, it isn't him I intended to touch; it is the colour.

"Hit by a train," he answers. He doesn't say Daniel fell, or jumped or was pushed because he doesn't know. Only I know the truth. In the papers it says the case is still open but there have been no developments. Apparently, they can't find the footage from the station for that day. So I am still free for now. I am free and I wonder if I care.

"Were you close?" I stare into my mug, without giving him any attention. I fear that looking too closely into his eyes might remind me of Daniel too much. They have the same colour eyes and the way Thom's lips move when he speaks takes me back to that moment, when Daniel mouthed those words: *right on time.*

"I've lived here since I was twelve," he gestures to the room with his hands. "But, we weren't especially close," he admits, playing with his knuckle.

"Why did you live here?" I am wondering aloud and after I ask, I think perhaps 'normal' people wouldn't be so direct. Thom seems slightly stunned for a moment but quickly recovers; as though it is something he has programmed himself to do. I concentrate on separating the strands of my hair and examining them, waiting.

"My parents died."

My head jerks up, my mouth involuntarily jarred open. "Oh God..." I moan; my features running downwards like a painting soaked with water. My stomach is jumping. I can't believe what I have done to this man. He has experienced enough pain already. Yet I hadn't thought of anything that day, I just killed Daniel, whether he planned it or not.

Mum, how can I live with this?

"Do you believe in God?" he asks softly. I wonder if he is going to tell me he is at peace, he understands that God has a plan and therefore, he is dealing with all these lost people.

"No," I say, no explanation.

"Me neither," he agrees abruptly. I wonder for a moment why he brought it up. Is it just because I mentioned the word 'God'? Does he think I am a hypocrite for using the word when I have no belief in the concept?

Thom takes a gulp of his tea, completely unaware of my paranoid musings and burns his tongue. "Shit." He uselessly tries to cool his tongue with his hand and sucks in air. He doesn't notice me moving until I'm beside him. I want to cuddle him, for his parents, for his cousin, for not cuddling Michael. Most of all, right now, I wish it was you. This is the first time I have wanted to perform this action for years and I have no idea why Thom is the person I want to do it with.

I lift my arms and look at them as though they are not connected to me. Thom notices and forgets about his tongue for a moment, perhaps wondering if I am going to show him my wings or start a puppet show. His tongue still darts in and out of his mouth though, and I am suddenly drawn to it. I am looking at the lips that look so familiar and want to touch them, feel how soft they are.

I lean towards him and he doesn't move, curious perhaps. I wonder if he thinks I'm going to tell him a secret or blow on his tongue or spit in his face. His eyelashes flutter uncomfortably. I am a floodlight blinding him. Yet he doesn't move, even when I press my lips against his. At first, it is a still kiss as though I'm trying to give him CPR but it deepens and my tongue flickers against his for a moment. It feels hot against mine and I wonder if his tongue is burning mine by proxy. His stubble scratches my lips and, as I kiss him, I think I am remembering *something*... a red bedspread, the stench of lavender clashing with disinfectant... then I forget.

As I release his mouth from my hold, he uses his hand to stay upright on the sofa. Perhaps he fears he is in danger of simply falling to one side. I can see his lips trying to form words, his throat bulging with speech but he fails and only shakes his head. I start stretching out my curls, not focussing on him.

"I think God is a comfort blanket for people," Thom finally says. I have no idea why he is returning to the subject. It feels like the kiss hasn't even happened.

"It wouldn't make you feel better about your cousin…?"

"Daniel," Thom reveals, not realising I already know, and adds, "no."

"Why not?"

"Why did you do that?" he asks, almost aggressively and I wonder what is so offensive about my question.

"What?"

"Before… the kiss," he croaks.

"I don't know," I answer, honestly. I draw my legs up to my chest and rest my head on them.

"I have a girlfriend." Thom finally remembers.

"Okay," I say, surprised by how unaffected I feel.

"Emma," Thom emphasises.

"Okay," I agree, cold again. I suppose he thinks I should care but I don't. I don't have any real feelings for him, I just wanted to touch someone again. It doesn't matter who he is.

"Daniel…" Thom says, out of nowhere. "Sarah… You remind me of him, *a bit*." Thom's eyes are wide as though he isn't the one who made the suggestion.

"Really?" I smile faintly.

"You surprise me," Thom admits; his forehead growing more wrinkled with each word he says. I have no idea why he is telling me this.

"In a good way?"

"I hope so," Thom whispers, his eyes focussed on something in his head. I wonder if he is thinking about what he was reading in the garden, the thing that made him cry. "I've only had nasty surprises from Daniel."

I am afraid I have ruined this man. Although when I think about it,

I remember Daniel's hint that he planned for me to push him in front of that train. Has he left similar puzzles behind for his family, particularly Thom? Am I meant to confess to save him from this torment?

For a moment, I nearly say the words. I nearly tell Thom, his lip trembling like he is standing in the snow, *it was me. IT WAS ME!* I am the murderer who took him away from you. Then I think the word 'murderer' is too strong and that can't possibly be what I am. I just need to look after them. They need me. Someone needs me.

"You'll be okay," I finally tell him and he stares at me hopefully, like when I was a child and you told me the gerbil wasn't dead, he was just sleeping. And I wanted to believe you so much.

17 The Red Stain

When Thom waves to Sarah as she gets to the corner, he is practically in the garden a millisecond later. Yet before the notebook, he shrinks. He takes steps towards it but appears to be moving further away. It looks like a person who has jumped from a building; pages bent and twisted at awkward angles, opened with the words bare like a person's body ripped open on impact.

He kneels beside it, a parishioner atoning his sins, a man humbled by greatness. He touches the pages, feels the ink impressions that are harsh and definite and tries to press them flat. Yet, he can't force them to retreat; they are as strong as the day they were written.

Thom sags against the back of the house and drags the notebook onto his lap. He smooths down the pages and closes it. Even the cover isn't familiar to him. It is brown mock leather with a circular pattern moulded onto the front cover. It has a red stain on the back, which means nothing really, as it could've come from the lock up where it had been buried underneath a shelf of rubbish.

Why did he know nothing about this?

Thom can't read the words again, not now anyway. He just holds the notebook in his lap and traces the pattern with his fingers until he becomes aware, an indeterminate time later, that someone is in the kitchen. He grabs onto the window sill and hauls himself up, peering in through the net curtains.

He sees Aunty Val. She is at the kitchen table, carefully counting and stacking her penny collection into even piles. Thom can already see when she will finish, the piles of coins in straight piles across the table and an odds pile in the far corner. Then she will sweep them into her hand one by one and replace them in the jar. Counting the pennies calms her and she keeps them around as a form of comfort. Thom can remember only two times the pennies were counted *and* taken to the bank. Once, when Daniel decided to go to university and another when Richard wanted a moped.

The only other times Thom remembers using them is when the three of them used to play bingo together. They'd separate all the coins into even piles (or as close to); each put some in the middle and then drew cards from the deck. Thom always loved to be the caller, it made him feel grown up and responsible. Daniel hardly ever called "bingo!" even if he had the cards. He never wanted to attract attention but he still played – why? – nobody knows.

Thom is almost happy for a moment but the notebook grows cold against his hand, stinging him back to reality. His fingers tense around its body. It is a small snake that has slithered through his fingers and frozen in his hold.

Thom turns the doorknob and flings the door open. As the door flies open, it smashes against the table and the coins shudder, the piles jutting out of shape like vertebrae knocked out of position. Several of the piles spray over and mix with the piles next to them. Thom feels like an artist who has ruined the paints by mixing all the colours together.

"*Sorry,*" he whispers, placing the notebook on the table and pushing it towards her with one finger. It presses against the pennies and moves them in unison like one of those machines at the arcade, where you try to get your twopence to push some money off and create a chain reaction.

Aunty Val is silent. She is still staring at her fallen pennies. They are parts of her castle, falling down around her. Her mouth is twitching at one side and her hands are flat on the table, as though she is awaiting instructions. So Thom delivers one: "Read it."

Aunty Val plants her hands on top of the notebook and plucks it from the demolition, not causing a single penny to move a fraction. Her collectedness makes Thom envy her. Although, he wonders if she can retain it after sampling the contents. Thom waits as she opens the notebook to the first page with writing on, and her eyes begin to scan the words.

Five minutes pass before she puts it down and gathers her hands together in front of her, looking up at him. "And what is this about?"

"You've never seen *that* before?" Thom snarls, shaken by her lack of concern.

Aunty Val shakes her head and says, "Why? Where did you get it?"

"That's not important. What's important is that it has my name in it." Thom flicks open to the offending page and lets Aunty Val take a quick peek before slamming it shut. "How can that be explained?" Thom demands and wishes she will miraculously have an explanation that will calm him, which will make this whole wild set of events fade into the background and leave him to move on.

"I didn't know you thought of yourself as a *Downing*, after all these years." Aunty Val frowns, showing the first real sign of distress about the notebook but Thom can't help thinking she has missed the vital point.

"I didn't write that! Or... I don't remember writing it."

"What do you mean Thom?"

"I mean that I found this and I have no recollection of ever seeing it before or writing in it. Now, does *that* make sense to *you?*"

"Maybe you wrote it when you were younger," Aunty Val says plainly. She makes him feel like he has a splinter but is making it out to be a six-inch knife wound.

"I did think of that but I just can't remember doing this... at all."

"You were very upset then. You hardly spoke for a month and saw a counsellor." Aunty Val pats Thom's hand, dismissively.

"A counsellor…" Thom thinks for a moment. "Oh yes… I did, *didn't I?*"

"At least you remember that." Aunty Val smiles gently, a parent figure trying to encourage a pathetic attempt by her child.

"But why don't I remember this?" Thom slams his fist against the table and makes some of the coins jump in fright. Aunty Val doesn't flinch though. He feels bad for acting angrily when he notices the tissue poking out of her sleeve, reminding him of how fragile she still is.

"Did you really feel those things?" Aunty Val ventures, "the drowning, the fear we didn't love you, all of that…?"

"No," Thom interjects, "well, I don't think it was that bad."

"We always loved you the same," Aunty Val half pleads.

"I didn't ask you about that," Thom dismisses her and looks down to avoid seeing a tear carving its way down her cheek. Before Daniel's death, he rarely saw her cry. Now, it is a daily event. He can't handle it; it makes him want to run until his body twists in pain.

"Do you think someone else could have written it?" Thom mutters, still facing the table. There is a moment of definite silence from Aunty Val.

"Who do you mean?"

"I don't know. Anyone. Someone else." Thom focuses on her hand that is gripping the edge of the table.

"You're scaring me Thom," Aunty Val tells him. "You've been very quiet lately and now *this*. Has Daniel's death brought up old feelings about your parents?"

"Oh great!" Thom shouts, standing up and sweeping the notebook and coins from the tabletop. There is a sound of clinking and thudding as they hit the floor. "It's me who's the crazy one?" Thom spits. "There's all this shit lying around that I don't understand and you don't notice anything because all you do is sit around and wallow for fuck's sake!" Thom doesn't take a breath. Aunty Val's jaw has sagged, bringing out the wrinkles in her neck. Thom lowers himself onto the chair again. It has been years since he lost his temper this way.

"I know you're upset so I know why you did that. I just ask that you give me the same respect." Aunty Val holds back the tears and gets to her feet. Thom springs up to follow her but her turning to face him cuts him short.

"Please clean up those coins," she says and strokes the side of his face. Thom grabs her hand and kisses it and she nods, knowing what he means. Thom feels comforted by her but at the same time, sees how her eyes flicker under his gaze.

Thom wonders what Aunty Val would say if he told her all the parts he knew, about the note and the lock up, and whether she would still call him crazy then. Thom also wonders why he doesn't want to tell her, why he is keeping Daniel's secret for him, when he isn't even here to know about it.

18 Red Door

I try to return to my bedsit the evening after I meet Thom for the first time but, standing on the corner, I can make out Michael sitting in a car opposite the building. I am surprised he is wasting his time and partly touched by his presence. I wonder if Doctor Rosey is hovering too but decide she probably has better things to do.

There is no way I can sneak in. Michael has completely cut off my access to warmth and shelter. I have no choice but to make the streets my home for the night. I wrap the scarf tighter and walk in the opposite direction.

I think about Michael sitting in the car. Does it mean he cares about me? Or is he doing it for the good of society? After all, he considers me mentally unstable and probably dangerous. I'll bet that Doctor's been stirring up his fears too, putting detonators all over his mind.

It would be so easy to walk over to his car and ask him to help me. It would be so easy to let the doctors take me back to the hospital, keep the door closed 22 hours per day, make me swallow flavourless pills until I forget my identity and forget the sadness that hovers over it.

Yet, I am needed. Thom needs me. His family need me. They don't realise what I can do for them. Take today for example, I made Thom forget for a moment, I made him come out of his pain and confront something completely different. This is why I know I'm meant to help that family, why I know I have something special to share with them.

Without you, I have to find somewhere to be. You understand don't you, Mum? I'm not forgetting our family or you.

At the same time, I can't deny that spending time with them may give me the opportunity to find out more about Daniel. There are so many questions about him that need to be answered. I have made no progress in discovering what he meant when he said those words, before the train smashed him to pieces. In his destruction, all the answers shattered, like a plate thrown against a wall and scattering into dark undiscovered corners. You never find all the pieces when that happens. There is always a shard some place that the eye misses.

Overall, the only thing I know for certain is that I need to be with them. And without thinking, this is where my feet take me. I find myself staring at the house, which looks like an old woman, deflated and sagging. The door is painted red; something I have failed to notice, but the paint is peeling and flaking away in defeat. The curtains are half pulled in some windows and completely open in others. No one cares whether it is day or night. This house is in mourning too.

When I go in there again, I'll open and shut those curtains for them.

The thought makes me smile as I take residence on the bench opposite them, wrapping my coat around my body. My ankles are exposed and soon become cold but I close my eyes. In the darkness, Daniel wakes up and I start to follow him.

19 Red Scarf

Thom walks down the stairs the next morning, a flash of red stopping him by the hall window. He squints at the figure curled up on the bench opposite the house and instantly starts to run. He fumbles with the door and races across the street, nearly tripping over the rough grass in the front garden.

He reaches the bench, gasping for breath. She is wearing a large overcoat that has fallen open, revealing her bare legs and a few inches of her stomach where her top has ridden up. The blood red scarf is around her neck and trails over the side of the bench, looking as deeply asleep as she is.

Thom kneels down beside her. He considers tucking her curls behind her ears but as soon as he reaches towards her, his arm feels heavy and he lets it drop. Instead, he rests his fingers on the wooden slats, a few inches from her.

"*Sarah*," Thom whispers, too quietly at first, then louder a few more times. She begins to rock from side to side, a boat gently nudged by the current. Then as he persists, she shoots up as though he has shot her in the spine.

"Sarah, it's me," Thom says, grabbing onto her wrist. She jolts again but exhales heavily when she sees him. After a few moments, she even smiles and Thom feels comforted and cold in the same instant.

Sarah folds her legs towards herself so Thom has space to sit. Thom watches Sarah grasp the scarf in her fist and pull it towards her.

"How are you?" she mumbles. Thom almost laughs at her mundane question.

"I'm fine. And you?" Thom humours her.

"Fine," she answers, in a tone that is hard to doubt.

"What are you doing here?"

"I came to see you." She looks at him sheepishly and quickly refocuses on the scarf, pulling at the loose threads at the bottom.

"You did?" Thom leans forward.

"Yes. I just enjoyed our chat yesterday so much," she says in a voice so flat Thom gains nothing from it. She must mean it though, otherwise why would she put herself in a position where she could be humiliated? All of it is another puzzle. It seems she is just as empty as Daniel. So why does she fill him with so many emotions?

"I like your scarf." Thom gestures. Her head snaps up instantly.

"You like red?" She turns towards him and presses her fingertips against his arm. He doesn't answer straight away, enjoying even the minute pressure of her skin against his. He imagines he can feel her pulse beating with his own.

"I love red. It's very bold."

"It's a passionate colour," Sarah adds urgently.

"Yeah, I guess it is. We associate it with such strong emotions, contradictory ones at that: love and hate," Thom agrees.

"And sex and blood," Sarah tags on again and Thom sits back, unnerved by her words. She falls silent and leaves Thom thinking of how she is one of those people who cuts conversations in half, but is not bothered when social interaction is stopped short, like a film paused in the middle.

"You're wearing the same clothes as yesterday," Thom mentions.

"So?" She shrugs. It's a good question, Thom reasons. Why should she have changed her clothes? But then he notices her elbow, still blotted with blood and the grass stains on her knees.

"Did you go home last night?"

"Of course," she spits out air heavily.

"Where do you live?"

"Fennel Street," Sarah answers sharply. Thom snakes his hand along the edge of the bench and touches her shoulder. She watches his hand vigilantly, as though it is not connected to Thom and may attack her.

"You look like you stayed here all night. You can tell me, if you did…" Thom squeezes her shoulder. Shaking his hand off, she brings her knees up to her chest.

"I don't even know you." Her words are muffled by her knees.

"That's true but there must be a reason you're here." Thom puts his hand between them, his hand making a star against the wood.

"I did stay here last night," she admits. One of her hands dances along the edge of the bench.

"Why?" Thom asks, trying to catch her gaze. He wants to get closer to her, understand why her honesty makes his blood rush in all directions, causing it to collide and explode like atoms splitting.

232

"I'm having trouble with my landlord." She shrugs and he watches her hand, still doing gymnastics on the edge.

"We can't have you sleeping on the street," Thom tells her. He reaches forward and grabs her dancing hand, clasping it tight, afraid she might try to escape. Yet she squeezes his hand in return.

"You should stay with me – I mean, *us*."

"I can't. We don't know each other." Sarah gives Thom a coy smile.

"Stop saying that." Thom pulls her to her feet, for the second time in two days.

"Just come inside and meet Aunty Val. She'll fix you some tea."

Thom feels her hand spasm momentarily but thinks it is only a reflex.

20 The Mother

I watch her from the hallway as Thom talks in a whisper, explaining my presence. She glances towards the hall a few times and fiddles with her hair and her cardigan, obviously more annoyed she doesn't have time to fix herself up rather than the fact that Thom wants to invite a complete stranger into her house.

Yet, Thom doesn't think we are strangers. He likes me. He told me we *do* know each other. And he's right. We should be together. We should all be in this house, supporting each other, finding answers about Daniel.

I don't feel prepared as she walks towards me. I see everything I have observed from afar zoomed in: the cracked texture of her soggy tissue, the separate strands of her wiry hair scooped into a clumsy ponytail, the wideness of her pupils and the crowd of emotions leaving her eyelashes clumped together in a wet huddle.

"Hello Sarah." She offers me her hand, without hesitation. I take it and her touch is like a blowtorch slicing through my body. I stumble for a second and press against the wall, avoiding her face. If I look into her face…

"Are you okay honey?" the mother asks. She is looking at me like I am her own child or a beloved pet she is about to get put down. My vision finally stabilises and I'm forced to stare into her eyes. It is although I fear she will instantly know my secrets, but she does not. Apart from being full of water and emotion, her eyes are soft, making my feet steady again.

"This is Aunty Val." Thom smiles, unaware of the turmoil I have just recovered from. This moment is the happiest I have seen him and perhaps the happiest I will ever see him.

"It's nice..." I splutter, "to meet you." I realise I am still clutching onto her hand. She is a scaffolding for me but I am aware that I have to let go. Her hand drops to her side and I wonder why she seems fascinated by me, staring and smiling like a cheesy billboard.

"Shall we go into the living room?" Thom suggests. We all go inside and sit down together. Val brings us tea and custard creams. As Val mixes in my two spoons of sugar, I remember you. I smell the perfume you used to wear and how it lingered beside me when you had to go back to the kitchen, having always forgotten to bring the milk.

21 Curls

Her curls are like ribbons of dark chocolate, only blacker. Thom follows them around the room and when they're not there, he imagines their circular pattern curling into the edge of his view like paper burning, dissolving as quickly as it is seen. Everything seems to look like them too – the shadow of the curtain rings against the light, the winding grain of the coffee table, even the shapes he makes in the sky when he joins the stars together...

Thom doesn't know why he can't stop thinking of those curls. Even the few seconds when he manages not to, his thoughts turn to the edge of her red underwear he glimpsed beneath her skirt the day they first met. Then, he gladly returns to the curls before he can begin to blush or think of Emma.

Thom hasn't spoken to Emma in days, maybe even over a week... It's been eight missed calls, that's all he knows. He sits in the kitchen and watches the phone dance around the table until it either stops or plummets to the floor. He would almost feel relieved if it smashed apart but it has remained strong, unlike him. That's why he doesn't answer her. He can't think of anything new to say. He could easily listen to her small talk and pretend to care or he could say "Yep. Still grieving here." And then what? Would that satisfy her? And for how long?

Emma is far away; a distant planet that he knows exists but has no interest in exploring at present. Knowing she exists is enough. Yet if it's enough for their relationship, he can't tell.

In a similar vein, Sarah has become almost a fixture over the last few days. Sometimes he doesn't notice her at all, only her curls, as though they are a completely separate entity. Perhaps his fascination with her curls is only a distraction from his fascination with her. But he can't think about that right now either. Thom has to admit though, she has been a comfort. Sometimes he has been sitting in the dark without realising it and suddenly the room is flooded with light. Sarah isn't there but he hears her soft footsteps disappearing from the scene. Thom has ignored his body's needs at times too and Sarah has carefully deposited food near his door just as his hunger seems to have reached its peak.

Sarah seems to know Thom better than even he does. Yet she keeps her distance. The door to the living room where she sleeps is usually closed with little sound inside, and when she does appear, she helps Aunty Val with the washing or sits on the sofa with her legs pulled up to her chest. She looks like a fugitive, always afraid to be discovered. And maybe she is. He doesn't even know her; he just wishes he did.

Richard has barely spoken to Sarah. He tells Thom "I'm not sure."

"Sure about what?" Thom asks and Richard just shakes his head. He is acting like a dog who always barks and growls at someone, with reason or without, no one can ever ask the dog for its opinion. And Richard won't give Thom one. He can't mistrust Sarah on such a vague impression from Richard. Although, it's not like Richard to have a vague dislike for someone, without some foundation at least.

Thom is no closer to Daniel. He often puts out all the objects he found in the lock up on the floor and rearranges them, hoping they will suddenly fit together and unlock something. Yet they don't. He has re-read the note a million times, until the paper looks a hundred years old, but still it has revealed nothing more than the words written on it. He hasn't even looked up Mrs Tray yet, the mysterious beneficiary. He will do that soon.

Every morning he wakes up and feels like the world is a rhino sitting on his chest and he loses his determination all over again. It takes him hours to breathe easily again, to function. But tomorrow, he will make some progress. He knows Daniel must make sense to someone and every puzzle must have a resolution. Thom can't believe that reason will betray him on this one.

22 Swelling Blood

It is the fourth time I have stood in Daniel's empty room, including the time I snuck in during his wake. I have been staying at the Mansen's house for four days now, steadily becoming a fixture, whilst Daniel wilts with each passing day. Or does he?

The family and I are still transfixed on him. He is like that book, *The Catcher in the Rye*, because after you've read it cover to cover, you're not really sure what happened when someone asks you years later. And it seems neither the family nor me are really sure what happened with Daniel. Was it our stupidity, or was Daniel a genius who left behind an unsolvable puzzle? Or was he simply an ordinary man who wanted to die?

I sit on the bed. As I think about what his death has done to me, I realise it has awoken me again. For several years before his death, there are entire weeks and months I cannot recall. I have no idea of the length between my leaving the hospital and meeting him in the street. Even the days when I stalked Daniel seem a blurred series of photos, merging into one continuous film.

Yet since the moment I watched him fall, every sense has been on alert. I have smelt the sadness radiating from the house, touched the vibrancy of red, heard the guilt slinking after the family like a venomous snake, and watched depression grow from stubble to a beard on Thom's face. And I'd tasted him. I'd tasted Thom's guilt and confusion like heavy wallpaper paste gluing his tongue down, causing his words to huddle at the back of his mouth in a sticky trap.

I want to open Thom up. I want to cut his words free and examine his feelings; their colours, their textures, the way they fit together and interlock.

The door flings open then.

"What the hell are you doing in here?" Thom whispers loudly and checks behind him as he closes the door. "Aunty Val wouldn't like this at all," he adds.

I stand up and touch his arm. I notice that whenever I touch him, he stares at my offending body part with either disbelief or reluctant intrigue. "I'm sorry. I was just curious," I say gently. His lips are taut like they are two sizes too small for his face. Although, he tries to smile and appear casual by placing his hands in his jeans pockets, shuffling from one foot to the other.

"It's okay," he mutters, not convinced.

"I'll get out of here," I reassure him. He nods but as I start towards the door, his hand shoots out.

"I'm sorry... if, I frightened you." He squeezes my arm with one hand and then raises the other to grab hold of my other arm. He is holding me like I am a person who needs shaking.

"I just wouldn't want you to touch his things." Thom's voice breaks. "It's *too* soon to be touching... his things, his... life."

"Have *you* looked in any of the cupboards or drawers, Thom?" I ask, without thinking, regretting it as soon as I see his face. In an instant, his wet sadness is wiped off and replaced with frown lines.

"Why would you say that?" he asks, his grip tightening. He seems more distressed than he should be. He is biting his lips and already he has punctured them, a dot of blood marking his front tooth. "Why would you say that?" he repeats; both his words and his grip harder.

"I'm sorry. I just wondered." I shrug and try to pull away but a second later; he releases me anyway.

Thom walks over to the chest of drawers by the window. He looks over at me, a child asking for permission or seeing how far they can go without being told off, a person testing another's love for them by putting themselves in a dangerous situation. And all I can do is say nothing and wait for the inevitable.

Thom opens a drawer. He lets out a small yelp and for a moment, I hope that he has found something; a severed hand, a blood stained shirt, a weapon. Yet, when I look over his shoulder, there is nothing. Only the wood that the drawer is made of.

Thom catches my eye again. He has started to shake, a tree battered and relenting in a violent wind. He keeps my gaze as he places his hand on another drawer handle and slowly eases it open, a drawn out yawn and finally, he turns towards it.

Another yelp.

I know what he is feeling now. His heart is probably racing faster, his mind filled with the colour of that wood. Worse for him, he probably knows exactly what should be in that particular drawer and all of them. Whereas, I only expected something, anything…

Like a sense of déjà vu, he begins flinging everything open. He finishes the chest of drawers in five seconds, moving onto the drawers beside Daniel's bed, and flinging open the wardrobe. All empty. Gaping holes in everyday life, empty shells that are now devoid of function, life departed from the body it once filled.

There are no words for Thom. He is screaming like a baby who cannot understand anything yet. He is pushing the chest of drawers over and pulling the curtains down. He is punching the mirror on the front of the wardrobe and kicking the door in until it cracks in half, like broken ribs.

I watch the destruction of the empty room. I watch the blood swelling out of his knuckles and forget the whiteness of the room. The red is beautiful and I'm surrounded by it, a calm sea lapping against my brain, until I realise the lapping of the sea coincides with my pulse.

I remember. Thom. He is sobbing on the floor and smearing the carpet with blood, like a child finger painting. He picks up the slithers of glass and throws them at the wall but they only chime quietly and fall to the floor.

I dive towards him and take his hands by the wrists. I press them into my chest and don't let go. His blood soaks into my chest and I feel like he has taken a knife and slit my chest open.

I am alive. Mum, I am so alive. And Daniel is still dead.

23 Mrs Tray

The empty room tears a hole in Thom, literally with his slashed hands and, in another sense, perhaps intellectually. Either way, he has to mend this hole somehow. The only way he thinks this might be achieved is by getting some clarification, on anything he can. So he contacts the solicitors the next morning and after a bit of negotiating, he feels his hand moving in the shape of letters and when he replaces the phone receiver, he has an address.

Mrs Tray. The woman with a face like deteriorating fruit. The woman who silenced them all with the door. The woman with no reason for attending the reading, according to those who were meant to know Daniel. Yet clearly, they had been standing much further from him than they realised.

All night, Thom dreamt of falling through an endless white hole. Not the standard black hole dream, but a *white* hole. Obviously, the blank walls of Daniel's room were taunting him. The walls that have been painted recently, without anyone being aware. They are hiding Daniel's secrets. His room is a huge void, only filled now with Thom's blood and the smashed glass.

And now here Thom is, trying to get the woman with a face plagued with holes to fill his own. Perhaps she, as no one else has so far, will turn the whiteness of his mind some other colour. Even pearl would be something.

239

Mrs Tray lives in a cluster of flats designed for the elderly. It's a small community with a well-kept green in the middle that the flats surround. There is nothing remarkable about her front door. It is painted green but the green is like her skin, cracked and faded past its original state. He finds her name on the bell and presses it several times.

It's only now that Thom ponders about Mrs Tray. Is she a friend of Daniel's? If so, how did they meet? Perhaps she is a relative of one of Daniel's friends or girlfriends (though Thom isn't aware of many). Perhaps they met accidentally and formed a friendship. Or perhaps they had been having a sordid and, frankly, creepy affair. Thom relishes this idea for a moment but he fails to laugh. Whatever the details, there has to be something helpful he can find out here.

Thom hasn't noticed the door skulking open and he jolts slightly when Mrs Tray's cratered face floats ahead of him. She is smaller than he remembers and this time, she props herself up with a wooden walking stick, the texture as knotted as her hand that appears to have shrunk around the top of it permanently.

"Mrs Tray…" he says. It's the beginning of a sentence but he has no idea how to complete it. He hopes she will rescue him or ask him who the hell he is or invite him in without a word, yet she only stares. Her eyes are the colour of faded bark and they examine him closely, as though she is waiting for him to pounce.

"I'm Thom," he tells her finally. He wants to slap himself across the face. His stupid name means nothing to her! Perhaps he shouldn't have come. Maybe the answers he seeks so hard are also the thing he wants to run away from.

"You were at the reading of the will," she says. Thom feels like she has thrown him a piece of driftwood in the sea. Her voice is much softer than he would have anticipated and, even more surprising, is the gentle Irish twang to it. Her raspy face has given him false impressions. He should know better than to trust his own judgements at the moment, he keeps getting tripped up whenever he does.

"Yes. That's why I'm here!" Thom exclaims, too excitedly for the subject matter. He composes himself and holds his hand out. "Thom

240

Mansen. Sorry." Her hand moves upwards in slow motion and Thom finally grasps it. In situations like this, people often say 'pleased to meet you' but Thom isn't sure he is and doesn't want to lie to the woman.

"You'd better come in," she says, neither pleased nor displeased. It's all very lukewarm. Thom shrugs to himself and lets himself in. She directs him to a lit doorway down the darkened hall and ushers him ahead of her, the slow thump of her walking stick pursuing him.

"Sit anywhere," she shouts ahead and Thom sits himself in an armchair near the door. He digs his fingernails into the fabric and waits for the unknown to catch up with him. He closes his eyes, his blood thumping inside his head, the rhythm smashed by the door. Once again, her work is decisive and unquestionable.

"I wondered if anyone would come," she sings without trying and lowers herself, with some effort, into a chair facing him. He tries to look as disinterested as she does, hoping that it will have the strange effect of drawing truth from her. Thom has found this sometimes works with people (especially those who were trying to make fraudulent claims) who, so desperate for some clarification, end up spilling their secrets.

On the table he sees a pack of cards set up for solitaire. She is playing three-card draw and Thom instantly respects her a little more. What is the point of playing one-card draw? It is one of his pet hates.

"You took longer than I expected actually," Mrs Tray says and folds her arms. If anyone saw her now, they'd say she looks like any harmless elderly woman, yet Thom believes she is hiding something. Her face is full of nooks and crannies where she can conceal things.

"I've had a lot to do," Thom claims. When he really thinks about his words he wants to laugh. What has he actually achieved? He's failed to get out of bed, sat around in the darkness, invited a strange woman into his home, and sliced his hands open. It isn't exactly the traditional definition of 'progress'.

"I imagine so. Do you play by the way?" She gestures to her cards. Thom nods and leans forward.

"The seven of spades can go over there." He wonders if he

241

should've said it but she nods gratefully and performs the action.

"Sometimes all it takes is a fresh eye." She smiles but Thom gets caught up in her words, a wind stuck in a pipe, rattling and whistling. A fresh eye? Perhaps that is all he needs.

"Do you live alone?"

"I'm alone," she answers. The two words are small and quiet, yet they seem to pull at Thom's lips and like a puppet, he mouths them a few times: "I'm alone."

"Did you enjoy your inheritance gift?"

"Why would you call it a 'gift'?" Thom cocks his head, like a detective in a film.

He wants her to know he mistrusts her, but even he has no idea why. Some detective...

"Well, didn't your friend, Daniel, call it a 'gift' in his will?" Thom is disappointed that the explanation is so simple and picks up on the fact that Mrs Tray referred to Daniel as his 'friend'.

"He was my cousin," Thom tells her. She nods quietly, perhaps having suspected it and folds her hands in her lap. She gives Thom none of the usual 'I'm sorry' and merely waits.

"How did you know him?" Thom asks finally.

"I didn't," she says, "not really." The words are simple but Thom feels like his eardrums are pressured for a moment and he doesn't believe he really heard them. *I didn't* – what does that mean?

"I'm sorry?" he asks, using the phrase he expected from her.

"I didn't really know Daniel," she repeats, more forcefully. Thom watches her lips move and churns the sentence around in his chaotic brain, filled with all the things Daniel left behind.

"But why were you there? At the reading?" Thom splutters.

"He looked after my husband. In the hospital," she explains.

The hospital! Finally, something Thom knows about! For several years, Daniel worked fulltime at a hospital for those with mental health problems. He'd only taken a job as an administrator at first but later worked as a mentor for several patients. He hadn't spoken too much about it to Thom but Aunty Val often passed on stories. Thom often wonders how Daniel found contentment in the job, as he seemed to have limited empathy for others and preferred to be alone. Yet, Daniel spent around three years there and Thom heard of no complaints throughout that time. Why he left, Thom isn't sure. Yet it wasn't long before he died, perhaps six or eight months at the most.

"Your husband was a patient then?"

"Yes. He spent several years at the hospital but before Daniel arrived, he was making very little progress." Mrs Tray stops for a moment and smiles to herself. The gesture and its relation to Daniel seem foreign to Thom.

"Daniel helped my husband greatly. I think he finally felt like someone was listening and even that helped a little. But like I said, I didn't really know Daniel. I heard a lot from my husband, when he felt able, and met Daniel only a few times myself," she pauses. "He seemed like a lovely lad though. He was quiet, shy, but he helped my husband so much. I think my gratitude embarrassed him."

"He helped your husband?" Thom is asking himself to believe it, rather than asking her to clarify. How could someone who hardly said a word to his own family help a mentally ill man?

"Yes. So when he sent the letter, I had no reservations agreeing to his request."

"His request?" Thom repeats. Thom can't construct his own words; merely regurgitates those of others instead.

"He sent me a letter several months ago. He asked me to attend a meeting."

"The reading of his will?" Thom surges forward with his words.

"As it turns out – yes," Mrs Tray verifies. Thom sags backwards, his body jolting and struggling to function normally. Just breathe, just beat, just swallow.

"Did Daniel commit suicide?" she asks. Thom stares at her for a moment, wondering if she is really asking *him* a question. He thought she might have the answers but here he is, on the spot, as it were.

"I don't know," Thom says, "I've wondered..." His throat is getting smaller. He starts to cough like a cat trying to retrieve a hairball. Mrs Tray pours him a glass of water from a jug he hasn't noticed and he gratefully gulps it down. His hand shakes so much that he spills it down his shirt. "Sorry," he gargles as he slams the glass down on the table. "Do you still have the letter?"

Mrs Tray leaves the room and returns a few minutes later with a perfectly crisp envelope. It has been torn open with an old-fashioned letter opener, judging by the perfectly straight tear across the top of it. Thom looks up and Mrs Tray nods her approval. He plucks the letter from inside and places the envelope neatly on the table beside him. He unfolds it and Daniel's handwriting instantly drowns him.

Dear Mrs Tray,

I realised it's been a few months since I contacted you. I hope you are coping with the loss of your husband, a great man whom I have missed greatly since I left the hospital. Thank you for inviting me to the funeral, I was happy I was able to see him off properly.

I would have come to see you but it's just not possible right now. So I'm afraid I have to ask you a favour by letter. I know it's not polite to ask something of you, especially as my friendship was solely with your husband. Yet I have no choice and as you're related to someone I trusted, I feel like I could ask you and perhaps you would find it in yourself to help me.

It's a simple request. I need you to attend a meeting that will probably occur within the next month. The address is enclosed on a business card. You will probably be called nearer the time. I just wanted to ask you personally. Please be there.

Yours, Daniel

"He invited you to his will reading in advance?" Thom asks, holding the letter away from him as though it's diseased. All Daniel's paper trail seems to be offending him.

"I know. I don't understand it either," she says. Silent for a moment, she finally adds, "I guess he must've known one way or another he was going to die." The statement is the next obvious step but it knocks all sound from the room. It winds the situation and, for a few seconds, nothing and no one moves or breathes or comprehends.

"I found a note too," Thom reveals finally. He hasn't told Emma, Aunty Val, or anyone else since he found it. It has burnt its every curve and line into his brain, but he hasn't said it out loud. Until now...

"What did it say?" She is just as intrigued as he is about hers.

"It had the time and place of his death." Thom winces. He doesn't know what effect the revelation will have. He's been dreading it since he found it.

"Oh goodness." She shakes her head.

"So he knew," Thom vocalises their thoughts. "He either jumped in front of a train or he was pushed by someone he knew."

Thom feels an inappropriate waterfall of relief beating down on his shoulders and back. He wants to close his eyes and let it beat him unconscious. "I thought I was going crazy." Thom wants to scream and smash everything in the room apart. He wants to punch his way through the wall and draw blood again. He thought he felt confused but all he feels surging through him like a current is anger. Anger pumps into his heart and gets stuck, inflating it until it buzzes like a threatened beehive.

"It sounds like you have a lot to find out," Mrs Tray tells him. He has to clasp onto the chair in order to stop himself from hitting her or throwing something at her. *Obviously* he has a lot to find out, stupid bitch. That fucking bitch comes along with her sob story and one letter and starts telling him what to do. What does she know?

"I'm sorry about Daniel. I was so sad to hear about his death and now, it all seems so... sinister," she adds and puts her hand on his knee. Thom stares at it, wishing it would burst into flames.

"Can I have this?" Thom asks abruptly, snatching at the letter. Mrs Tray withdraws her hand quickly and nods.

"Please do." She heaves herself out of the chair and walks towards the door. "It was nice to meet you, Thom." Thom realises he has overstayed his welcome and probably frightened the woman. He would usually apologise but all he wants to do is lash out so he keeps his mouth closed, for fear of bees flying out of him and stinging her to death.

On his way out, he merely nods at her and crumples up Daniel's second letter until the creases mark the inside of his hand like a tattoo.

24 The Stranger

Thom dives into a parking spot just outside the house and turns the engine off. He lets his body flop. After all the adrenaline that has been surging through him the last hour, his muscles haven't relaxed once. He wouldn't mind now if a huge spaceship fell out of space and crushed him. It would save on a lot of emotional turmoil, and he wouldn't have to tell Aunty Val that her son was either murdered or planned his own death. All the questions she would ask him – why? What happened? What made him do it? How could he leave us all to deal with this? Thom has no idea, not one, to share with Aunty Val.

Mrs Tray had seemed an unimportant character. Yet she has really opened the can of worms, as such. She confirmed that Daniel had premature knowledge of his death. Either suicide, planned murder or even some psychic sense – Daniel knew. And now Thom knows. Thom knows and his heart feels like a steam engine in his chest, wheezing and coughing itself onwards. If he closes his eyes, he isn't certain he will open them again for hours or perhaps days. Yet when he does close them, it is alarmingly white so he is forced to open them again.

There are still things that make no sense. The notebook for one. Had he written that or had Daniel? And the lock up. What did the effort of doing that and the objects inside reveal? And the emptied room. Why would Daniel empty it and how did he do it without his family's knowledge? Aunty Val clearly hasn't noticed yet, as she hasn't mentioned it.

Thom jumps at a knock on the window. At first he thinks he imagined it but when he notices the shadow over his lap and the steering wheel, he lifts his head and sees a man standing there. This isn't a yellow line and he isn't blocking a driveway so the man's intentions are unknown to him. Thom unwinds his window.

"Yes?"

"Do you live in that house..." the man interrupts himself with a glance over his shoulder, "*that* house over there?" Thom pulls himself up and looks at where the man is pointing. Yes, that is his house. He can't see anything wrong with it – no fire, no broken windows, nothing visible from the outside. Is there something wrong? In the same vein, this man doesn't look like a fireman or a policeman, unless he is plain clothed.

"Yeah," Thom answers casually. He doesn't want this stranger to know he is alarmed and confused. The man keeps looking around. It seems he expects to be caught out by someone or he is about to reveal a secret to Thom.

"I've seen you going in and out of there," the man says. He is bending over to speak to Thom. Thom can see a defined bend in the bridge of his nose. His hair is a black lump of frizz and something about it seems familiar to Thom. *Familiar hair?* What is Thom thinking?

"I need to ask you about someone," the man finally continues. He is trying to get something out of his pocket but his hand seems to be shaking. Thom backs away slightly, yet doesn't roll up the window.

"I've seen you together," the man mumbles whilst he continues to struggle. Finally he pulls out a folded piece of paper. He opens it up. It is a photo. He hands it to Thom. "Do you," he pauses deliberately, "know her?"

The man looks excited, almost manic. Thom looks at the photo carefully. Of course he knows her. She is much younger in this picture. Her hair is shorter but her intricate curls still wind around his attention. She looks happier. Now, he always senses sadness in her. But he could hardly judge her for that; he hasn't been a barrel of laughs lately...

"Why are you asking this?" Thom pushes the photo back at him, reluctant to give in so easily. The man helplessly takes it back, but glances at it before placing it back in his pocket.

"I need to find her," he answers briefly. No explanations, no hints that he knows her well or is concerned about her. What does this man want with Sarah?

"Look, I don't know her that well. We only met once," Thom tells the man and makes a move to exit the car. The man pushes the door shut again and Thom wonders then what this man might do.

"She's been in your house…" he fumbles. "I know she has?" The man persists with a question, although Thom isn't sure it's not just the tone of his voice. His voice is bordering on a whine.

Thom opens his door again and this time, the man doesn't block him. Thom locks the door and turns back to the man. "If you know, then why are you asking me anything?"

"She'll just run if she sees me," he confesses, sagging against the car.

"What have you done to her?" Thom asks, feeling the adrenaline begin to pulse through his blood again.

"I'm trying to help her," the man insists. He grabs onto Thom's arm but Thom immediately shakes him off.

"I think you should leave; whoever you are." Thom begins to walk towards the house. Yet, the man chases after him, grabbing at his shirt. Thom spins around and bats at the man with his hand. "Just fuck off. I don't know what you want and I can't help you, okay?"

"You think she's fine but she's ill. I know her. I promise I just want to help." Thom can't decide if the man is genuine or whether he just believes his own lies.

"What's her name then? You haven't even said anything personal. How do I know you know her?"

Thom and the man are standing in the middle of the road. The sun is starting to set and the impending darkness doesn't seem attractive to Thom in his current situation. He has to get away from this strange desperate man.

"Her name is Alice," he says softly and Thom instantly starts to turn. The man stamps after Thom. "But I bet she told you her name is something else, didn't she?" His words chase Thom across the street and will never fully be lost inside his mind. "Let me ask you, does she seem strange to you? Does she talk about her family? Do you know that much about her?"

The man won't shut up so as Thom reaches the gate, he flings round and aims a punch at the man's face. Luckily, the man ducks and Thom misses. Thom doesn't really want to hurt him; he just wants to scare him away. Like a moth head butting a light bulb continuously, this man is becoming irritating.

"What are you doing?" the man shrieks.

"I told you to leave. You haven't convinced me of anything and you're wasting my time," Thom says the words but still inside, the moth keeps crashing into the back of his eyes and he knows he won't sleep much tonight.

"I don't want her to hurt herself or anyone else." The man seems weary now.

"You don't even know her name." Thom puts the front gate between them.

"That's not important. What about the other questions I asked you? What about them?" The man looks like someone dying pleading for a cure. Thom could easily give him a glimmer of hope and give into the doubts he has dismissed in order to have an easier life. He *has* wondered about her: why she acts so coldly, where she appeared from. Yet Thom is too tired to trust this man, too battered to let something else in his life fall apart.

"She has a lovely family. She's shown me pictures." Thom watches his words pull down the edges of the man's mouth like weights. Thom stares at him for a few more moments and turns away.

"I won't give up," the man vows to Thom's back.

"Do what you like." Thom shrugs. Thom opens the front door and slams it behind him, almost in Mrs Tray style. As he laughs at the comparison in his head, he looks up the stairs and sees Sarah watching him. Thom doesn't say anything, just returns the stare. He wonders if he should have protected her or if she will shed her skin and prove to be the monster the stranger warned him about.

25 Red Scars Beneath

He is bound to have them: questions, doubts. He hardly knows a thing about me; only the obvious physical attributes and a few snippets of information that can barely fill half a page. And when he sits down beside me on the steps, so close that our knees and thighs are squashed together, and says: "There was a man asking about you outside," I know he finally has to ask. At the same time, I know it's finally time for me to lie.

"What did he ask you?" I question, managing a convincing mask of concern.

Thom is instantly the gentleman, saying: "I didn't tell him anything."

I should've known he would be on my side. He is a sweet man and I can't help but reach up and touch his soft stubble. Like always when I touch him, he opens his mouth slightly and freezes, waiting for the moment to pass.

"So what did he want to know?" I ask again and Thom turns his head, making my hand fall away.

"He said he knew you. He said you were ill and you need help." Thom says the words cautiously and still doesn't want to make the air throb with awkwardness or cause the stairs to creak underfoot. He glances at me from the corner of his eye, trying to gauge my reaction.

"That's strange," I say casually. Inside, the drum of my heart thuds quicker.

"I couldn't tell if he was lying or not," Thom pauses but quickly continues, "are you in some kind of trouble, Sarah?" He is more concerned than playing the detective.

"I told you, I'm a little behind on my rent but that's all." I give him a sheepish look. He nods understandingly.

"He said your name is Alice," he adds and lets the name hang in the air for a moment. He seems to be watching it to see if it attaches itself to me or to see if I make a move to claim it.

"Alice? That wouldn't suit me at all." I laugh. Thom chuckles a little but it doesn't fit his mouth properly.

"Sarah does suit you," he agrees.

That's exactly what I always thought. I even wanted to change my name by deed poll but I had never done it. I'm glad I can be who I want now.

Do you mind that I left my name behind, Mum?

"Did you ever call Daniel 'Dan'?" I ask.

250

"No, it didn't seem to fit." Thom shrugs. "I guess nicknames are familiar and playful. Daniel didn't really go for that type of thing." Thom picks at the skin around his nails as he picks at his memories.

"That's sad," I say quietly.

We fall silent and listen to the house, humming and creaking.

"Aren't you going to ask what the man outside looked like?" Thom asks abruptly. I almost believed we had left the subject behind but Thom is scrutinising my every pore, line and muscle for weakness.

"Oh… I meant to ask." I fumble slightly. Thom seems a bit suspicious for a moment but he gives me a brief description nonetheless: short black frizzy hair, the beginnings of a beard, a brown overcoat, and a bend in the bridge of his nose. I shake my head in response and say, "I don't know who that is, sorry." Thom seems disappointed but nods again.

"He had a picture of you," Thom adds. He has been quiet for a few minutes and I have been listening to his puckered breathing. He seems distressed about something, unable to even let the air slip easily through his windpipe. What is wrong with my Thom?

"He did?" I ask, unable to think of anything else just then.

"Yeah. It looked like you were a bit younger in the photo," Thom pauses. "How do you suppose he got that?"

I have to think fast. At that moment, I hate Michael more than ever.

"I didn't want to tell you about this but I suppose I have no choice," I hear a voice saying. Thom is looking at me with keen interest and I realise it's my throat that is vibrating with sound. "About two years ago, I was raped." The words hang in the air like poison gas and neither of us knows whether to breathe in or out. We stare straight ahead for a few minutes.

"You were raped," Thom repeats. I know he instantly believes I am weaker. Everyone does when they hear that. So many people didn't know how to speak to me afterwards, that's what made it more isolating.

You kept me alive, Mum. I wouldn't have survived without you. But you aren't around to pull me out of the quicksand anymore; I just keep sinking until even the numbness doesn't feel anything.

"What does this have to do with that man?" Thom asks quietly but his fists are already wriggling with his assumptions.

"He was my boyfriend but we broke up." The lie feels like fur on my tongue. I want to stick my fingers down my throat and make it come gushing out. I want him to see the blackness inside but at the same time, I want him to love my black curls instead. "He didn't take it too well," I add. Thom is biting his lip so hard I can tell there is blood gathering beneath his teeth. It is slowly throbbing out of him like the blood that oozed from his hands in Daniel's room. I resent him for a moment, for being able to see some of his pain in the burnt scars beneath his bandages whereas my scars are inside, hidden beneath the bandages of my skin.

"That man hurt you," he says but his teeth and his clenched expression muffle his words. I nod and this is enough to answer. Being so close, every movement is like an earthquake between us.

It all happens so fast. Before I can blink, Thom is on his feet and has managed to jump most of the staircase. He is advancing on the front door, his body arched like a hedgehog preparing to defend. I stumble after him and manage to reach him just as he grabs at the door handle. I push him against the wall.

"That won't help anyone," I tell him but he squirms underneath me. His head is so furrowed I want to shake him. I want to make him look sad again. Anything would be better. "Please Thom," I say and press my face into his shoulder. He smells of sweat and cold.

In the next moment, I feel him push me away gently. He has stopped shaking. His anger has been replaced by concern for my gesture. What does it mean? What do I want from him? If only I knew myself. Never did I think I would confess my secret to this man. Even though I'd lied about the person who'd committed the act, I wasn't lying about the incident.

I wish you were here, Mum. You were looking after me and you didn't finish. I need you still. Yet maybe I'd asked too much and that's why I lost you.

"I can't promise I won't do something if I see him again but I'll leave it," Thom says, "for now." I nod and take a step back. He is pressing himself against the wall. He takes a side-step towards the stairs but before he can take another, the doorbell rings.

We both look at one another but neither of us moves.

26 The Visitor

"Emma," Thom croaks when he opens the door. She isn't smiling but she doesn't look angry either. The wind is making her loosely tied hair dance and she has goose bumps on her arms. He is slow to react and she gives him an impatient narrowing of her eyes. "Oh sorry, come in." He ushers her in and glances outside to see if the stranger is still there, but he is nowhere to be seen. He closes the door.

Sarah is still standing just inside the door. She and Emma are facing one another. They both look as though they are owed an explanation. Thom feels like two opposing forces have met and are pushing against one another but he doesn't know why – no one has moved or spoken.

"Who's this then?" Emma finally asks.

Thom is about to answer but Sarah lifts her hand up and informs her, "I'm Sarah." Emma returns the favour but her mouth slants down to one side as she speaks. After all, she is no clearer on who this strange woman is.

Thom clears his throat and both of them turn to him expectantly. "Sarah, could you leave us please?" he asks, feeling like a traitor. Sarah just nods quietly and makes her way upstairs (without making the stairs creak, when he still does after walking up them all his life).

Emma turns to him. He remembers her appearance as though it's been years since he last saw her. He recaptures the three-freckle cluster beside her earlobe, the way she twitches her mouth when she feels uncomfortable, her slender fingers that press against his arm now.

"Let's go in the living room," Thom says and leads her by the hand into the darkened room. He turns on a lamp, closes them in and they both settle on the edge of the sofa. Sarah's bed sheets are in a pile by the chair, like dog shit that neither of them wants to acknowledge or clean up. Emma is staring so hard at him that he feels she can see everything he has done in the last few weeks – his obsessive detective work, his tears and depression, his explosions of anger, his taking in of a mysterious woman he knows nothing about. Yet she can't know. She has come here because she doesn't know what he's been doing, or what he's been thinking.

"What happened to your hands?" she asks as she lightly traces her fingers over the gauze.

Thom hesitates for a moment, on the verge of confessing but instead says: "I dropped some plates and cut myself a few times." This is the second major lie he has told her. It all started with the note and his first lie. Now, he is lying again to stop her entering the world he has been living in since his first deception.

"You've grown a beard," she comments. She is noting the changes one by one, hoping to get past the surface. Yet Thom hopes she gets lost in unwrapping the bandages and his clump of facial hair.

"I just haven't shaved. No reason," Thom tells her, wiping off the small hint of a smile on her lips.

"I've been trying to call you, as you've probably realised..." Emma drops her eyes to her lap, probably not wanting to hear what he has to say about this. What explanation would be a good one?

"I'm sorry. I needed some time... and quiet."

The couple know there is an undertone to the conversation, words and thoughts that are being trapped beneath their tongues and inside their heads. The words and thoughts are cockroaches that struggle to surface in view of others and prefer to scuttle around in the safety of darkness.

"I know you needed time. I've left you for three weeks, wondering how you are every day. I only called because I thought it'd be easier if I made the first move." Emma is leaning closer but Thom shrinks into the arm of the sofa and ignores her.

"You were probably right to think so," Thom agrees blankly.

"Then why didn't you answer one of my calls?"

"I'm sorry. I just had nothing to say." He shrugs. Emma doesn't respond to this, she falls silent. For several minutes, they both find sanctuary in the rhythm of the clock on the mantelpiece. It chugs onwards, regulating their jumpy heartbeats for a small period at least.

"Who is that woman?" Emma finally ventures.

"We met about a week ago. She's having trouble with her rent so Aunty Val invited her to stay."

"Where did you meet?"

"In the front garden, if you must know," Thom answers, realising it sounds completely insane as he hears it. Yet, he has accepted it readily as it happened, as though meeting people in the front garden is a regular occurrence.

"In the front garden?" Emma repeats slowly, like someone who is speaking English as a second language.

"I know it's not ordinary but that's how it happened."

"What was she doing in the front garden?" Emma persists but Thom cuts her down, "Look, I don't have to explain my whole life to you."

"That's not what I'm asking," Emma tells him, folding her arms.

"I'm sorry about this," Thom says quietly after another few minutes of silence. The room feels hot so he goes over to the window and pulls it up. The cold wind hardly affects his bandaged hands. Across the road, he sees the stranger with the photo getting into a car and turning the ignition on. With one last look at the house, seeing Thom, the man pulls off quickly and his lights disappear within a few seconds. Thom almost wonders if he imagined it.

"I think you want to talk to me but you're holding back for some reason. What is it Thom?" Emma can't help but let her affection for him resurface. After all, as far as she is concerned, until about ten minutes ago, nothing had been different between them. Thom's head droops, disgusted that his love for Emma seems to have become buried between all the half-clues and mysteries surrounding Daniel's death. Where have his old feelings gone? All he feels now is curiosity, anger, and infatuation.

"I have things I need to do," Thom reveals, not answering her question. Emma waits for something more and Thom only adds, "I can't go back to my old life now."

"Everyone has to go back sometime. Everyone has to get over losing someone," Emma says, not understanding the situation. Yet, it is not her fault. Thom has kept her separate.

"It's not about that. It's not about losing Daniel. I just have to find answers."

"Have you spoken to the police, Thom? Did they tell you what happened?"

"They haven't even bothered with him. They don't care enough."

"I have no idea why you're isolating yourself, Thom."

Thom watches her approach him in the reflection on the window pane. He doesn't move away, yet doesn't turn to greet her either. He watches her bow her head.

"I'm not. I just can't explain all this to anyone, even if I tried. I need to work on things. I need to learn more myself."

"Have you spoken to Aunty Val about all this *stuff*?"

"Only some. No one would understand it. I have to wait." Thom is being deliberately short, almost relishing the air of mystery he is creating. He imagines he is a renegade detective who will win the case in the end and reveal his amazing discoveries to all those involved! Yet Thom knows real life isn't like this, he is no Sherlock Holmes or the like. He is an ordinary man who is just as lost as anyone else would be given the same facts and clues.

"You sound a little crazy," Emma tosses his way.

"Sarah doesn't think so," he bites back.

"Right, *who* is this woman and what the hell is she doing here?"

In response, Thom does something he himself doesn't understand. He spins round and laughs. After weeks of depression, he finds himself laughing, when there is nothing amusing around him. Emma immediately withdraws a few paces. She is looking at him as if he has just cut his own hand off. He simmers to a chuckle and then only smiles. Still watching him in half-fear and confusion, Thom approaches her, grabs her and kisses her. Emma is rigid in his hold but lets him continue, opening her mouth slightly to allow him in. When he lets her go, she settles on the back of the sofa like someone who has merely tolerated something.

"Who is she, Thom?"

"Sarah. She's a nice girl who's been no trouble to us. She needed help and we were there for her. Is it okay to help someone else or not?"

"You know I wouldn't mind that," Emma says, taking a breath and trying to rephrase it, "I'm just not sure you should be welcoming strange people into your life right now. You're the one who needs some help and you need your close family, me – people you can trust." Emma has a good point of course, but Thom won't allow her to win.

"I *can* trust Sarah. You don't know her."

"You hardly seem to know her," Emma argues hopefully. Thom can't understand this himself. He feels as though someone has written Emma out of the story of his life and Sarah has been written in instead. Yet he can't tell Emma these things. He can only push her away and hope she realises how deep he has fallen into a white hole where there are endless possibilities and directions he can go.

"I love you," Emma confesses. Thom freezes, taking in her sincere tone. He has flashbacks of them laying in bed at weekends, tangled in the covers, her soft voice whispering those words, the movement of her throat on his shoulder where she is resting it. He is sure the movement and vibration would be exactly the same now. Yet he closes his eyes and the white world recaptures him.

"I'm sorry Emma," Thom manages. He feels certain in his mind, or at least he thinks he is. His body, however, seems to be swaying slightly, his eyelid twitching.

"I'll come back, Thom. Just to see how you are," Emma promises, gathering up her handbag and coat. "I didn't realise you would still be in such a state."

"I'm not in a state," Thom sulks. "I'm getting things sorted now."

"If you say so, Thom." She nods, unconvinced and makes her way towards the door. Just as she opens it, Thom's legs go soft. He grabs onto the edge of the sofa.

"Emma," he calls out. She peeks back around the door at him, her spark still not diminished. Perhaps this is why he says, "There's nothing going on with Sarah," because she still believes in him.

Emma nods and asks, "So she doesn't know about these 'things' you need to sort out either?"

"No she doesn't. She doesn't know anything."

Thom and Emma both seem comforted by the words, neither knowing quite why. Thom likes to think it is because he is neither together with her, nor together with Sarah so that's some consolation at least. There is a way back for them.

"You know my number," Emma tells him, clearly hoping this isn't the end. Thom nods and lets the door close behind her.

27 Red Trail

Who does he think he is? *I know nothing?* How dare he tell that stupid bitch that I know nothing? I've been around him more than she has the last few weeks. He hasn't even phoned her back. But why does he care what she thinks of me anyway? I can tell he was just trying to reassure her, let her know that she's not the only one in the dark. But how can he say that?

I've definitely seen what's been going on: his moods, his obsessive examination of certain strange objects, his comings and goings, his relationship with his aunt. I may not know exactly what he's thinking or doing but I do know more than he told her.

He pretends that I'm not really in his life, yet he seems to want me around. He wants to protect me, as I saw with Michael. He wants to be near me but at the same time is afraid. I know these things, probably more than he does himself! And now, I am only more determined to find out something about Daniel. I will find out how and why Daniel planned for me to push him, and that way I'll prove I know more than Thom thinks. He'll be shocked when I tell him all the things I've found out.

Mum, we'll prove him wrong, won't we? Of course, I won't tell him

I pushed Daniel; that's our secret.

It had been hard to listen through the living room door but I managed to catch most of it. My skin burnt hearing them together, sharing a connection, her trying to crawl underneath his skin and see the damage. After all, where has she been all this time? I have been the one turning on lights for Thom, leaving him food, watching he and his family day and night, swabbing Thom's slashed skin. I deserve to hear his plans, his need to find things out and discover what things mean.

The first thing I have to do is talk to Thom; perhaps even find out exactly what he's been up to. He might be willing to tell me, everyone likes to halve a burden when they can. And I am the perfect outlet. He doesn't want to hurt Val, and Richard isn't interested in anything being harder than it is.

Why can't Thom see me? Why doesn't he tell me about the objects he stares at for hours? Why won't he stop being afraid?

I really thought that Michael might have succeeded in turning Thom against me. Yet fate seems to have saved me. Perhaps because fate knows that this family needs saving and I am the one who can protect them. Yet at this moment, all I want to do is prove I can find out the truth, the plot that led up to the climax as the train bulldozed Daniel out of the family's lives, the reason he led me to them.

When Thom lets Emma out, I am sitting at the top of the stairs again. As he turns back, his face drained, he sees me. He freezes for a millisecond, clearly wondering if, or what, I heard. I smile, writhing inside. Reassured, he returns the gesture and walks slowly towards the kitchen.

Later that night, as he sleeps, I creep into Daniel's room again. Closing the door quietly, I turn the light on.

This is where it begins Mum; the answers...

From the doorway, all the way across the carpet, there is the red trail of blood that Thom left behind. I tiptoe across the trail and arrive at the wardrobe, still gutted. I peel the door away and place it on the ground. The cracked pieces of mirror make a jingling giggle against the carpet. I reach inside the wardrobe and let my fingers dance along the wood inside, each surface, the corners. I find nothing.

Next I open the small drawer at the bottom of the wardrobe. Nothing either. Yet just as it is about to close, I see it. On the left side of the drawer, carved in red pen, is a combination. Underneath that there is a street number and a street name. I wrench the drawer out and it tumbles onto my lap.

Mum – it's here!

Remembering where I am, I sit still for a moment and listen to the movements of the house. Yet there seems to be only ordinary noises, no one has awoken. I give my attention back to the tattooed wood and feel blood rushing to my fingertips that I press against the words. I almost don't have to read them with my eyes because I can feel their shape. If I've ever seen anything more beautiful, I forget then. These carved words are a salvation, a way into a maze that I have only just realised I want to enter.

I memorise those numbers and words. In a few days, I'll follow them to wherever they want to take me. Weeks and months after his death, Daniel is still leading me. This revelation once again is like a set meal, easy and comforting in one sense, yet depressing and controlling in another.

As I am returning the drawer to its place I hear the click of the door handle. The door begins to open as I get to my feet. Although instead of Thom as expected, it is Richard who materializes.

"What's going on?" he pulls at his left ear as though it is helping him wake up.

"Nothing. I thought I heard something in here."

"And is there anything in here?" he persists, looking doubtful.

"No. There's nothing," I say but inside my heart dances with my discovery.

"No ghosts? No poltergeists?" Richard mocks. He is scanning the room, perhaps surprised to see the trail of blood and the carcass of the wardrobe, yet he doesn't mention it.

"Why, have you seen one?" I retort. He has hardly spoken to me. Every time he sees me, he looks at me as though I'm wearing a prison uniform or brandishing a knife.

"No," he answers; his lip and nose curling upwards.

"Well then, let's get back to bed then."

I make to move past him but his hand springs out and grasps my arm. His face is close to mine. His eyes seem to be flickering, like he is staring into fire and the heat is twisting its tongue in the air in front of his face.

"I don't know who you are," he tells me, "but you'd better not hurt my family. They've had enough." He reminds me of a child standing up to a bully for the first time, worried it will result in a heavier beating.

"I don't want to hurt your family," I say truthfully.

"What do you want then?" Richard's hand seems to be trembling slightly. Goose bumps have risen on his bare arm from the cold of the air or the cold of my manner. This must be what keeps him away from me.

"I want to be their friend." *I want to understand your brother Daniel,* I add to myself.

"Okay," Richard whispers, as though I had been asking his permission. As far as I am concerned, he is irrelevant.

"I'm going to bed now," I tell him and without realizing, glance behind at the drawer that contains the secret message I have discovered. When I have left the room, Richard stares in the direction in which I glanced and tries to see something revealing but all he can make out is a broken wardrobe, a door laid out like a body having jumped to its death and the blobs of blood scattered on the carpet like paint splattered without consideration.

28 Red m & m's

"I bought you some m & m's," I tell Thom and take the place next to him on the front step. He is open-mouthed for a moment, looking like I have just handed him a bar of gold and then smiles brightly.

"I love m & m's. Thanks." It is pure joy beaming out of him and although I still feel angry with him about last night, it makes me proud in the same instance.

He tears open the packet and unashamedly begins his ritual of eating them in a certain order. I have only watched this from afar several times and I can't help but stare. Now that I am so close to him, I can see the chocolate melting into his fingerprints, the m & m's brand on each sweet, hear the crunching of the shells and nuts under his teeth.

He has eaten four when he offers me the pack. Despite holding it towards me, I see he is biting his lip. I doubt he is being greedy, more concerned that his ritual is being interrupted. I reach carefully into the packet and luckily; my fingers emerge with a red one. I squeal quietly.

"You got your favourite," he notices and after several seconds' hesitation continues; "my favourite is the yellow." He is currently making his way through the blue ones. He hasn't touched any but the brown and blue ones. Next, he will progress to the red, the green and finally his beloved yellow.

"They insist they all taste the same but I've tried them all and I'm happiest when it's the yellow last." He lowers his head as he talks.

I want to tell him I love his quirk and could watch it for hours. Yet, I don't want to scare him so instead I say, "You have to do what you enjoy." He appreciates this, rolling a red sweet around on his tongue and finally biting into it.

"It's nice you didn't laugh at me."

"Has anyone before?"

"I've had some strange looks!"

For the first time in weeks, Thom seems relaxed. His muscles are allowing him to smile. How long will it last though?

"How was Emma last night?" I ask, almost pushing him to lose his smile. He falters slightly but manages to shrug it off.

"Okay, I guess. I just can't be what she wants at the moment."

"And what does she want you to be?"

"My old self." Thom shrugs again, finally moving onto the yellow. He takes each one and holds it in his mouth, letting his tongue absorb the luminous taste.

"What are you like now?" I am desperate to know. Part of me

wishes I'd seen him being his 'old self'. Would I have liked him then?

"I have more in my head," he says but frowns instantly, unsure this is what he wants to say. He opens his mouth again but, straight after, closes it and shakes his head.

"What's in your head?"

"Lots of thoughts and questions and ideas."

"Isn't that what everyone's head is filled with?"

Thom appreciates the comment, giving me a small smile. "I guess it depends what all those things are related to."

"And yours are related to Daniel?"

"I guess that's obvious to you, being around me." Thom takes his last sweet and considers it before devouring it like the rest. He crumples the wrapper and stuffs it into his pocket.

"Can I help you with anything?"

"No," Thom says, clasping his hands together. "I think the only one who might be able to help is Daniel." He grimaces, reminding himself of the impossible.

"What's so confusing about it all?" I ask, wondering what it is that Thom knows. Does he know Daniel was pushed? Is he looking for me without realizing it?

"I'm not sure I should be talking to you about this," Thom begins tapping the step with his clenched fist. "I should've talked to Emma, if anyone. She cares about me but... she's just been so far away." He is toiling with himself in front of my eyes. I know I must act in order to get him to trust me, so I reach across and place my hand on his knee. He looks up sharply.

"I'm here for you Thom," I vow. He doesn't know how much I mean it but even a fraction of it is enough for him. His ignorance over my physical attention is beginning to lose its simplicity. He must acknowledge me soon, either positively or negatively.

"You're right, you have been. And that's what I told Emma..." he reassures me, hoping he won't have to get any closer to me for now. I can't tell if he would like to or not, now or ever...

I wish I could ask you what you think, Mum.

"I do want to talk to someone... but when she asked me last night, I

263

knew it wasn't her I wanted to tell." Thom is thrashing with his conscience, guilt, and the desire inside.

"Who do you want to tell?" I ask; praying *please say me, please say me*.

"I can't be sure of anything anymore." Thom ruffles his own hair as though he is trying to perk himself up. Then unexpectedly, he leans his head onto my shoulder. Like a parent who hasn't been in their child's life for years and suddenly is faced with comforting them, or a person who hates animals and finds themselves having to care for one's wounds, I don't know how to respond initially. I just let his head rest there. Somehow a shoulder is always a perfect pillow.

My heart is thudding heavily – heavier than the moment before I pushed Daniel onto those tracks? I can't decide. I can only think clearly about the present: Thom's beard poking through my jumper, the dull smell of chocolate on his breath, his increasingly wavy hair squashed against my neck.

"I think Daniel knew he was going to die," Thom mutters, just when I have started to believe my heart can't race any quicker. Or rather instead, stop completely.

The world is swaying slightly, yet the cars continue to chug by, the trees continue to stand motionless in the icy air, and Thom continues to hold his breath.

"What?" I say because it's the easiest thing to say. In a million films and books and useless conversations, people have said 'what' in response to questions for lack of something better. I am disappointed I have joined the masses on this one.

"I've been finding things he left behind..." Thom whispers, keeping it a secret from those cars and those trees. "It all points to him knowing."

A shudder makes my back spasm and I am sure Thom feels it but perhaps he attributes it to the peculiar notion he has just suggested. It is probably how he first reacted when the facts finally crystallized into sense.

"How could he know?" I splutter. Thom reaches his hand across my stomach and grabs onto my rib. I wonder if this is the moment when he will reveal he knows, when he will squeeze me so hard that my heart will suffocate and die. Yet he doesn't move after the initial movement, just grasps onto the place where he has seized initially.

"He left a letter, a note, notebooks and clues and rubbish. I don't know what I'm supposed to do with it all." Thom isn't crying but his fingers are beginning to clutch so fiercely that they are settling into the structure of my rib bones. It's as though he wants to dig a way in and hide himself.

"What did he write?" I almost plead. Thom doesn't notice that I am asking the wrong question. He accepts it because he doesn't know what to ask either.

"He wrote terrible things or maybe I did, I still don't know." Thom sinks into my shoulder further, a rock sinking in quicksand. "He knew when he was going to die," Thom adds so quietly I almost don't hear it, or maybe I just wish I hadn't.

I'm glad that Thom is on my shoulder because although he thinks it's for his benefit, to hide his face, I am relieved he can't see mine. If he could, he would see my curls shivering and my eye-lashes flicking in unison. He would see guilt screaming out of my pores and features like a spontaneous eruption.

"Did he know how?" I ask, realising that Daniel did but trying to gauge what Thom knows.

"He wrote down the train station," Thom answers and begins digging into his pocket. This causes him pain, as his palms are still raw underneath the bandages. Finally he drags a piece of paper out, as wrinkled and as ragged as his beard. He hands it to me and I can barely move my fingers to open it. Before me are words, words that would seem irrelevant to someone else, someone who didn't know Daniel, someone who didn't push him.

Highbury and Islington station. 15:30 Sunday.

I stare at the words until they seem as hard as brick, as though Daniel is head butting me. And I have only one thought: it says the wrong time; it should say 15:32.

29 Disclosure

Once Thom shows Sarah the note, and tells her about his beliefs, his investigation seems to spill out of him. One tiny incision and Sarah has unleashed a waterfall. Unknown to him, Sarah has struck at exactly the right time and will easily gain the knowledge she thought she would have to work much harder to attain.

From the front step, Thom takes Sarah upstairs and shows her the notebook (but doesn't let her read it), he shows her the collection of items he took from the lock up, he tells her about the lock up and how Daniel left it specifically for him, he tells her he met someone who has proof Daniel knew about his own death in advance.

Despite Thom's disclosures, Sarah doesn't reveal her own clues; such as the combination she discovered last night. She makes the noises of someone who is surprised to learn about Daniel and the prior knowledge of his own death. Yet there are some surprises. After all, Sarah has no idea there were such a multitude of clues and taunting items that had been left behind.

Thom can't help drawing parallels between Sarah and Emma, in particular the way he has responded to both asking the same questions. What does that mean for him and Emma? What does it mean for him and Sarah? Thom feels he might already know the answer but he shrugs his thoughts away.

Sarah seems fascinated by his discoveries. He imagines he is a detective again, revealing all the answers to a less superior counterpart, and he delights in showing her some of his findings and delights equally in holding parts back.

He lets Sarah touch the objects from the lock up but it physically pains him. With each fingerprint she leaves on them, he feels his muscles tensing. Eventually he has to collect them up and put them away again without explanation. She begins moving towards the notebook but Thom snatches it up.

"I'd rather you didn't," he says and shoves it into a drawer. Sarah tosses her hair, unconcerned and runs her hand over the note, which is still on the bed in front of her.

"So this was your first clue?" Sarah questions, not looking up.

"Yes. I found it in Daniel's room just before his funeral."

"I thought nobody was supposed to go in there?" Sarah half-mocks him but he doesn't appreciate it.

"Well I have more of a right than you do," Thom snaps and throws himself down on the end of the bed. Sarah instantly apologises. Silence fills the room like a flood and Thom closes his eyes, letting it conquer him.

"Have you told Val or Richard about this?" Sarah asks after a few minutes. Thom reluctantly reopens his eyes and turns towards her.

"Would you?"

"It would be pretty devastating for them."

"Do you think I should tell them?"

"*No*," Sarah answers harshly, and then coughs gently, "I mean… it probably wouldn't help anyone if you did." Thom nods gratefully but doesn't realise Sarah is only protecting herself. Yet, Thom also knows he is running on a stopwatch, sooner or later Aunty Val or Richard will start asking questions about his behaviour and actions. If the positions were reversed, he would've asked ages ago.

"It feels good to share some of this," Thom tells Sarah, who smiles whilst wrapping her hair around one of her fingers. It does feel good but, equally, Thom feels as though it's been easier than it should've been. How can the words slip off the tongue like soft butter, yet have such a heavy impact like a bludgeoning? Thom feels betrayed by his secrets.

"I'm so happy you decided to tell me what you've been thinking."

This troubles Thom. Has he really told her what he's 'thinking'? No, he has shown her some physical things that he's been consumed with. Has he told her how he feels isolated? Has he told her how he feels guilty and sad about Daniel? Has he told her he can't stop thinking about her red underwear and her black curls? No to all the above. She thinks she has submerged her head in his mind but she has only dipped a finger in.

"What are you going to do now?" Sarah persists.

What a question. Thom thinks and thinks more. He imagines he is in an interview and tries to think of an answer rapidly but it's not possible. After several minutes of bending his fingers backwards and forwards he says, "I'm going to keep trying. I don't know how but I'll keep trying."

As Thom speaks, he studies Sarah. At his words, he notices an odd flick of her head, a jut or a tick. Her chest is rising rapidly. Her forehead looks clammy. If he saw her in a lift now, he would guess she is having a panic attack. Yet she isn't in a lift, she's sitting on his bed having a quiet discussion. What is happening?

"Are you okay?"

"Yes, I'm fine," Sarah answers hastily. She gives Thom a wide-eyed look, pleading for him not to assault her and suddenly he thinks of her being attacked by the man in the street. He doesn't want to make her feel afraid. Why is he always so suspicious? Perhaps she is just hot or feeling a little ill, what business is it of his?

"Sarah, tell me about your family." Thom changes the subject, hoping this will relax her. Instead her face goes through several expressions in succession and Thom wants to kick himself. Her family were probably killed in some freak accident, he sighs inside.

"What do you want to know?" Sarah attempts a smile and Thom gets a sense she is stalling. More paranoia? Probably.

"Anything. I don't mind."

"Okay." Sarah pretends to be selecting information or memories but really she is constructing lies. Thom waits patiently, allowing her more time than he should.

"I have a brother called Peter who's three years older. He lives in Scotland now," she pauses and hastily adds, "my Mum and Dad live in the country so I don't see them much either."

"When is the last time you saw them?"

"Probably one of their birthdays, I can't remember exactly."

"Do you all get on?" Thom is getting nothing from the questions. What he wants to ask is; did the stranger tell the truth about you? Why haven't you mentioned your family before?

"Yes, mostly. All families have their problems sometimes," Sarah dismisses him confidently; anyone would've believed her.

"When you were having problems with your rent, couldn't you have asked them for help?"

"I was embarrassed really." She shrugs. It's moments like these she's had recently, when Sarah has begun to feel like a 'normal' person, who can have a conversation, who can answer unpredictable questions. Other times, she regresses and implicates herself without even trying.

"I understand. Sometimes it's hard to ask for help, especially from those closest to you."

"I'm glad I didn't ask them because I wouldn't have met you otherwise," Sarah says quietly, bowing her head as though she has just told him the most humiliating thing that has ever happened to her. She is a frightened innocent in this moment and her hushed confession makes Thom's obsession with Daniel thaw, for a few moments at least.

Thom gets up and moves next to her. She doesn't look up as he scratches her cheek with his thumbnail. He wishes he didn't have these bandages on anymore. He wants to press his palm against her warm cheek. Thom moves his thumb over her lips and she opens her mouth slightly, still keeping her eyes down. Thom wonders if she is only complying with his touch out of fear. Should he stop?

He can hear her swallowing, frozen except for her tongue brushing a layer of moistness over her lips. Thom touches the wetness with his thumb and imagines it is his tongue instead. Sarah hasn't met his gaze yet and Thom worries briefly, she is staring at his erection. Yet with most thoughts in this area, the worry quickly disperses.

Thom is about to boil over with tension, her icy ignorance acting in reverse. Hoping she won't scream, he kisses her. She finally meets his eyes, wide but not afraid, and grabs onto him. They kiss like they are grappling; it is hard, oddly diamagnetic. He finds, although she tries so hard to seem cold, her skin is as warm as other women's.

Thom isn't sure who pushes back first; he is still kissing her in his mind. His unfounded obsession with her has been partly indulged; he has felt those lips again and crushed her bouncy curls between his fingers. Strangely he also feels the desire to do it again turning his stomach like a violent urge to vomit.

They stare at each other for a few seconds, perhaps unsure that what they have done is 'right', perhaps still shocked that it has occurred, perhaps wanting more. Sarah stands up, smoothing her top as she does. As she passes Thom, she grazes the side of his neck with her fingers. Thom closes his eyes and a second later hears the door being closed with the same tenderness.

30 The Red Lock

I don't leave the house until the next day; bathing in the moment Thom removed the gap between us, holding our desire and curiosity in a violent whirlpool. He has calmed the waters with his soothing kiss and transferred the whirlpool into my stomach and my bouncing heartbeat.

I spent the evening sitting across from him whilst the family watched TV together, remembering the tough bristle of his stubble making my chin grow a rash and go slightly pink. Later, I stared at the rash and only felt happy. In the living room as I sat across from him, he looked over only once, neither smiling nor frowning, perhaps winking at me without moving at all.

I have forgiven him for telling Emma I know nothing, as he has now confided in me. He has let me get closer to him. She is irrelevant now. He can't want her if he kissed me, can he? He must think about me too. He must want me to help him like I always thought I needed to.

Yet I am still following up the address I found. Daniel must have left it there for me. I have an obligation to go to the address and see what is there waiting. Perhaps it is just something to tease me, perhaps there will be nothing there at all, or perhaps there will be something important there like I fear.

I can easily give this up, I tell myself. I can easily go back to the house and take Thom to bed with me, make him forget about Daniel too. I'm sure if I try I can dominate his attention and make Daniel release his talons on Thom's mind.

More than half of me wants to take this option. More than half of me wants to jump on a new train and leave Daniel's one behind where it belongs. Yet like the blood will always remain in traces on that tunnel wall, on the platform, underneath its chugging feet – similarly, he will chew on the corner of my mind until I do as he wants. He has left this message for me, as he'd left the note for Thom and we are pathetic to his remains. We are both like animals picking at his carcass.

This is why I am standing outside a post office with an address written in my mind. This is why I am reeling it off and checking it against the street sign on the corner. This is why.

But, Mum, I'm so afraid of what I might find. Will you stay with me?

The post office is a discreet looking building. There is nothing spectacular about it. As the clock had spoken to me on the day I pushed Daniel, the post office is tipping his hat to me. He is opening the door repeatedly, asking me inside. He is poking his tongue out.

I finally grab hold of his tongue and enter the post office. It's much more spacious inside than I expect, it is as wide as a concert hall. There are people queuing with their parcels, letters, and bill payments. I am searching for where the address intends to lead me, panic swelling up my throat. Finally, the sign floats into vision that reads 'Lockers'. An arrow points towards the back of the building.

This way, Mum…

I skip towards it; past the lines of people sending things to those they love or know, to the place where I think someone might have cared enough to leave something for me. Although what could Daniel possibly have left here? And do I really want to see it? The point is, he knew I'd find the clue. Thom missed it because he couldn't see things properly; it may as well have been invisible. This clue is definitely mine.

I greet the lockers with an ecstatic cry, as though I am meeting old friends. I reach out and touch their metal bodies, checking they aren't apparitions. They are definitely real. They are cold and smooth and beautiful. Dancing around the locker room, I count up the numbers until I finally reach my beloved – locker 11.

I chuckle to myself at the sight of the red lock securing it. He really has thought of everything and then with that thought, I frown. He has planned so much. He knew more about me than I seem to. How did he know I love the colour red? He has used it several times to speak to me. How did this stranger know all about me? And be certain that I would push him to his death?

I shake the thoughts away and instantly begin to turn the dials to the four numbers from the drawer, not shocked by it; I line them up like perfect soldiers to combination *1530*. Again, I want to correct it. Perhaps I should reset it to the correct time and afterwards go home and change the time on Thom's note with a red pen. That would be irony for Daniel, wouldn't it? Correcting his note like a schoolteacher, with the only colour appropriate for such tasks.

The lock gapes open in my grip, allowing me to twist it sideways and rip it away from the body it has hung from like a piercing. The locker is now unlocked, ready to be opened, ready... *Go!* I tell myself and fling it open, expecting ghouls to fly out or a hammer to swing towards me and crunch every bone in my face.

Yet everything is still. Nothing comes towards me out of the locker. Nothing is hiding in there to bite my fingers off, one by one. Inside there are only a few small objects. A red scarf, origami shapes made from red paper, a brown file and a few letters with the name Daniel written on the front. The handwriting looks familiar yet I can't place it. The red shapes mean nothing to me, the scarf seemingly useless when I am wearing one exactly like it. The file is fat and bulging, squashed together with two fat elastic bands, holding its secrets inside.

Mum, what do you think it all is? I wonder if you'd tell me to just shut the locker door and leave it all here. But how can I do that?

Checking nobody is watching, I empty all of the contents into my bag. The fat file is a monster, its corners pressing against the closed zip, bursting to spill its contents. A few strands of the scarf get caught in the zip but I stuff them back inside and hastily pull the bag onto my shoulder. I close the locker and hang the lock back in its place, locking it without thinking.

I hug my bag as I pass through the crowds, anxious someone will try to steal it or that some undercover policeman, who has been following me without my knowledge, will suddenly reveal himself and demand I hand it to him. I wouldn't be able to hand it over though, not even Thom could prise the bag handles from my bloodless fist.

31 The Intervention

As Sarah is searching for a safe place to examine her items, Thom is on the living room sofa, staring at a family picture. It is a photo from about four years ago when Aunty Val and the three of them took a day trip to a theme park. They are all smiling in the photo, all the outward 'signs' point to a happy family but Thom wants to rip it apart now. Underneath Daniel's shy smile there is only hate and the desire to destroy others, to destroy all of them.

Thom is so engrossed in his dark interpretation of the photo that he only notices the others when their shadows drift over it. He lifts his head up reluctantly, yet is still undeservedly warmed by Aunty Val's smile as she lowers herself beside him. Richard enters the room behind her and before taking a seat in his usual armchair opposite, empties his pockets of a screwdriver and some nails. For some reason, he thinks carrying these things will keep him prepared or something. Yet, can he fix us all with some nails and a screwdriver?

Aunty Val notices the photo he is holding and runs her hand over it, her mouth stuck like a cross, a smile overlapped with a frown. Her fingers linger over Daniel for a split second and then fall into her lap. She wraps her other arm around Thom and squeezes him to her. Part of him melts into her familiar form, the part that also wants to find Sarah and melt into her warm moist mouth. Another part doesn't want to be squeezed in case all his dark thoughts and questions and anger gush out.

"Can we talk to you, Thom?" Aunty Val asks gently, like someone approaching an addict who needs rescuing. Thom smiles weakly and

273

nods. He glances over at Richard, who has his hands clasped together in front of him, seeming like a doctor or a CEO delivering bad news. Thom has an urge to simply jump up and run.

"Richard saw what happened to Daniel's room," Aunty Val begins warily and continues gently as though Thom is a landmine, "and your hands have been injured recently. So we put two and two together..."

"If you want to ask me about something, why don't you just do it?" Thom says flatly, staring her directly in the face until she blinks rapidly and looks down.

"Thom, did you smash up Daniel's room?" she asks quietly.

Thom casts a glance in Richard's direction and announces, "Yes, I did."

With his omission, the air in the room tightens. "Why would you do that, darling?" Aunty Val's expression is that of Thom having peed all over her favourite possessions. A storm is churning inside Thom, and he can't look at Richard or Aunty Val for the next few moments or he fears he will detonate. One sight of them will split him in two and he doesn't know if he will be able to fuse the nuclei back together and exist as before.

"Did you look around in there, Aunty?" Thom doesn't want to do this but she is forcing him. It's her own fault if she wants to find out this way.

"No. I just stood in the doorway and looked in. I still can't do that."

"And you Rich, did you check anywhere?" Thom persists.

He hears Richard shuffling in his chair. "No, I just saw the wardrobe," he pauses, and even from the corner of his eye, Thom sees him tugging at his ear lobe. "What are you getting at?"

"I didn't want to tell you," Thom moans.

"Tell us what?" Aunty Val whispers but her voice is so tight Thom can see she wants to cork her ears. She still feels like a pane of glass without a frame. She has lost one child and another of her 'children' has become consumed by something ever since. What can she do to save the one who still lives?

"It's all empty." Thom shrugs, almost bored with the revelation. He and Sarah have both seen this revelation through each phase and they

274

have reached the surface again, not wanting to go back for those still struggling below.

Richard sits forward in his chair. "What's empty? Stop talking in riddles, Thom," Richard chides.

"When have I ever spoken in riddles?"

"We spoke to Emma. She's worried about you," Aunty Val adds, trying to quell the rising argument, not realising she is only sparking more anger in Thom.

"She's just trying to get back at me because she got knocked back."

"You shouldn't be so rude about her," Richard says.

"Do *you* always act the way you're supposed to, Rich?" Thom snarls.

Richard shrinks back in his chair and gives him a shocked smile. "Of course not, but what does that have to do with anything?"

"You've both come in here to judge me, haven't you? Because you don't agree with how I've been acting, because you think I wrote those horrible things in that notebook, because I haven't acted the same as *you*." Thom spits each sound. Aunty Val begins to breathe shortly beside him and he has to use all his strength to scream at his body not to attend to her.

"We just want to know what's going on." Richard stands up and waves his hands around in the air, someone drowning or waving to a boat pulling away from him. Thom leans forward, rubbing his eyes into his palms.

"I tried to tell you about his room, didn't I?"

"*What*, that it's empty? What does that mean?" Richard stares at Thom.

"Exactly what I said!" Thom barks back.

"Why would his room be empty? He was living in there, Thom. The day before he died, he slept in there." Richard is pacing the space in front of the sofa, as if he is a coach trying to decide what to tell his team at half time. Thom hates to see Richard troubled, he hates to see him pulling at his ear again like the day they first discussed Daniel and smoked together in Thom's room. Yet, this is what they are both asking him for – discomfort, awkwardness, and revelations.

"I don't know, Richard. But... the drawers are empty, the wardrobe is empty, there's not a scrap of anything in there. Believe me, *I've looked*." Thom is jerking in his seat, so much that Aunty Val reaches over and presses down on his leg. Thom tries to regulate his breathing, in the same instance wondering why Aunty Val seems so composed.

"How could there be nothing, Thom?" Aunty Val asks quietly.

"You think I know? I've thought and thought and thought again about all this and I have no answers. If you were expecting me to help you out, I'm afraid I'll have to let you down."

"Why are you being so aggressive about this?" Richard is leaning towards Thom, his hands stretched towards him, yet he doesn't touch Thom. "Does this have something to do with Sarah?"

"What have you got against her Rich? Leave her alone," Thom cautions him and continues angrily, "I've been dealing with all this for weeks and suddenly *you're* interested. Oh woe betides me, I've known this fact for about five minutes and I want all the fucking answers!"

"Thom, please don't swear," Aunty Val says. Thom is about to say something biting when he looks into her eyes and changes his mind.

"Who cares if he swears, Mum? Have you heard what he's been saying?" Richard kicks the carpet. All his muscles and veins are Braille on the surface of his skin. "He says Daniel emptied his room somehow, without our knowledge! He's been really rude about his girlfriend and he's started hanging around with some strange woman. And when we ask him to help us understand something, he completely turns on us like a stupid dog. You have to get him to talk normally Mum, *please*."

Richard slumps into the armchair and stares at the ceiling. Perhaps he is praying and, if he is, Thom wants to tell him that God doesn't exist. Like he told Sarah, He's a fabrication. He's a lifeboat that people search for in a violent sea but one that deflated itself for him after his parents died.

"Richard, would you mind leaving us alone for a moment?" Aunty Val asks as softly as ever, seemingly oblivious to the last ten minutes. She sits next to Thom with a straight back and with her hands placed by either leg. Thom remembers, in that pose, why he respects her so much. Why has he been pushing her away?

Richard stares at her, yet after a few seconds, he pushes himself to his feet. He gives them both a concerned frown and leaves the room with a few large strides. As he slams the door, Aunty Val swivels her body round to face Thom and makes him do the same. Thom hears the clock again and with the slam of the door, the hands instantly get down onto their knees and begin to crawl around the clock face.

"Aunty, I'm..." She puts her hand up and Thom closes his lips immediately.

"Thom, I want to speak." She massages her forehead briefly. "Darling, I'm so worried about you. And I have to tell you..." Aunty Val's lips are choking on shapes. Thom reaches up, sweeping her cheek with his fingers briefly, meeting her gaze. "I have to tell you something..." she resumes, "I'm afraid, Thom. More afraid than I've ever been." Aunty Val has weighed down the life-raft and must empty the excess out before she sinks. Thom isn't sure he wants to hold all her excess though.

"Aunty, I don't..."

"I'm not finished, Thom," she warns. Thom bows his head.

"What I'm trying to say to you is... well, you know how important you are to me, don't you darling?" Thom nods quietly. "Well, when your parents died, I felt so worried about you. I didn't know if I could help you..." Thom doesn't know why they always seem to be talking about this subject lately. Why does she want to keep returning to this? Why does she want to poke and infect the wound? He wants to tell her that their deaths are necrotic tissue that he would be happy to surgically remove.

"You are so important to me. I love you so much darling. And I'm so proud of you, do you know? Well, I'm sure you do. I'm just saying that I'm proud of you for everything but most of all, for how you dealt with it. How you rebuilt your life and let us be your family..."

"Aunty Val, this isn't helping anyone," Thom pleads; tempted to gouge his eyeballs out and stuff them in his ears.

"Thom, please, I've always been so amazed by your strength. I know you can get yourself back on track." Aunty Val grabs one of Thom's hands between hers. It is a clamp, Thom can only dream of escaping it. All the while, he is chuckling inside his mind at her use of the word 'track'. He is on a track that's true, just not the one she hopes he is on.

"What's been worrying you? Why have you been so angry?"

"My cousin dying isn't enough?" Thom challenges. Aunty Val squints and looks away as though he has squirted lemon juice in her eye.

"Of course it's enough... But I asked you about more than that."

"I told you about his room Aunty Val. If you don't believe me, check for yourself!" Thom tosses her hand back to her. She stares at it, an invisible gash leaking blood down her arm.

"But you haven't said why you think it happened. Was he moving out? What do you know about it, Thom?"

"I'm trying to protect you." Thom grinds his teeth with each vibration of his tongue. Aunty Val is putting her organs on a stick and ramming them into a fire. Why is she asking him to hurt her?

"Sometimes you look so much like him," Aunty Val whispers.

"*What?*" Thom feels his brain splitting in two. "Don't say that ever again."

"Why?"

"I don't want to look like him or be like him or remind anyone of him *ever*. Do you understand that?" Thom speaks the sentence slowly and she doesn't appreciate it.

"Fine, forget that." She bites her lip. "But what are you hiding about Daniel? If you're sad about losing him, we can understand. We've felt all the emotions too." Aunty Val grabs him by both shoulders and holds him steady. Thom curls his hands into balls and stabs his own skin.

"He's the one who hid things Aunty."

"Is this my fault?" Aunty Val asks suddenly.

"I'm not saying you're a bad parent. This isn't about you."

"Have I been there for you, Thom?" Aunty Val pulls him closer. Her breath makes his cheek moist.

"Yes Aunty, yes," he stutters, trying to regain a distance between them. "But I have to tell you something."

"You're frightening me, Thom."

"I'm frightened too." Thom is shaking to emphasise his point.

"Just tell me. You *can* tell me." She is gritting her teeth. Her mouth is twitching. He is worried what he will do to her. He might as well stone her to death. This way he is instead throwing her overboard into an unsure sea that could drive her anywhere and even make her lungs so heavy she might sink.

"He knew, Aunty Val," Thom manages to say. Again, he has failed to articulate the whole sentence he intended. Speech has floated away from him once again.

"What did he know?" Aunty Val shudders, her voice shrill. Thom gets the sense she already knows something, she seems too quick to panic. Yet she hasn't given any hints before. Is he being paranoid yet again?

"That he was going to die," Thom surrenders.

Her eyes instantly roll, and she collapses.

32 Red Gifts

I scurry through the city, a fugitive, a dirty rat trying not to get stamped on, and finally settle underneath a tree in a small green. I spend twenty minutes scanning the surrounding area for spies. I even focus on several nearby bushes and monitor them for irregular movement and stare up into the branches above, watching the sway until I feel I can trust it.

I'm so glad I have you with me. I can't face this alone, Mum.

Unzipping my bag, my chest grows increasingly hollow the wider the mouth opens. I wonder what will happen when I reach inside, whether I will fall in and keep sinking. Trembling, I close my eyes and plunge my hand within. I let my fingers drift around the items, trying to feel Daniel's presence pulsating from them. Yet there is nothing and

I fear I have lost him, my pulse racing for someone else instead.

I pluck out the red origami first and examine each one. One has been made into a swan, another a flower, another looks like a horse. There are six altogether. Someone has obviously taken time making these, each fold is precise, each structure complex. I place them in a line next to me, assembling an army.

I take up the scarf; hold it to my nose as I did with his scarf after the push. It doesn't smell of him. I am even more disappointed because he has faded from the original scarf too. Slowly I am losing him and I can't weave him back into the threads. I toss the scarf aside, making sure it doesn't mix with my original scarf that at least has some sentimental value.

I decide to tackle the letters next. I stare at his name on the front trying to decipher the author, yet I am blank. Something is familiar in the way the capital D is slanted, aggressively sharp and with a slight dip in the top half. I know who wrote this, why can't I place them?

I lose patience and turn the envelope over. The seal has already been broken, the lip is cracked and tattered, the adhesive clumped together and dried. With tremors still echoing through me, I fumble with the opening until it slowly gives in. Inside I see white paper folded into three. Holding my breath, I snatch the paper from inside, the swiping sound of its exit like a guillotine rushing towards a helpless neck.

I unfold the paper and find a letter. Looking at the first word it stops me dead: *Daniel*. I feel like I have been hurtled into a brick wall, not just because of what the first word is but because I finally connect the writing with the owner. Like my shadow finally catching up with me, I realise the author is me.

Mum, mum, why is my writing on this page?

After stalling on the first word, I eventually manage to break through the current and begin to take in the rest of the letter:

I can't stop thinking about you. I love the gifts you sent me, as always. I take them out when everyone is asleep and stare them. I like to imagine your hands when you were making them, how you wanted to make me smile, how you snuck them in for me without the others seeing.

I have to hide your gifts under one of the floorboards so at night I feel like I am freeing them. I wish I could show everyone how thoughtful and loving you are. I really don't deserve to have you giving me attention but I thrive on it, it keeps me positive every day I am in this prison.

The doctors have been asking about you but I won't tell them anything. They just want to catch us out. They don't want me to be happy or connect with anyone, and they want to keep me in here forever.

I will never forget when I first met you, how you kept trying to make me smile because I looked so sad. I hadn't spoken properly to anyone in months but you managed to connect with me. I actually feel like you care for me. I haven't felt that since my Mum and before that, the only person I thought loved me ended up hurting me in the worst way.

I know you won't hurt me. I can't wait to get out of here and spend time with you in the real world, among the birds, the wind that thrashes in the trees, the coldness of the lake outside the window I can never touch.

I particularly love the bird you made me. It gives me hope that I will escape one day. I can't wait to see you again; I'm waiting for you here.

There is no signature. Yet the letter needs none. This is written by me, there are no doubts. If I needed clues, I could even authenticate my identity by underlining the references to not having you around anymore and someone who I cared about hurting me 'in the worst way'.

You know all about it, don't you, Mum? We can't deny that it's me in this letter.

This is my handwriting. This is a letter written in a hospital. This is a letter to the man I pushed in front of a train. All the details point to me being the author yet I can't understand this. I am submerged in water; my fingertips are burnt to numbness, my nose clogged with blood. What do these combinations of black marks really mean?

This letter is a classic example of a yearning lover writing to her beloved. Even when I reread it several times, I have a notion it must be a prank or something that Daniel wrote to torture me. Yet the handwriting is undoubtedly mine. I can't deny it more than I can deny my own reflection.

I drop the letter and tear open another envelope. This letter contains much of the same musings. I toss this one down and grab the next one, shivering as I read yet more similar expressions of adoration. I almost scream when I get to the bottom where in shaky writing, I see: *I think I love you Daniel.*

I screw the paper up and hurl it aside. I jump up and stamp on the origami army beside me before they can lead a mutiny against me. I start beating my fists against the tree behind me and kicking it until my toes bruise and groan in my shoes.

How could I have written these things? I have no recollection of any of these words, their combinations, or even the thought of picking up a pen to scratch them out. It is as if I am staring at a pile of vomit confined to a page, I have no idea where to start picking it apart to make sense.

Is it true that I cared for Daniel, Mum? And if I did know him at the hospital and had all these feelings for him, how did it result in my pushing him in front of a train? I wish you were here to help me understand this. I wish you were here to hold me and stop me shivering.

I slump next to the tree again, my breath a rag that seems as filled with holes as my memory. Trying to refocus my heartbeat and sensing the water layer over my eyes blistering, I drag the file towards me. I figure things can't get much worse.

I fight off the elastic bands around the file, imagining I am a child prodding my fingers into a mousetrap. I have to succumb though. I have no choice but to continue with my journey into the darkness of my unknown past. The file opens easily and I prepare myself for a shotgun to annihilate my dizzy head.

The first page is nothing alarming. It is my admission record to the hospital, all the standard details: age, name, gender, date of admission, current drug treatment, notes on special requirements, the reason I'd been sectioned.

There are several dull pages of this. Then something different; some handwritten pages making notes on some of my counselling sessions with Doctor Rosey. None of this is particularly new to me either. I can't recall the memory of actually talking to Doctor Rosey but the subjects seem familiar. The subjects are those I discussed even just before I left the hospital. The guilt over losing you, the helplessness of being taken advantage of, the confusion over why you left me, the anger and fear of living a day-to-day life. I have no idea why they let me out of there…

Still pondering the failures of the system, I come across another strange document. On the header it has the address of the hospital and the word 'memo' written in large red letters. Underneath are the words 'Attention: Serious Issue Reported'. I continue reading. The memo describes an incident of a staff member being caught acting inappropriately with one of the patients. Apparently, the reported staff member was suspended (pending investigation), but the memo also notes that several witnesses had come forward saying the staff member and patient were definitely having an inappropriate relationship. Furthermore, the staff members had stepped up their vigilance on this particular patient, a certain patient named Alice…

The evidence is a mountain that towers above me. The branches are waving at me. I watch them stretching higher in the sky or maybe I am sinking into the mud, or the tectonic plates of the earth have hiccupped underneath me.

33 The Awakening

As Thom cradles Aunty Val on the sofa, the door blasts open. Richard rushes over to Aunty Val and wrestles her out of Thom's arms. "What have you done to her?" he asks, shaking her gently. She is already stirring but keeps her eyes closed. Richard is staring at Thom like he is holding a knife covered with blood.

"We were just talking. She's fine."

"She doesn't look fine," Richard screeches.

"I didn't hurt her, Richard," Thom says, yet swallows heavily. Is he sure about that? He just told her about her recently deceased son knowing he was going to die? Surely that is hurting her, not physically, but nonetheless…

"I can't believe the way you're acting. You're being exactly like him before he died." Richard is stroking Aunty Val's hair. She is mumbling but Thom can't understand a word.

"What?" Thom sits on the edge of the sofa, trying to look open for negotiations.

"He hurt her too," Richard tells him, shaking his head as if he should have known this would happen. Thom can't believe Richard could draw these comparisons between him and Daniel. How long has he been thinking these things? Why hasn't he said something before?

"How did he hurt her?" Thom asks, not bothering to defend himself again. He doesn't think Richard wants to hear it; he is convinced he is Aunty Val's protector and Thom the attacker.

"He hit her," Richard answers flatly.

"What? When?" Thom lurches towards them, making Richard hug Aunty Val even closer to his chest. Thom settles back again, not wanting to frighten Richard's information away.

"About two months before." Richard's answers are curt; his lips so tight Thom can't see even a minute fraction of his usual smile. Thom can't remember seeing Richard this angry. In a way, Thom is proud to see him stand up for something, yet he wishes he didn't have to be the receiver.

"Why Rich?"

"She wouldn't say." Richard gestures to the awakening Aunty Val. "I just came home to see this horrible purple bruise on her face. She tried to lie but I could tell straight away. Something had been going on with them for months."

"Why didn't you mention this before?" Thom jumps to his feet. "Maybe it would've helped with everything, with finding out…"

"Shut up!" Richard shouts, so bloodthirsty that Thom halts instantly. "This has nothing to do with your stupid quest or whatever it is. This is about him and now you, hurting *my* mum."

Aunty Val opens her eyes and stares up at her devoted son. I envy her for having someone whose job it is to protect her, who will always love her no matter what. Even though Thom has pretended he can play that role too, he isn't her real son and he isn't doing a good job of protecting anyone, even himself.

"I love her. I wouldn't hurt her on purpose," Thom insists, squeezing his bandaged hands until they begin to ache. He deserves the pain so he increases the pressure the more they throb.

"But you still did!," Richard shouts.

Thom feels like someone has stabbed a needle into his lung and is letting all the air rush out of him. He remembers the day he received the phone call from Richard, the tears in Richard's voice. He has failed them.

"I'm sorry Richard… Aunty. I haven't meant to do anything bad."

"I should smack you in the face like I did him," Richard swears but Aunty Val grabs his clenched fist and holds it against her cheek. He slackens the tension but gives Thom a dark look, warning him that he is still capable.

"He didn't do anything, Richard," Aunty Val says, letting him help her to sit up. He holds onto her torso like a human stabiliser.

"Why were you unconscious then?" Richard persists, feeling like a child being lied to. He is certain he has missed something and wants to be included.

"We were just talking, weren't we Thom?" She reaches a long way in order to touch Thom's knee again, nodding in a discreet way only he understands. She doesn't want him to tell Richard what he told her. Why? Yet, Thom nods quietly anyway.

"I just felt a bit woozy." She waves into the air and proceeds to gently peel away Richard's hold from her chest. Richard stares at his rejected hands.

"What were you talking about mum?"

"It's nothing darling." Aunty Val gives him a broad smile. Thom's stomach spins at the sight of it. He can't help feeling she is a mother protecting her last innocent child from the world. Thom is already lost, Daniel already dead, she only has Richard now. He wants to hold out his hands and beg her *save me too; I need you to keep me from falling apart*. Yet Thom can't make his muscles tense to speak, they are tumours impeding function and he doesn't know if they will ever be granted freedom.

"I think you should leave, Thom. At least for a few days," Richard suggests coldly. Thom doesn't hesitate; he ejects himself from the sofa and attempts to eject himself from their lives. Feeling he is now the tumour, he decides to hack himself out as quickly as possible.

"No, Thom," Aunty Val chases and grabs him by the hand. "We need you here."

Thom shakes her off. "He's right, I think we all need some space." Aunty Val grabs tighter so Thom pulls away more roughly. He may as well have kicked her to the floor. In the next moment she sinks to her knees anyway.

"I need you Thom."

"Aunty Val *please*..." Thom dismisses her, with a desire to stab himself in the heart instead of watching this sad display. Richard stands up behind her and presses her against him. She is still on her knees so she holds onto him through his legs. He is staring at Thom, a solemn lip clashing with his furrowed eyes.

"You have to come back," Richard tells him firmly. Thom nods, fascinated by the words. Come back to where? To the house? To his old self? To them?

Thom turns sharply and shuts them in, pausing in the hallway. He glances up the stairs, expecting to see Sarah on the top step or hoping to visualise his way back. He takes the few small steps to the front door and leaves the house. The wind whispers to him outside *come back, come back*. He doesn't see Aunty Val peering out of the front window, her face raining on the inside.

34 The Nose Bleed

I run all the way back to the Mansen house, doubled over with breathlessness and sickness by the time I arrive. Crouching in the middle of the road for several minutes, I gasp and suck in air, not concerned if a car were to speed around the corner and bulldoze me into the asphalt.

My bag feels like it's swelling with rocks but I haven't been able to let go of it. I don't want to lose the evidence or let my past escape from my memory ever again. I want to be able to say I have knowledge of something, even if it's something bad.

Mum, it's time to get the past back. It's time for me to realise you can't help anymore.

I think about going back to the house but my feet don't want to go that way. They walk down the middle of the road, slowly and even leisurely, until I reach the part where the ascending road begins to roll downhill again. I reach my hands into the air and begin saying 'Michael', louder and louder until I am screaming and sobbing.

I am sobbing heavily when the figure appears out of the darkness. He presses me against him like he wants to seep into my body, trying to calm my moaning. His familiar smell wraps around me like his embrace and I run through several memories in my mind of a time when we were happier, when we didn't stand on two opposite ends of a scale that were never level.

"Oh Alice..." He coos and kisses my forehead. "Are you okay?" he asks and I wonder why I have been running away from him for so long. He does love me. He didn't mean to disappoint me by deserting us. I can tell by his digging fingernails that he is sorry.

"I'm not okay," I snort, burying myself into his clump of curls. I feel like I am reacquainting with myself, his hair so similar to mine, his bony nose the mirror of my own. I'm returning to the life I thought I lost and it is easier than I imagined. I can talk to him. I can act human. There is hope for me.

"Whatever it is, I'll help you," Michael promises, holding my face between his hands like people do when they are being earnest. I rest my forehead against his, reminding myself of his clammy blemished skin. "I love you Alice, I'm so sorry about everything. I won't let you down again."

For some unknown reason, I believe him. I have been trying to escape him for weeks but hearing his voice now, it is as strong and honest as a piece of steel. I need him anyway. I can't deal with these new revelations alone.

"Will you tell me the truth, Michael?"

"I will if I can." He stares into my eyes, not shaken by the increasingly cold wind thrashing all around us. I feel like we are in a bubble that nothing can touch, everything is frozen except the two of us.

"Tell me about a man named Daniel, then," I say. Michael's eyes protrude in response. There is no attempt at disguise.

"How do you know…" Michael rolls silence around his tongue for a moment but finally finishes, "…about him?"

My insides instantly sink. He has confirmed it. It's true. I don't even need to ask any more questions, the file is a hub of answers. Yet to keep our interaction going, I say, "I found a file from the hospital."

"I wish you hadn't found out about this." He lowers his head.

"Why didn't anyone tell me?"

"We thought it would make things worse." Michael pouts. "But if you want to know more, maybe we should take you to see Doctor Rosey."

I instantly pull out of his hold. He stiffens up and reaches his hands out towards me. "Please, don't run." He is standing like he is ready to chase me.

I shake my head and reassure him, "I'm sick of running."

"Thank goodness," he sighs happily and brings his feet back together. I want to throw my arms up in victory at this small gesture. It seems that suddenly Michael and I are communicating.

"I don't trust that Doctor. She wants to take me back to the hospital."

"I won't let her," Michael slants his head, "…not again. You can come and stay with me."

"But your family…"

"My family will get to know you and support you." He nods seriously. My chest is threatening to rupture with elation. Another small part of me wonders if Michael is merely trying to trick me. It has happened before. What makes this situation different?

Reading my mind, Michael adds, "you can trust me this time Alice. I won't let you down again. I've realised..." he inhales deeply, "I should've been there."

"I want to believe you." I begin pulling at my hair and letting the curls spring back. Michael watches, a smile rising on his lips.

"It's so good to talk with you like this again."

"I'm still ill Michael." My admission makes him smile even wider.

"That's a good step." He takes me by the shoulders, a brother praising his little sister. It's obvious but I enjoy every moment. I've done nothing for him to praise the last few years.

"Come and see the Doctor now, we'll talk to her together."

Michael starts leading me towards his car but suddenly he is wrenched backwards. I spin round and see Thom standing there. He is shaking like an infected dog, salivating as he stares at Michael.

"Get your hands off her," Thom snarls, his jaws crunching loudly.

Michael instantly remembers Thom and doesn't take him seriously. "What business is it of yours?" Michael stares Thom down. What Michael doesn't realise is that Thom thinks he's a rapist, that Thom has just been accused by his cousin of hurting his Aunty, and that Thom would love to skin someone alive.

"She told me about you." Thom jabs him.

I jump in front of Michael and raise my hands. "Thom, you don't understand."

"No, I do Sarah," he growls. "And I won't let him scare you anymore."

"You have the wrong idea," I appeal to him again.

Thom's nose is hooked upwards with disgust, his nostrils flaring like tunnels. I want to pull him close to me to make him settle but equally I can't stand to see his face, taunting me with the living vision of the man who has made me sick with obsession and perhaps even love?

"The wrong idea?" Thom cries. "This bastard raped you." Thom jabs Michael over my shoulder. Behind me, Michael lurches forward like a spring and I am pushed aside.

"What did *he* say?" Michael shouts, turning white. "Are you crazy?"

"You have the nerve to call *me* crazy you fucking pervert!" Thom shrieks and grabs Michael by the throat. I hear Michael cough and grunt, trying to claw at Thom's hand. I pull on Thom's arm but he shoves me backwards, making me stumble over. I can only watch Thom pushing Michael against a car, throwing his fist into Michael's face. Whilst I try to hoist myself up, my legs suddenly numb.

Michael is attempting to push Thom off him, his face swelling with desperation and blood. When Thom finally releases him, I am holding myself up at the end of the car, blowing out the air I have been holding. Yet my relief is short as in the next instant, Thom begins punching the still recovering Michael, as if he is a piece of meat he needs to tenderise.

As Michael slumps down the car, with blood exploding from his nose like a dam battered by flood, I squeeze myself between them. Thom narrowly misses striking me with yet another punch intended for my brother. He leaps away from me. I think about saying something to him, then shake my head and turn away.

Michael is lying face up on the floor, leaning his head as far back as he can, staring up at me drowsily. He is probably thinking about what a terrible person I am, or what a terrible person Thom is, or why he is being called a rapist when he is not.

I kneel next to him, bowing my head close to his body, atoning for my lie and its bloody offshoots that pierced him like shrapnel. He grabs my hand. I stroke his sweaty forehead and press my scarf against his bloodied nose until he squints and groans. This scarf is no longer a bind; it is a bandage.

"What the hell are you doing?" Thom yelps from behind me.

"You have no right to hurt him."

"But he hurt you!" Thom cries as I help Michael sit up, and then turn to face him.

"I told you it was fine and you ignored me anyway. Why didn't you listen?" I hit at his chest, hoping to bruise him.

"But you told me he hurt you. I don't understand." Thom holds his head with clawed fingers, backing away from the source of his throbbing confusion.

"Why did you tell him that, Alice?" Michael coughs, equally as perplexed.

"Don't call her Alice." Thom snarls and kicks Michael in the ribs, who yelps sadly and slouches sideways. I drive forward and shove Thom into the middle of the road. He stumbles as if he is standing on one leg. He holds his hands up, to help him balance and to reach out.

"Stop hurting my brother," I spit. A current of shock mixed with awareness thrashes over his expression. He drops his arms, his body a balloon wailing into a slump.

"Your brother?" Thom squeaks, glancing at Michael on the floor, who is pushing himself up with a half press up.

"This is Michael," I say blankly.

"But you told me..."

"I know what I told you," I interject before he can repeat my poisonous lie. "I told you that because I didn't want you to listen to Michael." I step closer to him but he immediately backs away the same distance, afraid I have a disease that is airborne.

"Why Sarah?" Thom's words seem to froth from his mouth. "Or Alice or *whatever* your name is," he sulks.

"I've been ill for a long time and I haven't been ready to face up to that. I didn't want Michael to disturb my life."

"You were ill?" Thom repeats, his tone lacking surprise.

"I have had some issues... well, I still do." I hear the words and feel them clear and bold in my mind. There is no static or interference. I see the truth like a fact in an encyclopaedia. "I've been running away from dealing with them for ages. Even though they let me out of the hospital, I'm really not better."

"The hospital?" Thom shouts out. His mouth moves like he is a dummy being manipulated by somebody else. He isn't thinking about talking, he is merely performing it.

"I spent time in a hospital Thom. And just for the record, I *was* raped."

"Why should I believe you now?" he mumbles dejectedly.

"Would I really want to tell you all these bad things about myself if they weren't true?" I move towards him again and manage to sweep my hand across his.

"Well, you told me your brother was the one who raped you," he reminds me and I bow my head.

"I shouldn't have done that," I pause and look into his face again. "I was afraid that he would tell you all these bad things about me and you would hate me. But I should've realised it would have been the best thing to get this all out, to realise how sick I've been."

Thom shakes himself out and begins to turn away, then snaps back, kicking the floor between us. "This is all crazy. You've been lying to me this whole time."

"You didn't actually ask that much about my past. And when I told you anything, you just accepted it." I don't mean to criticise but Thom has no other way to hear this.

"You're blaming me?" he cries, his mouth hanging open. I want to reach over and press it closed, fix one of the growing holes in his life.

"No, I'm sorry."

"I can't believe this Sarah." Thom screws up his face. In this moment I feel superior because he is falling apart. I decide to close the gap between us and take him by the hands, as Michael had done with me only ten minutes before.

"It's not your fault. I shouldn't have lied." I want to hug him but his bruised knuckles stop me. Thom's legs are wobbling, his face a piece of paper gradually crumpling, creating passages for his tears.

"I can't deal with this right now. I need *you*…" he whimpers.

"You're okay Thom, I know you are," I say but I am lying again. Yet this is a lie that is needed, an exit clause and a scaffold.

"But Richard thinks I'm trying to hurt Aunty Val." Thom pulls me towards him and grabs onto me. I have to push him away. "He told me to leave and now… now you hate me too." He tries grabbing me again for a few seconds, I instinctively squeeze him but remember to urge him away again. Thom's posture drops and he shuffles backwards.

"What did you do, Thom? Why did he tell you to leave?"

"They don't understand Daniel," Thom sighs and looks ready to lie on the ground and wait for the tyres to crush him into a pile of slush and chunks. Although Thom thinks he has nothing left, his words actually repair the smallest thread of our relationship. It is a microscopic fragment on a large tapestry. If anyone can empathise with the damage Daniel has done, I can.

"You can stay at my place. It's a horrible bedsit but at least it's somewhere," I say, giving him the address and the key. Thom nods at the gesture and holds the key tightly in his hand, a hook and line keeping him attached to the shore, no matter how weakly.

I force myself to turn my back on Thom and finally help my brother to stand. Michael leans against me and we walk towards the car. I hurriedly help Michael into the passenger's seat and he reluctantly hands over the keys when I fasten myself in the driver's seat.

In the mirror, I struggle to pick Thom out in the darkness of the street. He is a thin line amongst trees and lamp-posts and the buildings. I shake the dull smudge of him out of sight and start the car, knowing I have to get to my bedsit before he does.

35 The Copper Smell

After we leave Thom in the road, merging into blackness; we stop by the bedsit. I tell Michael to wait in the car, his blood drying and cracked, and make my way inside.

I have to knock on the landlord's door and ask him to let me in, saying I have lost my key. Thankfully he is so drunk he can't even climb the stairs, so he is forced to lend me his keys and leave me grope-free on this occasion. He asks me to return them when I've finished.

The lock opens with a crack, adding sound effects to my desertion. *If I'd had the choice, I'd never have come back so count yourself lucky*, I chide the door. Then I toss the thought away with a quick shimmy of my head. Exactly that kind of thought made me crazy in the first place…

The room is dark inside, so to avoid surprises I switch on the light and shut the door behind me. *So I'm back*, I tell myself, pursing my lips. The plants are much further into their decomposing process, the rat and insects are still motionless on the floor with several additions, and it still smells of damp and emptiness.

I instantly see some of the incriminating pointers that I must remove before Thom arrives. The paper from the day of the murder is buried in the duvet, thankfully folded so I don't have to see the photo of Daniel again, the menacing photo that now looks even more eerie with the knowledge I now have. I thought he had been speaking to me when I first saw it and I was right. Yet I still have no idea how he made me kill him.

I think about keeping the paper but decide it's too much of a risk. Thom could easily look through my things and find it. Why would I have kept this paper and no others? I go to the kitchen cabinet and collect a plastic bag, dumping the paper inside. I use a dustpan to collect the dead insects and rat, and pour them inside too; sadly adding the deceased plant. Everything here is dead.

This place always seemed like a desperate and dank environment but looking around now, when I feel like each breath is clearer and deeper, it appears much worse. How could I have ever lived here? How had I not grown diseased or died out of solidarity with the fading plants and insects?

I can't see anything else in the bedsit that can alarm Thom. The other links to Daniel are the scarf, which Michael has, and the contents of my bag, that are safe in the car at present. In fact there is little in this room that reveals much about me. There is the bare amount of clothes, a few books and tapes, basic living provisions. This place has never been my home and for a while the concept of 'home' hasn't been as prevalent as it should have been, too focussed on my stalking Daniel.

Yet I want a home now. I want to have somewhere that isn't full of decay and sucks the breath from any living object forced to live within its walls.

More contented, I tie the bag up. I don't bother to say goodbye to the bedsit or take the vision of it away inside my mind. Instead I have an urge to close my eyes whilst I walk to the door, not wanting to risk accidentally memorising the details. I fling the door open to leave, turning the light off with my back to the room. I feel for the handle and pull the door up against my back, sighing into the hallway.

I post the keys through the landlord's door and deposit the bag of rubbish into the bins at the front of the building. As I close the gate, I glance back at the building and can't help thinking this is the second prison I have managed to escape in a matter of months.

The car is alight where I have left Michael. I skip towards it and jump in. Michael opens his eyes at the noise. He looks like he has been dosing. The stench of dried blood smothers me, and I imagine sheets of copper nailed all around the car, blockading us inside.

"All sorted?" he mumbles.

"Yes, I needed to do that."

"Where are your clothes?" Michael asks, noticing my hands are empty. I stare at them for a moment, remembering I had told Michael I needed to collect some clothes to take to his house.

"Oh, I decided to make a new start." I shrug.

"Okay then," Michael agrees, closing his eyes again. "Let's get to the house. I think I need a shower and my bed."

He does need a shower; he looks like he has eaten a messy hot dog and is now smothered with ketchup. The loss of blood and the trauma has left him sagging.

I start the engine, pulling away quickly. I have to take my brother home. I have to be the one to carry him back to his haven. As I cast a quick look into the wing mirror, I think I see a dark shape standing by the space the car had just occupied. Yet before I can begin to add detail to it, a car flashes its lights at me in the road ahead and I focus on that instead.

36 The Bedsit

Thom watches Sarah pull away from him and can only stand in the space that the car has departed from, not wanting another car to take its place. Perhaps if he keeps the space empty she will definitely come back to fill it once again. Can she just leave him like this? Can she completely forget him?

Thom resists the plan to simply sit down on the ground and wait for her return. He makes himself turn towards the house behind him, a towering cracked form that seems to sway. Although if it falls down whilst he is asleep tonight, he isn't sure he will care. It certainly won't be something to deter him.

He has kept the key safely in the inside pocket of his coat, where he will return it once he is inside her bedsit. He doesn't want anyone to see what she has given him, a small token of rescue, a passage carved out after an avalanche. She has lied to him sure, but he stills needs her, still wants to call her by any name she wants him to. Sarah has watched him bruise and break her brother's skin and she nonetheless has offered him somewhere to rest his equally broken body and mind for the night.

Thom tiptoes up the stairs, thinking how dark this stairway is, not like the lightened and warm passage to upstairs at Aunty Val's. There is no carpet on the steps so each positioning of his feet, despite him being on tiptoe, makes a loud tapping sound. He can hear someone's TV talking behind the wall next to him and hopes the bedsit will be quieter. He fears one whisper will throw his fragile mind against the floor, smashing it into tiny shards that he won't be able to reassemble.

Thom finally reaches the door, his feet aching as though he has walked for days. He even imagines the tight squelching of blisters rubbing against his shoes. Shaking the thoughts away, he unlocks her front door and closes himself in. For a moment, he lets himself be immersed in the rush of darkness, glad to forget his physicality.

As his eyes begin to adjust, he sadly flicks the top light on and sweeps the room with a squint. He can see why Sarah would refer to it as 'horrible' but he accepts it for what it is – a refuge and a decent bed where he can bury himself for the night.

As he thinks what to do next, he hears a beeping noise and looks down at his pocket. It is only then he remembers his mobile, a distant friend he hasn't connected with for weeks, and wonders how it even got into his pocket. He has no recollection of shoving it in there, but here it is, telling him he has a message. He presses open and reads:

I spoke to your family. Are you okay? Did you find somewhere to stay?
Em x

Thom throws himself onto the bed. He stares at the words. He feels his heart slowing down for the first time in days and lets himself fall back on the bed. He wonders why he feels so alone when there are all these people talking about him – Richard, Aunty Val, and Emma. Can someone really be alone when others are talking about them?

Thom releases the phone and lets his hands plunge into the bedclothes. They are used, soft, and Thom is sure he can detect a faded whisper of Sarah. She has slept in these sheets; she has thrashed in them during nightmares. Sarah has let him borrow her sheets for the same purposes.

What kind of things has Sarah been through the last few years? How can Thom ever understand them? He may not ever comprehend her experience of being raped or even her mental illness but what he does understand is her fear. Fear of being judged, fear of alienating those you care about, fear of being discovered, and fear of facing up to yourself.

He doesn't hate her for lying to him but he wishes she could've been honest. He is just so tired, his senses and perceptions fuzzy clouds that used to be sharp shapes that fit correctly into specific holes. Now he keeps pushing everything into holes that are too small or the wrong shape or holes that appear out of nowhere and extend for miles without a visible conclusion.

Thom remembers his phone and picks it up, rereading the message. He is nearly warmed by it but feels like a shard of ice slithers between him and this extension of concern. His eyes glaze over and he can hardly look at the screen. From memory of where the keys are, he types a message and when he finishes, turns over and falls asleep almost instantly.

Somewhere in another part of London, Emma receives a reply to her message and can only guess at what Thom might have been trying

297

to tell her:

4 am mk. Stazing with a eriemd. Uhbnks 4 gettimg 4n tovch. I mis7 u + I'n rorry. H wish I 2ovld gn ba2k btt its ton late. Notiinh makes sdnsf. Tjom

37 Red Recollections

Walking around Michael's house after my first night as a guest, I touch the objects he sees and uses every day (the blender, the kettle, the radiator, the taps), and I feel I am returning to life with each sensation. I can use these things. Maybe I can even live how I did before all of this.

You believe me, don't you, Mum?

When we lived together, we owned all these things too. Touching them, I remember their sounds, their texture against my skin. I also remember you; standing in the kitchen in the early morning, waiting for the kettle to boil for your tea, smiling and tapping your spoon against the side.

I wish you were here now, the kettle's boiled…

I am still busy thinking of you when Michael calls me into the living room. I am forced to leave you before the kettle has stopped spluttering. Yet I freeze in the doorway to the living room when I see Doctor Rosey, sitting with her clipboard, her legs crossed, pen poised for action. I expect her to click her fingers and have me dragged away or to press a button and have a cage drop down around me. Yet, she merely smiles. A-tiny-line-on-a-large-piece-of-paper smile.

"Alice. It's so good to see you again," she tells me as I sit opposite her. Her tone couldn't have been more stretched. It is a tired balloon that has been inflated too many times. She bites her lip as she takes me in. She is probably wondering just how insane I still am. I come incredibly close to making a strange screeching sound and rolling around the floor but looking up at Michael standing between us, for once, I don't want to fail him.

298

"Doctor Rosey," I spit. She notices my tone and immediately scratches something onto her board.

"I think it's time you put that down and answered some of *my* questions," I tell her firmly. Doctor Rosey's face drops at the suggestion but Michael repeats the same request, translating it for her. She then does as she is told and places the clipboard beside her. I want to laugh as her fingers claw into the sofa and unconsciously spread towards her treasured sidekick.

"Tell me about Daniel Mansen," I say. Thinking I have already drained her face of colour, she surprises me by turning even paler.

"Don't lie to her," Michael adds; crossing his arms and taking a seat on the arm of the chair I am sitting in. Doctor Rosey looks instantly betrayed and straightens herself up.

"I presume you've already discussed it with Alice," the Doctor addresses Michael.

"You can talk directly to me." I wrestle into her attention and she is forced to meet my gaze, nodding rigidly.

She takes a deep breath. "What do you know?"

"Why don't we start with what *you* know for once?" I challenge her again.

"Okay, I'll tell you what I can, if you promise one thing…"

"And that would be?" I lean forward.

"Not to take any action against the hospital." She squashes her lips together and waits for my reply. I glance at Michael who half smiles and raises one shoulder in a sign of passivity.

"Okay, I promise. And Michael can be your witness."

"Good." She nods sternly, recovering her authority for a few minor seconds. Yet she doesn't speak immediately, she rolls her tongue around in her mouth and repositions her body several times.

Finally she says, "Daniel originally worked as an administrator at the hospital but, over time, he demonstrated his ability to create a rapport with several of the patients. Some even showed a marked improvement with his support." Doctor Rosey gazes into the air above our heads, recalling a star pupil. Although, she quickly scolds this admiration with a downturned mouth.

"We decided to increase his duties, make him a mentor to some of the patients who had taken to him. He had shown himself to be trustworthy, or so we thought…" She sighs here. "What we didn't know was that he had designs on one of our patients."

"I'm guessing you mean me," I predict flatly.

"Yes…" She shakes her head as though she is faintly trying to escape a net. "You made no progress for months after you arrived and only began to speak when Daniel made an effort with you. We were happy to see you talking, at least, but we had no idea what price it came with. You understand that, don't you?"

Doctor Rosey is on the edge of her seat. I fear she might attempt to touch me so I sink further into the chair. Yet she doesn't move; her soggy eyes work on her behalf to show me an extended hand.

"Don't you monitor things in there?"

"We do Alice but on this occasion, we just missed it…" Doctor Rosey has transformed before us. I am the one asking questions, she is the one smashed to pieces by the bludgeon of guilt and shame. "And to our miniscule credit, we don't think anything physical took place between the two of you before he got caught."

"*Your credit*?" I laugh. "*You* let some strange man take advantage of me. You have no credit!" I am ready to leap from my chair but Michael pats on my shoulder softly and this is sufficient. Yet, it doesn't stop my eyes from tearing Doctor Rosey into strips across the room.

"You're right. We failed you," she agrees, glancing aside at her clipboard for comfort, but it doesn't move. "He was immediately fired of course," she adds.

"Oh that makes me feel *so* much better." My mouth is oozing.

"I can only apologise and explain this to you."

"How could you have let it happen? He groomed me… influenced me. How could you not see it happening?" Michael grabs my hand and squeezes it. Glancing up, I see the purple bruises smudged underneath his eyes like tribal face paint. It reminds me of all the casualties Daniel has triggered, directly or indirectly. He is the first wave that pushed us all into each other, with numerous reactions spinning and colliding like sparks wrestling in flames.

"He was a clever man. Like you said, he groomed you so he didn't have to worry about you telling on him. As for the staff, they trusted him and as for me… I just didn't see it. I couldn't get through to you and he did."

"So he's better at your job than you are?"

"There's no need to be so cutting. After all, I did help you in the end, didn't I?"

"I wasn't well enough to leave," I whimper, covering my face with my hands.

"We decided you were well enough, with supervision, of course." Doctor Rosey defends her decision. She can't face the idea of failing me twice.

"But I know now I wasn't well enough," I insist, sagging into the chair. Michael puts his hands on my shoulders and attempts to lift me back up again. I try my best on his behalf. "Why don't I remember what happened?" I ask, resting my head in Michael's lap. He doesn't move at first, staring down at me, and only after a long pause does he massage my neck with his thumb.

"You were very ill and when we caught Daniel, you were still *very* ill. As soon as he left, you seemed to forget about him and only after a few more months did you start to talk about anything at all," the Doctor explains.

"We thought you had enough to deal with, Alice," Michael adds from above and I cast one eye onto him, which is enough to make him turn his head away.

"I'm sorry," Michael whispers.

"You all lied to me."

I move myself out of Michael's lap and shake my head. My head is filled with helium, all I want to do is cut the cord and let it float away.

Mum, I know I shouldn't talk to you anymore but I think I need you still. All these people, they've lied and let me down but you never did.

"We didn't lie Alice, we just didn't discuss this with you," the Doctor claims but Michael betrays her with his clammy hands that leave sweat marks on the side of the chair.

"You don't know what this has done to me." My voice is a metal beam bending under the weight of tonnes of rubble.

"What has it done to you, Alice? What does that mean?"

"You let him get inside me. You let him lead me. You let him influence me to..." I feel as if I might be sick and stumble out of the chair. "You let him mould me... how could you?" I hold onto the arm for support as the room swirls like paints being blended into one. "You don't know what you've done," I squeak as my throat closes up.

The train is coming towards me. The lights knock me to the ground as I try to scramble away from it. Yet the train is skulking closer, the reversed stalker. Daniel's lips are moving again but I can't hear or guess the words he is trying to say. The cold fingers of the track have locked me in place and I wait for the monster to churn me into pulp. I scream and call for help but the blurry figures on the platform don't respond or move.

Mum! Mum! Help me please!

The only figure is Daniel and he is beside me, then inside me, then I hear his voice in my brain, *right on time right on time* to the pulse of the monster, to the pulse of his heart, to the pulse of my own organ scratching against my rib cage. The raspy breath of the train louder now a scream, a flood of light...

38 The Hospital Visit

Thom wakes up in a strange room. It takes him several minutes to realise where he is. He rolls over and finds his phone stuck within the covers. It is 9:42am.

His neck is aching and his left arm is numb from the way he has been sleeping. He can't remember closing his eyes last night. He hasn't even switched the main light off and he is surprised that he'd been able to sleep with it on.

Thom familiarises himself with the room. He decides that it looks even more tragic in the daylight and opts to leave the place as soon as he can. He takes a fast shower in the bathroom down the hall, dries himself off with a stained towel, and throws on the same rags he came in with. He hopes the spots of Michael's blood on his sleeve aren't noticeable to anyone else. The grey swelling on his fists only underlines his shame further.

When he has his hand on the front door, Thom realises he has no idea where he is going. He slumps back onto the bed and considers his options. First, he could go back to the house and face Aunty Val and Richard. Second, he could go and look for Sarah and talk over the revelations of yesterday night. Or third, he could try to discover more about Daniel and why he died.

Out of fear and perhaps tiredness, Thom chooses the most familiar. He will keep investigating Daniel. He can't talk to his family yet, and finding out more about Sarah's lies can wait. Just because everything in his life has changed so much, it doesn't mean he can forget his task. He has to find out about Daniel.

But where should he go now? The lock up? Mrs Tray's? Yet Thom feels like these are places he has already been, places which make up the past and are not to be revisited. Where or what is he missing?

Thom thinks back to when he met Mrs Tray and the way she played solitaire. What did she say to him? *'Sometimes all it takes is a fresh eye'*. And Thom remembers how the phrase slithered into his ear and solidified there. He has been caught in a whirlpool for weeks or months now and he needs to break out. As he always hears them say on the news, he needs 'fresh leads'.

So what places or people has he left out? Well there's the station where it all began of course, but Thom isn't sure he's ready for that. He hasn't even been in a tube station at all since Daniel died, let alone the one where he was smashed to pieces.

The only other 'lead' he can think of is the hospital. Thom has never known enough about Daniel's time there, and Mrs Tray made the link to it when they had talked. Therefore, this seems a sensible plan to Thom and he finally feels able to turn the door handle and leave the frowning room behind.

Outside the air is cold and instantly stings Thom's cheeks. He zips up his coat and makes his way towards somewhere where he hopes he can catch a bus in the vague direction of the hospital. He knows little about this hospital but he at least knows which one it is.

Two long bus rides later, he is standing somewhere in South London, in front of an unassuming building which is actually a hospital. People walk by without even looking at the building, which Thom finds troubling as it is a grand and stony character. There is a large wall guarding it and only a small entrance at one of the sides, guarded by one man sitting in a booth, as though no one ever tries to gain entry to it. Or perhaps no one ever comes out?

Thom hesitates as he stands on the pavement scrutinising the entrance. Standing here, the normality of the crowd threading past reassures him. At least here, his 'madness' of late is concentrated by all the other bodies and their sanity. But inside that hospital, his 'madness' will be spiked by all the insanity of the patients. In there, will he finally fall apart and reveal his strange thoughts? Will he finally tell someone he isn't sure whether he can ever rejoin the life he left behind?

Thom forces himself to approach the guard. He explains he is considering placing a relative into the hospital and wants to discuss his options with the managing director. The man reluctantly replaces his cigarette with the phone receiver and makes a hushed call to someone. When he replaces the phone, he nods towards the hospital and mutters, "see reception." Thom does as he has been instructed; walking gradually towards the hospital he fears can undress him.

Thom takes on the stairs like a warrior certain he is climbing to his death. The door of the hospital grows with each step, a mouth that will swallow him. Yet when Thom finally grasps the handle, he feels reassured by its cold stillness, and manages to navigate his trembling legs through it.

Inside, he is buzzed through another door and is greeted by a young woman. She tells him the director would be happy to see him and discuss admissions, perhaps even give him a tour should he want one. She asks him to take a seat but Thom barely grazes the chair when he jumps up again.

"I don't have a sick relative," Thom confesses. The receptionist freezes and for a strange moment Thom believes he has stabbed her in the spine and she is paralysed. Yet after a few moments of silence, she turns to face him again.

"So what is it you want exactly?" the woman asks, her hand creeping towards the edge of the desk. Thom suspects there is an alarm there and he doesn't blame her for reassuring herself with it. If the position were reversed, and he was the one looking at a clammy-faced man with his clothes stretched to all sides and hanging off his shoulders, he would press the alarm instantly.

"I want to ask about my cousin." Thom attempts to straighten his clothes, as if this will help the situation greatly.

"Who is your cousin?" She doesn't take her eyes off Thom.

"Daniel Mansen." Thom is watching the woman equally as closely as he says the two words. These two words seem to spit glass in all directions whenever they are mentioned. These two words make Thom want to duck down after he's said them and wait for the screams.

"Daniel," the woman repeats, letting her arm move back towards her body. She lets go of the physical alarm in response to the alarm in her mind.

"You knew him," Thom states.

The woman slowly nods and takes a step towards Thom. "Why are you here?"

"Daniel is dead," Thom tells her. The woman bites her lip and looks down.

"I'm sorry," she mumbles, drawing even closer to Thom. "But why have you come here *now*?"

"I know he left his job here, but I don't know why."

Thom is standing next to the woman now; they are huddled beside the reception desk, speaking in quiet tones. Thom guesses the woman can feel his pinched sticky desperation and he can see her guilty curiosity that made her let go of the alarm.

"He didn't tell you?" she sighs.

"I feel like I'm really missing something here," Thom admits. He has just summarised his feelings throughout the whole investigation. Yet Thom guesses this is the nature of an investigation: always being in a state of lack.

"I am sorry Daniel's dead but I don't think I should tell you anything."

"I'm sorry to ask this but I need..." Thom rubs his hands over his face, "I need to know what happened. I know it's something bad, so you don't have to worry."

"But the hospital..."

"This is about people, *not* about this hospital," Thom wrestles in. "Look, I promise you I won't say anything to anyone. I just want to know, *for me*." Thom pronounces each word precisely.

"I understand how you feel and I'm sorry..." she persists, shaking her head.

"No, don't say that again. You have to help me, no one else can. I need to find this out, to help me understand him. I can't ask him, can I?" Thom knows this is unfair but he is grasping at anything, showing only traces of his once noble self.

"What is your name anyway?"

"Thom," he answers and holds his hand out.

"Kelly," she nods, taking his hand. Thom is glad he took the bandages off this morning. After all, they had been covered in Michael's blood. "You know, Daniel and I were friends. I was shocked when I heard he'd been fired..." Kelly pauses, expelling air loudly, "and the reason, it made me sick..."

"Daniel was fired," he repeats. It is meant to be a question but it comes out as a fact, a brick wall suddenly complete. Thom can't believe he hasn't thought of this already. He should've figured this out by the fact that no one in the family ever discussed it, yet at the same time it hadn't seemed crucial when it happened. But now, everything is vital, everything is a grain that gathers together to form a giant textile. Thom wishes he didn't have to collect all of the parts so slowly.

"He was caught with a patient," Kelly adds, after a few minutes of cold silence.

"What?" Thom snaps his neck up, too fast, and massages the ache that mushrooms across the back of it. It takes about thirty seconds for it to fade.

"He was caught kissing a patient."

"Oh fuck." Thom punches the desk. Although he is ninety percent sure Aunty Val might've known about Daniel being forced to leave his job, he bets she doesn't know the reason.

"How could he do that?" Thom covers his face.

Kelly hovers next to Thom, her fingers twitching beside his arm but not making a connection. Thom doesn't notice this and when he uncovers his face a minute later, she has moved her fingers away.

"I can't tell you anything else Thom, I'm sorry." Kelly shrugs. "And I wish I hadn't had to tell you that." She smiles gently.

"I don't know why I'm surprised. I've been finding out so many things about him and most of them not good." Thom is tired, he wants to hang himself over the desk and close his eyes. How much more can he take? Was Daniel a bad person, or a good person who'd made some bad mistakes? Had Daniel felt so bad about himself that he threw himself in front of that train?

"Daniel seemed like a good person, but he really abused that patient's trust, the hospital's trust." Kelly seems almost as broken as Thom. Yet he doubts the cracks extend as deep as his.

"What happened to the patient?"

"She got better." Kelly smiles.

"That's good."

"I can't believe Daniel's dead..." Kelly shakes her head.

"Me neither."

"I'm sorry, Thom, but I have to get back... to work."

"Okay." Thom takes her hand and relishes in the warmth for a few seconds. Kelly smiles again and takes her hand with her, when she returns to her seat behind the desk. Everything is as it should be again, she behind the desk and he in front of it like a visitor. Their moments of sharing have finished.

Thom reaches the door, still rolling the new information around in his mind and his heart. As he stands in the doorway looking out, his feet seem to curl up into balls, making his balance uneven. He holds onto the door frame to stop himself from falling. Taking a few breaths, Thom suddenly thinks of Sarah. He thinks about the revelations she shared with him yesterday night and before he has even considered this properly, he swings round and says, "Kelly, what was the name of that patient?"

"I don't think that's relevant," she dismisses.

"I'd just like to know, out of curiosity…"

"Okay." Kelly leans across the desk on her elbows, like a little girl unloading a secret to her best friend. "The patient's name was Alice."

39 Red Bruises

I wake up in Michael's guest room. The sheets are moist and my curls are pasted to my forehead. As soon as I attempt to push myself up, Michael appears at my side.

"Don't move," he says quietly, stroking my sweaty curls. He lowers me back onto the pillow. I don't want to do as he says but I feel weak and my body doesn't have the same determination to defy him. I wonder how long I have been unconscious.

"Alice, I'm so sorry," he whispers, bowing his head. "We've really hurt you by keeping this secret. I mean… just look how your body reacted." Michael's eyes are glistening in the semi-darkness of the room. "You just flopped on the floor and…" he breathes in shakily, "and I was so scared. I feel so responsible." He grabs hold of my hands and squeezes them between his. "I threw Doctor Rosey out by the way," he adds and I can't help smiling slightly. Michael lifts his lips to one side, knowing I would appreciate this.

"I understand why you lied," I confess; pushing myself upwards so I can sit against the headboard. Michael waits for me to continue. "It's just that I think he influenced me and it's affecting me… now." Michael brings his eyebrows together in a slanted V at my words.

"How has he influenced you now?" Michael asks. This is my cue, the moment I could reveal my nasty deed to him; the moment I tell him I am a murderer. Yet, I can't bear to have him let go of my hands in shock, or have him look at me with the same confusion as he did a few days ago.

"I saw an article in the paper, saying he had died," I venture, not sure where I am leading myself.

"I saw that too." Michael nods. "I hoped you wouldn't or if you did, you wouldn't remember."

"I didn't remember that I knew him," I say, my chest seemingly filling up with air that is blocking movement and function. Yet, here it is: another lie. "But I felt curious for some reason. So I ended up going to his house."

"What?" Michael jolts in his chair.

"I know, it's crazy but I just felt some unconscious need to go there," I pause, "and now I know why I found myself drawn there." *Drawn to him,* I add to myself. Finding out about me and Daniel being together at the hospital probably did explain my fascination with him, the decision to follow him, perhaps even the decision to kill him. He'd been leading me for months before the push and he wanted me to know with those horrible words: *right on time.*

"I just needed to look at the house, for reasons I couldn't place. But as I stood there looking at it, one of his family came out and started talking to me…"

"You left, didn't you?" Michael interjects hopefully.

"No Michael, I stayed. We talked and he invited me in."

"It was that Thom guy, wasn't it?" Michael asks, running his fingers over his still swollen nose. I nod faintly, anticipating his anger or disappointment. Yet, Michael lowers his head and shows me his bald patch, mumbling, "If I'd been there for you, maybe you wouldn't have gone to him."

"I don't know. I clearly felt some link to Daniel."

"Does he know you knew Daniel? And how are they related?"

"They're cousins. And no," I emphasise with my eyes, "he doesn't know I knew Daniel." I grimace appropriately.

"You're *not* going to tell him?" Michael places his hand on my arm.

"I don't want to and I'm not sure it matters."

"Is he a decent person, Ali?" Michael continues, calling me by a name he hasn't used since before you died. I relish its familiarity for a few seconds and give my brother a warm smile.

"He's not a bad person, Michael. I know he hurt you but he just thought he was protecting me." I lift my hand up and brush his cheek, trying to dull the red-grey stain that has blossomed there.

"And you two… are an item?" He winces.

"No," I say, convinced this is what he wants to hear, "we're just friends." As I use one of the clichés people always use, *just friends*, I wonder what Thom and I actually are. Yes, we kissed the other day, but does it mean anything? I've supported him for a few weeks, he'd invited me to stay when he thought I had nowhere to sleep, but isn't that merely friendship? Only that one violent kiss hints at anything more and now after all the lies, what does he think of me now?

"I think you should be careful with him, Alice." Michael grapples with my eye contact in order to stress his point. "I've only met him twice but he seems unsteady… I think he's capable of something…" Michael scrunches his mouth up and looks aside, imagining what Thom is 'capable' of while staring at the wallpaper. I sit up and take his hand.

"What might he be capable of?" I ask, all the time thinking of what Michael is unaware of. He doesn't know his own sister is capable of murder. He doesn't know his sister is also a liar, a manipulator, still fascinated with the colour red. The whole time the two of us have been talking, I have been imagining his nose gushing with blood again and thinking of the scarf soaking it all into its body, a parasite sucking on my brother's lifeblood.

"I wish I could tell you. I mean; we've already seen he can hurt people. I just don't know…" Michael stares at the wallpaper again and finishes, "just how far he could go." Michael is unconsciously running his fingers over his bruises again. I think whenever he sees Thom, even weeks from now; he will stroke the areas on his face where Thom struck him.

"He's a good person," I say, shaking my head.

"Good people can still do bad things." He frowns and suddenly pulls me towards him. He hugs me tight and continues to hold me for several minutes, his uneven breath humidifying my neck.

As I am in my brother's arms, I think about good people and bad people, good actions and bad actions. I consider how they are all interchangeable and question which way the scales tip for me: am I a bad person who commits bad actions? Or am I a good person who commits bad actions?

40 Alice

Thom doesn't remember what happens for a certain amount of time after he hears that name again. It seems to crack against his head and make him lose consciousness, although he somehow manages to still walk and breathe. He next finds himself back at the bedsit, standing in the doorway. The clock above the kitchen sink says 1:27pm.

He doesn't remember how he'd slumped against the wall at the hospital, or how the receptionist shook him, or how he'd sworn and muttered incoherently about things even he couldn't have made sense of, how he'd pushed the woman off him and sped out of the door into the street, into the city, into more unknown things and more unknown people. Even the people he thought he knew have become false.

Standing in the doorway of the bedsit, the room seems to pulsate and all the objects in it begin to contort. Thom rubs his eyes and shakes his head. Yet the phenomenon continues and he slowly lowers himself onto the bed, pressing against the mattress to steady himself. Thom fears he is about to vomit when a voice distracts him.

"Thom." A happy tone but tight. A familiar voice but distant.

"It's you," he says, not using either of her names. He doesn't know which one fits her anymore. Like the objects, the names warp at the thought of attaching to her.

She smiles and takes a seat beside him. She doesn't move to touch him. Instead, she stares at his still purple and grey knuckles. He wonders how long this will be the case and, at the same time, wonders how much he cares. He is in the middle of a field with space stretching in every direction with nothing else in even the farthest sight. Which direction should he choose? Which might lead him to somewhere familiar that won't implode?

"How are you, Thom?" She takes a strained breath, clutching onto her left arm with her other hand.

"I don't know what to call you anymore," Thom says, not answering on purpose. She meets his gaze, trying to remind him of the exact colour of her metallic blue eyes.

"Call me Sarah..." she says and adds hopefully, "if you can."

"If Sarah's what you want." Thom shrugs. She nods happily, reaching across and clutching his fist in her hand. "How is Michael?"

"He's okay, still a bit bruised."

"You shouldn't have lied to me." Thom's face crumples. He snatches his hand out of hers and massages it. He doesn't want her poison seeping through his skin. All he can think about, as he looks at her, is her kissing Daniel. Had she enjoyed it? Which one did she prefer? How can she have kissed them both?

"I'm so sorry," she says quietly. As Thom listens to her words, he realises how human she sounds. When he first met her outside Aunty Val's house, she spoke in a methodical way, every word considered. Now, she seems to speak more impulsively; perhaps more honestly. After all, what is there to consider when you're telling the truth?

"You understand why I did it, don't you? I'm ill Thom, and felt completely ashamed and afraid that you would push me away if you knew." Sarah bows her head knowingly. "I didn't realise my lies were hurting people..."

"You told me you had a different name, a different history, you told me your brother raped you. You didn't think *that* would hurt anyone?" Thom enunciates each word, his saliva thick with distaste.

"I didn't think you would hurt him." She kneads her forehead.

"I was just trying to defend you," Thom snarls.

"Let's not go over all this again. It's not helping either of us," Sarah says, turning to face him and lifting her head up with effort. "I came to tell you about everything."

"*Everything* as in...?" Thom leans towards her expectantly.

"Why I was in the hospital," she tells him solemnly. He wonders if she will include the part where she met Daniel and then somehow ended up living with his family after his death. *Doubtful*, he decides.

"Okay. I'm listening." Thom pushes himself back and leans against the wall. Sarah copies him, smiling at him gently as she settles. It feels like they are two children sharing secrets. Thom is tempted then to reach towards her and press his hand over hers that is squashed against the bed.

"Right, well... I guess I should start... I guess... the start is..." Sarah trails off. Thom is mesmerised by her fumbling. When he'd found out she had been lying to him and he'd found out about her knowing Daniel, he felt sure he would only hate her. Yet as he watches her lips struggling to form words, he feels an explosion of warmth rising inside. This unexplained warmth is what troubles him, not the hate.

"I was raped," she finally begins, holding her breath, as though she is the one who has been told something difficult by him. He merely waits for her to continue. "I didn't lie about that, Thom; I promise you on my life." She meets his eyes, water flooding them, as she pulls desperately at his sleeve. He nods gently and she lets go of his clothes. "It ruined everything. I dropped out of uni, I couldn't go out, I was afraid of men... I couldn't trust people." She shakes her head, still unable to comprehend all these facts even now.

"Is that when you ended up in the hospital?" Thom asks, trying to rescue her. She seems to be sinking into the mattress, her past suspended over her like a noose.

"No," she sighs. "I wish." She chuckles sadly. "My Mum... she really helped me get through it, or she did until..." Sarah rolls her eyes upwards, wishing she could shoot through the ceiling, away from him, away from the truth, "she died," she exhales quietly.

"She died," Thom repeats. He can't tell if he is unconvinced. If someone can lie about rape, can they lie about death? Yet Thom can't imagine she would lie to him about this. It seems too large a lie to slide out of her small delicate mouth.

"I came home one day and she was lying there, her slippers were...

313

she was cold, and there was blood and she didn't move..." Sarah looks like she is lost in the middle of a supermarket, beginning to cry loudly and crush her curls until Thom thinks they will flatten permanently. Perhaps to stop her from losing her curls, he gathers her up and presses her against him.

Thom cradles her but, at the same time, has an urge to crack her neck. Just one sharp pull like the snap of a Christmas cracker...

Her words are now tiny injections stabbing at him through a waterfall of tears. "Her skin... so pale... a line of blood... twisted legs and bruises and... she didn't move..." Thom feels her words have physically penetrated him and he checks his arms for puncture wounds. He worries that when she moves away from him again; she will uncover holes she has made in his chest and allow the blood to ooze out like uncontrollable foam blistering from a champagne bottle.

She pushes back from him. Her eyes are swollen and bloodshot, her eyelashes clumped together in a moist huddle, her hair glued to the sides of her face as though she has dipped her face in a sink full of water. Thom feels nauseated by the display of raw emotion. Much like Aunty Val, he feels like he is being forced to hold Sarah up.

"So *that's* when you ended up in the hospital?" Thom asks again but is greeted by Sarah's shaking head.

"I didn't understand, Thom." She squashes her lips together, trying to stop them from trembling further. "I think I've only just fully accepted it."

"What do you mean?" Thom snaps, slightly impatiently.

"I stayed in the house with her, for weeks... I still didn't know when they took me to the hospital and even months after... I don't think I knew properly until recently."

"That your mum had died?" Thom clarifies. Sarah closes her eyes and takes a few deep breaths. Her eye twitches gently, her muscles stubborn and wavering at the same time.

"Yes, she's dead," she nods weakly.

"Wait, you kept her in the house... when she was dead?"

"Yes," Sarah admits tight-lipped. "I told you... I was ill."

"That's terrible. That's so sad," Thom spurts breathlessly.

"I was already distraught and I guess her dying just shoved me over the edge." Sarah holds her hands out in front of her and stares at them intently. Thom stares at them too, watching the veins swell and throb, watching the skin swirling as if he is looking at them through a kaleidoscope.

"Do you feel better now?" Thom inquires hopefully. Sarah faces him, her eyebrows creasing together in the middle of her head, thinking.

"I'm sorry Thom but I don't know yet," she smiles meekly. Thom's posture drops in response.

"You still feel like you're ill?"

"I've only just realised properly so yes, I'm still ill, whatever that means..." she trails off, still considering this. Thom puts his hand on her knee, his hand that continues to ache; his hand that looks like someone has drawn lines on it with a red biro.

"So that's everything? Everything you lied about?" Thom verifies, pressing down on her knee, staring into her eyes. She doesn't twitch, blink or look away.

"That's everything," she says. All Thom's ribs seem to crumble apart in one rapid moment. All the air in his chest sucks downwards, to where he can't tell, but all he is concerned with is the fact that he can't feel his own heart.

"Everything, huh?" Thom echoes, taking his hand off her knee and burying it in the duvet. He crushes the duvet with both his hands to stop himself from crushing her neck between his fingers.

"Thom I think I should go now. We've said enough for today." Sarah stands up. Thom jumps up after her and feels his muscles locking, except for his facial muscles that keep rolling into different expressions.

"There's nothing else Sarah?" Thom persists, almost desperately. His tone is strained. He is a man asking for the truth, for the piece of information that is the hook to pluck him from the angry sea he has been battling in for weeks.

"No Thom," Sarah says firmly. She bends her head sideways, with an expression of confusion, a trace of anxiety? She pushes her shoulders back as he stares at her, a hard stare that hammers into her.

"You're *really* sure?" Thom offers her a last chance.

"Nothing else," she reiterates hollowly. She is insistent but unconsciously falls back slightly, hiding in daylight. Thom can't help the chuckle that vibrates feebly in his throat. Sarah's mouth quivers momentarily.

"So you don't want to tell me about the hospital?" Thom moves closer. Sarah has to force herself not to move back, Thom sees it in her shaky legs that are set apart like someone about to burst into a sprint.

"What do you mean, Thom?"

"What do I *mean*, Sarah?" Thom's words are clouded by the thunder of his heartbeat. "What-do-I-mean?" he shouts. Sarah gives a distasteful glance at the spit that jumps from his mouth onto her body. She doesn't say anything. What can she say except to tell the truth? And apparently she doesn't know how to do that, despite her attempts to prove otherwise.

"Were you ever going to tell me you met Daniel at the hospital?" Thom snarls, the blood thrashing at his cheeks and tears assembling in the corners of his eyes, preparing for an assault.

Sarah doesn't react initially. She watches him, his arched back and his teeth sharpening, her expression unchanged. For a moment, she reverts to the woman he met in the front garden of Aunty Val's house with mechanical movements, thoughts and functions.

Then a full minute later, the signs of shock set in. Her eyes widen as though he has jumped out on them, her body stiffens like an exclamation mark and she suddenly spins towards the door. Taking a few desperate leaps, she reaches the door and scrambles with the handle. Before she can manage to make her fingers function properly, Thom pounces on her and slams her against the door. She groans as though he has punched her in the stomach and sags in his hold.

"You'd better tell me, Sarah. I'm tired of your fucking lies," Thom spits as they both fall back onto the floor. She looks exhausted, as though he has clubbed her with a blunt object. He feels a moist patch on the back of her head and worries it might be blood but gratefully realises it is only sweat. Thom wrenches her up to a sitting position and pushes her against the door.

"If you lie to me again, I think I'll go insane," Thom whimpers. Sarah nods and tucking her curls behind her ears, she opens her mouth.

41 The Red Secret

"I promise you, I only found out a few days ago," I tell him, grabbing onto his arms.

He is on his knees before me, a man pleading for honesty.

"What?" he growls. His dark expression makes him look strangely attractive, but I don't think this is the time for sharing these types of thoughts.

"I didn't know I'd known him," I swear, tightening my fingers around his arms like a clamp. He doesn't move. Perhaps I am holding him up or perhaps he is too weak to move away.

"How could you not know?" Thom shakes his head hopelessly. If he's ever been certain of anything, I think he's finally lost his last ties to it. He seems to have no comprehension of the divide between certainty and uncertainty anymore.

"I don't remember a lot of things from that time. I guess... I guess I blocked it out or something. But I only found out when I read the letters."

"The letters?" Thom's neck snaps up. His eyes are burnt wood still lit with a tiny ember.

"I found a combination and an address in Daniel's room," I admit quietly. How could I have trespassed on their grief the way I have?

"You were in his room..." Thom broods but instantly shrugs it away and adds, "how did you find anything in there? I searched *everywhere*." His mouth is slightly open, with an expression of minor admiration at someone doing better at investigating than he has.

"It was inside the closet drawer written in red pen. It wasn't easy to find."

"But *you* found it," he says sulkily.

"I think it was meant for me to find." I smile gently, hoping he will accept this. He shrugs. A moment later he reaches up and pulls at one of my curls, making it spring back at my face. After he does this several times, he moves his fingers over my lips, dabbing them as though he is pressing against tacky glue.

"So the letters..." he reminds me, squashing my lips down with his thumb.

"They were in a locker," I mumble incoherently, due to his probing. He takes his thumb away for a moment and waits for me to continue. "There were letters inside. They were written by me," I reveal, still unconvinced by them. I cradle my head in one hand, remembering the handwriting that looked so familiar. *Of course it was familiar – it was yours!* I hadn't seen my handwriting for so long; it is no wonder I didn't recognise it. And the things my own hand created!

"They said horrible things about... about me... and Daniel." I feel the nausea solidify and mushroom up my throat. I have to close my eyes and concentrate on trying not to vomit on Thom. When I open my eyes, Thom is staring at me. He moves his arms so he is holding onto me instead. I blink and nod my head in gratitude.

"They sounded like love letters, Thom," I moan, kneading my eyelids until the threatening tears are squashed out. With my eyes closed, I jolt slightly when I feel his warm skin clashing with my clammy cheek. I reopen my eyes and gaze into his.

"Do you think I loved him, Thom?" His hand drops.

"I hope not," he mumbles.

"I can't believe I don't remember meeting him."

"Is this the truth Sarah? Is this really the *truth*?"

"Yes, Thom," I vow.

"But why did you end up at the house? You can't tell me it's just coincidence?" I shrug his hold off and move away. Thom scrambles after me. I watch his movements, a lost infant chasing a parent, and my heart feels like someone has plunged a skewer through it. Although I want to tell him the truth about everything, this is the blockade in the road.

"I saw the article in the paper and I don't know what happened... I just found myself..." I pause, "...at the house." I stand by the window looking out at the street. I imagine myself walking along the pavement, under the quivering trees, inhaling the fumes and the sharp air. Thom hovers behind me, hanging on the silence. "I didn't know you would talk to me," I stress.

"If I hadn't found out," Thom moves to stand beside me, "would you have ever told me?" I don't look in his direction but I feel his awkward stance contorting in my peripheral vision.

"I can't tell you that."

"At least that's honest," Thom says. He is silent but I feel he isn't finished. This is clarified when he grabs my arm and pulls me in his direction. "Can you tell me Sarah?" He stammers for a few seconds. "Was it nice... to kiss him?"

This isn't the question I expected. I fall back on myself. The bind between our gazes seems unbreakable. I think about the question and wonder if I even know where to begin. Do I really remember kissing Daniel? Since reading the letters and talking to Michael and Doctor Rosey about it, there had been vague flashes about the hospital and Daniel. Yet, I can't be sure I actually remember anything. After all, I could've invented recollections now I have the information.

I haven't spoken for several minutes. I only realise when I see the colour draining from Thom's face. His body begins to quiver quietly, but he pushes his shoulders back and tries to maintain the gaze we are sharing.

"I'm sorry, Thom, but I don't remember..."

"But you must have some recollection now," Thom insists.

"I wouldn't trust any memories that came to me anyway." Thom slumps at my words and finally snaps our stare. He turns away. I reach out and touch his back gently, feeling his back muscles tensing and bulging.

"I love your curls," he says suddenly. I move closer, circling him with my arms. I think he will flinch but he leans back into my body. He smells of sweat, as though he has been running for days without stopping. I am so close I can see his broken strands of hair, the loops that have formed at the back like an army waiting to conquer the rest.

"Since I first saw you, I couldn't stop thinking about them," he confesses. I can't see his face but I imagine his cheeks have rashes of blood rising on them.

"I didn't want to kiss him, Thom," I say. His body shudders in my hold but he quickly recovers himself, knowing I can feel each movement. "But I wanted you." My whisper claws its way through his beard and up to his ear. Some of my hair is stuck to his beard as though it is Velcro and when he pulls out of my hold, it clings on until it has to accept defeat.

I am sad that we are apart. Yet as soon as I think this, Thom takes hold of me by the hips. Unlike the first time when we wrestled, this time there is an awkward approach. There is a slow draw between us, the clash of breath, and the replacement pressure of his thumb with his lips.

I pull back after several seconds and gush, "Michael says I should be careful with you." Thom smiles briefly, glancing to one side for a long moment before he gradually turns back to me. He opens and closes his mouth like a goldfish that never intends to speak. Then another cheeky grin later, he pushes me into his lips and fills his silence.

42 The Red Slippers Revisited

Getting into the car outside my bedsit, I avoid looking up at the window where I know Thom is standing. I am certain my lips are flashing or my cheeks are still flushed, yet when Michael nods 'hello', he shows no signs of suspecting anything. He starts the car and with a glance in the mirrors, pulls away.

"Is he okay?" Michael asks, although I'm not sure he is actually interested.

"He's okay," I say, staring at the world rolling by outside like a continuous rapid slide-show. Michael fiddles with the radio and after several options, settles on one station. I don't recognise any of the songs they play. It feels like years since I listened to music, either religiously or just as background music. What kind of music am I actually interested in anyway? I can't remember.

"What did you talk about? You were in there a long time." Michael says after two songs have passed.

I look over at him, fiddling with my hands in my lap and tell him, "We talked about lots of things. Thom had questions too." Michael nods at my words and stops at some traffic lights.

"Did he get angry?" He glances over.

"Why would he?" I snap.

"It's not that unreasonable an assumption." He narrows his gaze at me, making sure I have to look at his bruises once again. I sigh, knowing he is right.

"Well, he's fine." I shrug. Michael keeps looking at me but I don't acknowledge him. Finally, he sees the lights have changed and is forced to concentrate on driving again.

"I thought we could go to the house," he says quietly. Jumping in my seat, I look at my brother, trying to decide if he's being serious. Only I would understand which house he means. To anyone else, it could be any house in the whole city. But to me, it's *your* house.

"You didn't sell it?"

"No Alice." He appears he is pouring petroleum onto a fire and is waiting for the backlash. "I thought you might want to see it again," he mentions it as though he is talking about buying some milk. "I just told you I did, because I thought it would be easier, for the time being..."

"I don't know Michael..." I splutter, wringing my hands and leaning forward in my seat. My chest is tightening. I have to focus on dragging the air into my lungs and letting it slide back out easily. I hold onto the dashboard, steadying myself slowly. All I can think about is the staircase, your crooked legs, the unnatural paleness of your skin, those slippers...

Mum, can I go back? Will it still feel like you're there?

"It's okay Alice, we don't have to go," Michael says, taking his hand off the handbrake and patting my leg quickly. His obvious lack of surprise angers me though.

"No, we'll go," I blurt.

Michael looks over again, almost forgetting he is driving and nods gently, "If you're sure..."

We arrive outside the house twenty minutes later. The closer we have travelled to the house, the more my throat has swollen up and my breathing has grown raspier. Michael has said nothing.

The car stops and is silent but I can't make my hand rise up and grab the handle. Michael leans across me and swings the door open for me. I throw him a look as though he has just smacked me in the face. He sits back in his seat and stares ahead, waiting for me to move first.

"I don't think I can do it Mike," I confess, pressing my back into the seat so hard that it begins to ache across my shoulder blades. Michael grabs my hand, hearing my wavering tone, and hearing me calling him by the name I barely use when addressing him.

"You can Alice. *You can.*" He squeezes my hand.

"Michael, can you call me Sarah?" I glance at him. His forehead burrows in a sudden avalanche of skin.

"Your name is Alice," he tells me, as though I have forgotten.

"But I really prefer Sarah."

"Okay," he mumbles. "I'll try Al—*Sarah*," he adds, pronouncing Sarah as though in a foreign tongue. He shakes his mistake away.

"Thanks," I tell him and swing my legs out of the car. "I should be able to do this," I inform myself out loud.

When I am standing outside, my legs seem to dissolve and I grab onto the car. A second later, Michael is propping me up. Even though I want to let him hold me up, I push away and tell my legs to work properly. The least I can do for you is stand up by myself.

That is all you'd wanted for me especially, Mum, before you died.

"Do you have the key Michael?" My voice is as shaky as the hand that I extend towards him. I hear him fumbling in his pocket and he places the key in my palm. It feels light and cold. It is a small object but when I use it to open the front door, a waterfall will thrash into me, submerge me with the emotions and memories I have locked away since the day I found you there.

The walk towards the door is quick and easy, when I feel it should be a harrowing journey through mountains and rough currents. I don't look back but I know Michael is behind me. Just a few days ago, I wouldn't have trusted him to be there, but I have a different sense of him now. Even the air around him seems firmer, a commanding building looming over a skyline.

"Okay," I say to the door and jam the key into the lock. It feels stiff as I turn it and the door sticks as I try to push it open. After a brief struggle, the hallway opens up to me. I sway slightly, Michael's hands instantly steadying me.

"That's where I found her," I reveal quietly, stepping across the threshold. I point to a spot on the carpet, unremarkable to others' eyes, and circle it, hunting the memory. Michael stays in the door-way, watching me in the throes of interest and guilt, gnawing at his bottom lip.

"She was on her front, her face bent towards the door, her legs bent in weird directions, her slippers..." I move towards the stairs, "One was here. I put it back on her." I can see you like you are before me now. I can feel the rubber texture of your skin; see the chalky tone of your face. When I had picked you up, it felt like there was an anchor attached, dragging you away from me.

Don't worry; I haven't forgotten you, Mum.

"Did you know..." Michael holds his sentence hostage again, "she was dead?" He speaks quietly, so quietly I'm not convinced he wants to hear the answer.

"I don't think I did. I think I just really 'lost' my mind..." I give him a pleading look. "Can you understand, Michael? It was like someone flicked a switch and I just couldn't figure things out anymore..."

Michael stares at me. I begin to think he will regress into his old judgemental self and get me locked up again. Yet after a few minutes, he drops his stare to the space on the carpet. "I can't imagine what it must've been like for you," he says, surprising me. "After what happened to you with Harry, I don't blame you for taking Mum's death badly."

"I don't want to talk about him," I spit.

"I know, I know." Michael holds his hands up and moves closer. I study his steps as he walks over your outline. I cringe, imagining your floppy limbs being trodden on. Michael skips a few steps when he realises what he has done. "I should've realised at the time," he continues, taking my hands, "it's just hard *Sarah*. I can't ever completely understand it. It still confuses me how..." Michael shakes his head, "look, it doesn't matter. I'm just trying to say I'm here for you now, even if I can't understand it all."

"Thanks," I mumble, taking my hands back. "Michael, I'm going to look in Mum's room now and I'd like to go alone." Michael steps back on himself, grasping at his thinning hair.

"Must you?" He croaks.

"Yes," I answer simply and turn away.

Leaving Michael behind, I'm instantly lost in the soft padding sound my feet make against the carpet. I remember the sound of you, Mum. Outside my room; your slippers flashing underneath the door, the slice of light as you checked on me whilst you thought I was asleep. The truth is I could never sleep until I heard you check on me. Even now, it's a struggle to drift off without imagining the flash of light and the click of the door.

The door to your room is shut. When I touch the handle, it feels as cold as you did when I touched your cheek several days after the fall. I pause, nausea swirling in the pit of my stomach. How had I been so deluded about you?

I push the door open. The first thing that strikes me is that your bed is missing. I step inside and close the door, taking in the space. Examining the floor, I see the darker square of carpet where the bed used to be. Where has it gone? Why has it been taken? The bed is the last place I saw you and now it's gone. This absence physically stabs me all over my body like pins and needles.

I enter the empty space and try to conjure you back into existence. If I concentrate, I even believe I can smell the scent of your soap but then the sense is overrun by the last smell of you, when your body had started to radiate the stench of death. Tempted to vomit, I go over to the window and wrench it up, putting my face next to the gap and sucking in air.

I sag to the floor. Sitting in the room now, years later, I can't see it how I did then. I can't imagine what steered me to take the actions I did. How could I have brought you up here, talked to you, cooked you food, tucked you in and propped you back up? Yet all these things were done when you were quite clearly cold, unresponsive, dead.

Although I realised the fact long ago, and have since become more familiar with it, this is the moment when I really understand that you are dead. The absence of the bed proves the absence of you. The clear lines on the carpet that are less faded by the sunlight seem to make the realisation sharper inside my mind. It has been lost in there for years and I have finally pinned it down. I feel its cold body, the overwhelming taste of salt, the sound of screaming and sobbing, the smell in my nostrils of stale furnishings.

Forgive me, Mum. I've held on too long…

I don't hear the door open or Michael softly crossing the room, avoiding the space where the bed is no longer, and kneeling beside his rupturing sister. The first thing I am aware of is his voice. "You shouldn't have come in here," he says, tucking my curls behind my ears and pressing his hands against my sodden cheeks.

"No Michael, I'm glad," I say, muffled by the onslaught of tears. "She's dead. She's really dead," I tell him firmly, as if he doesn't know.

Michael frowns, bowing his head, his bald spot baring itself to me again. It is only after several seconds that I realise he is crying too. I instantly pull him towards me. I think he might resist, yet he tumbles into my messy hold and allows me to comfort him.

"You're so much better," he says, a sad smile on his lips. I am too busy staring at his wet skin. I haven't seen him act this way since we were much younger. I almost think he has just come out of the sea and is wearing a skin coloured wet suit and when he takes it off, he will show me he hasn't been crying at all.

"Everything's much clearer now." I lean back, gazing through the still open window. I think about how I haven't been able to let you go, thinking that keeping you in the house back then somehow meant I would never lose you. Yet looking out at the sky now, I know that although you are dead, I will always have you in some sense.

Mum, I'll look after Michael, I promise. And even though I know you're dead, I'll still talk to you sometimes. Yet it's not the same. I have to talk to real people now – like Michael, and Thom, people at the shops and people in the street.

Mum, you're dead and we both have to let go.

If only I had been able to see that a couple of years ago, perhaps I wouldn't have pushed that man onto the tracks.

43 The Secret

Thom still has the taste of Sarah on his lips when he retraces his route back to Aunty Val's house in the numb darkness of early evening. He feels like he has been absent for so long; the paint on the door looks more cracked, the weeds droopier and extending their talons closer to the gate.

Is he ready to go back in there? Is he ready to face Aunty Val and Richard?

He stands at the front gate as though it is an obstacle to his entry and runs his tongue over his lips, closing his eyes and imagining he is back in the bedsit with Sarah. He doesn't understand why she left or why he'd been abandoned in the cold damp room immersed in the memory of her warm kiss.

It is only a few hours later, after Thom decides he needs some fresh boxers, that he makes his way across the city and back to the house he ran away from only days before. After all that has happened, he feels like he is an explorer who has returned after months of rough expeditions that have taken him to the brink of death.

He finally slinks through the gate, tiptoeing around the cracked paving, wondering how broken his family are inside the house. He reaches the door and somewhere in the depths of his pockets, rediscovers his keys. It takes him several seconds to direct the key into the lock at first; then he turns it in the wrong direction.

Eventually, Thom pushes the door open. The hallway is a murky crossing. All the lights are off, the darkness huddling in the corners and threatening to smother him. Thom takes a step inside, the soft pad of his feet on the carpet sounding like a stick clashing against a gong. Thom winches and closes himself inside gently, the lock making only a whisper as he guides it into the frame.

Thom stops and listens to the house, hearing nothing but the central heating humming and the natural creaks of the structure, like bones cracking spontaneously. Thom sighs loudly, adding to these sounds, becoming a human instrument. Thom closes his eyes and enjoys the way his breathing is in harmony with the moaning of the house. Is it sad? Like all three of them?

Thom still has his eyes closed when he realises that someone else is in the hallway. The music in Thom's mind is interrupted by the ragged breathing of another person; sounding as though they are catching their breath after inhaling smoke into their lungs. Thom opens his eyes and sees Aunty Val standing in the doorway to the kitchen. She slowly tiptoes her way towards him. She stops in front of him, giving him half a look before staring at the wall. After her tearful pleas the other night, Thom isn't expecting this.

"I didn't know if you were coming back," she says quietly. Thom has to strain to hear.

"Of course I would," he insists. He considers reaching out and taking her hand but decides not to. The only person he wants to touch in any capacity at the moment is Sarah. His hands have hurt too many people lately. His hands have been prying into things blindly with serious consequences.

"What happened to us?" she asks, locking her fingers together and twisting them. Again, Thom expects her to cry but she seems calmer. Perhaps she has finally accepted that Daniel is dead.

"We lost someone," he tells her, "and we found out more than we wanted to."

"Do you wish you hadn't found out that he knew about his death?"

"Sometimes I do." Thom shrugs. "But at other times I'm glad I can finally understand Daniel more than I did when he was alive." Aunty Val gives him a tight smile, not sure how she feels about this comment. Perhaps she has similar thoughts but, as Daniel's mother, can't justify vocalising them.

"Shall we sit down Thom? We can't talk properly here."

He nods and follows her to the kitchen where they both take a seat around the table. The table; where numerous family arguments, dinners, birthday parties, board games and bingo have taken place. What is this occasion? And will it restore the family that has been deteriorating revelation by revelation?

"You were right about Daniel's room," she starts quietly. Thom simply nods. "Where do you think it all went?" she continues.

"I have no idea." Thom answers and he really doesn't know. Perhaps Daniel burnt everything, or donated it to charity, or it is all stored in another lock up somewhere. They will probably never find out.

"How did you find out that Daniel knew about his death?" Aunty Val thrusts at him, nearly giving Thom a head rush. Thom thinks about how this all started – *the note* on the day of Daniel's funeral. An ending and a beginning in such close proximity. Why hadn't he just told them all there and then?

"I found a note in his room," Thom confesses, relief hissing out of his mouth.

"A note," she repeats slowly and continues, "what does it say, Thom?"

"It has the time and place that he died." At his words, she slams her hands down on the table, the thud echoing through the groaning house. Thom stiffens in his chair, regressing for a moment, and then tells himself to sit forward again.

"Nothing else?" Her voice creaks.

"No Aunty," Thom insists, his face flushing with heat, despite telling the truth.

"Why would that be in his room?" She grabs his sleeve and shakes his arm violently a few times. It is as though he is the one who wrote it.

"I don't know. I just found it," Thom pleads, pulling his sleeve out of her hold.

"Why didn't you say? Where is it?" She barks, shoving the table towards him so it crunches into his ribs. Thom sags over the table and massages his chest, winded. Aunty Val immediately sprints to his side and pulls his chair back. She rubs his chest in an attempt to apologise but he pushes her off.

"You just had to ask." Thom jumps to his feet and digs into his pocket. He drags out the crumpled note that he has carried everywhere since he found it. It looks worn and faded, a shadow of the pristine clue it had once been. It seems as overused as Thom's thoughts that have circled around him like a whirlpool, sucking him down and vomiting him back out.

Aunty Val hesitates. It takes her several seconds of staring into Thom's face to reach towards the note. She flattens it down with her palm and bends towards it as though she is peering over the edge of a cliff. Thom watches her expression twitching and contorting as she reads the words, her eyes rolling from side to side as she reads. It seems like she is reading a long book, not a one-line note.

Thom thinks about comforting her, placing a hand on her shoulder, but he doesn't. He waits beside her, arms crossed, ribs sore. Aunty Val begins smoothing out the paper again, scratching out the creases with her fingernails but it hardly makes any difference.

"Does this mean he did it?" she finally asks quietly, a tear slipping beyond her control and crawling down her cheek.

"Did what?"

"Killed himself?" She nearly chokes on the words.

"I think he did." Thom swallows hard.

"The police called and said that," she whispers, wrapping her own hands around herself, "but somehow I thought, maybe he didn't… But I guess there's too much proof now." Her teeth chatter, although the room is boiling.

"The police called?"

"Yes. They just said it's an open and shut case."

"It figures…" Thom shakes his head at the police's tendency to take the easy way out. "You know, I kept thinking that perhaps he just knew someone was trying to kill him, as crazy as that sounds… But I met that lady who came to the reading, Mrs Tray, and she showed me a letter from Daniel asking her to come to the reading in advance."

"Why did you go and see *that* woman?" she asks, her voice shaking on her body's behalf. She is looking at him as though he has done something wrong. Much like the note, him keeping it from her is a betrayal.

"I wanted to know why she attended the reading. I thought it might help me understand more about Daniel and why he died." Aunty Val grabs his hand and wrings it between hers. Thom wants to cry out but he holds it inside, the screaming roaring until he feels his head begin to throb.

"I know why," she says noiselessly but he only understands because he is staring into her face and sees the movement of her lips. The throbbing intensifies, yet Thom only hears the silent words in his mind "I know"… "I know why." Thom thinks he understands what the words mean; he thinks he remembers the definitions he learnt for them. Yet they don't seem to make sense, in any order, in any context he has known before.

"What?" Thom eventually murmurs. Aunty Val grips his hands harder until they begin to numb. She is trying to push him against the table, make him take a seat but he resists and pushes back. She lifts her hand up, pressing her clammy palm against his facial hair. Her sweat soaks into his beard.

"I know why he killed himself," she tells him again, louder, but she is looking at the floor.

"I can hear you but I don't understand," Thom confesses, grabbing her by the shoulders and shaking her gently as if the meaning will fall out of her. "If you knew something all this time, why wouldn't you have said?" Thom persists, grabbing the note from the table and wagging it in her face. "You can tell I've been going crazy with it all, tearing myself in pieces... *Why* didn't you save me?"

"That's all I've tried to do," she insists; grabbing him by the face and making him look into her eyes. Thom shoves her backwards, the blood throbbing through his veins so fiercely he feels dizzy.

"You were *saving* me? How exactly were you doing that?" he snarls.

"I'm sure he would've told you himself, if he hadn't died..." Aunty Val's chin crumbles as she fights her tears. "But then he died and I didn't think it was important... But I guess it was the reason." She stares into the distance, and Thom has to jab her in the arm in order to attract her attention again. She almost looks surprised that he is still there.

"He was dying anyway," she explains, a sob stabbing at her body so that she folds for a second, holding onto the table for support. Thom stares, wide mouthed, waiting to receive the words. Why do they sound so distant? Why does it sound like a language he has never heard before?

"Daniel was ill," she adds, sucking in air continuously but with little effect. She is bent over the table, as though she is about to give birth.

"What are you talking about?" Thom spits. "Daniel wasn't ill. I would've known. Richard would have known... we *all* would have..." Thom stumbles over words like he is jumping hurdles with his legs tied together.

"I'm sorry," Aunty Val moans, pressing against her eyelids to force the tears back into her eyes but they gather under her eyelashes anyway. "I'm so sorry Thom. I've been a terrible mum." She sobs harder, bending further towards the table as though an invisible force is pushing her down.

"What are you talking about?" Thom pulls at his hair. Aunty Val turns and pulls him towards her, her nails digging into his arms until he is certain the skin will break.

"Daniel was dying," she repeats. "I should have told you but I just didn't know how to. After he died... I didn't think it mattered anymore."

"Of course it matters." Thom shoots his words at her, causing her to cower away from him slightly. "Do you understand what you're saying?" Thom screeches. "Do you understand?" He screams louder. Aunty Val bows her head, her tears now dropping straight from her eyes onto the wooden floor with a loud splat.

"I wanted to tell you but Daniel got so angry when we talked…" she trails off, closing her eyes, remembering. Her eyes are clenched like tiny fists. "I know he didn't mean it, he just got so angry…" She lifts her hands up, still holding onto him by the wrists, and presses his tensed hands against her cheeks. She is performing his actions for him.

"Is that when he hit you?"

"How do you…?" Aunty Val begins but loses her words in her stuttering.

"*Know*?" Thom finishes for her, taking his hands back. "Richard told me the other day when you fainted." Aunty Val's face plummets instantly.

"You shouldn't think he was a bad person. *Please Thom*. You believe me, don't you?" She raises her arms again to reach out to him but she drops them at his flat expression.

"He must've been upset. He just found out he was ill, maybe dying." Thom shakes his head, some of the puzzle he has been twisting and turning around for weeks finally making sense. "I guess he just thought jumping would be quicker."

"I don't think that's why he jumped," she says. This time her words are clear, like bells echoing in his ears for minutes afterwards. Thom stares at her, feeling faint.

"I think you need to explain that."

44 The Donor

Initially, Aunty Val doesn't say anything. For a moment, Thom wonders if she remembers what she has just said, how she has just ripped his feet from his legs so he can barely stand. She gives a short exhale, pulls out a chair and seats herself. Thom watches her, clasping her hands together in front of her, staring straight ahead. Thom finally takes the seat opposite her.

"You know why he jumped?" Thom asks sternly. Aunty Val blinks for several seconds, her lips taut and dry. It is so silent Thom can hear her swallowing; it is the loud and elongated sound of fluid squeezing through a tight pipe.

"Yes," she whispers, not wanting to reveal the secret she has been keeping from him for months. Thom feels livid and guilty, because although he should be mad for Daniel's sake, he mainly feels angry for himself. How can she have lied to him? How can she have let him comfort her when she knew the truth?

"I'm sorry, Thom," she mutters.

"I'm not interested in that, just tell me," Thom says viciously.

"Okay," she agrees. Thom is staring at her, wondering how the person he has always trusted and respected can look so hazy and stained across the table.

"About nine months before he died, Daniel asked to talk to me. Well you know how he never liked to talk much... so I sat down straight away to listen," she pauses, each letter an obstacle course from her brain to the atmosphere. "He said he was ill, he said he'd been to the doctor's because he'd been feeling really tired. He thought nothing of it... but they called him back in and told him; he had leukaemia."

"How could that be?" Thom leans forward, the word 'leukaemia' striking him in the face. There hadn't been an inkling of this or even the hint of an inkling.

"I know Thom... *leukaemia*. I had no idea about it. I always imagined children got it, not young men..." She keeps gulping in the middle of words, chewing on their sounds and leaving them ragged. "I didn't take it very well Thom. After all these years just the four of us, it felt like part of myself was torn away." She hopes Thom will say something, perhaps sympathise with her, but he remains silent. "For one of only a few times, he looked scared, Thom. He was nearly crying. He *even* let me hold him."

"Did they say they could help him?" Thom asks quietly, imagining the scene at this very table as she describes it. He can't see Daniel though; he can't see Daniel in the pose she describes.

"A few weeks later, Daniel went to hospital. They told him he would have to have chemotherapy and after that, might need to get a bone marrow transplant," she explains sharply. The end of the sentence is pronounced but Thom thinks there is a lot more she should be divulging. She can't end the conversation here, although she seems to want to.

"So what happened?"

"Well, Daniel wanted to be prepared for everything involved with the treatment." She pauses, taking a few deep breaths. "Do you know what that means, Thom? About the bone marrow?" Aunty Val takes his hand. She seems to be tugging on it gently as though she is trying to stay afloat. Thom ignores this but when he looks into her face, finds it harder to ignore the sweat that has swollen up underneath her fringe.

"How does it work? I might think I know but I probably don't."

"Full siblings are usually the best match. Their healthy marrow is meant to encourage the growth of blood cells or something like that. I asked a friend to look it up online but I don't remember everything now."

"I did hear some things like that," Thom agrees. She nods and begins rolling her head, rolling her thoughts around. They splash out in her expression like water slamming against the sides of a deck.

"I have something else to tell you Thom but... I'm scared."

"Why he did it?" Thom tries to pull it out of her. At his words, she lets out a quiet whimper. Her secret seems to be fighting its way out.

"I have wanted to tell you for months, well – for years."

"What the hell is it, Aunty?" Thom snaps. She reaches out, letting her hand hover near his face but instantly takes it back. The conversation has been plagued by half-gestures and withdrawals.

"Daniel wanted to ask Richard if he would be a donor," she says, every sentence seeming like the start of a novel.

"Did Richard say no?"

"No," Aunty Val answers quickly. "Daniel never asked him."

"Why not?" Thom yelps.

"When Daniel told me he was ill, he asked me if I thought Richard would help him," she pauses, her breaths growing shallow and rapid, "but I told him that Richard couldn't help him, even if he wanted to."

"Are you saying what I think you are?" Thom finally believes he understands something in the whole scheme of facts that have been eluding him.

"They weren't full siblings." She lets out a muffled sob. Thom gets up and moves to her side. After some hesitation, he puts his arms around her. She leans back into him.

"How could you have never said something before?"

"I don't know..."

"So there's no chance Richard could have helped?"

"Not *no* chance," she admits, tightening her grip on his arms.

"So what happened? Why didn't Daniel talk to Richard? Why didn't *you*?" Thom feels like he is accusing her of something but he doesn't know what. He tightens his grip around her but not in need of affection, instead possessed by anger.

"It was too hard to talk about." She shrugs.

"Don't you know who their fathers are?" Thom taunts her unfairly. She instantly throws his arms off.

"Of course I do," she spits.

"Well which one of them has a different dad to Uncle Peter?" Thom leans against the table, looking at her sideways. She tears at her hair, which has become unloved and clumped together.

"Daniel," she confesses in a whisper.

"Shit," Thom twitches. "Can you imagine how heartbroken he must've been? He probably thought he might be saved and then he finds out that they weren't real brothers." Thom shakes his head. "And more than that, it meant life and death for him."

Thinking about Daniel, he wants to sob on his behalf. Thom wants to tear the cupboards from the walls, pull out the pipes and let the water spray out like punctured vessels.

"Did you tell him who his dad was?" Thom asks, not able to look at her. He turns and stares outside the window into the garden. He sees the chair where he sat after finding the notebook, the notebook that said terrible things and claimed he wrote them.

"I told him."

"And how did he react?"

"He went crazy," she whimpers, "but I didn't expect any less. I deserved it..." she trails off, too traumatised to cry. She locks her eyes on an indistinguishable spot on the wallpaper and begins to sway.

"You should've told him but it's not your fault for being with someone else." Thom tries to comfort her but his words feel like wood being eaten from the inside, ready to crumble at the slightest touch. Thom slides into the chair next to her, feeling slightly dizzy.

"I wish it was that simple." She finally turns to look at him. With a small toss of her head, her whole appearance seems to have changed. Her face is still and not wet with tears for one of the first times in weeks.

"There's still something else, isn't there?" Thom narrows his eyes. "I can't even fathom what it might be, but there's definitely *something*..." Thom ventures. He wonders if Daniel's father is violent or a murderer or some obscure relative of Aunty Val's.

"You're such a clever boy." She smiles, forgetting the situation for a brief reflex. Similarly, Thom bathes in it for the millisecond it lasts.

"Daniel's dad, well it's complicated... he and I weren't in a relationship."

"That's not that complicated."

"No Thom," she stops him. "This is important for you too." She is staring so violently that Thom has to look away.

"How is Daniel's dad important to me?"

"Daniel's dad is important... to you... because..." Her voice shows her weakness again. It sounds like a radio losing reception. "You have the same father."

45 The Red Threads

The house is sinking. To everyone else, it looks the same as it always has but I know the truth. Its insides are rotting and crumbling. The imploding ceilings are striking them all on the heads so they leave the house feeling dazed and detached from everyday life. Soon perhaps they will be stuck inside because all the doors will be blocked and the stairs a pile of dust, shaved down by pressure.

When I'd been falling apart, I didn't see this all clearly. I saw their grief painted on their sullen faces, their ragged clothes and ragged skin, in their diminishing forms. Yet with the house, only the edges of the wallpaper had begun to peel and fall off. The red paint on the front door had begun to crack, the grass in the front garden grown wild and unshaven.

Looking at the house now, even in settling darkness of night, it looks like a person slumped over. How can it be saved? How can I push the bricks and windows back up so they are standing as they should be once again?

I wonder if Thom is in there now, what they are saying to each other, whether they will ever understand each other post-Daniel's death. Will Daniel's ghost ever release the house? He has removed himself from that room but the house won't forget. The people inside are connected to him with an invisible thread that will follow them for years, through their daily lives, in relationships with others, during sleep. Just as the scarf has never quite released me, they are trapped forever.

The vain part of me thought I could save them. Yet I am the one who needed saving and still do. I have managed to get a hand above the ground but I am still buried in the past and all the things I have done. If I stay near them too, I will never get away from Daniel and what he made me do.

But Thom... I think I love him. I can't help thinking about him, letting him press his lips against mine, letting his madness fester in front of my eyes. It must be real love if you can still love someone when they are losing themselves. Or is it blindness? Can you really love someone if they don't know their own feelings?

The questions are infinite now. Before this, I have no recollection of what I thought about all day. What flashed through my mind as I walked down the street? Or whilst sitting in my bedsit? What did I dream about?

It seems when you died; my life was severed. And now, I have been severed from the life I have been leading since then. I'm no longer who I was the last few years, but I'm no longer who I was before you died either.

If I just tell Thom the truth... Maybe he can understand? No. He does understand what Daniel can do to a person but murder... why should he understand that? Either way, whether coerced or voluntarily, I killed that man.

If I tell them all, will it really help any of them anyway? It isn't the fact that he is dead that pains them the most; it is the confusion and the unanswered questions. Thom looks so helpless sometimes, when all he wants is someone to tell him why Daniel left all these things behind. They don't want to know how he died, but why. Maybe it would help if I could tell them why he made me push him. But I don't know that. And if I did, could I put myself on the line for them? Would Michael put me back in the hospital and never trust me again?

All the questions make me wish I could recede into my madness, yet madness makes no sense to me now. I see it flaring up in Thom and I don't know what to do to rescue him from its grip. I hope his family will do that for me, as Michael rescued me. When I met Thom, I asked myself how I could've hurt this man for no reason. Now, I ask how could Daniel hurt his own cousin, and why and why and why and why?

46 Reverberations

Thom doesn't know how it happens but the next time he is aware, he is sitting on the kitchen floor. His elbow is throbbing. A chair is lying beside him. Aunty Val is peering over the table at him but doesn't move to help.

"Did you hear me, Thom?"

"I'm not sure," Thom mumbles, cradling his elbow with his other hand. He wants a sling so everyone can see there is something wrong with him. How will people be able to tell that he has been split in half when there are no signs on the outside?

"You and Daniel have the same father," she repeats. Her voice keeps slicing through him like a glacier.

"But that would mean he and I were..." Thom can't even say that word, though it is only two syllables.

"Yes, brothers," she finishes.

"But that doesn't make any sense." Thom heaves himself to his feet, supporting himself with the table. He retakes his seat.

"It makes sense if you know the details," she tells him and pushes her chair back, the scraping of the chair rupturing his insides further. She walks past him, her familiar smell touching him in the way she can't now, and opens a cupboard behind him. She places a set of papers on the table and steps back.

"What is this?" Thom demands, focussing on her lips, hoping they will lie.

"Read it, Thom."

Thom reluctantly obeys but it takes him several seconds to focus on the words at the top. Finally, Thom sees them: *Contract of Surrogacy*. As soon as his eyes absorb these words, his eyes instantly blur again. "What the fuck..." Thom mumbles, the word 'surrogacy' repeatedly crashing against his forehead.

"Your mother and father couldn't have kids together," Aunty Val says quietly, as she sits opposite him again. The table sits between them like a mediator. "After years of trying, they finally got tested and

339

found out your mother was infertile."

"What the hell are you talking about?" Thom snarls.

"The truth, Thom."

"How could my mother be infertile? And what the fuck does this have to do with me and Daniel having the same dad?" Thom thinks he should faint but instead, he feels like he has seized up, ready to attack.

"They came to me one day and they asked me if I would consider being a surrogate for them," she says, a brief smile passing over her lips. Yet, they quickly darken with a guilty frown. "After thinking about it for a while, I decided I would do it. I just wanted to help my sister, *that's all*."

"So you're some saint are you?"

"If I were a saint, I would've told you years ago." She bows her head.

"What exactly are you telling me?" Thom slams his hand against the table and winces as discreetly as he can when it begins to throb. Aunty Val grabs it, squeezing it hard to enforce the words that follow; "I carried you. You were twins."

Thom rips his hand away from her and jumps from his seat, wrenching the table upwards and launching it across the kitchen. Aunty Val stays in her seat, as though she is expecting the table to return and she can once again lean her elbows on it. Thom doesn't move again. Inside his mind, moments and words are gathering together like a puddle at the bottom of a gutter.

When he entered the room after the wake and Aunty Val turned white…

The way Sarah seemed so fascinated by him instantly and kissed him…

How Daniel left him clues to make him question everything and everyone…

The number 11 on the lock up door...

Why hasn't Thom realised? Daniel has been trying to lead him here from the moment he died. In the face of leukaemia, Daniel discovered something so hurtful that he didn't want to live anyway. And through these clues and his departure, he wanted to show Thom how similar they are, so similar because of a genetic bond neither of them knew about for most of their lives.

Thom shakes himself. "So who is the woman?"

"What woman?" Aunty Val says, sticking to the chair. Thom paces around her as though he might swing an axe and behead her.

"The woman who gave her egg for my dad... you know, to put in you." Thom feels like a child again.

"Thom, I thought you understood," she says in a high-pitched tone. Thom stops in front of her.

"Understood what?"

"Your mother asked me to do it, so it wouldn't be some stranger. I'm the one," she tells Thom, cowering, shaking. Thom sags into nothing. He once again finds himself being looked down on, staring up at her from miles away, her face shivering behind a curtain of tears.

"You are not... you're not..." Thom splutters and crawls away backwards. "How can you say you are, when I already have a mother? You're just sick and lonely and you want to keep me here because Daniel's dead." Thom pushes up against the wall. "Well, I'm *not* staying here with you, no matter what lies you tell me." Thom doesn't take his eyes from her as he heaves himself up near the kitchen sink.

She edges closer. Thom glances at the back door, trying to gauge how far away it is. He also stares at the hallway behind her, wishing it would chew her up. Yet nothing happens and he doesn't escape. In the few seconds he has been thinking, she is only inches away and when he realises this, she has already grabbed him.

"I *am* your mother," she declares. "I've tried to tell you so many times but it's been so hard. Your parents kept promising they'd tell you and then they died and I didn't know if you'd be able to cope with it. I didn't want to take their memory away from you... I'm so sorry, Thom."

"Say this is true..." Thom begins, nauseated by the mere notion, "If you gave birth to us, why did we get separated?" Thom feels smug; sure he has discovered the minute snag in her claims. Yet she remains in the same position, with the same expression and his hopes begin to plummet.

"If you read the contract, you'll see. We changed it after you were both born. We only found out it was twins much later in the pregnancy and when I gave birth, I just couldn't let you both go..." She is sobbing.

"Your parents weren't happy and it took a lot of talking and thinking but we decided – well *they* agreed, to let me have one of you," she pauses, a sour smile on her lips. "It's scary and terrible and I don't think either of us were truly happy with it but thankfully, they understood how terrible it would be to have to give up two babies at once."

"I can't believe this. You said I was early, that's why we were both born then..." Thom shakes his head violently. Then his attention turns, "How did you decide anyway? Did you flip a coin? Did you play highest card draw? How exactly did you choose a baby to give away?"

Her shoulders are slumped, her eyes red and soggy, her mouth a drooping flower that cannot be revived. "You don't understand, Thom," she cries, sobbing and moaning, "If you knew what it's like to give up a child, let alone two..." Thom swivels his arms and grabs hold of her by the arms, shaking her.

"And you think being lied to your whole fucking life isn't hard?" he screams, his spit jumping out and clinging to her skin. "How could you do it, Aunty...?" Thom demands and instantly feels like a fool. "Or whatever the hell you are," he adds, starting to sink once again but she holds him up.

"I didn't want to give either of you up but we'd agreed, Thom. I couldn't back out because even if I'd tried to take them to court, the lawyers said I would've lost."

"Daniel and I deserved to know."

"I couldn't tell him without you being told too and your parents kept saying 'when the time is right' but then they weren't around anymore."

"You're blaming them? I guess that's convenient for you now they're dead." Thom feels like his blood is boiling in his veins. He looks at the back of his hands to check bubbles aren't rising underneath his skin. However, his skin retains the normality he can no longer see in this kitchen, in his 'Aunty', his whole stupid lie of a life.

"I think your mother felt very hurt she couldn't even provide an egg. I think she couldn't bear to tell you she wasn't your biological mother."

"You won't take her away from me," Thom tells her firmly.

"I never wanted to, especially after they died. I didn't want to take those memories away from you, you'd lost everything else." She tries to pull him into a hug but he pushes her back.

"I hadn't lost everything then, but I have now." Thom drops her arms. He moves away from her towards the door but before he can reach it, he bends over and vomits. His body convulses violently as it forces its way out of his throat. Thom can't fight it, he lets it overpower him and watches it elongating on the floor below him.

When his stomach is empty, he pushes himself up and swallows several times, the sour taste of vomit lingering. He remembers having the same reaction after finding the note. He remembers the guilty sick stain on his sleeve that he stared at throughout the funeral.

"You haven't lost me, Thom," Aunty Val says, placing her hand on his back without looking at his indiscretion on the kitchen floor.

"What am I supposed to do, Aunty? Start calling you *mum*?"

"No, Thom. Not at all. But we can sort this out."

"Daniel didn't think so."

"I hoped I wouldn't lose both of you because of this." She shakes her head sadly. Thom can't help looking at her now. When he considers her features properly, he can see the truth. He can see the shape of her mouth that he and Daniel shared, and he remembers the shade of her natural hair that matches his unkempt mop. He has never seen her properly before. He has spent his life with foggy eyesight, his beloved Aunt elevated so high that he could never see the frightening similarities.

"Why didn't you tell me?" Thom's face crumples. He looks down; ashamed to show her how she has torn him apart. "Why has everyone been lying to me?"

"Who else lied, darling?" She cuddles him. He is tempted to resist her again but he is too weak. He lets her hold him up, like he did for her on the day of the funeral. Somehow telling the truth has made her stronger, for the both of them.

"Sarah. You. The only people that matter," Thom muffles into her shoulder.

"Sarah matters to you? What about Emma?"

Thom pushes back. "Is it really your place to be grilling me?"

"No, of course not. I just didn't know." She touches his unshaven cheek and scratches his beard playfully. "I miss talking to you Thom."

"I've missed you too," Thom admits, "but we can't just go back."

"I love you, Thom. Please work at this with me." She leans her forehead against his. He stares into her eyes, his heart clunking. He wants to ask her thousands of questions, he recounts times when she started telling him something but then changed her mind. Why hadn't she ever finished the sentence?

In the next moment he thinks about the last time he was here. He thinks about how he told her that Daniel knew he was going to die and how she collapsed. Had she been afraid he'd found out about the leukaemia? Or had she been afraid he had found out they were brothers?

"How *did* you choose, Aunty? How did you pick?" Thom presses his head into hers until he thinks he hears the bones crack. The words poke her in the eye. She blinks several times.

"There was no decision, I took one baby and your parents took the other."

Thom shoves her away. "That's it? A lottery to choose which child you take?"

"It would be more horrible if we'd had some criteria, don't you think?"

"That's why he hated me," Thom says suddenly.

"What?"

"The night I arrived, I took over his bedroom. And you were always giving me all this special attention. He must've sensed it all along and when he found out... no wonder he left me all this shit to figure out." Thom crushes his hair in his fists, his brain unfreezing.

"What stuff did he leave?" Val asks.

"Nothing, nothing…" Thom dismisses her. "He must've always known something but I guess he didn't really believe it. He just couldn't deal with it."

"Stop it, Thom. We couldn't have changed things. People take things how they want to," she says, resigned.

"You're actually blaming *him* now?" Thom advances on her.

"I'm not blaming him."

"You've ruined us." Thom starts to sob. He moans and attempts to bury himself in the wall. Yet he can't push himself inside and hide. She can still see him; she can still claw at him and try to comfort him.

"I love you, Thom. I love you so much," she cries. Her sobbing and her words seem fake to him. She is a lying bitch who has torn his heart out, who has watched them grow up in her lie, who has taken away his parents forever.

Before he can stop himself, he swings around. The first thing he knows about what he has done, she is leaning against the worktop holding her lip. The blood doesn't appear until a few seconds later. Thom watches it swell out between her fingers.

Thom tries to speak but all he can do is howl.

"It's okay, Thom. I know you didn't mean it." She lowers her hand, the blood spotting her hand and lip. Yet she doesn't wipe it away. He stares at it until it appears to spread across her face, turning her entire face into a red mess. This is the blood that made him. This is the blood that runs through his DNA.

"I'm so confused. I can't work out… I don't know how… Please tell me…" The words get lost inside the avalanche steadily blocking exit points through his synapses, his mouth.

"It can be different this time," she says hopefully.

Thom hears her words but can only think of how everything isn't different at all. Like Daniel, no one really understands him anymore. Like Daniel, he feels angry and betrayed. Like Daniel, he has found out his whole life has been a lie. He has hurt her too. He has kissed the same woman Daniel had.

Thom begins to back away into the darkness of the hallway. She reaches out, tries to speak but realises it is useless. Her lip quivers hopefully, like a person still clinging onto the faith that after everything, it can't possibly be over. Yet Thom feels like a full stop has been stamped on his heart.

He is swallowed by the darkness, becomes an outline and flashes briefly in the light from the street lights outside, before disappearing completely.

47 The Bloodied Scarf

The air covers me like a hot flannel. My skin feels numb so I can't feel the sweat dribbling down my face. I only feel it when it gathers above my eyebrows and I have to wipe it away with my sleeve.

I guess I knew I would end up here at some point. After all the confrontations with my past lately, it seems apt and only fitting that I face up to the location of my crime. Yet, it doesn't stop me shivering in the muggy cavern.

After sitting outside the Mansen house yesterday, I realised that I had to come back. This station, the trains, the smells, those oversized posters and the silence of death – they have all been haunting me since that day. I can't run forever.

The scarf trails behind me, darkened with my brother's blood. I slowly approach the place where I stood on that day. It seems wrong when I see the clock says 13:45. I am early. Yet I won't be meeting anyone here. No one knows where I am and the people around me are all strangers, with no inkling that I'm a murderer returning to the scene.

I wonder if any of the others on this platform were here that day. If as they watched helplessly; they screamed in horror, had been unable to tear their gaze away from the broken body crushed and flung by the train, the spray of blood marking them forever. Am I the only one who walked out of the station on that day unable to remove the image of that falling man caught by the train in mid-air?

I am standing on the spot. Nothing about it distinguishes it from the rest of the platform. There are no marks, no blood, and no red tape prohibiting others from stamping all over it. It sickens me how life continues so easily. How many people have stood here since that day? How many trains have passed through the tunnel? How many people have seen the clock at 15:32?

I look down at the tracks and see nothing but dirty metal and a few pieces of rubbish. When I try to imagine Daniel's face, I can't even remember how he looked. All I see now is Thom. I wish then that Thom could be here, holding my hand tightly to stop me jumping into the escalating wind. Yet how could I explain to him why I need him here in this spot?

The wind begins to thrash against me until I nearly topple, the scarf fluttering madly beside me. Others begin moving forward and I look back at them, wondering if one of them will push me in front of the train. It would be fitting after all. The tunnel is lightening, the spotlight approaching, honing in on me – the culprit.

I am sure I am a beacon, a firework spinning in circles. I am certain I am screaming out loud but it is only inside my mind. This is the scream I didn't give Daniel on that day. I killed him without surprise, without emotion, without my eyes rolling in water. I believed that I knew exactly what I'd been doing but I'd been miles from reality, standing in a bubble where the only thing that could reach me was Daniel.

The air seems clogged with dirt, thick with the sweat pouring from me. I try to breathe but the opening seems blocked. The train's nose is poking out of the tunnel and within moments, rushes past me, without hesitation. I realise how quick the transition is, how I must have taken the precise split second to kill him. He must've been proud of his work. He must've loved saying those words to me. *Right on time...*

I suddenly realise I am standing in the way of the doors and people are barging their way past me. I move aside. When the last person has exited, a man waves me to go ahead of him, but I shake my head and tell him, "I'm in the wrong place." He frowns gently but I turn away and make my way off the platform.

It is only when I reach the surface that I feel I can breathe again. I gulp in so much air that I feel dizzy. At the same time, I feel so alive. Although I believed killing Daniel brought me to life, I know now that facing up to everything has made me alive again. No matter how hard this all is, I am living a normal emotional and complicated life. My feelings are more realistic now.

I am aware now that I am connected to only some things in this giant maze of a city, not connected to everything. I can't see emotions in the air anymore. I can't save that family from implosion. I can't make up for the murder by joining their lives. I can't blame anyone but myself.

In a sense, I am limiting my world again but it feels good. By realising my limitations, I am setting myself free again. I am putting the objects and people and thoughts back in the 'right' places. When I look at the street now, I am fascinated by the shop signs, the signs telling people what to do and what not to do, the traffic lights, the paving slabs set in lines – how controlled everything is and how everything is there to warn and instruct.

This is the world I left behind several years ago. It is coming back to me like a lover I rejected, still enthralled by me. I am remembering its beauty, the way it merges together and functions. Having imagined my own messages for so long, I realise they are naturally here all around me. Yet, I have ignored them. Now their messages are like kind words sent to a recovering relative.

I can never rewind time and take back my actions. It is too late to save Daniel but I can save myself. I can feel regret. I could go as far as to report myself to the police but I am not brave enough and I can't see the benefit. After all, what I did is exactly what Daniel planned. Can you be a real murderer if someone led you to do it?

Beginning to shiver, I'm suddenly aware there is a sharp wind whipping at my face. I pull my coat around myself and begin to walk away from the station. Looking back a few times, I see the cars continuing to jam and crawl and argue. I see the people passing but not noticing one another. I decide that life is continuing for them so it should continue for me. He is gone. Not even the platform remembers him.

48 The Beginning

Thom misses Sarah by only moments. He may not have seen her anyway, as he is in a trance, his feet leading him to the one place he hasn't allowed himself to investigate.

The first time he is aware of anything, he is standing in front of the barriers, which won't open. Thom thinks for a moment and decides it's money he needs. Digging a few coins from his pocket, he slots them into the machine, buying the first option he sees. He hasn't come here to travel; he's come to see the place where his 'brother' died. The brother he never owned, the brother he has lost before he even had him. Can this all be true? Can the woman who saved him after his parents' death really be half of what made him?

Thom feels nauseated whenever he even tries to think about it. He had spent the entire night walking through the city, darting through the backstreets, believing he could hide from himself.

He shakes the thought of his 'Aunty' away and gets through the barrier. The world can't get through though. In the station, it is only he and Daniel. This is what Daniel wanted, to show him the truth, to punish them all for their lies.

He follows the signs for the platform. He remembers reading the platform direction in the paper and thinking it an odd addition. It was probably just to explain to everyone why the tube service was disrupted that day...

As Thom takes each step, he begins to shiver. He thinks it's the wind but he realises it's his legs softening and failing him. He feels humiliated, letting some people pass while he recovers himself. Was Daniel afraid? Did he clutch onto the banister with sweaty hands? Did he consider changing his mind?

Thom decides that he must move quickly or he won't get there at all. He almost runs down the last ten steps and lands on the platform he has been running from since the day of Daniel's funeral. He hasn't been in a station for a long time. Yet it looks the same as most others. There are people dotted along it, a countdown machine reporting on the train destinations and times, large posters faded by dust and soot, an empty track.

The track is a snake that can sliver to life at any moment. It can take him into its dark mouth. It seems to wrap its chain-like body around his chest and leave him gulping for air. He leans against the wall and tells himself to breathe. When he finally feels calmer, his hand comes back to him covered in dirt. Like the lock up, he will leave dirtier and more damaged than when he came.

"Are you okay?" a woman, who is standing several feet away, asks. Thom nods hastily and moves hurriedly past her, further down the platform. Thom realises then that he doesn't have a clue where Daniel jumped. Was it that end nearer the entrance? Or this end nearer where the train comes from? Thom wishes there is some kind of marking, or a sign: *This is where he jumped!* Yet, there is nothing that can tell him anything about that day.

This is useless, he spits in his mind. He stamps his foot so hard that some people give him a sideways look, too afraid to stare in case he becomes vicious.

The wind begins to increase and Thom hears a faint roar. If he really concentrates, he can already feel the platform vibrating. The increasing rush revives the crowded air. He closes his eyes and thinks about the lights of the train, the people inside who don't know what awaits them, the driver thinking about his dinner plans, and Daniel.

The roar gathers momentum, the sound making Thom's heart bang to its rhythm. He is no longer a person; he is a beat, a heart standing alone with its scars and holes. The train is speaking to him in a language that only he can hear.

Thom is hypnotised by the train. Thom is captured by the track. He doesn't realise how enthralled he is until he feels the train whip just past his nose, a fraction of a millimetre away. He is being dragged back by something. He tries to pull forward but he can't escape. He has a knot in the middle of his back and it won't release him.

"What are you doing?" a voice cries out by his ear. As the doors of the train slide open, Thom finds himself sagged against someone. The other people on the platform stare at him; the passengers coming off the train step over him and look back.

Thom pushes away from the person he is lying on and sits up. He turns to see a man, breathless and still clutching onto him. He is wearing a luminous waistcoat and Thom recognises the London Underground uniform beneath it. His face is wet with sweat. Thom is sweating himself, his t-shirt clinging to his body.

"What are you doing?" he cries again. The crowd of people who have got off the train have gone away, but some linger to watch the two men tangled on the floor; unaware they have just avoided screeching breaks and chaos. The doors of the train have snapped shut and the train is now moving off.

"I'm sorry," Thom mumbles to the man. He can't force himself to stand up. The man finally lets go of Thom's coat, satisfied he can no longer harm himself, and gives him an encouraging pat instead.

"I'm Sam," the man tells Thom and offers his clammy hand.

Thom thinks about refusing but decides he is just as sweaty, "Thom."

"Let's get you out of here," Sam says, pulling Thom up. Thom leans on him, like an injured footballer limping from the pitch. Thom leans on this stranger because he feels like he hasn't got anyone else.

Sam takes Thom to a door along the platform. Thom has never really noticed these doors before, or not properly anyway and experiences an odd stab of adrenaline thinking about what could be behind it. Yet when Sam struggles with the key and heaves it open, there seems to be nothing spectacular there. There is only a harshly lit corridor that Thom can't quite see the end of. Sam carries Thom inside and locks them in.

Thom can now see the doorways lining the corridor. There is the sound of a television or a radio coming from one room, the smell of burning toast and the faint hint of smoke hanging in the air. Sam directs Thom to the second door on the left and deposits him on a rundown looking sofa. Thom feels quite comfortable on this, as though a new sofa would offend his state of mind.

"Tea?" Sam asks. Thom nods and watches the man disappear out of the room. Thom leans into the chair and seems to breathe for the first time since he entered the station. Perhaps for the first time today.

His whole life is irreversibly changed. There is no way to retrace the steps and go back, no sense in which his existence isn't different. Everything he thought he was, he is now not. He is not a nephew, not a cousin, not a boyfriend, not an employee, not a detective, not a victim...

"Here." Sam appears beside him and hands him a mug. Thom accepts it and wraps his hands around it, letting the warmth of the mug attempt to melt the icicle speared through his heart. Thom knows it is meant to be tea but he can't taste anything. It could be blood or poison and he wouldn't be able to distinguish it.

"Don't people usually say thanks for saving their life?" Sam jokes, sitting on the arm of the chair. Thom looks up at him, almost amused, wondering why he doesn't feel thankful.

"I guess they usually do." Thom shrugs and rethinks, "thanks for doing that."

"So were you going to do it?" Sam says quietly. Thom considers the question for a long time, staring into his tea.

"I don't know," Thom admits. "I didn't even realise what I was doing."

"Someone was hit by a train not long ago."

"You saw it?" Thom jumps, spilling a few drops of his drink on his trousers.

Sam sits upright in his chair. "You sound like you know something about it."

"It was my... brother." Thom exercises the term. He has been an only child all his life, an orphan since twelve. Now he has a brother, a mother, and a half-brother. If only it didn't all come from lies, he could feel happy about it all. Yet he only feels betrayed and lost. He didn't even know about him and Daniel being twins until it was too late...

"Your brother?" Sam gasps. "And what were you doing? Going to join him or something?" Sam's heroic act is now undermined. Has he merely saved someone who is ready to die?

"I just came to see where he died. I didn't plan on anything... like that."

"But you were about to do it. You were about a millimetre away!" Sam wriggles, biting his lip hard.

"I'm a bit of a mess. I have no idea what I was doing."

"But what if you'd died?"

"Then I guess we wouldn't be here." Thom shrugs. He even smiles, although it isn't funny. Sam's mouth also curls into a small smile in response, not knowing how else to put his face. They fall silent for a few minutes, the trains rumbling on the platforms, the smell of burnt toast weakening.

"Did you see him die? Were you on the platform?" Thom finally asks after the silence nags him into speech.

"I was in the surveillance room that day," Sam tells him. The full stop on his sentence seems so final that Thom's suspicions instantly swell out of him like a scab forming, forcing him to scratch.

"So you saw it happen?" Thom looks up at Sam, who is staring into his mug, with an expression as though he is falling into a black pit.

"I saw it, yes. That's why I've been watching people even more," Sam confesses. "I don't want it to happen again."

"What did you see, Sam?" Thom asks desperately, appealing to the stranger like he is an old friend. Yet, this man owes him nothing. And equally Thom knows nothing about this man except what he can see: a broad-shouldered man with a hint of a Jamaican accent, wearing a loose-fitting London Underground uniform, with a wedding ring that clatters against his mug. Does this add up to disclosure?

"I can't believe I'm talking to that guy's brother." Sam shakes his head.

"His name was Daniel," Thom tells him, hoping the personification will appeal to him. Sam nods and exhales heavily.

"What do you know, Thom?"

"I know he's dead, that's all." Thom doesn't tell the entire truth, that Daniel knew about his own death, that he left behind clues to let Thom know. It will only confuse this man if Thom tries to explain.

"I think I need to show you something." Sam stands, scratching at his short afro. He puts his mug down on the table. Thom does the same. "Come on," Sam gestures and leaves the room. Thom scrambles after him.

He takes Thom further down the corridor, stopping in front of a door. The sign says *surveillance room*. Sam enters and Thom slowly follows him, the room seeming like a tunnel leading into a deep cavern. Even if he physically exits the room, will he ever be able to really take himself out of here?

"Do you really want to see this?" Sam asks as he takes a seat in front of a screen. On the screen, people are standing on the escalator, staring ahead or playing on their phones for the last time before they are cut off. Thom meets Sam's eyes and nods weakly. Does he want this? Does he need this?

"I didn't think about a video," Thom mutters inaudibly, shrinking into himself.

"I'm sorry," Sam says, digging under the desk and retrieving a DVD. He checks the date on it as though he is checking which film he recorded from the TV, nodding to himself in agreement. "I may have held onto it for a few days afterwards." He flashes Thom a guilty look, bowing his head as he pushes the DVD into the machine. "But I gave it to the police last week. Didn't they call you?"

Thom guesses that it explains why Aunty Val has only just heard from the police, simply to be brushed off with the words 'open and shut case' and 'suicide'. Thom begins to speak but, as the fuzzy screen flicks on, Thom's head feels just as fuzzy.

The platform appears on the screen, a time and date tattooed on the edge of the screen. It says 15:29. It is nearly time. Thom guesses Sam has looked through the footage and recorded only this part. Perhaps he has watched it several times, wondering why Daniel jumped too.

The camera must be at the far end of the platform, near where the train will soon shoot out of the tunnel. The platform looks crowded. Lots of the people seem to be wearing scarves, hats or a football shirt. If Thom didn't know better, there would be nothing remarkable about this scene. In fact, it wouldn't even be worth his attention.

However, he is searching for Daniel in the crowd. The people look blurry and Thom has to concentrate hard to distinguish them. Yet eventually, he manages to recognise Daniel. Thom finds it strange seeing him again: moving, breathing. Thom has the urge to touch the screen so maybe he can feel Daniel's life once again. This is his brother, minutes before death. This is his brother, and he hadn't known.

Thom focuses hard on Daniel. At a few points, Daniel's head seems to turn as his curly hair flashes in the camera. As Thom locks his gaze on Daniel, Sam stares at Thom. Strangely, Thom feels safer knowing someone is watching him.

Thom can hardly understand what he is watching. The clock is rolling ruthlessly fast, indifferent to the fact it is counting down to the moment that Thom will lose Daniel forever. Thom wonders what Daniel had been thinking at this moment. Thom wonders if his legs had ceased up as he waited. Thom wonders if Daniel hesitated. Thom wonders how much longer Daniel would have lived otherwise. Thom wonders and thinks until his mind is a vacuum.

Thom doesn't realise he is sitting on the edge of his seat. He is gripping the sides so hard that his hands are turning numb. Yet all he can do is stare at the screen, helpless, wanting to climb inside and pull Daniel back. Why hadn't he wanted to be Thom's brother? Why was this a better alternative?

Then Thom sees it. Some people's hair has started to move, their clothes flapping from a wind that Thom cannot fully understand. He can't feel it, and he wants to, more than anything. He wants to have the air rushing towards him as Daniel felt it in those few seconds. The only way he could relate was standing on that platform before, hoping he could connect to Daniel, too late.

Then the train is there. 15:32 – his note is two minutes early. And Daniel is falling. In a snap second, Daniel disappears and the train keeps rocketing through the picture. Thom screeches, rocking in his chair but unable to let go. Sam jumps up and switches the screen off. He grabs Thom by the shoulders and tries to look into his eyes. "I'm sorry," he whines breathlessly.

"Put it back on," Thom orders. Sam stands up, his forehead furrowed, putting himself between Thom and the screen.

"I really don't think…"

"Put it on!" Thom shrieks, jumping up and pushing Sam out of the way. He jabs the 'stop' button and then 'play' again. It's 15:29 and Daniel is still alive.

Thom watches it all again. Thom counts down the longest three minutes. Thom grabs the sides of the screen and is so close his nose is touching. It is almost time when he sees something. Behind Daniel: a person. This is not spectacular at all, being a crowded platform, but Thom knows this person.

Thom has been fascinated by this person; her strange mechanical voice, her dark curls, her evasive love. The only woman who has kissed them both. She is there. Thom turns and grabs Sam, pointing at her.

"Do you see her?" he asks desperately, pushing Sam's head close to the screen.

"Who?" Sam asks; trying to push back but Thom holds him there.

"The woman with the black curly hair. Do you see her?" Thom wheezes.

"Yes," Sam nods. "I see her."

Thom releases Sam. *So he isn't imagining her...* She is standing right behind his brother on the day he died. She is there and now she is in Thom's life. How did she get from this platform to his lips?

Thom is gawking at Sarah. Daniel is now a secondary character in this short film. The crowd sways and swells as the train approaches. He loses her several times but keeps his eyes on the space where he thinks she is. He barely notices Daniel is gone until the train shoots through the left-hand side of the screen.

The crowd is moving back like it is being showered with glass. Faces are contorted with shock. The doors remain shut as the whole platform seems to freeze. Thom has to look at the clock to see that time is still moving.

He is searching the spot where she'd been standing. And then he sees it. As the people continue to move back, he sees a hand outstretched, holding a piece of material. This could mean nothing, but Thom knows inside, that it is her. He also knows that despite the fuzziness of the screen, the material is a scarf. And although it is a black and white picture, Thom is also certain the scarf is red. It is Daniel's.

49 The Video

Thom presses the eject button and snatches the DVD. Sam immediately tries to block Thom's exit but his body is slumped slightly, showing that he isn't convinced he has the right to.

"Are you going to stop me, Sam?" Thom dares him. "Are you going to stop me having the video showing my own brother's death?" Thom shakes it in Sam's face. "Would it be better to leave it here so it can collect dust?" Thom spits.

"I shouldn't have even shown you it." Sam shuffles on his feet. "And you seem to be obsessed with that woman in it. Are you going to try and find her?"

"I don't need to. I already know her," Thom tells him, smugly.

"Are you going to hurt her?"

"Did you show this to the police?"

"Yes I did, last week – *I promise.*" Sam nods vigorously, emphasising to Thom that he has completed all the 'right' actions, although delayed.

"And they didn't see that he was pushed?" Thom's limbs are flailing beyond his control. Sam is pressed against the door, looking as though he wishes he were on the other side of it. "They said it just looked like a jumper," Sam repeats and winces as he speaks, waiting for the repercussions he doesn't personally deserve.

"A jumper?" Thom laughs bitterly. "A fucking jumper? Are they blind?" Thom screeches. "She's standing right behind him. She's holding onto his scarf."

"I don't think they saw what you saw," Sam argues, holding his hands up.

"No one seems to." Thom is feverish, his clothes drenched, the sweat from his hair dripping onto the dusty floor. "No one can see what I see. That you're all liars, that you all betrayed us, that he only wanted to show us the truth."

"Take it. But please don't hurt anyone." Sam moves away from the door.

Thom holds out his hand. "I need your keys."

"Did you hear me tell you not to hurt anyone?" Sam lets his hand linger above Thom's as he gives up his keys.

"I heard you," Thom says, snatching them and flinging the door open. "But I don't think I can promise that," Thom calls back as he runs towards the exit. He unlocks the door hastily and throws the keys on the floor.

As Thom bursts out onto the platform, he knocks out a man with the door. The man sags to the ground, cradling his head. Some people quickly gather around the man, and one of them bends down, trying to look at the injured man's face.

Someone begins to confront Thom but cowers away when he sees that Thom is wet with sweat and all his veins are thick underneath his skin, like pipes about to burst. Thom quickly forgets the scene and runs towards the exit. He passes many people, he barges through the barrier behind someone else, he dodges the cars in the road, yet he feels immune.

If Thom had been thinking, he would've known there is no other place he can go. With the DVD clenched in his aching hand, he looks up at the building. It has become his comrade, the friend he keeps around who reflects his mood. It is the place that still connects him to her.

As he unlocks the front door, he thinks about where he is. He thinks about how there is only a slight chance she will actually be here. Yet Thom feels his heart honing in on something or someone and with each step, he feels more certain. As he turns the key in the lock, he can see her turning towards him, smiling?

Yet he is greeted by no one when the door of the bedsit creaks open. He sags against the door frame for a moment, before accepting it and wandering inside. He slumps onto the bed, the DVD still fastened to his hand, almost cutting through his skin.

The bed is still unmade since he was last here. He looks at the disc in his hand and shoves it into the covers, burying it.

Thom gets up and walks to the window. He tweaks the blind, the dust coating his fingers. He leaves his fingerprints on the slats, so if a policeman investigates later, he will know that Thom has been here. He will be implicated. They can accuse him of stealing something or hurting someone because he has left something behind.

"Thom?" a voice says from behind him. He wonders why it is a question. She must know it is him. Who else would be in her bedsit? Who else looks like him? Except Daniel... That thought makes Thom's chest flush cold as if someone has pulled the toilet handle.

"Sarah," he says, turning. Sometimes when he says her name now, he blushes. After all, it isn't really her name but he is holding onto it, as he is holding onto her.

After seeing her in the video, he thought when he saw her, he'd attack her. He thought he'd scratch her pale cheeks, tear at her bouncy curls. Yet, as he looks into her eyes and she smiles at him, the coldness rushes out of him and his blood flushes instantly warm instead.

"I hoped you'd be here," she says, closing the distance between them. At first, Thom jumps back, crashing against the blinds. Her face momentarily twitches, yet she shakes out her curls, dismissing it. "I've missed you." She smiles, holding up her hand in openness. Thom stares at her fingers, shaking in the air and finally locks his hand with hers.

"Have you really missed me?" Thom asks quietly. She reaches up with her other hand and plucks at some of Thom's hair. He shakes her touch off, but smiles faintly. He feels like he is seeing her through a heavy fog. He can't help grasping onto her hand for fear he will lose her, for fear he'll slip further into the fog and never climb his way back out.

All the time he is looking at her, half of his mind is preoccupied with the video. He is playing the scenes over in his head. They are flashing across half her face like a horror film, and he is helpless to change the ending. He wants to rewind everything, never let the clock reach 15:32. Yet it isn't to save Daniel as much as to save himself.

"Where have you been?" he asks, pulling her into him. Her heart drums against his body. He wonders what she has to feel so anxious about. Has she seen the DVD buried in the covers somehow? Is she going to leave him? Thom squeezes her tighter at these thoughts, trying to decide which option is worse.

"I've been thinking a lot. I've been resting," she answers simply. Yet Thom knows there is much more she is leaving out. Does she know she killed Daniel? Or has her damaged mind hidden it from sight underneath the madness and delusion?

"You feel better." Thom nuzzles his words into her neck. She smells like soap and toast. Thom thinks about eating breakfast with her, about reading the paper with her – ordinary things they have missed out on since they met. How can he really have a relationship with this woman? This murderer?

Yet the word murderer offends Thom. How can he possibly attach that evil concept to his beautiful Sarah? Even if she pushed him, there must be a reason. Daniel must have hurt her, or he has imagined it all.

"I'm much better than I was." Sarah nods gently. Thom presses his thumb against her cheek, her pulse and his pulse mixing together until he can't separate them. Thom doesn't think he can ruin her now, after all, she has made progress and she looks happier. When she smiles at him now, it makes him want to slap her and squeeze her in the same moment.

"I'm so happy for you," Thom croaks. Yet his eyes are welling up with water and threatening to spill over like an avalanche gathering momentum. Sarah grabs him by the wrists.

"You're *not* okay though are you?" Thom wants to let his legs melt. He wants to sink. He wants her to love him so much that he will forget everything on that disc and everything he knows.

"Sarah, I need to…" Thom begins, yet he can't finish. He won't only be finishing a sentence; he will be finishing both of them. He digs himself a burrow in her arms. Her chest is sticky against his cheek. As he inhales her sweat, he looks down and sees the top of her breasts.

Thom thinks then about the day of the phone call. The moment he stopped, as though in preparation for the news that would jar his routine forever, jab a stick into the spokes of the wheels that make his world turn. He'd been worried he wouldn't be able to move from the desk, wouldn't be able to meet Emma and lie next to her in bed. And now, all he can think about is touching Sarah instead.

Thom lifts his head up, catching the softness in her expression as she'd been looking down at him. She instantly corrects herself, as though her feelings are a secret she doesn't want him to discover. Thom stands face to face with her, their toes touching, their hands grasping onto one another's. He is thinking about how it is so simple to kiss her and, at the same time, how his fingers are tingling in anticipation of strangling her.

So Thom kisses her instead. The throbbing anger and confusion suck desperately at her, trying to recover something caring instead. It strikes him that getting these things from a murderer is a paradox but he can't stop. Her lips seem even softer than only a few days before. The longer he kisses her, the more he wants to kiss her and get dragged into her mouth, into her body.

She brings him closer and slides her hand underneath his top. It feels cold, so he tracks its every movement over his stomach and chest. She digs her nails into his side and feels the grooves of his ribs that have become more prominent over the last few weeks. Thom wonders whether he should touch her and decides that she made the first move, so why not? He has one hand on her hip, on top of her clothes and he now moves the other underneath her top and up her back.

Her backbone curves beneath his touch. Her body wriggles in his arms; pressing so hard into him he almost falls backwards. In the next moment, she is pulling off his shirt. It almost pains them to part for those few seconds. Their lips instantly spring back together as Thom's top lands on the floor.

The longer Thom kisses her; each second feels like he is withering inside. As his hands grip onto her and his muscles tense and relax, he feels like he is shrinking inside. He begins to feel like he is floating or that he is standing on top of a high building, staring at the dizzying lights below.

Sarah pulls back, sensing Thom's distraction. His eyes directed at the floor, as though they are being circled by sharks. She takes him by the hand and leads him over to the bed. Thom suddenly remembers the DVD buried there and rushes forward, flinging the duvet towards the wall.

Sarah raises an eyebrow at Thom, worried by his sudden surge of energy and by just how keen he is to get her into bed. Thom realises these same things as Sarah thinks them and instantly says, "The sheets haven't been changed," blushing. Sarah nods dismissively and sits beside him.

Thom has forgotten that the last person she kissed before him is Daniel and, before that, she was raped. And Sarah has forgotten that he attacked her brother, that he is Daniel's relative and that he is slowly losing grip on reality. There are only the two of them, in this darkened room filled, for once, with life.

As the thought that she has murdered his brother flickers through his mind, it sparks him into leaning forward and giving her a long hard kiss. She grabs hold of his face and pulls him even closer, moaning quietly and pushing her lower body into his side. He imagines he can feel her clit, hard against his hip.

He forces himself to pull away, staring into her eyes for a moment and slowly moving his hand up to unbutton her shirt. She watches his hand moving down her top, smiling faintly to reassure him, until her stomach and breasts are exposed. He gently releases her bra, then instantly presses her body against his.

Sarah pushes Thom down onto the bed, moving on top of him. She closes her eyes, imagining he is already inside her. She bends down, kissing him and reaching down to undo his belt and trousers. Thom almost gags at the speed of this, and can't help remembering the man who hurt her. Why does she trust Thom? He is a violent and reckless person who knows her secret.

Thom thinks about confronting her then but his resolve is broken. He is torn between the curiosity he has inexplicably felt for her since he first saw her in the front garden and the desire to avenge Daniel. Yet as Sarah eases his trousers off and her own, and continues to move against him, the moment overtakes. All Thom wants then is to get inside her.

Sarah is afraid but thinks taking control will help her. She reasons she also trusts Thom, that she loves him, and therefore he is the right person to open up to once again. Feeling certain of this, she eases herself onto him and presses her body down until he is fully inside her. She winces half in pleasure and half in pain, adjusting to the feeling again. Thom feels her getting wetter, his eyes closed as he moves her up and down by guiding her hips.

Thom lifts his hands up to her breasts, rubbing them over her erect nipples, making her squirm for a moment but then relax, pushing her body down on him harder. He is watching her, the display of her pleasure, still asking her in an unspoken way if this is all okay.

She presses down on his chest, his heartbeat thudding under her hands, sweat gathering on their skin. Time seems to have slowed down but only a minute or two has passed.

When Thom sees Sarah close her eyes, leaning backwards and her chest reddening, Thom allows himself to come. He thrusts hard several times and finally feels release. Sarah moans softly.

As Sarah falls on top of him, her breaths rapid against his cheek, Thom finds he can't do the same. He tries a few deep intakes of air but his chest feels constricted. Sarah unknowingly nuzzles into his neck but he pushes her off. Looking hurt, she begins to speak but stops as Thom jumps to his feet.

He presses against his chest, trying to force an opening for air. Yet, he still can't breathe. Sarah gets up and tries to comfort him but he shakes his head, his vision beginning to recede. A huge circle of darkness begins to burn at the corner of his eyes and slowly spreads. He thinks that this must be how it happens – this must be how he dies.

The darkness is nearly complete and Thom is being surrounded by a tunnel, closing its mouth around him. In the last flash of light, he sees Sarah. Staring out of the darkness, Thom knows she is waiting for him, as she waited for the train to emerge from that tunnel, in order to kill his brother. Falling now, Thom realises he can't escape the truth, the video, the tunnel. For one last moment, his body tries to keep him from all these things.

50 Blood and Truth

Thom screams and claws himself out of the dark. He can't help thinking this is a familiar feeling since the moment he answered the phone and had been told about Daniel's death. The ink on the note only dragged him further into the darkness, the unknown, the unrelenting pull into a set of jaws that keep chewing him apart inch by inch.

He realises Sarah's arms are around him. He smells the dampness of the room before his eyes slowly adjust to the light. As he rolls onto his side, he notices a few dead insects on the floor under the window and a layer of dust coating the floor. His body is aching as though he has been running for miles. Part of him thinks that this is apt, as he has been running from his old life and the truth for far too long.

"I know," Thom grunts as he heaves himself to a sitting position. Sarah is still only a fuzzy shape to Thom. Despite this, Thom feels a definite alteration at his words. It is as though a sudden beam of light has appeared or the room has slowly begun to slant.

"What do you mean, Thom?" she asks quietly. She is pulling on clothes as she talks, as though planning to flee. Thom refocuses on her face. He realises then that he is still naked and grabs at his t-shirt that has been deserted on the floor. Then he struggles to pull on his jeans, nearly toppling as he tries to zip them up.

"I think you know exactly what I mean," Thom sneers and adds for emphasis, "I mean that what you've been running from is exactly the thing I've been chasing."

Sarah narrows her eyes at his words, trying to decide whether he is hinting at what she thinks he is. He wonders what questions are going through her mind like a whirlwind: what does he know? *How* does he know? What should she do now?

"Thom…" she starts but he cuts in.

"No." He stamps his foot. "I've had enough lies from you."

"I don't want to lie to you anymore…" she whines, holding her hands out to him. He takes them without thinking. When he looks at them, he can't see Daniel's blood covering them but at the same time, he can't ignore the fact that they are the reason he is dead.

"I saw the video of the day he died," Thom tells her. When he had imagined this moment as he'd run away from the station, there was shouting and crying and perhaps even blood. Yet looking into her face now, seeing her struggling to meet his eyes and her shoulders weighed down with guilt, he feels calmer. He loves her, despite everything.

* * *

I shudder inside as he says the words. Why did I never think of a video? I should've got there first, to stop him ever finding out. Surely he will lash out now? I have killed someone, and this someone was his cousin.

Lots of pointless words come into my head at once. I filter each one, deciding they will be even more useless to Thom. Although, one feeling overwhelms everything: relief. No more hiding, no more running – I can stand before him and he can see every dark crevice and glaring scar.

Mum, I'm coming clean about everything. You would be proud of me for that at least.

"You haven't said anything," Thom notes, looking for something to fill the heavy silence. I inhale deeply, my head beginning to swell out like there has been a tumour hiding behind my eyes for some time, waiting to pounce.

"What can I say, Thom?" I swallow heavily. "That I killed him? That I knew who you were when you chased me out of your garden? That I have no idea why I pushed him and I still don't?" As I speak, Thom bites his lip so hard it nearly disappears underneath his teeth.

"You're admitting it, just like that?" Thom asks, shifting on his feet. He hasn't expected it to be this easy but I am tired, ready to let the stone, I have been holding in place, roll out of me and disappear into the distance.

"I've tried to hide this from you for too long."

It seems like we are discussing a tea party or what we watched on TV last night, not a murder. Where is the shouting? Where is the heart-wrenching emotion? Perhaps we are both too exhausted. I can see the bags under Thom's eyes; they are parachutes that have deflated before they have left the ground.

"You know what I don't understand?" Thom exclaims suddenly, raising the sound level, throwing my hands down. "How you could lie to me all this time, how you could sit there and listen to me going on about what he did and how I don't understand it all… Didn't you feel bad? Didn't you at least feel sorry for me?" His hands are in fists; his teeth clenched as he stares at me, like a dog I have kicked for no reason. I instantly feel the ceiling sagging above my head, threatening to collapse.

"It's the worst I've ever felt in my life," I answer honestly.

"Worse than you felt after you pushed my brother onto those tracks?"

* * *

"Your brother?" She asks dismissively, thinking he has made a simple error and will correct himself. Yet Thom gives her a twisted smile, almost mocking her for being so stupid all this time, as he has been for most of his life.

"*Of course.* Didn't I tell you that Daniel and I were actually brothers?"

"What are you talking about?" Sarah grabs him by the arms and squeezes gently, trying to bring him back to sense. Thom doesn't push her away now. He thinks that her gesture is born out of affection for him and part of him enjoys it, despite everything.

"Aunty Val had a secret all these years. Apparently Daniel found out and he wanted me to know too."

"Are you saying Val isn't your aunt? She's your… *mum*?" Sarah pronounces each word carefully, except the word 'mum'. That word falters on her tongue, partly held back as if she doesn't want to let it go.

"Yes. Apparently she's my real mum. She and my dad put their genes together and ended up with twins. So they flipped a coin and decided which one she should keep and which she should give to my parents."

"I'm sure it wasn't as easy a decision as that," Sarah says quietly. Thom laughs and reverses the hold, so he is now holding onto her, and pulls her close to his face.

"You really think so, do you?" he spits.

"Thom, I'm sorry." She stares into his face, determined not to be frightened by him. Thom shoves her away roughly but she manages to catch herself and doesn't fall.

"You're sorry, she's sorry, we're *all* sorry." Thom counts on his fingers. "All it means is that my whole life has been a big fucking lie. And Daniel's too." He closes his fist around his own fingers, cutting himself down.

"You must feel completely betrayed," Sarah hazards. Thom raises his head, one side of his lip hooking into a smile. His cheeks are reddening and even from here, Sarah can see his eyes flashing with water.

"You know…" he begins, twisting his hands as he talks, "I wanted to believe you so much." His words have a twang of tears. "I guess that's why it was so easy for you to fool me."

* * *

"I didn't try to fool you Thom," I insist. I am desperate to close the space between us, have him against me again, skin on skin. Yet I can't move, knowing I will be rejected.

"Oh so what do you call it, Sarah?" Thom can't stop a few tears escaping from his eyes and running down his face. "I mean, that's not even your real name. *I'm* a fucking joke." Thom digs his nails into his arms. His body is shaped like an arch weighed down by tonnes of stone. As he coughs out his words, his tears fly towards me in the air and land on the floorboards.

"Please Thom. I never meant to make a fool of you." I falter, knowing that my intentions and my actions are completely separate. He is right.

"But you did Sarah. I believed in you, despite everyone telling me I shouldn't. Richard didn't trust you, Emma didn't believe you, and even *I* wasn't convinced." He chokes on a suppressed sob. "But I am so broken that it was easy for you."

"I'm broken too," I tell him. He jolts as though his body is offended by this comment but after a moment, he nods gently.

"Did you know what you'd done at the station that day?" Thom asks cautiously, seemingly jabbing a lion in the eye with a stick.

"My body and my mind weren't connected properly. I remembered I'd done it but my mind wasn't connected to reality. I can't even tell you what I was thinking," I pause heavily, "even now, my mind isn't right…"

It feels like I am talking to a therapist again, but this time, I am making some progress at least. However, looking at Thom, each word I say seems to punch him down. His body is swaying slightly, his eyes squinting at the world he can't escape.

"So when you met me, you already knew. And you didn't feel shame or remorse?" He is pacing the room now, trying to look like an excellent sleuth but his wobbly steps defy him.

"I didn't really feel remorse then. You helped me with that."

"Me?" He stops.

"Yes. Spending time with you taught me how to feel again. You really saved me, Thom," I tell him earnestly, grabbing at his hand. He glances down at my touch, as though he has forgotten he has hands.

"But you're still a murderer." He shakes me off roughly.

* * *

Thom watches her body droop. For a few seconds, he thinks she might faint, but she slumps onto the bed instead. A strange stab of guilt pricks Thom in the side. How can he still care about her? Shouldn't he be getting his revenge for Daniel? Or did he feel she is just as much a victim as Daniel? Even after all these weeks, he is just as torn as he was when it first began. It seems like since the note, he has been torn in two – the grieving relative and the detective. Although his detective work leaves a lot to be desired; the culprit has been right in front of him for weeks and he has been blind to suspect her.

"I sometimes thought you were alike," she says, playing with her

368

hands in her lap and peering up to see his response. Thom allows her to speak this time.

"Every time I saw you, your hair or your voice, would remind me," she pauses, "and every time I saw your grief, I felt like I was killing you too. But I realised that although what I have done is completely wrong and unforgivable, I wasn't aware of what pushing him really meant."

"You're defending yourself?" Thom scoffs, kicking the floor-boards. A haze of dust floats up between them.

"Not defending, Thom, *explaining*."

"Should I really care about your explanation, your reason or whatever you want to call it?" Thom says, his limbs flailing as though independent of himself.

"You're right," Sarah admits, shrugging, "but there is something I want to tell you." She lets the silence fill the room for a moment until Thom can stand it no more.

"What then?"

"He said something to me, Thom."

"Well you knew him before, didn't you? At the hospital? It's hardly surprising he spoke to you!" Thom turns away, laughing to the side of him, as though he has an invisible friend standing there.

"No, I don't remember all that," she corrects him. "I meant when he fell."

Thom's head jerks back towards her. She instantly feels as though a stark light is shining into her eyes and she lifts her hand to shield it.

"Don't people always say something when they get pushed in front of a train?"

"Not like this," she insists, "I thought at first I imagined it, as you might expect a crazy person could. I thought I'd seen it wrong... but I'm so sure that I'm right..."

"Are you ever going to tell me?" Thom cries, bouncing on his feet like a man standing on hot coals.

"Yes," she reassures him. "As he fell, he said *right on time*." She stares into the distance. She expects Thom to react to this, yet he seems almost unflustered.

"Right…" He agrees, as though they have been comparing notes.

"You don't seem that surprised'.

"I'm not really." He nods, a small smile growing on his lips.

Sarah isn't sure what to make of this so she continues talking: "I thought about it for days and days afterwards. And I decided I had to know what he meant."

"So you came to our house?"

"I followed you first. I tried to find out more about him by watching you."

"You were following us?" Thom says; looking more disgusted than when she admitted she is a murderer.

* * *

Looking at myself through Thom's eyes is now an altered and disturbing experience. From his unrelenting faith in me, he is now losing his adoration word by word.

"I told you I was very sick."

"You love telling me that, don't you?" he says roughly.

"People find it hard to see. Even I did before this happened to me…"

"Talking isn't helping. It doesn't change all this, does it?" Thom looks so tired that all I want is to lie him down and let him sleep for days, forgetting everything.

"We should've talked more before," I tell him, unsure of what else to say.

"You're right," he says quietly, pained by the fact he agrees with a murderer and a crazy person. "The thing I'm most sad about – how all this started – is the lack of talking." He leans against the wall. For a moment, he looks like a tramp hitching a ride to another town. His hair is unwashed, his brow dirty with sweat and dust, his eyes darkened by lack of sleep.

"If she'd just told us in the first place, if she'd been honest enough, Daniel wouldn't have been so angry. I could've saved him, *and you* wouldn't have pushed him. He must've made you do it, I don't know how… But all *this* could've been avoided." Thom gestures to the room around them as though it holds their lives. He walks towards me, his gaze so focussed that I believe it is compensating for his broken mind. He takes my hand.

"But the person I'm most upset about is you," he tells me, his lips trembling uncontrollably. Yet he doesn't cry. He is too shattered and drained to actually cry again. "I loved you. I really loved you." He squeezes my hand until it feels numb but I say nothing. "If after everything, I could've trusted you, maybe I wouldn't feel like there isn't anything left."

"Please Thom…" I say sadly but can't think of how to end the sentence. Please Thom, change your mind? Please Thom, let me love you? Please Thom, let's forget everything and start again? None of them seem right so I say nothing.

"I wish you knew what to say to help me now." Thom's words transform into a moan. "But you've *all* let me down." He snatches his hand back, although he is the one who initiated it. "And I let Daniel down because I am so stupid that I never saw the truth… I let everyone lie to me because I can't handle things."

"Thom, don't say these things about yourself."

"Well it's true," he spits. "I've never been able to deal with anything. I've sat in a cosy office talking to people on the phone, never really dealing with anything. And do you know why Sarah?"

"Why?" I ask reluctantly.

"Because I don't really know who I am." Thom shrugs, not even sure his words are true. "I thought I was a son but then my parents died. I thought I was a cousin but it turns out I'm a brother. I thought I was a nephew but I'm a son. I thought I was an insurance officer but I can't even remember where I work. I thought I was a detective but I've been fooled all along. I thought I was a boyfriend but I'm a cheat. And I thought I was a man in love but… *I don't know anymore.*" Thom stares at his palms as though they are morphing before him.

"I know you don't want to hear this but I can understand how you feel."

"Oh, you can?" Thom sneers, clearly unimpressed by my empathy. "I can't believe you're trying to liken yourself to me. After everything..."

"We're not so different, Thom. Daniel fooled me too," I say quietly. Thom's face instantly softens as he digests this.

"You're right," he croaks. "He changed your life forever. You can never go back." Thom pauses briefly, finishing, "just like me."

When he moves, I think he may be coming to embrace me but he brushes past me. I don't move, too drained to really think of doing so. What's the point? I know I can't leave him here. But I should be out of this house, since I tried to escape it for months and have been so close...

Thom's presence arrives behind me. I turn towards him. His eyes are bloodshot, his body straight like a nail sticking out of the floor trying to catch my toe and drag me down, his arms bulging with veins, the knife sparkling in the light from the half-opened blind.

I open my mouth but he grabs me roughly with his free hand before I can protest, plead or even utter a syllable. His mouth is wet with spit, a few specks on his beard. I am frozen for a moment, staring at the knife in his hand.

Mum, I know I said I'd stop talking to you but I'm really afraid...

"Sarah," he whispers, looking down at the knife himself. He moves it between them and pulls me even closer. I can feel it through my top, like a vein throbbing beneath the skin; subtle but something that cannot be ignored. I meet his gaze, wondering what has happened behind his eyes. What has happened to the man I can trust? What has happened to his hope?

"Thom, you don't have to do this," I tell him firmly.

He shakes his head. "I have to do something," he insists, pulling me even closer. My stomach leaps at the thought of it being punctured, but the pressure of the blade only increases, although doesn't draw blood yet. Our foreheads are touching, and from afar, I imagine we look like lovers.

Thom begins to shake, his unrealised tears making his whole body shudder. I want to grab hold of him, keep him still but the knife lingers between us and I'm afraid I will push it into one of us, or both of us. Instead, I reach up and touch his face. I move my fingers across his bristly beard, the softness of his lips amongst it, his clammy skin.

His body slowly stills again. He nuzzles his head against mine, moaning gently. Yet all I feel is his grip on the knife, which doesn't falter. My wrist is still clamped in his other hand, drawing me closer to his body and perhaps closer to death.

As I move over the back of his neck, he jolts suddenly. His body shoots up straight, his expression darkening. I feel the knife press harder into my stomach, the pressure beginning to mark the skin underneath. His eyes are wet but his mouth is hardened by his clenched teeth.

"While I've been standing here..." He speaks in a throaty voice, as though he has been screaming for hours. "All I can think about is two things," he pauses, "kissing you and... *killing* you." The space between us is now non-existent; there is only the knife to separate us. His face is close. I can feel his breath on my lips and as he moves his head a millimetre forward, his beard scratches at my skin.

"You can't let him do this to us," I insist. I don't want to plead with him. I don't want to be the murderer who can't face up to death. If anything, he should've killed me as soon as he found out.

Thom finally lets his tears throb out of him like lava pulsing out of a volcano. His face flashes with sadness and anger each millisecond. It seems like I am watching him through a kaleidoscope. Then he moves a millimetre forward and presses his lips against mine. They are shivering and cracked.

I see the red before I feel it. But it's the sudden push backwards and a thrust that really occur first. It punctures the skin violently, delving inside where no one can see what's been ruptured. It is seconds later that the blood actually begins to swell out of the hole. Yet, after the initial swell, the blood spreads like a fire tearing through the material. The shock follows. Neither of us moves. Our eyes are locked, our mouths gasping for air.

Still locked together, we fall to the floor.

The door bursts open as we land. The blood covers my arms. I'm holding onto the knife so hard that my hands are sliced open. "Alice, *no...*" a voice says. I realise Michael is pulling me up, leaning me against him. He is searching for the wound, flailing his jacket around, ready to plug the hole. I have forgotten he had been waiting for me at all.

"No," I push away, as he realises what has happened. I scramble towards Thom, lying on his side, staring towards the blank TV screen. I lift his head onto my lap. Michael belatedly presses his jacket against Thom's stomach, causing Thom to groan and recoil. Yet after a few moments, he doesn't seem to notice anymore.

"Why did you do it?" I shake him. He looks dazed so I slap him gently on the cheek until he focuses on my face. He smiles gently, as though he has forgotten everything. Perhaps this is exactly what he wanted – numbness, oblivion. Yet I don't want to let him go. I start to sob as Michael calls an ambulance.

For once, I don't find blood beautiful. It makes my head dizzy. It makes my chest tighten and spasm. It makes my stomach twist as if the knife is actually stuck inside me, ripping my organs apart.

"I had to," Thom says quietly. "You're getting better..." He whispers, leaning his head into my chest. Does he mean that only one of us can survive? That he thinks he will never 'get better'?

He closes his eyes but I refuse to let him leave me. I shake him awake. He drowsily reopens his eyes, and I think he will start telling me how he is cold or numb. Yet he doesn't need to. His body is shivering in my hold and he seems unaware.

"Don't die," I tell him. Thom barely responds. He is going limp.

And all I see is you, Mum. I am holding you in the hallway. The line of blood is drawn down your chin as though you have misapplied lipstick. I can't feel a heartbeat as I lay my head against your chest. You are still. The world is still. Yet somewhere in my mind, I refused to accept it.

I rest my head against Thom's chest and hear his heart beating, slowly, slower, slower, slow. I think I hear the ambulance wail somewhere in the street. Yet I can't be sure I haven't imagined it. All I know is this time; they will need the sirens. He isn't dead. Not like you or Daniel. We can get out of the tunnel. We aren't paused forever.

Still beating, beating, beating, beating, it still beats.

51 Red Fingerprints

Michael pulls me closer. I let myself flop onto his shoulder, not knowing what else to do with my body. My arms are covered with Thom's blood, now dry. Somehow I believe this is the blood that should've marked me after I pushed Daniel. After all, they were made of the same bloodline.

Even though all the information is before me, I can barely draw faint lines to connect them. I know I pushed Daniel. I know he planned it. I know he left clues for Thom. I know Thom and he were actually brothers. And I know that Thom uncovered my secret.

Losing a relative is enough to break anyone, I completely understand. But finding out your whole life is a fabrication... that is enough to destroy someone. And Thom knows this now. Everything he trusted has twisted out of familiarity and transformed into something else. No wonder Thom has responded to everything as he has.

Destroying a person takes time. And Daniel had had that time. Creating questions and doubts through his clues, bringing unfamiliar people into Thom's life to unbalance him and distract him, holding back the vital clues to keep Thom chasing him, making Thom's whole life flip upside down until his head was so full of blood it needed to explode. He'd been clever and perceptive and, most of all, evil.

Even now, I can't recall the hospital properly. I have faint flashes of him sitting on a bed, perhaps holding my hand? Yet I can't trust my thoughts. I have the letters now and they give me enough ideas to create something. It makes me shudder thinking about what he must've said to me, how he influenced me, how he somehow knew me better than I did. However, I guess a fragile mind is easy to manipulate.

As I followed Thom down to the ambulance, I saw the DVD lying on the floor. Picking it up, it seemed to scream in my hand. I didn't need to put it on to know what I would see. I shoved it into my coat pocket and it is still hiding there now. I wonder what I should do with it.

The moment I pushed Daniel seems like a dream. I have rehearsed the simple action in my head but it never seems to be real. The only thing that makes me believe I will live with the guilt is the fact that he led me there.

It is then that I realise Michael has fallen asleep beside me. I slowly lift myself off him, only making him stir for a moment before I slip away. I have to wash off this blood. Looking for the nearest toilets, I see they are down the hallway. I shuffle towards them, clamber inside and rush straight to the sink. I pull the taps on to full and let the spray lash at my clothes. My torso is instantly soaked and I imagine it is me that was stabbed, not Thom. Yet there is no pain for me.

Splashing the water up my arms, I scratch at the stained skin until the blood grudgingly re-moistens and slides off. The sink water turns pink and eventually drinks it all. I only stop when the water turns clear again.

I switch off the taps but as I do, catch myself in the mirror. My hair, my left cheek, and the bottom of my neck are speckled with blood. I grab some paper towels, dropping a pile of them in the process, and hurriedly rub at the stains until all that is left are red tension marks. I douse my hair and hope it has caught most of it; but I will have to wash it several times when I get home.

Although, this will never truly wash off.

As I leave the toilets, water dripping onto the dusty floor from my hair and the bandages on my hands, I see them. Richard and Val are standing in the corridor, holding hands. Richard has his head down and even from here; I can see him holding onto Val so tightly that his arms are bulging with muscles. He squeezes her and lets go of her. I begin to duck but thankfully he walks in the opposite direction, digging into his pocket as he walks, filling his hand with coins.

I watch Val for a moment. She is looking around as though she is lost. I can already see the withered tissue peeking out of her sleeve. I am taken back to the first time I saw her, leaving the house I'd been watching for days, her eyes sore and a tissue flapping behind her. I consider turning away and even take a step backwards but in the end, I walk straight towards her.

She barely notices me approach. She only looks up when a drop of water lands on her arm. She lifts her face up with great effort, her wrinkles appearing deeper with each movement she is forced to make. She stares at me for several seconds before she nods in recognition. "Sarah…" she says in a raspy whisper. Her cheeks are raw with tears, her lips cracked. She reminds me of the last time I saw Thom. The only difference is a purple bruise making a small bulge on her lower lip. Where did that come from?

Considering her now, I see the similarities with Thom. She has the same shaped face; a slightly rounded nose, long eyelashes (although hers are glued together in clumps by the mascara and her sobbing), the same downturn of the mouth that makes a smile even harder.

"How is Thom?" I ask. She instantly begins to sob as though I have flipped a switch. I hesitate but finally draw her into a hug, wondering if by being this close she will be able to feel that I am a murderer. She doesn't seem to flinch though. She simply buries her head in my curls.

"How is he?" I repeat, more urgently. She says something into my hair. I have to push her backwards slightly, yet her words are still muffled like she is speaking through a pillow. "Val, please." I shake her gently.

"He's not good," she finally manages.

"What did they say?"

"They say he's struggling. He's lost a lot of blood," she tells me shakily, digging her fingers into my arms. "What will I do?" she asks me desperately. I deliberate on how to answer the question: "*you'll cope, we all do,*" "*he'll be okay, I'm sure of it,*" "*don't think about that now, let's wait.*" I can't help thinking I am the last person who should be comforting her. If Thom had punished the right person, he wouldn't be 'struggling' to stay alive.

"Let's see what happens first." I choose a variation on one of them to comfort her. She nods but her face is still twisted in anguish.

"The only thing is; it's all I can think about," she admits.

People are filtering by but she doesn't seem to notice that they are staring at her, wondering if we know each other and wondering if there is somewhere they can move her, so they don't have to see her pain.

"It must be horrible for you," I tell her. I feel terrible imagining how I would respond at the possibility of losing two children within a few months; especially as one has only just found out he is her child.

"I don't think I can cope with this again..."

"I know." I squeeze her.

I imagine she is you, Mum, alive again. I let her warmth smother me. Her salty tears sting my cheeks. If only you hadn't left me, maybe I wouldn't need to drain this poor woman of her last drips of energy.

"You were with him," she says, easing away from my hold. "Did he say anything about me?"

I remember every word that Thom said in the bedsit. I could've recited every word and every intonation to her. Yet now I have begun to feel normal again, I recall that the truth doesn't always help. If I tell her how angry he'd been, how confused and desolate he felt, would it really make her happier?

"He told me what happened. But he didn't say too much."

"Then why did he do that to himself?"

"I'm not sure. He didn't make much sense." I shrug, hoping she is as confused as she looks. She shivers as though I have thrust an icicle into her chest and wraps her hands around herself.

"Did he do it because of me?" she asks quietly, unable to meet my gaze. I think about this carefully before even thinking of opening my mouth. It's definite that she has some weight in his anger and pain, but is it because of her? I decide the answer is safely no. Without Daniel and myself, he wouldn't have done it. Under normal circumstances, I believe he may have even reconciled with her one day, despite the years of lies.

"It wasn't you," I say, bending towards her lowered gaze to emphasise this.

She nods weakly and says, "I'm his real mother, you know."

"He told me." I nod. She seems satisfied, looking away to compose herself.

"Do you want to see him?"

"Yes," I answer instantly. Since I'd been forced to let the paramedics take him away, I have only thought about the moment I can see him again. I want to see how they have repaired him, fixed the gaping hole in his skin. She takes my arm, the broken leading the broken; towards the person we both love.

As we approach the cubicle, with the curtains drawn around the bed, I try to catch my breath. I can't believe I will actually see him again.

Unlike you Mum, I won't be losing him forever. I won't have to stand at a funeral and feel my mind float up above my body, never quite able to reconnect.

Val peeks through the curtain discreetly, as I hop on my feet. She lets out a small yelp. I push her aside and tear the curtains apart. Before us, the sheets are dishevelled and twisted, alarmingly empty, like a robbed grave. The machines beside the bed are dead. I bend down and see the plugs have been pulled out. The wires connected to the machine are tossed on the bed like haphazard veins leading to nothing. There are a few bloody finger marks on the sheets, on the bedside table, on the curtain to the left.

I follow the blood marks, chasing them into the next cubicle where a surprised family turn to face me. I run around the bed and keep following the marks, diminishing with each gauzy curtain, becoming more elusive with each bed. There are three I pass before I reach the corridor at the end. I check all the doorways for signs of him and after several, I find the faintest mark on the door to the stairway. I fling the door open and fly down the stairs.

I imagine I am a policewoman in pursuit, only a whisper behind. Yet, when I reach the bottom, the door is firmly closed. No one has been here recently. I open it anyway, feeling the cold night rushing towards me. I think about Thom's clothes and how the knife has torn them, how he could be shivering in an alleyway, or worse, dying.

I step out into the night, looking to both sides. Ambulances are pulling in, a few people loitering in the car park, a few nurses smoking near the corner, but no Thom. I focus my eyes on each spot in my sight but see nothing unusual. I somehow believe that if he is out here, I will find him, despite the darkness and the stinging wind.

Checking the floor for blood, I pace up and down. I look in doorways. I walk in between the cars and search for bloodied fingerprints or smashed windows. I walk to the street and search for movement or a group of people huddled over a body. Yet I find nothing.

I can't find Thom.

Wrapping my arms around myself, I let myself sink against a car. I look at my arms and remember the stains of his blood and now can't believe I ever washed it off. This was my last link to him. I may never see him again and I have washed him away out of guilt.

"Thom," I call into the wind. "Thom!" I scream. The only response I get is from a fox that is slinking across the road which casually glances over and, after a long stare, continues padding onwards. I slide further down the car, leaning my cheek against its cold body.

I know he can't hear me, wherever he is. Yet I hope he knows I came looking for him, that I called for him, that I am frozen by the heartbreak. This is all I can do for him now. Unlike me, I hope he knows that someone is thinking about him and believes in his ability to heal.

Oh Mum, what should I do with myself now?

Several minutes later, when I drag my body from the floor, I wonder if wherever he is, he will think about me too. And when he does, will he think of me as a lover or a murderer? No matter what I do in the future, there will still be a person who knows what I am.

Yet if I saw him again, just once, perhaps I could tell him I love him and it would change his mind.

Lynnwood

Thomas Brown

Thomas Brown

Thomas Brown has spent the best part of his life reading and studying fiction of all kinds, but his heart beats for Horror and Fantasy.

In 2010, he won the University of Southampton's Flash Fiction Competition for his short story, 'Crowman'. In 2014, he won the Almond Press Short Story Competition, 'Broken Worlds'. In the same year, his first novel *Lynnwood* was a finalist for **The People's Book Prize.** In 2018, he completed a doctoral degree at the University of Southampton examining the limitations of language and how to navigate them to better communicate meaning through fiction.

He lives and works in a small market town bordering the Cotswolds, where he still writes every day.

Dedication

For Christopher Robin, who was so patient,
and provided wine when it was required,
and often when it wasn't.

Acknowledgements

My greatest appreciation to:

Aamer Hussein, Peter Middleton, Alison Fell, Rebecca Smith, Will May, Anna Alessi, Brian and Gillian, for helping me to realise this somewhat strange story.

I must also thank my friends and colleagues at the Coffee Shop, the Hounds of Thirty-One and my fellow Creative Writers in Southampton, for their relentless love and support. My gratitude goes to Philip Hoare, for such encouraging and insightful praise.

And finally to you, the reader, for taking a chance on me and my voice. Without you, the writer is a lonely man or woman. If nothing else, enjoy.

Thomas Brown
June 2013
Oxfordshire

@TJBrown89

'And this also...
has been one of the dark places of the earth.'

Joseph Conrad, *The Heart of Darkness*

CHAPTER ONE

When Freya discovered the pig's remains, on the third of September, they stirred unseemly urges deep inside her. She often circled the village with Eaton, keeping to the surrounding paths, and this day was no different. They passed beneath the alder trees, which grew near Mawley Bog, and around the outskirts of Lynnwood. It was a Sunday, both in name and temperament; an air of sleepiness hung over the village, its inhabitants reluctant to rise, save a nameless few, undaunted by the hour.

As she moved beneath the trees, her thoughts turned to the village's history. There were few in Lynnwood who did not know it well. The village dated back to the fourteenth century when settlers first flocked in real numbers to the Forest, and by all accounts it had changed very little since. Ancient oaks hemmed in the village, and beech and yew and holly. Together they kept the place their own. There was a single bus that went as far as Lymington, which left and returned once each day, and one long, vermicular road. These were the only ways in and out of the village. Many visited the Forest each year, drawn by the herds of wild ponies, the allure of the woodland and its seasonal beauty; the wild gladiolus, found nowhere else in Britain; the carpet of late summer heathers, a sliding scale of purples; even snowdrops, when winter was nigh and the days were at their shortest. It was no wonder that those who ventured into Lynnwood chose to remain. What sane man or woman would want to leave such a place; the sweet, isolating scent of flowering viola, the old Forest paths, the light?

Freya set a brisk pace that morning, her hands buried firmly in her Parka pockets. Tall, dark green wellingtons protected her jeans from the worst of the mud and blonde hair spilled out beneath a faux coonskin cap. It fluttered fiercely in the wind.

The dog, Eaton, caught the scent first and as they broke from the tree line he slipped under the wooden gate, bounding into the adjoining field. At first Freya was unconcerned. Even for a Lurcher,

Eaton was a spirited animal. She had bought him for her thirty-fifth birthday, almost eight years ago, and he had been a part of the family ever since. She could only imagine how exciting the world seemed to him and his keen canine senses; the scent of rabbits, of edible things concealed in the grass, even other dogs, a number of which they would usually encounter each morning. Even when she caught an acrid tang on the air, she gave it little thought. McCready must have been burning things. He often ventured into the village, his hands still black, his clothes stinking with smoke.

"What've you found, boy?" she said, smiling into the wind. "Yes, aren't you a clever dog! What's that, then?"

The corpse of the pig stopped her in her tracks. The lingering damp of Mawley Bog was replaced by the smokiness of scorched flesh, which carried on the breeze. Shivering, she brought her hand to her mouth. Fat had bubbled and popped across heat-cracked bone, then cooled in slick, waxy pools between the ribs. Even the surrounding grass was dead; a crisp, ashen elf ring. Flies hovered over the corpse, accountable for the buzzing sound that filled her head as her eyes settled on the skull. It grinned back at her with a sooty, feral smile.

* * *

She left McCready's field quickly, dragging Eaton from the pig by his collar. Arriving home, she first cleaned the dog with a towel. Then she headed upstairs to the bathroom. She wouldn't usually shower after each walk, but that day it felt important. Her skin still shivered, her body unclean, the stink of burned flesh haunting her nostrils.

The blasted pig had deeply unsettled her, but worse were the feelings it had stirred: loathing, fear and the fluttering of hunger. She told herself that she had been mistaken. She had felt a ripple of revulsion, perhaps; the knotting of her stomach at the sight of such a horrid, unexpected thing in the grass, but not hunger! The very thought of bringing her mouth to the charred flesh, of tasting it, cold and crisp on her tongue, was monstrous.

Hot water splashed her skin. For what seemed like the longest time she stood under the spray. Eyes closed, she relished the water as it ran down her body. An antique mirror hung on the opposite wall from the shower, rectangular in shape and framed with golden ornament. Green Men studied her from the frame, their faces wreathed with vines. Her mother had been especially fond of the mirror, and many were the times Freya had stood in the doorway, when just a little girl, watching the older woman as she made herself presentable; hiding the human beneath lipstick and blusher and long, black lashes.

There was no hiding as Freya stepped from the shower, a smudge of exposed pink in the reflection. She glanced at herself only once, then dressed with her back to the ornament. Birds sang whimsically outside the window while she clothed herself.

Changed and refreshed – physically, if nothing else – she returned to the kitchen. She filled the kettle and prepared a drink, moving stiffly, as though dazed. Eaton followed her around the room, an auburn shadow at her feet.

She had not eaten meat since Robert left her. Though she encouraged her children to eat it, she had not touched it herself for over ten years. She associated the food with him and their last meal together, which stuck so vividly in her mind.

Steam whistled from the kettle's spout like the scream of burning swine. Moving the kettle from the hob until the shrill sound trailed off, she poured her tea and drank it. They said that tea was good for dealing with shock. She poured another, which she supped more slowly, savouring the sweet warmth that rose from the surface of the liquid.

* * *

It was a dizzying experience to walk the frosted village in December. Cobbled pavements were slippery and hard with ice. The warmth of mulled liquor and brandy burned throats while the cold weather bit red cheeks. Carollers moved from cottage to cottage, singing righteous songs in celebration of the season. Nor were theirs the only voices to be heard, for the night was Midwinter and on that night, without fail, the dogs of Lynnwood tossed back their heads and added their own anxious howls, their chorus carrying far over the New Forest. The skies were cloudless, the constellation Orion, the Hunter, visible as he chased his quarry through the blackness and the stars.

From the comfort of her front room, Freya watched, as she did every year, a small group of children finish carolling at Granary Cottage across the street. Their failing voices were whisked away by the wind. The ancient hymns made her happy, infusing her with festive spirit. She wasn't a religious woman, like Ms. Andrews of the Vicarage, but it warmed her heart to see the children playing together. They skittered across the icy road, past the parked cars and street lights to the next cottage, and she turned from the window, the dark silhouette of her reflection doing likewise in the glass.

The house was lively, excitable. An air of anticipation filled the rooms, which she cheerfully attributed to Christmas. Baubles glittered like silvery apples on the potted pine tree in the corner. From the kitchen came the sizzling scent of roast chicken and the crisp, root aroma of potatoes. Her mouth became wet and anxious and she followed the smells and the sounds of cooking to their source.

Where the front room was dim, lit only by lamps and the flickering lights of the tree, the kitchen shone brightly. Exposed oak beams lined the ceiling, an AGA cooker – black from use, even then – dominating the back wall. Robert stood by the dinner table. He stooped to pour two glasses of white, the wine making delicious glugging sounds as it decanted.

"My favourite wine for my favourite woman," he said, turning and pressing a glass carefully into her hand.

"I'm your woman now, am I?"

He grinned, teeth bared in mockery of an ape, and tapped his chest with his fist. "Now and always."

"Misogynist," she said, smiling and sipping from her glass.

"What can I say? I'm an animal."

"You're not the only one." She nibbled his ear as she passed him, her breath sharp and zingy with the white. She tasted it against his lobe and on the air. He shivered bodily between her teeth.

They ate dinner quietly. Even when the dogs began to howl, the peace wasn't ruined. There was something beautiful and primal in the chorus of their cries. She decided then that they should get a dog of their own. He said it was a wonderful idea. Something loyal, to look after their little girl, Lizzie, and recently-born George. Both slept upstairs, lulled by the lingering howls.

It was strange, how well she could recall the details of that meal. Every flavour seemed suffused in her tongue, taste memories; of moist chicken breast, succulent and spiced; of rich gravy, thick and salty; of those hot, slender vegetables, asparagus, still crunchy, and carrots slippery and soft. She ate and drank with abandon, her head thrown back, eyes closed, mouth agape, as if the bestial howls of the dogs erupted from her own throat –

* * *

She didn't see Robert again after that night. Though she could never forgive him for walking out on her, she had loved him once, enough to share a house, a life, to father her children, and the thought of abandoning that drew a roaring panic inside her. Feelings had been unfettered in that field, frightening and seductive, threatening her last memory of her husband with promises of crisp crackling, succulent flesh and dripping grease.

Alone in the kitchen, with only the dog as witness, she stepped slowly towards the black, cast-iron pan, hanging above the hob, and the bottle of cooking oil beside it.

When her children finally dragged themselves downstairs, almost an hour later, they were greeted by the sizzle of hot fat, the splutter of eggs and the rich, salty scent of fried bacon. They smiled sleepily at their mother and seated themselves at the dining table, oblivious to the half-eaten rasher at the bottom of the bin or the guilt behind their mother's eyes.

* * *

Though she did not know it then, Freya was not alone in her private distress. Nor was she the first in Lynnwood to suffer. Ms. Andrews, of the Vicarage, dreamt she saw a woman in the Forest with the face of a fly and great, glassy wings. Mr. Shepherd, at his bench one afternoon, crafted seven intricate brooches, each in the shape of a gaping maw, before he realised what he was doing or how long it had taken him. And McCready was woken one night by screaming. Following the sound to his sties he glimpsed a skeletal figure crouched over the body of one of his pigs. Neck craned to the night sky, it shrieked a ditty from McCready's own childhood:

Scads and 'tates, scads and 'tates.
Scads and 'tates, and conger.
And those who can't eat scads and 'tates,
Oh! they must die of hunger.

These things were not dwelt on. Dreams were disregarded, as dreams so often were, though Ms. Andrews took to wearing her rosary beads beneath the collar of her nightdress while she slept. Mr. Shepherd melted down the ugly, unsettling brooches, except for one, which he secreted into the bottom drawer beside his bed. And once McCready had finished the whisky that he saved for occasions such as this, he dragged the pig's carcass into an empty field, doused it with lighter fluid and burned it. Afterwards, when he woke quite suddenly, sweating and cold in his bed, he couldn't be sure that he had left his pillow at all.

Outside, as a new day broke across the blue autumn sky, the pig's blackened bones cooled in the grass, unobserved by all except one woman and her dog.

CHAPTER TWO

Having felt the playful nip of that hunger, which risked revealing something wild inside her, Freya clung to old habits, finding herself among the village congregation next Sunday. She held no special love for Allerwood Church, but like many of the village's residents she felt a hollowness inside; a quiet corner of her being, forever empty. Some felt this most at night, when their kitchen lights failed them, or when they passed through the Forest in the evening. It was a human thing, she knew, to fear this darkness. Theirs was an epicurean herd, grown fat and contented on life. They had no mind to be stripped of their lives at the trough, by death or any other means.

For others it was dogs that frightened them; the wet stink of their fur, or their animal howls, which carried so easily over Lynnwood. Like the darkness, they reminded of human things; race memories, rank and coppery, best left forgotten. The same swine of society heard the dogs' howls and they buried their faces deeper into their feed, and their lives went on in pleasant Lynnwood.

"The service seems busy this morning," Freya said, when she greeted their vicar, Ms. Andrews, on the church steps that morning.

"Indeed, the promise of winter brings many guilty gluttons to our doorstep." The elderly woman smiled, then winked at Freya's children. "Besides, the more the merrier. We need the bodies."

"I'm sorry?"

"To warm the church, my dear. The building is old as anything in the village. Even filled it doesn't hold heat well."

Darkness held no fear for Freya; she who had been left in the dark already, and there was familiarity in the cries of the dogs that conjured up memories of her last night with Robert, when they had sat at their dining table and eaten to the chorus of howls. Rather, it was the fragility of that memory that kept her awake at night and in a moment of madness, alone in her kitchen, she had threatened that...

She left the old woman to her greetings, leading her children past the alcoves, where there were fewer people to disrupt. They slipped into the third-row pew and waited while the rest of Lynnwood's churchgoing residents found their seats. The cruciform ground plan was typical of fourteenth-century traditions. Sitting in the third row, she had a clear view of the altar, the high place on which it rested and the transept at the head of the room. There was little of the ornament boasted by grander churches, but theirs was a practical parish. The pews were varnished oak. A table by the entrance held a vase of white-lipped lilies and the collection bowl. White plaster covered the walls and although some stained-glass windows overlooked the nave, these were of a simple design. It was a place of worship and nothing more; a church for a parish which needed spiritual nourishment, when the nights drew in and the dogs began to bay.

Beside her, George fidgeted in his seat. He looked distracted, she thought, as did his sister, their eyes staring but not seeing. She didn't judge them. Church was no place for the wild spirits of children.

* * *

"Do I have to come?" Lizzie had said that morning, when Freya stepped into her room and flung open the curtains. The room was dark, stuffy and filled with a menagerie of shapes in the half-light; the products of her daughter's art classes. It smelled of adolescence, and the perfumes used by teenage girls to mask it.

"Yes, darling," she said. "This is family time."

"But it's pointless! You think there's some All-Father sitting up there, nodding when you go to church and frowning when you're bad? You think Dad lived by those beliefs? We're not a parish of medieval sinners. No one believes in God anymore!"

"It doesn't matter what you or anyone else believes," she said, unlocking the window to let some air in. "It's the done thing. The least we can manage is a Sunday, here and there."

"This is stupid," said Lizzie. "Mark Thomas's parents take him to beer festivals, and Rachel's mum cooks her three-course dinners when they need family time. With cheese-boards. And pâté starters."

"You don't like pâté, darling, and neither do I."

"That's not the point," said Lizzie. "You're not listening to me. I'm saying church isn't normal anymore."

"Your skirt's on the bannister," said Freya, unfaltering. "You've got twenty minutes, young lady."

* * *

Freya had heard it said once, when shopping with Robert in Lymington, that the hungry were quick to forget. This was true of the conversation; they were enjoying afternoon tea at a small café and the table beside theirs had entirely forgotten what it was they had ordered. She remembered the café well; the miniature sandwiches filled with wafers of smoked salmon, the lace tablecloths, even the serviettes, printed in patriotic colours and folded carefully for each customer by their place mat. People loved the café, as they loved all places where they could gorge themselves under the pretense of propriety. They were modern predators, snouts speckled not with blood but tea and breadcrumbs.

The saying was also true of Lynnwood, however. Perhaps that was why she had felt such guilt at her appetite, the Sunday she encountered the pig. She could not explain that morning's weakness, which stood against everything she had upheld for over ten years, except that even as she remembered it her mouth began to fill with hot, wet anticipation. For the first time in a decade she had felt temptation, and she had succumbed to it in a moment. They might not be medieval, as her daughter had suggested, but Freya had sinned, and while she continued to sin there was Allerwood Church. The Dark Ages, it seemed, had endured to the twenty-first century, hidden beneath the boughs of the trees and in their hungry hearts.

* * *

The sky was grey and heavy with cloud when they left the service. They took the gravel-stone path through the churchyard and around the back of the church. The little chips made crunching sounds beneath their feet, like hard, dry cereal between her teeth. The three of them moved amid the headstones.

As with most old parishes of its kind, an intimate, if not generous number of graves had sprung up in its grounds over the centuries. The very first graves, the earliest, were those nearest to the church. Some of them were little more than rock piles, their inscriptions long since eroded, or hidden beneath moss. These were the first settlers of Lynnwood, resting beneath its hallowed grounds, from where they might continue to keep a quiet watch over their village. There had been a petition to have the graves restored, she remembered, several years ago. Quite a number of signatures had been gathered from the village's more spiritual residents. They had a more than vested interest in the maintenance of the graves, she supposed, as regular attendees of the church.

Her signature had counted among those collected. She could still recall doe-eyed Ms. Andrews and Sam Clovely from the village council standing on her doorstep that morning; their beatific smiles as they talked to her about heritage, history and remembrance. She had signed, for what it was worth. They weren't bad people and nothing had come of the appeal anyway. Clovely had disappeared one night, halfway through the local campaign, and all the signatures with him. She struggled to remember the details, which were unclear in her mind, but seemed to think they had found a book of his – a journal – in which he had written of noises at his window, late into the night, like the scrabbling of rats or light-fingered children. The general consensus was that he couldn't have been of sound mind, the poor man. The money had gone towards refurbishing the village hall instead, and the leftovers used to fund some cookery classes there. She had attended one with Lizzie, in the spirit of the community. Her daughter seemed to have enjoyed the lesson well enough, though she had found it lacking.

The further they walked from the church, the more recent the graves became. They were still old but their condition gradually improved. They stood higher and straighter in the soil and in many cases the names were still legible where they were engraved into the stone. The most recent dotted the outskirts of the churchyard. The names were still clear, some only a year or two old – if that. They must have been people she knew, to have been buried so recently, and yet she could think of only a handful of people who had passed away in this time. She inspected the family names on the nearest two headstones: Richards and Collins. They meant nothing to her and slipped easily from her mind.

They were almost at the gate when George wandered from the path. She waited while he approached the nearest memorial. For almost a minute he stood in front of the headstone, which was roughly his own height and fashioned after the stony style of its forbears. She couldn't see his face, standing as he was with his back to her, but she watched as he lifted his hand to touch the grey stone. The scene was strangely affecting, stirring something inside of her she couldn't explain. It might have been the sight of one so small, standing alone between the gravestones, or it might have been his fingers on the stone; the living crossing the boundary of the dead. It might have been something obscurer still; her flesh and blood remembering the forgotten. A bouquet of flowers rested at his feet and it brought her some relief to know that someone besides her little boy was caring for the graves. Someone in Lynnwood remembered the buried dead, even if she could not.

CHAPTER THREE

As if that first breakfast had unlocked something inside of Freya, they became a regular habit in the mornings. Any guilt at her activities, the violent shudders of her stomach, faded beneath the sizzling scent of hot fat, the wetness that flooded her mouth and the quick, primitive beating of her heart as she bit into that which was tough and fleshy and once a living, breathing thing. Her lips glistened with grease from swollen sausages and bacon – sometimes rare, other times as crispy and black as that horrid thing melted into McCready's field. The very act of eating became sensual and primal as she remembered that last meal with Robert to be.

Her children remarked on the readiness of cooked breakfasts, and the kitchen stank perpetually of smoke, but beyond that nothing was said. Nothing could be said, for her feasts were private and she always ate alone, before her children woke. The virtue of her vegetarianism was maintained, as was that of her motherhood, and life went on in Lynnwood.

On the thirteenth of September she saw her children, George and Lizzie, return to school. Hollybush Manor was not an outstanding college of learning but it was built, like most of the village's heritage, on old traditions. These aged values gave it strength. It was also blessed with being the only school in Lynnwood. Those children – or indeed their parents – with an appetite for education had nowhere else to turn without driving the distance through the Forest, to Lymington. The school owed much to that hunger.

That morning Freya walked with her children to school. George was more than capable of looking after himself, when left to his own devices, but the other children weren't so accommodating. Only last summer she had been called in for a meeting with his headteacher, Mrs. Morecroft, when it had emerged than Daniel Collins and some of the other boys from George's class were bullying him.

"Good riddance," she said, as they set off from Haven House towards the village green. Nobody had missed the Collins family since they had moved last Christmas. Between their troublesome boy and Mr. Collins's penchant for drink they had made terrible neighbours, undeserving of Lynnwood's good name. She could never remember quite where they had moved to, or the precise date, though truthfully she gave such things little thought.

"I feel sick," muttered George, from where he walked beside her. He refused to hold her hand, no matter where they were, not since his eighth birthday when she had taken him to the park and another boy had laughed at them.

"You feel sick, darling? Where is it, your tummy?"

"Yes, my stomach," he said. "It's cramping."

"Maybe you ate your breakfast too quickly." She paused, crouched to his level and brushed the stray hair from his forehead. "Did you rush your food? You know this happens if you don't chew properly."

From several paces behind them Lizzie snorted. "Maybe you should stop force-feeding us fry-ups every morning."

"Yes," Freya said. "Yes, I... I probably should."

They had stopped on the roadside, by the Old Dairy. The sky stretched pale grey, promising rain. The wind rushed against her face, stinging her cheeks and bringing tears to her eyes. She blinked them dry.

Though the dairy had long since closed down, the field behind it was still used to graze cows. As she watched through the slats in the wooden gate, the nearest lifted its head from the grass and brought its sidelong gaze to bear on her. For several moments she stared at the cow and the cow stared back, its mouth slowly working the cud. And if it seemed as though the cow was chewing something else, something darker, fleshier, as she later thought when she tried to remember what she had seen, she knew that she was mistaken. Cows were herbivores, and largely placid animals at that. They didn't eat meat.

"Hurry up, Mum," said Lizzie, "or we're going to be late. He's not sick, just nervous. I get it all the time when something important's coming up."

"I didn't know that," Freya said.

"Sure you did. That's why I didn't eat before my GCSEs last year, remember?" Shouldering her school bag, her daughter marched ahead.

"Exams or not, you should always eat breakfast, Elizabeth Rankin. It's the most important meal of the day."

"Come on, I think we've all established that much already..."

Presently the grey, moss-flecked brick of the Manor rose into view. Freya knew all about the building, having once helped George with a piece of History homework on the subject. The school was first commissioned in 1698 when the wealthy merchant, Peter Young, passed through the village on his way to Lymington. So struck was he by the idyllic air of the village that he committed his thoughts to paper, a modern translation of which could still be read in Southampton's City Library. Freya had found a scan of it on the Internet.

"Knowing the area of the Royal Forest, the New Forest, so well and being so familiar with its surroundings already, which are nothing short of pleasant, I was entirely taken aback by the little village of Lynnwood. I call it a village still, although how it has not yet flourished into something more I cannot fathom. Surely, I challenge anyone who spends more than an evening here, or the day thereafter, to display anything other than reluctance at having to leave this place, or regret at not choosing to stay longer. The soul of this village, its wholesome spirit, is without doubt the public house, The Hollybush. The ale flows freely here, as does the custom, and nary on my travels through the Forest, indeed the county, have I encountered such friendly faces. But there is more to Lynnwood than its tavern. The air tastes clean, unlike that of my London. The cottages are quaint, modest buildings and everywhere I look I find trees, lush and green as any I have ever seen. They must feed well here, and must have done so for many years, to have grown to such heights. Beyond these things, I cannot identify the nature of the village's charm. It is quite plausible this itself is the source of my being contented. An air of underlying pleasantry, which dulls the senses, illuminates everything so softly, and infuses me with a delightful hunger only Lynnwood can appease..."

The children of Lynnwood were at this time educated in the village hall, although poorly and without much in the way of direction. Peter, a firm advocate of the merits of teaching wherever they might be imparted, sought to rectify this and Hollybush Manor was commissioned, named after the pub he had found so charming.

That morning, neither Lizzie nor George was late. She left them to enter the grounds themselves, kissing them both before they went. Then she made the ten-minute walk back to Haven House. She stopped only once, as she passed the field behind the Old Dairy. This time the cows did not stare at her but stood and chewed, as only cows can.

* * *

October became November, the air grew colder, but the Forest still retained the russet glow of autumn. Red leaves clung to the branches, and orange and brown, so that it seemed as though the trees had patchwork quilts draped across the branches. Much of the ground was similarly coloured, where the leaves had started to fall, and the pathways were littered with puddles. These were the best indicators of the subtly changing seasons; even long into the afternoon the puddles retained the icy glaze of morning. Many were cracked, where they had been trodden on, but those that were undisturbed showed no signs of melting. Mawley Bog, when they reached it, was similarly chilled. Sheets of ice spread from the banks across the surface of the water, like hardened wax. Nor was Freya alone in her observations; gone were the swarms of flies, usually seen dancing just above the water level, and the frogs, which seemed to fascinate George so much, were nowhere in sight.

"They're hibernating," he said, when she asked him about their absence. "They crawl into holes beneath the ground and wait out the cold."

She didn't blame the frogs. She had anticipated a mild winter, thrown off, perhaps, by the lingering golden brown of the trees, but walking through the Forest she knew she had been mistaken. There was nothing mild about the air. Her faux coonskin cap protected her ears, and she had even seen need for a scarf.

They took the long route around the water. Of the two ways around Mawley Bog, this was the path her parents had always preferred. Often her father would take her for walks but sometimes her mother, Harriet, accompanied them.

* * *

Freya chased the dogs beneath the trees. The year was '76 and she was nine years old. Though her chest heaved and her feet flew, her legs were only little. The dogs barked playfully as they dashed ahead, noses close to the ground. The earth was a spill of shadows and soil.

"Careful, Freya, darling, don't run too far!"

She didn't heed her mother's advice. It was a wonder she heard it at all. The Forest was not Haven House. Propriety held no sway here, only sharp branches and soft leaves and the damp Forest mulch beneath her shoes. Here she could run as fast as she wanted, as far as she wanted, with her faithful hounds by her side.

"David, she's going to hurt herself."

"Let her run," he said. His voice seemed to carry through the trees. "She knows to keep to the paths. And look at her, look at that smile. Have you ever seen her so happy?"

"She's easily pleased. Unlike her mother."

David's voice thawed into laughter. "You're telling me."

"You'd hardly think we were related, looking at her now. A wild child of the Forest."

"Oh, I don't know about that. Look at how her hair streams behind her. And her cheeks, when she turns around. Tell me you don't recognize those cheeks..."

Freya's parents continued talking until they faded out of earshot. Still she ran after the dogs. Exhilaration burned her chest as Ralph and Jack led her deeper into the trees. They came upon the hollow of an oak, where leaves had fallen, or been blown into a pile. She slipped between the dogs, kneeling before the hollow. It felt colder here, though not unpleasant. The air smelled ripe. Poking through the leaf-layer, like a child's emerging tooth, was a small bone. She touched it tentatively at first, feeling the smoothness of the creamy surface, dry and light. Then she grasped it firmly and pulled it from its bed of leaves; a tool with which to repulse her mother and impress her father. How proud he would be of his brave little girl! How her mother would shriek!

* * *

Harriet had been a vain woman, the product of modernity, but even she hadn't been able to ignore the allure of the Forest, as though some part of her under that false face longed to be beneath the trees. It was a longing that had kept her from the Forest, in the same way that the hungry sometimes deny themselves food, for fear of overindulgence. Freya knew that now, although such a thing would never have occurred to her younger self, who only delighted that both her parents were walking with her. She drew comfort from that delight, from the old paths, the memories of simpler times.

She wrapped that comfort round her like a blanket. More than the cold or the arrival of winter she detected something else in the Forest; a gnawing uneasiness at the back of her mind. She didn't see or hear anything untoward, but she couldn't deny the weight she felt, pressing in from all around.

"What's that?" George said suddenly. Lost in her thoughts, she had almost walked into him. He was standing in the middle of the path. She followed where he was pointing to a bird, a solitary magpie, perched on a sign.

"That's a magpie, George."

"No, not the magpie. I know what those are," he said. "I meant the other thing."

"What other thing?" She studied the Forest.

"There was a figure, by the trees. A person, I think, except it was hard to see properly because of the shade."

"It was probably another person then," she said. "You know, plenty of people from the village walk their dogs around here, like we do."

"It reminded me of someone. My friend from the train tracks."

"Your friend?"

He looked up at her with wide, impressionable eyes, the darkness of the Forest reflected in his pale face. "My friend. The man who lives in the tunnel."

* * *

The memories are so clear now. She can hardly think, hardly breathe, for their clarity, after so long in the dark. That which was once clouded has run clear until she can think of nothing else. They sluice like the brook through her mind, its waters swollen with spring.

She pauses, pen in hand, and turns to the AGA cooker. The ache inside her redoubles, crippling in its intensity until she cannot move except to clutch her arms around her stomach. But these are not hunger pangs; they are aches of a different kind. It is not her stomach wrapped in her arms but her abdomen and the womb beneath, where her little ones first came into being, where they grew and from where they were born into this wilderness world. They are children of Lynnwood and now Lynnwood has them again. She feels hollow. Lightheaded at the thought of what they have become. They are lost to her, devoured by the same hunger that threatens to consume their mother.

She moans helplessly, a low, bovine sound, before dropping her pen and clasping a hand to her mouth. Her eyes flicker to the window. Evening is fast fading. Shadows lengthen, spilling from the empty windows of Granary Cottage opposite, moving where all else is still. The building is tinged with the lingering pink of dusk. Soon there will be shadows of other things too; bony silhouettes peering into her house, crawling through the streets, slender arms reaching for her door. And she will answer them. She will open her house to Midwinter because there is no fighting it anymore...

There is not long left but there is still time, if she writes quickly. She retrieves the pen from the tabletop and places the nib to paper. With the smells of the Forest filling her nostrils and the haunting laughter of her children in her ears, she writes.

CHAPTER FOUR

The more that she ate, the more she surrendered to those instincts she had for so long been conditioned against, and the more she began to remember. It was a therapy of food; slim rashers of crisp pig, bursting sausages, eggs beaten to within an inch of their lives by her practised hands, as though not eggs but something else, transformed into dripping omelettes. It was only natural, she supposed, that these memories manifested in her dreams at first. What else are dreams, but memories of the past, the future; of what could have been, or might yet be?

* * *

She dreamt first of the Forest. She couldn't see the brook from where she walked but she could hear it; a lively rushing of water through the trees. It was dark here, but not oppressively so; light broke through the dense canopy in wide pools, which scattered the shadows of the forest floor. Occasionally the path would take her through a glade or clearing, where more light reached, uninterrupted by leaves or branches. It must have been summer; delicate elf rings dotted the grass, inviting her to run through them, to jump from circle to circle, and dandelion seeds drifted languidly on the air.

Another figure moved behind her in the Forest. She could feel his presence; the press of his footfalls on the ground. She knew without looking that it was her father and that she was a little girl. The trees were taller, so much taller than she remembered them being, the grass much closer to her face. Wood pigeons warbled softly in the trees, as did a number of birds she couldn't identify. She didn't suppose it mattered; the birds sang and the forest air was pleasant. These were the important things. This, surely, was why the memory had endured, hidden for so many years. She felt dizzy with nostalgia.

Father and daughter moved deeper into the Forest. She saw other shapes now, twin shadows in the undergrowth: their two Cocker Spaniels, Ralph and Jack. The dogs moved through the shrubs without stopping, their noses never far from the ground. Occasionally they would collide, as the same scent brought them together. Playful yelps ensued, scattering through the trees, followed by laughter. She realised it was her own, and that she was smiling.

The brook drew closer. She could see the gap ahead, where the trees grew slightly apart, and she hurried towards it. She moved faster now. She seemed to be skipping.

Bauchan Brook, named after a local legend of Lynnwood, said that visitors to the water were watched by someone or something between the trees; a spirit of the wilds or perhaps the trees themselves, standing guard over the clear waters from which they drank. She had no such memories, no encounters that she could recall, but she couldn't deny the presence that hovered over the place; a quiet watchfulness, seeming both young and old.

Except, this time when she stepped from the tree line, as she knelt to dip her hands into the water, she thought she did see something. A silhouette, crouched across the brook. She saw only its reflection first, broken and pale in the shining waters. Filled with curiosity she looked up, the figure across the brook doing likewise. Their eyes met and she felt a deep, irrepressible urge inside of herself, the likes of which she had never felt before. Then the brook seemed to expand, breaking its banks as the light washed down through the trees, and the trees themselves rose taller and thinner until there was nothing but that shining, liquid light and she woke, wet and hot, in bed.

* * *

Though Freya never actually saw her father in these dreams, he wasn't far from her thoughts. David Heart was as shrewd a businessman as he was a devoted father, and he had always been there for his daughter.

"He was tall. And broad. I remember him being broad," said Catherine, her eyes sparkling devilishly over a glass of white one afternoon. "Big, strong arms."

"Catherine Lacey. You're awful, do you know that?"

"Would you have me any other way?"

Despite growing up in the same school year as Freya, Catherine still seemed the more youthful of the pair. Her rotund face concealed age, and her portly figure, with her thick neck and generous arms, suggested a voluptuousness Freya's slender shape lacked. Even so, the two remained as close friends as they had ever been. Where they had run through the heathland as little girls, now Freya's dog gambolled over the grass. The poetry they had read at school filled Catherine's bookcases. One collection comprised of Catherine's own verse, though Freya had been forbidden from ever reading it. And the squash that they used to drink had become darker, stronger and much more alcoholic in nature, though they drank it with no less relish. Catherine had always possessed something of a nose for "the good stuff," ever since they first started sneaking bottles from her parents' wine cellar after school. Raised on these fumes, it was only natural that the woman had grown up with a taste for them.

"I've been thinking a lot about him lately," said Freya, staring over her glass into the garden. "About what happened to him, the unfairness of it. The disease took everything from him. That business was his life."

"Everything! Remind me, did the business fail?"

"Well, no," said Freya. "He sold his shares long before the end.

404

There was no other way. He couldn't run a company with dementia."

"There we go," said Catherine. "The wheels of industry kept turning. Some poor soul will have risen to replace him and that was the end of it, as far as they were concerned."

"You're saying his business lived on without him. Is this supposed to be comforting?"

"Yes! Consider that Sam Clovely. He took his seat on the village council so seriously, but what good did it actually do him?"

"He was mad, Catherine..."

"No, he went mad." She rolled her eyes. "When you get down to it, it's not work that matters, it's not job titles or a place at the head of the business table. These things go on regardless. It's Haven House. It's your memories. It's you."

"Me?"

"You, your father's seed, his flesh and blood –"

"You're growing vulgar again," said Freya, winking. "It's too early in the evening for that yet."

"Dress it up however you like." Catherine took a large mouthful of her wine. "You know what I mean. There's working and there's living."

Birdsong sounded from the garden. It was light, without worry. Freya watched as one of Catherine's cats stalked a sparrow through the undergrowth. "I've been dreaming about him again," she said.

"Your father?"

She nodded and Catherine smiled wickedly.

"I've been dreaming about him too. What would your mother have said?"

The cat sprang, the sparrow vanishing beneath its claws.

* * *

When not in Catherine's company, Freya found herself increasingly drawn to Allerwood Church. She had lived a privileged life, all things considered. Her father worked hard to provide for his family and she had inherited generously on her parents' passing. She visited the churchyard in the afternoons, once Eaton had been walked and the

405

children were at school. The dreams gnawed at her resolve, their little teeth nipping at wounds long since healed until they were red and raw.

"It is clear you have something on your mind, my dear," said Ms. Andrews, after they had exchanged pleasantries one afternoon. The vicar made her way through the graves, to stand by Freya's side.

"Is it so obvious?"

"Indeed," said Ms. Andrews. "I have a view of the church grounds from my windows. It's really quite beautiful, in the summer. Pardon my saying, but you're spending near as much time here as the dead. Is there anything I can help you with?"

"I don't think so. Thank you, though."

"You are sure, Freya? God is healing, you know, and failing that I have an excellent brandy in need of drinking."

"I feel... I'm remembering things, that's all."

A curious look passed over Ms. Andrews's face at these words. The woman seemed suddenly older and younger, almost childlike in her expression. She toyed with her hands behind her back.

"We're all remembering things. Winter, it seems, has brought a host of memories this year." She stared into middle-space for a moment, her wet eyes glistening. Then she smiled. "Come inside, let us talk and eat."

CHAPTER FIVE

Shadows and a vacuous quiet filled the Vicarage with a rigid presence that seemed, momentarily, to still the waking hunger inside Freya.

With shaking hands, Ms. Andrews unscrewed a dusty bottle and poured two splashes of amber coloured liquid into glasses. The old woman sat across from her in the drawing room, which had the same stale air, Freya thought, as Allerwood Church. An effort had been made to soften the room and make it more hospitable, but not a great one. Varnished elm bookcases lined the walls, filled with volumes of texts, and a vase of lilies wilted on the windowsill. A plate of scones filled the table between the two women, small pots of jam and cream beside it. The smell of brandy blossomed in the room.

"Lynnwood is an old village," said Ms. Andrews, sipping slowly from her glass. "The old ways still hold sway here, though there are few who see it."

"Yes, we have a longstanding heritage here –"

"I see it, though," she went on. "I notice these things. I know what to look for, especially of late. So I realise the importance of our church here in Lynnwood."

"What do you mean?"

She indicated wildly to the bookcases, a drop of liquor spilling from her glass. Again, she did not seem to notice. "There are books, parchments and diaries here, which date back to the earliest days of the village. There are still more in the study. I have read many, although it would take another lifetime to read them all. These matters interest me."

They sat in silence for some minutes. Freya expected Ms. Andrews to continue, to expand on her observations, but she seemed distracted, her eyes fixed over her drink. Freya had a short sip of her own brandy, which tasted as it had smelled, then prepared her scone out of politeness. They were freshly baked, she noted, probably bought at market that morning.

She was spreading jam when Ms. Andrews chose to speak again.

"We didn't always have such comforts. Those early days were dark ones. I was unsurprised when I learned our church was among the first of the buildings to be fashioned here."

"I had read similarly –"

"People always turned to God in those times. He was a means of coping, a source of spiritual strength, a means, they thought, of elevation from the beasts of the earth."

Freya was surprised at the note of disdain in the vicar's voice. "You think this has changed?"

"Of course it has, Freya. People don't come to church anymore, not for God anyhow. I'm not sure if they ever really did come for Him.

People's reasons are generally their own."

Freya felt herself blushing, but nodded and took another hurried sip of alcohol. It stung her tongue and cheeks.

"But enough of that," said Ms. Andrews. "Tell me, what is it you remember?"

Warm and liberated by brandy and the frankness of her host, she recounted to Ms. Andrews honestly the dream that had filled her sleeping thoughts for over a week now. All the time that she spoke, the old woman watched her, nodding occasionally. Otherwise she was silent. Those loose, watery eyes stared right into her own, unafraid; an adult, listening to the anxieties of a child. Encouraged, Freya then spoke of her uneasiness, of the unrest she sensed in Lynnwood.

"It is strange that you dream of the Forest," Ms. Andrews said finally, when she had heard everything.

"Is it?"

"Yes, you see, I too have been dreaming of it. Not memories, or pleasant, energetic dreams, as yours sound, but dreams all the same."

The words that spilled from Ms. Andrews's mouth that afternoon took firm, wild root in Freya's head. She talked of horrible things, made all the more so for the righteous voice that spoke them. Freya couldn't help but worry for the troubled mind that formed such fantasies, or worse, endured them, night on night.

* * *

Ms. Andrews's dream was always the same; a woman with a housefly face and wings like stained church glass. Only each time she dreamt it was longer and longer before she woke from them. No matter how much she prayed when she rose each morning, or how softly she appeared to sleep, it was the same. And as her dreams deepened, playing out longer in her mind, she found herself approaching this figure in the Forest. She was helpless to move otherwise, no matter how much she struggled to turn, to run back through the trees, to the Vicarage and home.

The figure under the trees was a horrible sight to behold. Ms. Andrews had thought she had seen her fair share of suffering in her lifetime; her sermons preached often of lepers and she had worked with other, more unfortunate souls during the years of her service. But this woman, if she could even be called such, was by far the most abhorrent. Each night that Ms. Andrews dreamt, the figure took a step closer, and each night a little more of her became visible under the fading light.

Smooth, supple curves made up her human parts; pale, Elizabethan skin, soft and naked. Her legs were long but well-proportioned, her hips broad, as Sarah's, blessed mother of Isaac. Then she saw the face of the woman, her large head that of a housefly, like the ones that crawled behind the curtains in the drawing room to die. Its flesh was mottled and leathery and its eyes were like fractured glass, or, she thought, morality, from the way that it looked at her; a thousand glittering facets, strangely human, staring from across the clearing.

And most unsettling to Ms. Andrews was that each step across the forest floor brought the uneasy apparition itself closer. Every step that she took was mirrored by the horrid, fly-shaped figure opposite; until she knew one evening they would meet.

It was always with this realisation, she said, that she woke, sweating, damp and with a thirst only alcohol would slake.

* * *

Every resident of Lynnwood knew its vicar, though few found need to call Joan Andrews by her first name. A polite, private woman to meet, this changed when she preached, as if in doing so she was forced to expend herself, to draw deep from within. The lessons of her life became the subject of her sermons. And they were righteous speeches. Her voice, deceptively strong for one so physically frail, carried far over the pews.

Freya had sat through more than enough of these sermons to piece together the old woman's past, without their own private conversations taken into consideration. The rarer details of her history were imparted over cream tea and drink, such as they had taken the afternoon they discussed their dreams, and if she was an outspoken woman with a long life story to share, brandy only served to loosen her tongue.

Ms. Andrews was born and bred of the village. Christ was in her blood, she said; passed down from her father, and his father before him. She was the first and last woman in her lineage to take the title as vicar of Lynnwood. She had never seen fit to marry and, at seventy one, was childless.

There had been one man in her life, beside the Lord himself; a Frederick Mangel, travelling from Brittany the summer of '63. Already in Normandy visiting family, it had been the small matter of a ferry across the waters and he was among the Forest. He had remained in Lymington for three days before venturing deeper into the trees. It was his purpose to see as much of the place as he could; he had desired to visit for many years and, with business growing – he ran a small recruitment agency – he doubted he would have the time again for months to come.

On the fourth day he discovered Lynnwood and that, as Ms. Andrews put it, was that. A Romanticist at heart, he found an intense, spiritual satisfaction in the dappled light of the trees, the intoxicating freshness of the air, the carefree birdsong in the branches.

Ms. Andrews first met him in the churchyard while laying flowers by the headstones. He asked her to dinner. She accepted and they ate matelote, which he cooked himself using fish from Bauchan Brook. She could not remember ever having eaten such delicious food and it was true to say she melted somewhat under the warmth of that sharp cider stew.

It wasn't meant to last, however. That very Christmas – on the twenty-first, to be exact – he excused himself politely from dinner, citing reasons she couldn't since recall. She couldn't remember seeing him leave the Vicarage, or whether he had packed any clothes. All she did know was that she never saw him again. He flashed behind her eyes sometimes, when the dogs howled or the winter air rattled at the windows. All other times he was a shadow. A ghost of her past. He had proposed only three days prior to his leaving and, against every doubt, every pang of uncertainty, she had said yes.

That, she confessed over a glass or three of mulled wine two winters ago, was her one regret. She had been quite tipsy at the time and the confession had brought tears to both of their eyes, for Ms. Andrews deserved better. She was mild-mannered but stern, loving but fair, and charitable. When she encountered those people down on their luck, drinkers and the homeless, she would often sit and talk with them. Sometimes she gave them her blessings and when she prayed they were never far from her thoughts. Such charity, she said, cost nothing.

It was this grounded sensibility, this honesty and good nature, that endeared her to Freya and ensured that, when she voiced her unsettling dream, Freya listened. These were not the ravings of a mad old woman. Ms. Andrews was no Dickensian spinster, no matter her circumstances. And had they been ravings, she would have humoured them with her time anyway. Joan Andrews deserved that much.

CHAPTER SIX

One week to the day since her conversation with Ms. Andrews, Freya found herself on the banks of Bauchan Brook. She stared out over the brook for several minutes, watching the rushing waters run their course. They leapt and fell in smooth, undulating motions, curving around pebbles, sparkling in the afternoon light. Though bright, the air was still very cold, her gloved hands finding homes in her pockets. The sound of running water filled her ears. More than once, she thought she heard voices on the wind, of far-off people talking between the trees.

She had continued to gorge herself each morning. These feasts were without conscience; she ate until her jaw ached, her stomach turned and her hands were slick with grease. It was the grease that she craved so much. Even after finishing, if it could ever be called such when she was always left so dissatisfied, she would lick her fingers clean, sucking the fleshy flavours from them until there was nothing left to taste.

At first she would cook the food. Such civilised habits were hard to break, even in the throes of abandon. But as days became weeks and her appetite grew, so her impatience grew with it. There was no tolerance in gluttony, after all; no lenience, no admirable qualities of any kind. It was a dark pit of self-gratification, from which the hungriest figures clambered forth with ravenous intent. In her impatience she forwent the act of cooking. The kitchen became a different place then; filled with the wet, bestial sound of chewing as Freya tore into raw meat and other such foods however she could find them. It was into this kitchen that George tumbled, the morning he almost caught her.

* * *

Neck-deep in the refrigerator, only half-aware of her son's sudden presence in the doorway, Freya froze. She spoke to him without turning, raw egg spilling from her lips.

"You're up early today and on a Sunday, too."

"Couldn't sleep," he said, moving to stand behind her. She felt his hand as he tugged at her dressing gown. "What's for breakfast?"

"You couldn't sleep?" She swallowed down the gelatinous albumen, before too much of it escaped her mouth. The rest she wiped on the back of her sleeve. "Why couldn't you sleep, huh?"

"The man from the tunnel keeps coming to my room."

She struggled to remember, to place his words. They came to her slowly, as if through a dream, a parting veil. "Your friend?"

"He's not my friend anymore."

"Don't worry, darling," she said, turning and hugging him tightly. He stood quite rigid while she embraced him. "Nightmares aren't real. They can't hurt you."

"I know. What's for breakfast?"

"What would you like for breakfast?" she said.

He seemed to think about this. "Eggs?"

"We're fresh out," she said, standing and swallowing. "How about some cereal, does that sound good?"

He shrugged and seated himself at the table.

It was a bright November morning, most of the clouds having rained themselves out the night before. Sunlight streamed in through the kitchen window, cold but pleasant, catching the raindrops that lingered on the glass. It promised to be a lovely day. The perfect weather for a walk through the Forest.

"What were you doing?" George said, watching her from the table.

"When?"

"Just now, when I walked in."

She frowned, opened her mouth to speak, then thought the better of it. "Waking up," she said, smiling. "Just waking up."

"You were eating raw eggs," he said.

"Don't be silly, darling. People don't eat raw eggs."

"It's all down your sleeve and at the end of your chin."

She moved into the hallway and examined her face in the mirror there. A string of cloudy egg white hung from her chin, like saliva from a dog's mouth.

"I don't know..." she started hesitantly. Wiping her face clean, she returned to the kitchen. "I can't remember." Then, more certainly: "You shouldn't eat raw eggs, George. Some of them contain salmonella. That's a disease that you can catch from certain foods, if they're not cooked properly."

"I know I shouldn't. And I know what salmonella is, I read about it in a book. And you were eating raw eggs. There's evidence."

She heard Lizzie on the stairs; the last three always creaked, then her daughter was standing in the doorway.

"Morning, Mum..."

"Morning, darling."

"What's for breakfast?"

"Not eggs," said George. "Mum's eaten them all."

"I haven't eaten any eggs, George!"

"I don't mind, except that you have and it's not very safe."

Lizzie crossed the kitchen, also in her dressing gown, and seated herself opposite her brother. "Eggs aren't unsafe. They're really good for you."

"Not when they're eaten raw, as Mum likes them."

"George, enough!" snapped Freya.

"Mum!" said Lizzie, "what the hell?"

Slamming the refrigerator door shut, Freya rounded on the dining table. "I haven't been eating raw eggs. The consumption of raw eggs isn't advisable and I never want to see either of you risking your health that way. Understood?"

Silence settled over the kitchen. She stared at her children and they stared back. Outside, from the back garden, two blackbirds took up song, broken only by a single, delicate crack, as an egg rolled from the work surface to the floor.

"I'm going back to bed," said Lizzie.

"You haven't eaten anything," said Freya.

"Not hungry." Lizzie rose and left the kitchen.

George began swinging his legs, in time to the blackbirds' chirps. "What cereal have we got?"

* * *

It had been a long time since she had born witness to the brook in the flesh. She had stopped coming here after her father had died. It hadn't felt right, walking the paths they had walked together without him. She could still remember the tales he used to tell, which had so frightened and fascinated her as a child...

The wind whispered louder in her ears and she fancied it was the Forest's voice telling her those stories again; of the Bauchan, who haunted the hungry waters, luring careless young girls to their wild, watery deaths in the brook of its namesake, and how it would claim her, too; if she strayed too far from the paths.

Such tales were nonsense, of course; stories concocted to keep children safe, if not obedient. She had lived long enough to know the power of fear. Their society was built on it and the order it maintained. She thought this was what Ms. Andrews had meant, when they had spoken in her drawing room. The church upheld peace. It promised life everlasting to the good, the docile. And those who strayed from the path... She had only to open the pages of a Bible to read these things; the eternal damnation that awaits the immoral, the armies of Sin that plagued the land and other Christian legends. There still existed statues of those same Sins in the churchyard; fickle creatures, so much like men and women but twisted and monstrous as the vices they personified.

Fear fulfilled its purpose. Her father had told her these things not to scare her but to keep her safe. In Southampton and London, children were taught the dangers of traffic, of unsafe streets and knife-crime. Their urban Bauchan went by other names; Rawhead and Bloody Bones, Jack the Ripper, the Bunny Man. Even now, younger, no-less horrible apparitions existed, the urban legends of today. Fear was nurtured, fed like an appetite, until it had grown into something bloated and undying.

Reaching for a stone, she tossed it underarm into the brook. It vanished instantly beneath the rushing waters, but she continued to stare after it, deep in thought. Lynnwood's dangers were different, of course, but no less cautionary. They warned of older things, more insidious than traffic or knife-crime; those of the wild woods, of becoming lost, of drowning beneath the trees.

Instead of visiting the brook alone, she had played behind the Old Barn with the other children. She had gone to church, walked the safe places and lived a good life. Without fear and the order it maintained they were little better than the beasts of the Forest.

* * *

As the afternoon wore on she wandered even further down the brook. She wasn't sure what she had expected, as she followed the delicate music of the water downstream. A torrent of memories, a welling of emotion, the Bauchan, thin and hungry, standing opposite her on the bank...

She smiled to herself as she wandered by the shallows. Her father would have encouraged her to return here. It wasn't a place to fear anymore but somewhere pleasant, somewhere genuine and beautiful. She vowed to come again soon, with the children. Lizzie would love the visual spectacle of the brook; the sheets of broken ice that covered the banks, the sluice of the currents, the dead leaves, which were swept helplessly away. And as she walked with George she would speak to him in hushed tones of the Bauchan, and the legend of this particular forest spirit would live on through the telling, as it had done for so long already.

It occurred to her, as she shouted for Eaton through the trees, that this might have been the reason for her dreams. They were calling her, as readily as she summoned the dog, back to the wild waters and the place of her memories. Dreams were one thing, but even their lucidity could not match the brush of the breeze against her face, the glittering brook in the afternoon light, the roughness of the bark when she dragged her fingers over the trees.

Eaton broke from the undergrowth and pottered into the shallows. His fur was matted with burrs and sticks but it was the bird in his mouth that drew her eyes and held them; a magpie, chewed almost beyond recognition, iridescence flashing from its tail-feathers.

Wincing at the sight, she bent to retrieve the poor bird, only half aware that, distorted by the currents, her reflection might have been grinning as it stooped to snatch the dog's prey from his mouth.

* * *

That evening, at dinner, George wept over the fate of the magpie. There was no escaping the influence of the Forest; the rank, metallic breath of mortality. They were all mercy to the wild whims of the trees, which could one moment bear them to peaceful epiphany, even as they cast their chill shade over Lynnwood.

George disclosed to her that evening that he had only two friends in Lynnwood, the first of whom was a magpie, which had that very afternoon failed to show at its perch for the first time in nearly a year. And what horror – his face pale, small lips quivering, mouth agape with something else than hunger. More familiar than most his age with the harsh brevity of life – the insects he admired lived brittle, brutal existences – the death of this bird represented something entirely different. His grief was a testament to the loneliness she had always worried he felt, but had never before admitted to herself.

George often wandered down by the old train tracks, tracing the line through the Forest. All manner of insects made the tarnished metal sleepers their home and he went there to hunt for them beneath the rotted wood beams and cold, dew-slicked sleepers. This, he said, was where the magpie lived, where they met each afternoon at around three o'clock, when he finished school for the day.

The line had been important once, linking Lynnwood to Brockenhurst and, from there, the rest of the county. Built in the 1890s, it had meant a great deal to Lynnwood, which had until then been isolated by the very Forest that sustained it. The line had brought the first meaningful waves of visitors to the village, opening it up to Hampshire. For all its benefits it had not lasted. Lynnwood seemed incapable of supporting the industrial intrusion; the Forest unwilling to tolerate such a hungry competitor. The Old Places were so often indifferent to change, Freya knew. The Oldest seemed almost opposed to it.

The bird would always greet George from where it perched, on the rotten remains of its tree. He said its tree, not because it nested there or ever had done, to his knowledge, but because that was where it waited. Indeed, it never seemed to move from the spot, except to cross the clearing, or settle nearer to him as he moved down the track. Occasionally it would emit a gleeful croak; a raucous sound, like the rattling wings of a giant cicada. He hadn't named the bird. What difference did a name make except to belittle something, to make it less than it actually was? Its scientific title was *Pica pica*, he knew, not entirely dissimilar from the sound it made, and that was enough for him.

A keening sadness sprang inside of Freya as her son recounted these things, but he seemed genuinely happy in his own company. Nor did he know any better. Perhaps that was his saving grace; a wild streak, that of the lone hunter, sparing him the heartache of solitude. Even as she thought this, she knew it wasn't true; why else would he be brought so low by the death of the bird, unless it had meant something to him? Through these sobering realisations she began to perceive the nature of her son more clearly.

They were eating roast chicken at the dinner table when he learned the horrid news. The cooked bird was golden and large, served with all the trimmings. This in itself had caused a quiet stir between her children; Freya hadn't sat down to a roast with them in living memory.

"You're not eating very much," she said to Lizzie between forkfuls.

"And you're eating chicken," replied Lizzie.

"I'm making an effort," she said, feeling herself redden before her children. Steam pressed heavily against the inside of the windows in dripping, opaque smears. She thought quickly, then realised she needn't lie. "I haven't been feeling myself recently."

"Me neither," replied her daughter. "Too many fry-ups. They're making me sick."

The kitchen fell silent, disturbed only by the slow scrape of cutlery on plates. She tried to concentrate, to counter her daughter, but found her thoughts numbed by the rich aromas of the food. Instinct swelled under those scents, pressing against her chest, filling her mouth with juices. Inside, she screamed to throw herself across the table, to take up great handfuls of food, to tear the legs from the chicken and force them into her open mouth, so hungry, so desperate to be filled –

Somehow, she held herself in check. Instead she sat quite still, contenting herself with one forkful at a time.

Almost automatically, to fill the silence as much as reclaim some sense of self, of civility, she recounted the events of her day, and it was then, as she mentioned Eaton and the magpie, that her son's face fell and the truth of his circumstances came tumbling out. With them came his tears, uncharacteristic as her appetite for meat.

* * *

The nib of her pen buries into the page. Her hand is shaking, her fingers white as the sheets of paper beneath. Words seem to have momentarily lost meaning and there is nothing but the memory of her son's face; tear-stained at the upheaval of death, of the wild spirit leaving that magpie's body, its cold, decaying remains, left to be devoured by the dogs and the beetles.

His face shines before her eyes, so pale, so vulnerable, and her chest heaves; a generous, violent movement. Then she swallows, as if consuming the memories might make them leave, as it has made everything else disappear. It is not what has become of her son that upsets her; she knows he is in a better place. She sees that now. He is wild, free as the magpie to which he was so endeared; to move between the trees, the light, the dark, to relish in unbridled freedom beneath the vast sky, to run and hunt and eat as appetite desires...

But she misses him. The emotion endures because, like the hunger, it is instinct. She realises that now. Her son as she knew him is gone. She is nothing to him, or he to her, except memories, and soon even they will be devoured.

Except for the ones recorded by the fading light, in dark blue ink across the half-filled pages beneath her.

CHAPTER SEVEN

The morning Freya accompanied Ms. Andrews to the Forest was the last time she, or anyone else in Lynnwood, ever saw the old woman.

Ms. Andrews's dreams had been growing worse, she confessed after service the following Sunday. There was no escaping the fly-faced woman or the nightly visitations that brought her closer. She felt constantly drained and had taken to drinking herself into a stupor each evening. This, she discovered, was the only way to ensure a restful night, if alcohol-induced sleep could ever be called such. True to her words, the woman's breath burned with brandy. Her eyes were shallow pits in her face and her frame had shrunk, so that she resembled a wrinkly child or the husk of one of George's insects, left too long in the damp. The woman seemed to have aged years in a matter of weeks.

The sky was bleak; a vast expanse of distance, grey and empty except for the thin wind, which howled through the church corridors. They were standing just outside the entrance, on crumbling stone steps, and could hear the wind clearly as it sang through the building.

"Another insightful service," Freya said, "thank you again, Joan. What would we be without you?"

"You mean where, surely?" said the vicar, laughing.

"Yes, of course! Still, thank you."

"You're welcome. It's always a pleasure to see familiar faces gathered in one place. How are you keeping?"

"I visited the brook," said Freya, "after we last spoke."

"That's good, my dear. How do you feel?"

"I didn't mean to walk by that way. I just sort of ended up there. Looking back, my father wouldn't have wanted me to avoid it for so long. It really is beautiful this time of the year."

"I'm pleased to hear you're feeling better," said Ms. Andrews.

"It'll be the same for you, with the clearing in the Forest. Think of it as therapy."

As Ms. Andrews heard this, a curious expression swept her face. She gasped silently, like a fish left to die on the banks of the brook. She recovered quickly. "I'm not so sure I should follow in your footsteps. My dreams are not of your pleasant sort."

"Then, if anything, a visit to the trees will remind you."

"Remind me?"

"Well, that the Forest is not as you dream it." Freya smiled encouragingly as the two moved away through the graveyard. "We'll go together. Tomorrow, once the children have left for school. Eaton will need walking anyway."

After a moment of hesitation, Ms. Andrews returned a thin smile. "Yes, of course. Who am I, refusing the prospect of company on a Monday morning? I have a number of errands to run anyway. It will be good to catch up properly, and see that beautiful dog of yours."

"He's a wild spirit," she said, her laughter carrying over the graves.

"Aren't we all?" said Ms. Andrews. "Aren't we all?"

* * *

They met earlier than planned that Monday morning, Freya having also found errands to run. These were not dissimilar to Ms. Andrews's own and, after browsing the high street for almost an hour, they headed to McCready's farmhouse. The morning was misty with frost, the village cobbles treacherous. Cold light filtered through the clouds, which rolled like crashing waves through the sky. The air stung her cheeks and numbed her nose; winter, teasing her flesh with its teeth.

They made polite conversation as they moved towards the Old Barn. Freya spoke much of Lizzie and George; their art projects and school progress respectively. A great deal of fuss was made over Eaton, who was more than happy to oblige their attentive hands by presenting his belly and the backs of his ears. Ms. Andrews seemed well enough, although she still looked disturbed at the prospect of entering the Forest. Freya understood, given the lucidity of her own dreams. If Ms. Andrews's horrible visitations were anything similar, her apprehension was not unfounded.

Freya thought only of the healing to be found there, or if not healing then a freedom from the pressures of the village, of life, a primitive release. The delicate sound of the water as it ran its course, the rich aroma of bark, the feel of the Forest as it snapped beneath her wellies; Ms. Andrews would experience these things for herself, she would unbridle whatever beasts strained within and, relieved of these burdens, sleep would once again become restful.

The wind picked up as they approached McCready's farmhouse. Although she could see no smoke behind the barn or in the fields, she fancied she could smell the charred pig again, or the ghost of that smell, clinging stubbornly to her nostrils and the wet slip of her tongue; a smoky-lipped lover, pressing the taste into her mouth...

Moving past the barn, which seethed with the clamour of livestock; the metal sounds of riled fencing, bestial snorts and the clatter of unsettled trotters, they reached the farmhouse. Its proud, long-faced owner met them at the door. He was dressed in clean work overalls and his thin hair stood wilder than she remembered.

"Ms. Andrews, I hadn't realised you were coming so early. And Freya, what a pleasant surprise!"

"The early bird catches the worm, or so I hear," said Ms. Andrews with a tight-lipped smile.

He returned the expression, his long face softening somewhat. "I hadn't reckoned on lovely creatures such as yourselves hankering after worms, now..."

"Perhaps some bacon, then?" The words tumbled quickly from Freya's lips.

He stared into her eyes before replying. His own eyes were small, shrewd, set deep into the hollows of his face. Confronted with the unexpected challenge, she stared boldly back, relishing the unexpected thrill that raced within. It felt curious but not unpleasant; a bristling at the back of her neck, which coursed like blood through her veins, setting light to her nerves with animal fervour. The wind buffeted her face, scented with smoke and cold against the hotness of her skin. After what felt like forever, he spoke again. "Couldn't wait until market on Thursday, my dear? Not that I blame you, mind..."

"We're running low," she said, "the children have quite an appetite lately. I don't know where they put it all."

"I'm sure you don't," he said, still staring quite intently. Then, as though snapping from a dream: "Yes, I think I can stretch to some bacon. Here, come in. Let me take your coat. How about some sausages, too?"

"Why not?" she said, smiling, delirious with unspoken defiance. "Lead the way."

* * *

Despite moving to Lynnwood only nine years ago, John McCready had settled very quickly into the community. He was no stranger to village life, having lived in nearby Ashurst for many years before. The McCreadys had owned land there for centuries and were famously proud of their title as Commoners, which authorised them the care of their own land. The Forest was a law unto itself. They understood that better than most in Lynnwood.

The farm had meant everything to John's family. He had spoken at length with Freya about his childhood there, when first moving to Lynnwood. Mostly she had wondered what drove him from Ashurst, where so many of his roots were based.

"My sister," he said plainly that day, and she had known from the look in his eyes that she would not like what followed. "Mary was an unsettled woman. Even when we were children she would hear things. Noises at her window, or from the sties."

"Noises?"

"The pigs, screaming at night. Sometimes it was the cows. The farm was no place for a young girl."

"We're more resilient than you think," Freya said, smiling. He did not smile back.

"Have you ever heard a cow scream, my dear? Or a pig?"

"I haven't, no."

"Then let us hope you never have to." He took a long draught of his drink before continuing, his lips white with foam. "When my sister didn't get better, they took her to the doctor. Dosed her up on pills. Little tablets, all kinds of colours, to make her social, like. It seemed to work, I suppose, though she was never the same since."

"I'm so sorry, John."

"Happen the part of her that heard those sounds was the good part, the real Mary. The pills put a stop to that, anyway. For a while at least. She grew up right enough, though she was never fit to leave the farm again. Then one day, they stopped working."

"Just like that?"

"Just like that," he said. "I'd only recently moved back to the farm myself. Our father was not long gone and my mother couldn't cope with all the heavy work herself. So I came back, with my brothers, to help look after the place. That was when Mary started playing up again. Hearing things that weren't there. Seeing figures in the morning fog."

"Wasn't there anything you could do?"

"It all happened so quickly. Besides, what could anyone do, when she was struggling to surface? I swear it, the old Mary was trying to break free. It never did sit right with me, when they gave her those pills. Anyway, they said she'd built up some resistance, when they examined her afterwards, but I knew. I knew she was fighting.

"We found her in the stables one morning. Curled up in the corner, naked, stiff as the table here." He struck the wood with the palm of his

423

hand. "They said the cold got her. They said they were sorry. I didn't know what to believe, but I couldn't stay there anymore. All I could see was that shape in the corner of the stables, so old but so young-looking, and so vulnerable like. And I remembered Lynnwood."

He had visited the village several times, it emerged, during his formative years, and something of Lynnwood had remained with him ever since. She had heard similar stories before and was not surprised. The village had a way of sticking, in the mind and in the soul. So he had sold his shares of the farm and bought the rights to new land, here in the village, and had not looked back since.

* * *

The clearing stood near Mawley Bog, not far from the Hanging Tree. Smaller and more intimate than she had imagined from Ms. Andrews's telling, there was nonetheless room for the pair of them to wander. The old woman walked slowly, as though in her dream, twigs breaking beneath her tread. Sunlight shone down through the branches, which stretched overhead. Even the bark glinted silver with hoar frost, bright against the rotten branches on the ground.

"You see, Joan? No flies, just trees. They're just trees."

Freya's voice shattered the silence; a human voice, so out of place in this copse, this wild place, encased in a layer of cold. Only then did she realise how uneasy she felt. It might have been the stillness of the scene, or the hallowed quiet of the Forest in the absence of bird calls or the trickling brook, their dirges frozen on the air, as water to sheets of ice. And it was quiet. Every hollow snap beneath Ms. Andrews's feet echoed between the trees, until they might have been coming from anywhere in the Forest. The icy air pricked Freya's lungs with each savage breath, emerging again as a pale cloud when she exhaled.

"Lord in Heaven..." muttered Ms. Andrews, her back to Freya. "Oh Lord in Heaven..."

"Joan, what is it?"

"I'd forgotten... God forgive me. Lord! Forgive me for what I've done."

Alone together in the clearing, with only the trees and the cold for company, the enormity of those words crept agonisingly down Freya's spine. And with every word spoken, it seemed as though the trees crawled closer, the branches longer, the cold harsher. Her pulse thundered hot in her temples and it might have been her imagination but she thought she saw something between the trees; a thin figure moving swiftly around the outskirts of the clearing. Her throat tightened, her eyes distracted. The wind took Ms. Andrews's scarf, tossing it to the trees.

"Joan, what had you forgotten? What do you see?"

Another flash of movement, as something continued to circle the glade. She would have followed it except Ms. Andrews turned to her then. Never had she seemed so physically frail, as if drained by the chill air or the forest roots until only the ghost of Ms. Andrews remained. And yet there was a feverish light in her face, shining in her eyes, visible in those vaguely parted lips. Her scrawny frame trembled – from the cold, Ms. Andrews would later confess, as they walked back through the trees.

"Joan, I'm so sorry. I didn't realise. I didn't know you had... memories here."

"No flies," said the woman dumbly. "You were right... No flies."

"We should go. I can't apologise enough. Let's get you inside and warm. Have you seen Eaton? I think he ran into the trees."

Hearing the crunch of dead leaves behind her, she turned, to grab the dog, leash him and leave this wild, menacing place. Except the shape that burst from the undergrowth behind her was not Eaton, or any dog. Long, human arms reached for her. Bones clicked as the figure scrabbled closer, face twisted, mouth gaping, eyes fixed feverishly on her own –

This instinct was different. She fell back from the apparition, tumbling into the blanket of leaves. She could not challenge the sheer savagery of that vision, or the fact that behind the ecstasy in its eyes, the hunger that split its lips, it had seemed so familiar.

They hurried from the place; two small silhouettes beneath the vastness of the skies, the trees and the long, hungry howl of a dog.

425

CHAPTER EIGHT

Though no one confessed it, the residents of Lynnwood sought their missing vicar for their own savage curiosity as much as Ms. Andrews's welfare. When the news broke that she had vanished, they rushed from their homes and the village crawled with insatiable activity; figures moving swiftly, bent low with desperation, through the streets.

Once it was determined she was nowhere in the village borders, one question quivered, unspoken, on everyone's lips, hidden beneath the proper questions they voiced: what had become of Ms. Andrews since surrendering to the wild glamour of the Forest?

Joan Andrews's funeral was a formality. Lost to the trees there was no body to bury. The village gathered in the graveyard behind Allerwood Church where they prayed for their vicar, even as they stood upon the mouldering remains of those hundreds who had died before. Freya had never realised the hypocrisy of it, the sheer madness of such celebrations. Life was spirit, yes, but spirit made flesh; the kiss of the wind against one's face, the rushing of hot blood beneath one's skin, the swelling, irrepressible urges that flooded one's body with every hurried thump of the heart. In death, there were none of these things. Nothing but ethereality, reduced to insubstantial memory, so easy to scatter, no better than a dream, or the orange leaves of a tree in autumn. And then the body, stripped of the self; a cooling collection of limp limbs and ragged flesh, growing soft and syrupy with decay.

She attended the funeral with Catherine, two spectres in a congregation of famished ghosts. Mrs. Morecroft took the sermon. She spoke of Ms. Andrews's childhood in the village, then Frederick, and her role as vicar of Lynnwood. Others took the floor with their own memories, their own private interactions. Each anecdote pricked Freya until she thought she must be pink and flushed with shame. This was her fault. She had led Ms. Andrews to the trees. She had urged the old woman through the Forest, where she wouldn't have stepped alone. She had forced her into that place, which was so far from the village, and it had swallowed her whole with a verdant, vacuous roar...

She clung to the tears, hot and wet against her skin. Something had happened that morning in the Forest that she had not expected. The hunger had grown too great, too wild, bursting from every vein beneath her skin until she thought she might lose herself. Surrendering to her appetites whenever she felt them, she had not dwelt on how dangerous they were, or why they were repressed in the first place. She had thought them delightful, then wildly indulgent, but never deadly.

They must be reined in, she vowed. The feasting, her visits to the brook, these things must be stopped before they consumed her. Already, it seemed, they had nipped at her flesh, stealing bite after bite, and then in the clearing with Ms. Andrews, a monstrous mouthful, pale-faced and ghastly in the undergrowth.

She endured the rest of the ceremony in silence. Though there were no remains and, therefore, no grave, a traditional headstone was nonetheless erected. Once this had been appreciated and the ceremony concluded, Lynnwood's residents broke away, one by one drifting back into the village. As the last to leave, her face red, fingers pink from the cold, she was the only witness to Mr. Shepherd, the village artisan, and the gift he dropped quickly onto the headstone before himself departing.

Close inspection revealed it to be a brooch. Though ornate in design, it was hammered from little more than iron. She touched it tentatively. No bigger than the palm of her hand it proved smooth to the skin and icy cold, as if devouring the warmth from all around it. But more than the cold or the intricacy of the brooch, the depiction she saw in it struck her, causing a sharp inhalation of breath; the brooch resembled an open mouth, distended and ravenous, gaping up at her from the metalwork.

CHAPTER NINE

Freya thought often of the moment in which McCready's gaze had met with hers that day outside his farmhouse; the second when, challenged by his eyes, carnal instinct had bubbled to the surface. Civility decreed she fled; it taught to run from conflict, or to console it where possible, to neuter it as a dog relieved of its potency. But she had stared into McCready's eyes, bright with understanding, and recognised the hunger. She held his gaze unflinching, even as her lips formed the lies she had known they would. And though she concealed the truth, there was no hiding the lustre in her own eyes, as she had seen in his.

The memory served as a constant reminder of what lay beneath the skin, waiting to escape, should she let her guard down for but a moment. For weeks afterwards she clung to the commonplace, becoming a regular face about the village, where before she would have walked Eaton through the trees. The routine of Sunday service was unsettled but she didn't let this deter her from the church grounds. And if she thought there were more headstones of late, more graves than she could ever remember seeing, this could surely only be a good sign; the village becoming clearer and more solid around her, grounding her in the real, the now?

Her dream too began to change, as though subject to the turning seasons. The trees shed their leaves, branches seemed to twist and the dulcet song of the water fell silent beneath sheets of opaque ice. Winter had come to the dream-brook, and each time she glimpsed the thirsty figure opposite, with its hands dipped into the chill waters, it seemed thinner and less-kindly, until she began to doubt its motives by the pleasant brook, and dreaded the moment their eyes, for that one second, met.

* * *

The Knightwood Oak, two miles walk from the village across heathland, stood for all that was ancient and enduring about the

Forest. From where Freya waited with her daughter beside the small picket fence that surrounded the monstrous tree, the sanctity of the scene could not have been more apparent; the enormity of the wild, maternal edifice, reaching into the sky as it had done for hundreds of years, surrounded by a court of saplings; its children, cut from its own flesh and blood.

Even this mighty tree was not exempt from man's influence. Men dressed the practice up as pollarding, they validated their actions with reason, but this did not detract from the violence of their axes as they stripped back branches and brought the tree low for another hundred years. As though the tree would not have endured, not procreated, without their 'help', their 'encouragement'.

In that moment, staring up into the branches, she felt ashamed to be human. If it was the beasts who lived alongside the tree, who nested in its branches and hunted in its shadow, then let her be a beast, not the other; desperate to rise above the wilderness so inherent to man's heart. She could see that now.

Stepping closer, Freya took her daughter's hand in her own. Lizzie looked frail, as though the breath of wind that touched her hair might blow a little stronger and take the rest of her away with it. Freya hoped that she was happy. It had been so long since they had spoken properly, never mind laughed, or baked together, or played as they had used to, when Lizzie was little.

* * *

The blue light of winter shone through the kitchen windows, revealing an uncluttered room, sparsely filled, save for ingredients massed in one corner of the worktop. A calendar hung from the wall, beside the AGA cooker, marking December in all its festive glory. The year was 2004, though it could have been any winter's day; barely the afternoon, darkness already encroached on the village. A string of fairy lights hung from the ceiling beams.

"What are we making?" said Lizzie, her face caught in the glow of the lights. "Are we making cakes? Are we making mince pies for Father Christmas?"

Looking down at her daughter, Freya smiled. The girl's cheeks still shone from the cold. They had not long returned from the market, where it had begun to snow. Some of the flakes still lingered in her hair. "It's a bit early for mince pies, darling. We'll make some tomorrow, or the day after, so they'll be fresh when he visits. They taste the best when they're freshly-made."

"What are we making now, then?"

"Bread," said Freya, "using an old family recipe. Your grandmother taught me how to make it when I was a little girl, and her mother before her."

"But bread..."

"Special bread," she said. "It's extra tasty, you'll see. Here, help me weigh out the ingredients. It's important we measure everything just right."

They went through the ingredients one by one, sifting them into bowls and filling measuring jugs. Freya had weighed out everything beforehand; seven grams of yeast, a pinch of salt, fifteen grams of softened butter and one cup and a half of wholemeal flour, but that wasn't the point. It was the process that mattered. The activity.

"What next?" said Lizzie, her hands white, face powdery with flour. Against the redness of her cheeks she resembled a porcelain doll; one of the old-fashioned Victorian types, made up like proper ladies.

"You have to be patient," said Freya, "we're nearly done."

"Why do I have to be patient?"

"Because some things take time, darling."

"I don't think I'll be patient," said Lizzie decisively.

"When?" said Freya.

"When I grow up. It sounds boring."

A controlled burst of water, unleashed for one maddening moment, swirled inside the measuring jug, then Freya set to work. Taking Lizzie's hands in her own they mixed the ingredients together, as another girl had with her own mother, nearly four decades earlier. The gentle sighs of the mixture, as she worked it with her hands, filled the kitchen. The emerging dough felt soft, almost spongy, beneath her fingertips.

Nobody had made bread like Harriet, especially when generously spread with one of the Allwood's jams. The blackberry was always Freya's favourite as a girl. She remembered her mother's cakes, laden with succulent fruits; swollen blackberries, bursting raspberries, sticky and shiny with glaze under the afternoon sun. Though Freya had always been her father's daughter, the hours spent baking with Harriet were instrumental in their bonding. The act of creation, of making something out of nothing, was one close to every girl's heart, no matter her age, especially when those creations were crumbling scones, loaves of springy bread and glazed fruit tarts, sharp and sweet against the tongue; sheer sensuality, real and regenerating.

"Am I doing it right?" said Lizzie.

"You're a natural, darling. Much better than I was, when I was your age."

"Really?"

"Yes!" said Freya. "Maybe you'll become a baker one day. Then you could sell your cakes at market, like we saw today."

From where Lizzie stood, between Freya's arms, she snorted: "I'm not going to be a baker."

"You're not?"

Shaking her head, Lizzie looked up from their hands. Her eyes were sharp, bright, and suddenly there was nothing porcelain about her. "I'm going to be a runner," she said. "I'm going to run through the trees, faster than anyone else, and I'm going to keep running, just like Dad."

Freya's fingers sunk into the dough and remained there a moment. "Your father's run too far," she said. "He's run so far that he's got lost, somewhere in the Forest. Promise me you'll never run that far."

Lizzie promised. "You know, it seems to me a lot of people get lost in the Forest."

They spent the rest of the afternoon preparing the dough. When they finally finished, and Freya withdrew her hands from her daughter's, she noticed a faint red imprint where her wedding ring had pressed into Lizzie's skin. For a whole hour afterwards Lizzie pranced around the house, a dishcloth over her face, humming wedding songs and pretending she was to be married.

Only when the dogs began howling did Freya draw the curtains and usher Lizzie upstairs, mimicking the wolfish sounds as she chased her shrieking daughter into bed.

* * *

The Forest had grown dark this year, intimidating, alive with the movement of dead trees and memories, but when Lizzie had asked to see the Oak, Freya had been only too happy to oblige. She savoured this fleeting moment, in which the beauty of the trees was restored, this abused tree towering over its saplings, mother and daughter beneath it. She would think of it often, in the weeks ahead, when so much else became ugly and unkempt.

Presently they grew cold and hungry. As the afternoon set in and the light began to leave them, they set off for the village across the heathland, where the ponies ran wild as they pleased...

* * *

"I'm worried about Merlot," Catherine said, when Freya visited her old friend that evening for drinks. "She hasn't come home. Not since last night."

The cottage itself was beautiful. Freya had often thought it belonged in a fairy tale. Scarlet ivy crawled across the grey brick outside, stretching around the door to the first-floor windows. The roofing was dark slate that shone a gorgeous black in the rain and warmth suffused the inside of the cottage, so that on cold winter evenings there was nowhere nicer or more welcoming in the village. Beams lined the kitchen ceiling, from where wicked witches would hang their cauldrons. Catherine had opted for spice baskets and begonias. The room filled with the oaky scent of red.

"Spill the beans," Freya said, when her friend risked yet another glance at the window. Catherine's distress was palpable.

"What do you mean?" said Catherine.

"I haven't seen you this anxious since your father caught us swigging that expensive fizz the afternoon we finally finished school."

432

"That night..." Catherine smiled, her eyes flickering to Freya's. "I thought we were never to speak of that night again. We swore, remember?"

"We're not," said Freya, smiling back. "We're speaking of tonight."

They moved with their wine into the sitting room. Freya poured fresh glasses while Catherine sorted them some finger-food. It was cosier here, nestled into the sofas. The air was laced with languor. Freya took a sip of her wine, relishing the full-bodied taste of it, the feel of it slipping down her throat, while Catherine voiced her concerns.

Merlot was Catherine's cat, one of three, named after her favourite French grape. The animals meant a great deal to the woman, who treated them like her babies in the absence of children of her own.

"I'm sure she can look after herself," Freya said. "Isn't that the point of cats?"

"The point of cats..." Catherine rolled her eyes. "That's hardly fair. I don't quiz you on the point of dogs, do I?"

Freya laughed with genuine mirth. "I'm not sure dogs have a point, unless you count eating and trailing mud through the house, and I can hardly criticise him for that lately."

"You old bitch," said Catherine, laughing with her now. "What a pair we make."

"To Merlot," said Freya, raising her glass.

"To Merlot!"

They talked long into the night, Catherine's worries drowned beneath a cocktail of wine and memories. Many bottles were drunk, until there was no more Merlot of any sort in the cottage and Freya was forced to return home, before she lost the ability to walk. Retreating quietly from the cottage, she left Catherine where she had passed out on the sofa.

Only when Freya was outside did she trip, and curse her bra for being so restrictive, and almost fall into a flowerbed. The night seemed to swim around her. The alcohol had gone down well, she thought, as she stumbled home. Though she knew she would suffer tomorrow, she would drink again with Catherine soon. For Merlot's sake, if an excuse was ever needed, which it wasn't, in Lynnwood.

CHAPTER TEN

December settled silently over Lynnwood one night and with it an awareness; the worst kind, not of monsters or evil but the nature of the self, penned between the pages of a diary.

Night emerged from the Forest. It spilled from the dark spaces between the trees as much as the skies, rolling out across the village. There were no carols to commemorate its arrival, no children playing in the streets, no sounds at all, in fact, save for the muffled coughs of lonely silhouettes, bent low as they struggled home. Counted among them, Freya moved swiftly through the night. Her old Parka was zippered to her neck, so that only the tail of her scarf fluttered with the wind.

She should have returned home hours ago. She should have been there to meet George and Lizzie after school, to gather them up and lock the doors and comfort them. Instead she had remained at the Vicarage, poring over the books that Ms. Andrews had so diligently guarded all these years. Once she had begun, once she had deciphered the antiquated English with its wild scrawl and long-limbed lettering, she couldn't seem to stop until she reached the last page of each volume and felt the maddening truth of their echoes...

* * *

They raised the issue of the Vicarage three days before, while meeting in the village hall. Fewer than were expected attended the gathering but then the morning frost had been especially black, the air savage to breathe. Mr. Shepherd was a notable absentee, though McCready's sandwiches more than compensated for the matter, and Catherine arrived a little later with hot flasks of mulled wine to pass around. Gathered together beneath the exposed timber beams of the village hall, they ate and drank these offerings with abandon.

"There's always been an Andrews in Lynnwood to take care of matters such as this," said Mrs. Morecroft, when they had consumed their fill and drank much more. "As we all know, life had other plans for our vicar, God rest her soul, and we aren't afforded this luxury."

"We could hold an auction?" suggested McCready. "Happen we'd make a pretty penny, selling off some of the older items. Village heirlooms and such."

"That only raises more questions," said Mrs. Morecroft. "Which of the Vicarage's treasures were hers to sell, and which belong still to our church? There's local heritage to consider. Then, supposing we make sales, where does the money go? She left no will, no inheritors."

"The village," said someone else. "We could turn it back into the village. Get some decent roads down –"

"Roads! Through-traffic's the last thing we need –"

"We can't sell," said Catherine, blowing wisps of steam from an unscrewed flask on the table. Her eyes, filled with wisdom and wine, wavered through the heat. "These were Joan's things. This was her life. Have some respect for the woman."

They fell silent at these words, each afraid, as if they might have revealed too much of themselves in the presence of their neighbours. With some visible effort, Mrs. Morecroft roused herself to speak further. "This still leaves us with the question of what is to become of the Vicarage."

"We should clear it of her things," said Freya. She hadn't spoken yet, content to listen as the meeting unfolded, but she found herself talking then. The words moved through her mind like a swarm of tiny gnats, dancing above the surface of Mawley Bog in the ragged red of autumn dusk. "Give them away. The Vicarage's not her home anymore, and it's what she would've wanted."

"You're sure, Freya?"

"Yes, I think so. We spoke often enough. I knew her better than most, in the end."

Tension gripped the men and women of the village hall. Freya remembered the tightness of her bra against her flesh, the night outside Catherine's cottage. The feeling extended to the rest of her clothes; a second cotton-skin she sought to shed, revealing the real underneath. She knew the mounting urge to run, break free; to drop low, like dogs or ancient man, and race from Lynnwood into the half-light of the trees, as they imagined Joan Andrews to have done, and she knew she was not alone in feeling this. Some of the villagers, she would later learn, dreamt they had seen the old woman in the woods since; a wiry figure, naked and shrivelled, scrabbling through the trees.

The tension about the room grew tighter until she thought it might shatter like a stressed branch and splinter into a hundred pieces. Somehow, Mrs. Morecroft spoke. They voted in favour of clearing the Vicarage. Freya chose to tackle the study and the literature housed within.

* * *

She fled through the village. The night pressed down on her, a numbing blanket. She found relief in that numbness; a deadening of spirit and body, as though she drifted through the streets, born by the wind and nothing more. The sound of her boots as they knocked against the cobbled streets formed a frantic rhythm into which she was absorbed.

She should never have delved into the diary. But it had lain open on Ms. Andrews's desk, in that tired study filled with the accumulated dirt of ages. Crisp white pages had caught her attention, offset by the wide, frantic scratches of black ink across them, where so much else was dark and dusty with abandonment. The room itself looked as though it had not been used properly for many years, save certain marks, made recently in the dust. She followed these tracks, the lingering echoes of Ms. Andrews's last movements, and had found the diary, so innocuous as to be monstrous given the truths of which it spoke. Even as she had read it, curious at first, then with wide eyes and quivering lips, she knew them to be just that; truths, written and forgotten but remembered with the coming of the cold and the snow and Winter Solstice...

* * *

Taking the diary from where it lay on the desk, she turned the book over in her hands. The cover bore no name. Nor did its pages contain any obvious dates. Indeed, no effort of time-keeping had been made, as though that was unimportant. She leafed through the leather booklet slowly. Where the ink was older and more faded she discerned the earliest entries, but it was the most recent additions, in that long, hurried lettering, which were of interest to her. She read steadily at first, then with increasing quickness, as one who has glimpsed the horror of something and is thereafter unable to look away, both enthralled and afraid that they might miss something, or that the same horror should be worse only half-known.

Joan had written of her dreams; the clearing, the dusk, the fly-faced woman through the trees. Something about reading these visitations made them more real, certified by shaking hand and scratchy ink; the dreaming thoughts of a frightened woman, committed to paper. She wrote of other things too; the encroaching cold, the sounds of the Vicarage, the yellowing of the leaves of the alder trees by the church. Freya deduced from these things that it was October, though they were fleeting mentions. Always, it seemed, Joan returned to the dreams, as they returned to her each evening, when the sun fell and shadows filled her home.

Trepidation crept into the writing, or sleeplessness, characterised in the fragility of the lettering, the frantic pace at which it rushed across the pages. The trees, she wrote, seemed taller, the dusk dimmer, the fly-faced woman closer. There was night after night of this; each marked by a sole step across the deadwood through the dappled gloom. On reading these things, Freya grew quite sad. The feeling was physical; sickening in her stomach, mixed with pangs of regret. Who was she, to have suggested that walk through the Forest? So naïve to assume that it could heal, that it could help. She, who covered herself in clothes, who could not even bear to look at herself in the bathroom mirror, for fear of what she might see in the steamy glass?

Then came the inevitable entry, which she had been both dreading and eager to read. "Tonight we met halfway across the clearing, under the branches of the alders. I reached out and stroked the woman's

437

arm. There are few words to describe how lovely and horrid it felt, to feel her flesh against my fingers, so warm and familiar. Her human parts were smooth, and pale as milk in the fading light. I did not touch her face, not because I feared it by this point, but because there was no need. I have realised why I have been dreaming of her, and she is not a thing to fear. Instead I brought my hand to my own face, running it across my cheeks, my skin, the curvature of my head, and found it to be that of the fly. We are one and the same, this figure and I. She is me. I am the fly-faced woman, and I have remembered why I stand in that Gadarene clearing, night on night, alone and bearing the face of the Lord of the Flies, the Gluttonous One, the Prince of Hell...

"On touching my face and confirming these things, I found myself alone in the Forest. Either I had become the figure, or she had never been. One and the same, I fled from that place, overcome with a burgeoning sense of fear. The trees reached out for me as I broke through the brush. Leaves caught in my hair – I had hair, now, and my own face again – and breath blew in white clouds from my mouth. The sun had died and everything seemed frozen. And though I fled aimlessly, there were sounds ahead, growing closer and closer, not approaching me, but I towards them, and I realised – no, I remembered – I was chasing him through the trees, I was chasing him, I was chasing him, and then I felt it inside..."

The writing grew nearly illegible. Ink had seeped into the page and become faint, where wetness had made it run. Freya's throat felt dry, her lips cracked, her eyes narrow as she strove to read on. There was more scripture, and much talk of flies and demons, and then, on the last page, a confession:

"Only the Forest matters now. Heaven must wait its turn, if He will forgive me my actions. Have I done wrong by Frederick? Have I sinned, by chasing him through the trees that night and sating myself on him, by gorging myself on his flesh, his blood? My God, I can barely write the words, yet even as I do so my stomach grows impatient, my mouth wet with saliva. It is an abhorrent and monstrous thing I have done, in the throes of a hunger that was not my own, and entirely my own. I feared I was a Beast, and that Hell

438

awaited me. Then I realised this was not the case, or that we are all beasts underneath. There is no devilry in what I have done. Do foxes not pick at their prey? Do dogs and cats not eat flesh where they find it? He must forgive me, for I have acted only according to my nature, as it is all things nature to grow hungry and hunt.

"God made me in His image, and I am ravenous, as I once was, so many years ago. I must embrace this hunger, before it happens again in such a violent and uncontained fashion. I go to the Forest, where I shall run and be free and perhaps find Him in the trees and the earth, if not in myself."

* * *

At every turn Freya saw the terrible things of which she had read. Shadows formed silhouettes locked in ravenous embrace. The wind added sound to their feeding forms, Frederick Mangel's screams carrying through the years as his famished fiancée tore into him. And all the while Freya's boots knocked against the cobbles, matching the hurried pace of her heart, which raced, terrified and exhilarated, in her chest.

She saw the village differently now. Lynnwood had transformed in her eyes, reduced by ink and night into formless shapes; a meaningless collection of bricks and stone in the vast sprawl of ancient, untamed forest. Their ancestors heard the bellows of the Forest's breaths, the thrumming of the trees, the groaning of the earth beneath their feet, and in their horror they built houses and streets and a small church, anything to distance themselves from the roaring hunger of the trees, which so echoed the stirrings inside each of them. Each Midwinter families were found, broken apart across their sitting rooms. Husbands plastered bloodily to their armchairs. Wives in pieces down the landing. And both devoured; great strips torn from their backs, limbs and breasts removed, as though they were livestock and nothing more, like the pigs kept by McCready. Some years only the bones were left, sobering and sick in the cold light of morning, the occupants of Lynnwood, reduced to their grinning, fleshless cores.

Joan's diary was but one in a study filled with confessions.

Lynnwood had been built on a legacy on hunger, as far back as those earliest settlers. Though the forest soil was poor, there was little people would not do, or eat, when it meant the difference between life and death. Even in the winter months, when darkness dragged and bodies froze, there was meat to be found, if they would only eat it. There, perhaps, she had found the roots of Lynnwood's legacy; the earliest records of that nameless hunger, between the starving hollows of the trees.

And though the village had become a pleasant enough place in which to live, these hardships forgotten, their hunger had survived, carried in the blood and beneath the skin.

CHAPTER ELEVEN

Hear the music of the brook
Running through the trees,
Over pebbles, under stones,
Wherever it may please.

Smell the turning of the leaves,
Rich autumn in the bark,
The season sings a merry song
Its voice that of the lark.

See the water run its course,
The Forest, now awoken,
River shining in the light
And at its banks, the Bauchan.

He makes a very pleasant sight,
His long face pale and glowing
Of his hunger deep beneath
Why, none of it is showing!

His sopping lips spread wide apart

From them a pleasant song
He beckons so delightfully
Why, he could do no wrong!

But should you step onto the bank
Where earth and water meet,
He'll pounce on you, all tooth and bone,
Another treat to eat!

CHAPTER TWELVE

Standing in the window in her front room, as she had each day for a week now since that revealing night, Freya stared out over the street. Upstairs, her children slept. She clutched a tumbler of brandy – an old, thick-cut glass, inherited from her father – from which she took a sharp sip.

Lynnwood was quiet, but not peaceful as it had once been. It would never be peaceful again, tainted by the acts, committed in the dark places beneath the trees. She stood there for what seemed like forever. One by one, the other cottages down the street became dark, as Lynnwood closed its curtains, turned off its lights and became still. It was a ghost village, awaiting the arrival of the hungry dead; the bean sí, as one diary had called them. And in a matter of weeks they would come, as they did every Midwinter; not spirits, not demons but the ravenous people of Lynnwood.

Part of her – a very strong part – wanted the hunger to come. She invited its attentions. Let it take her, she thought, and that would be the end of it, of this two-faced existence. There would be no more pretending, no more forgetting, no more wandering the Forest, wondering why she felt so sick, surrounded by such beauty.

But there were other instincts, as primal and fierce as anything that night inspired. While her children slept upstairs, she could not abandon them. Nor could she bring herself to leave Lynnwood; her existence tied to that of the Forest. The very thought of packing up and driving through the trees brought a soft shiver to the back of her neck, as though on entering the Forest she might lose herself once and for all beneath its boughs, and her children with her.

When the last cottage fell dark she dragged her curtains together. She made her way back through the house, switching off each light as she passed. Night spilled into the hallway, the bathroom, the sitting room. Then she climbed the stairs to the landing. Long, oak boards lined the floor, which groaned beneath her tread. The sounds filled the silent house with their presence.

As each night now, she visited first Lizzie's room, then George's. It was her youngest she most feared for. Light spilled from the hallway across his clothes-strewn carpet as she moved to his bedside. She ran a gentle hand through his hair, compelled to touch him, to certify he was still there.

He turned, murmuring softly in his sleep. He really was just a boy; so small, so thin beneath his covers. She thought he would always be her boy, no matter how he grew up or what he became. And, of course, she would do her best to raise him properly, in the meantime. She refused to believe the inescapability of their hunger. She refused to believe that one day he would be driven to feasting beneath the trees. She refused it, as she refused to believe she herself harboured that evilness.

Their atrocities were monstrous, and yet each year they went forgotten. She thought that it was the human way, to deal with life and the horrors it brought. They had not wanted to remember – could not remember – for their own sakes. To remember would be too great a thing to cope with. It made her wonder what else she had forgotten over the course of her lifetime; memories that could not bear to exist.

The room was still and silent as the rest of the house. She licked her lips and continued to stroke her son's hair. It brought her comfort to see Robert's features in his face. It was his eyes, his mouth. These were the corner-marks of a face; defining features of character, of the person within. At least Robert had escaped this madness. At least somewhere he walked free beneath the night sky, and the stars that he had loved so much. She had thought it strange, once, that a man of faith might admire the stars and the shapes they made in the sky. He explained his God was not in Heaven but in the world around them; the trees, the soil, the constellations in the night. When he saw the stars, he said, he was reminded of nature's reach and its burning beauty. None captured that spirit better than his favourite: Orion, the Hunter.

Warmth flooded her limbs, which seemed heavy with brandy and remembrance. Lying down, she wrapped her son in her arms, closed her eyes and in that heady state of mind slipped from wakefulness into sleep.

* * *

She dreamt horrible things; new dreams that may or may not have been real. Shadows stretched for her son's window from all around; long, black limbs reaching for the glass. There was pale movement in the moonlight as scrawny figures clutched at the thatched straw of the roof, faces white and pained. Then sounds; clicking, like tongues against the hollows of mouths, or the cracking of many-jointed legs, and the foetid stench of unwashed teeth as the shadows swarmed closer, a hungry hive, descending on Haven House –

* * *

She woke suddenly in the darkness of the bedroom. Releasing George, she struggled into a sitting position. She felt cold, damp. Sweat plastered her chest and beneath her arms.

She thought to inspect the time. George's clock sat on the bedside table, but she couldn't see its face in the darkness. Beside it was a radio alarm, with a digital clock, but that appeared to have died. It must have run flat, sometime in the night. Rising carefully she slipped from the bed.

Shadows fled from the movement, the curtain caught a breeze, and for a moment she struggled to differentiate between dream and reality. The window was open, even though she was certain she had locked it. She moved quickly across the room, reached for the window latch and closed it. Wind buffeted the frosted glass, rising like a scream into the night, then was still.

Standing there, she stared out over the village. It was a very different place by night. The road stretched on into the darkness until she couldn't distinguish between the two. That seemed right, somehow. Gardens glittered with frost and everything else was black, as though coated in liquorice. She was reminded strangely of *Charlie and the Chocolate Factory*, which her father used to read her when she was young. All that was missing was the swarm of small, childlike figures, rushing through the darkness –

Another gust of wind, another scream, and her reflection twisted, unsettled. She put the thought quickly from her mind and was about to turn from the window, from the cold, empty blackness of the world outside, when she saw it. Long, apish arms clutching the window frame. And pressed up against the other side of the glass, as far away as she had been seconds earlier, a face. White, gaunt, like that of an old man, but horribly childish, staring at her through the first-floor window.

* * *

She woke, as before, in George's bed. Outside was the deep blue of dawn, growing gradually paler with the rising sun. Birdsong filled the air. She turned to her son, who was once more in her arms, and kissed his forehead. For the briefest moment, she felt at peace. She clung to the moment, savouring it and the soft waves of relief that lapped inside of her.

Then the feeling passed, replaced by another, more insistent urge. Unwilling to ignore it, to risk anything that might make her appetite grow, she rose from the bed and descended through the cottage into the kitchen.

CHAPTER THIRTEEN

When she noticed the brooch on George's windowsill the next

morning, she snatched it from sight and placed it in the pocket of her cardigan. She had been made privy to the darkness in Lynnwood, her eyes had been opened to the truths behind Midwinter, and the brooch seemed all the more horrible for it; a thing of delicate beauty in the shape of indelicate hunger, as though commemorating that night and the gaping mouths that filled it. Theirs was an insatiable society. Fine wines, foie gras, blue cheeses and long pork; they consumed these things without conscience. She supposed it was the natural way. Eaton had shown no remorse when chewing on the magpie, and she had lost count of the number of sparrows deposited by Merlot on Catherine's doorstep.

"Sit down," she told George, when she confronted him that afternoon. He hadn't returned straight home from school and it was almost five o'clock before he finally let himself into the house. She waited for him in the kitchen, her anxious hands knotted in her lap. She heard the door open then quietly close, feeling the air grow cold around her as winter rushed into the house. Moments later, his pale face appeared in the doorway.

"I'm home," he said. It was then she had instructed him to sit. He did as he was told. The placid hum of the refrigerator filled the room.

"George, what's this?"

He stared across the dinner table as she produced the brooch from her pocket. It shone dully in the lamplight, dark and grey against the rich grain of the wood beneath.

"It's a brooch," he said. "I think it's made from iron. It looks like a mouth, with teeth."

"And who does it belong to?"

Still staring, he shrugged his slight shoulders. "It doesn't belong to anybody."

"That's not true, George. I know where it's from and who it belongs to because I've seen it before. Why did you take it from the churchyard?"

"I didn't take it," he said. His eyes rose to meet hers, before falling back to the brooch. They swam dark against his pale face. "That would be stealing and stealing's wrong."

"Yes, stealing is wrong, but so is lying, darling."

"I didn't take it," he repeated. "It was a gift."

"A gift?"

"From my friend," he said. "The man in the tunnel."

Her mind jumped back several weeks, to the first time her son had mentioned the man. She remembered patchwork trees, damp soil, the ripe aroma of autumn, as the Forest softened and grew thin, like a piece of brown, shiny fruit.

"The one you saw in the Forest that day?" she said. After a moment he nodded. "I thought you fell out with him, darling?"

"I did. He scared me. But now we're friends again. I didn't know he'd stolen it."

She swallowed, her throat tight, lips pursed. "George, this man..."

"My friend," he interjected.

She forced a smile. "Do you really think you should be friends with him, if he steals?"

He seemed to think about this. The flicker of something, she couldn't tell what, crossed his face. "I'm sure he didn't mean to steal. He's nice to me. I feel better when he's around."

"George, I know things are difficult at the moment. The world doesn't feel like a very friendly place. But it will get better, I promise. In the meantime I need you to be honest with me, and with yourself. I think it's wonderful you have this friend, but you mustn't use him to lie for you, as a way of blaming others –"

"I'm not –"

"I need you to be honest with me –"

"I am –"

Pain flashed behind his eyes. His expression tightened, grew sad, such that she thought he might cry. She spoke quickly. "Can I meet him? Maybe if I asked him nicely, he'd put the brooch back where it belongs and none of this will matter."

"He doesn't speak," he said.

"He doesn't speak?"

"No, he just stares. And grins. Besides, you've already met," he said.

"I have? But when?"

"He visited last night, while you were sleeping."

Another face flashed before her eyes; long and white and filled with simian cunning. Imagined from the features of her son, it was all the more horrible; the predatory, formed from the placid. She drew a short breath. "He visits you at night?"

"Yes," he said, as though it were the most natural thing in the world. "He comes into my bedroom, through the window. How else do you think he left the brooch?"

* * *

It was mid-October when George first found his friend in the tunnel. Even autumn could not rob the Forest of its beauty. The trees aged gracefully, turning a hundred shades of brown and red and egg yolk yellow. Clouds gathered overhead, streaky in the dark blue sky, but rain was not unwelcome. Little egrets took to the swollen waters and earthworms turned in the soil. The village transformed into a vivid collage, one of those few places of quiet refuge, which were so rare.

Alone with his thoughts he marched down the tracks. He worked his way methodically from sleeper to sleeper, blissfully oblivious to their history as children are blissfully oblivious to so much of the world. His favourite trainers – the white pair, with light-up soles – found mud again, and a visible weight lifted from his shoulders. He liked to visit this place after school, he told Freya, when she asked him about that day and what drew him to that place on the outskirts of the Forest.

The grass had parted beneath his trainers, their dewy wetness licking the stains from his footwear with every step. He scanned the undergrowth for signs of his quarry; amphibious skin, yellow eyes, or the pink of earthworm flesh. It was perfect weather for hunting, he knew; the rain this morning had been torrential, an endless patter against the school windows, matching the excited beat inside of him as he watched it from inside.

"The streets, overflowin' with filth..." he mimicked, in a depth of voice still many years away.

Climbing the slippery embankment, he followed the tracks. When he was roughly halfway along he sat himself down and began to unpack things from his rucksack. The magpie watched him while he worked, from where it perched on the rotten remains of a tree.

A number of items appeared on the tracks beside him. There was a magnifying glass, two of the Allwood's jam jars – one clean, one still sporting the seeded remnants of preserve – a polythene bag filled with crumbs and, last to be retrieved, his pencil case. He set these things down carefully before proceeding to examine the underside of the metal slats and the surrounding mud. When he thought he might have found something he scrutinised it more closely with the magnifying glass. Mostly he uncovered earthworms, brought to the surface by the rain, or drowning woodlice.

The insects understood him. These weren't people with complex emotions. They didn't lie or hide things from each other and they didn't need fathers or school to raise them properly. They simply were. They existed to eat, to breed and, protected by their hard, chitinous skin, they did it very well. The other children found them disgusting. They threw them at each other, stepped on them in the corridors, shivered and squealed whenever anyone spoke about them. He remembered the case of desiccated butterflies, which Freya had hung on the wall in the sitting room; specimens of Papua New Guinea, a gift from an old family friend. Their faded, dusty wings retained an elegant beauty long after death, even skewered inside a display cabinet.

No, there was nothing wrong with insects. Simple creatures with natural drives, unencumbered by morality or conscience, they were respected. Admirable, even.

He stayed like this for nearly ten minutes, working his way slowly down the length of tarnished track, pausing to examine his findings. Only when he reached the very end of the track did he hear it; a slow, scraping sound. It was a harmless enough noise and yet something about it snagged his attention. He looked up slowly from the mud, the plants, the crumbling remains of rotten timbers, and found himself standing before a tunnel. It stared back at him, empty and vast and dark from the side of the hill.

He fell quiet as he recalled the entrance; a yawning chasm into the earth, where sunlight never reached. He remembered a smell; the moist, metallic tang of minerals. His face had tingled with unspoken fervour.

Standing before the tunnel he heard the sound again; like skin on stone or the scrape of his trainers against the playground tarmac. Except this time he felt it as much as he heard it; an echo in his blood, rhythmic as the drumming of hooves across heathland. He struggled to express the intensity of the feeling, lacking the language or experience to do so, but Freya guessed these things because she too had felt it, when staring down at the pig in the field that morning. It was the stirring of race memories, of those primal sparks long since suppressed beneath the skin; urges that even George, still wild of soul and untamed by adolescence, was unfamiliar with. She could only guess at the thrill he must have experienced; the terror of the unknown.

Though he could not see into the dark he felt a watchful presence inside; a silhouette, almost distinguished from the surrounding gloom. His heart raced, his blood pumped, his hands shook by his sides, but that same terror held him fast.

He never went inside the tunnel. Even before that day he never ventured into the cold, empty place. Freya had warned him often enough how unstable it was, that 'nobody maintains it, George; not since the station closed down.' He had heeded those warnings, it seemed, and for this at least she felt some pride in her son's judgement, even if his own reasoning stung her eyes with tears. He didn't much fancy a rock to the head, he had said quite unashamedly, not if he could help it. He knew that pain well enough already.

For one moment he stood there, surrounded by the damp air, the cold breath of autumn, the streaks of grey cloud overhead. Then he broke and ran. If he possessed the spirit of the lone hunter then it was also true that, faced with the hollow enormity of the tunnel mouth, his resolve broke. Instinct took over and he fled from that wild place to the village and Haven House.

In the days that followed Freya visited the tunnel herself. It marked the first time she had wandered from the village since learning its dark nature, but for all her apprehension she needed to witness the place herself. She needed to see what George had seen, to feel something of what he had felt.

Still, the tree line watched her as she drew nearer. Though she need not have crossed its borders to reach the tunnel, she felt too close to the Forest already; a shiver racking her nerves as its ancient breath, icy and deep, stung her face. Sounds filled her ears at her approach; long, drawn-out creaks, of wood put under stress, and the rare crack of ice, which echoed through the Forest. The tracks represented a middle-ground into which she had wandered; a halfway place between the village and the vast, verdant sprawl that surrounded it. Not a dozen miles away in Southampton, men and women would be waking and worrying; about morning traffic on the Itchen Bridge, the clothes they were going to wear, or wanted to buy, the bass drone of the cruise ships as they pulled into the city and regurgitated streams of tourists, hot and rank with their own meagre concerns, while in as many steps she would be swallowed by the boughs, lost to Lynnwood and society forever...

She found the tunnel empty. She stared into its mouth for several minutes, trying to replicate George's experience, but could discern nothing in the darkness; no movement, no sense of watchfulness, save that of the trees, in the corners of her eyes. Both relieved and troubled by the imaginary nature of her son's friend, she turned from the tunnel and headed home, following the path of the tracks into the village.

* * *

As a piece of fruit left too long uneaten, Lynnwood began to darken and turn soft; an apple, its brown flesh seething with movement. Once again McCready was woken by a screaming, which he followed this time to the hen house. The birds rushed madly in the moonlit pen, the cold air alive with frantic clucking. And at the centre of the enclosure, birds swarming around its calves, knelt the skeletal figure of before with that same long grin, a hen hanging limply from each hand. Nor was McCready alone in his night-time visitations. Weaker, or perhaps wilder, the children of Lynnwood stirred restless in their beds and dreamt of pale, hungry faces at their windows. And on abandoning his brooch at Ms. Andrews's graveside, Mr. Shepherd found himself unable to sleep. Night after night he tossed and turned, but rest would not come, his body filled instead with a hunger the likes of which he had never known, or could seem to sate with food.

A cry on his lips, McCready chased the figure from the hen house, which slunk like a fox into the blanket of birds and vanished. He woke the next morning with blood in his teeth, feathers stuck to his hands and a vile, coppery taste no amount of whiskey could remove. If the children complained of nightmares they were humoured, or comforted. Most did not, and though they might have seemed more tired than usual, their eyes brighter, their smiles sharper, their dreams went otherwise unnoticed. Mr. Shepherd, distraught at the absence of his brooch, fell upon his workbench with the ferocity of a feeding dog. He hammered iron strips into roughly-hewn pins, twisted metal in his vice, or held it in fire until it was soft enough to shape with his hot fingers. And each time his creations were the same; lips and teeth and lolling tongues. Mouth after mouth filled his workroom, until he couldn't move from his bench for the hunger he had wrought.

CHAPTER FOURTEEN

Freya returned many times to the study in the Vicarage. How could she not, knowing what was written within? The honesty that she found in those pages, however horrid, was nourishing. Mostly, it seemed to satisfy her hunger, or distract her from it, where it might otherwise have consumed her.

Some diaries, as Ms. Andrews's, were confessional. She read tear-stained accounts of feeding frenzies beneath the trees; residents racing through the Forest, converging like a pack of hounds on their human quarry. She read of panicked breaths, of lingering tastes in the mouth and the winter of '42, when the hunger claimed an entire train as it pulled into the village station. After that year the line fell into disuse. The carriages themselves were dissembled. Melted down. The metal, she read, was shipped off to the front line. It seemed an appropriate use for the blood iron, though the residents wouldn't have known this, to ask them.

Other books were more fanciful, their authors seemingly oblivious, poetry spilling like saliva from their lips. On this day in particular she stumbled on a written account of an old village legend. She found it moving for the memories it instilled; the warm security of her father's lap, his hands around her waist, his clear voice in her ears as he recounted the very same folk tale to a young Freya.

* * *

Once, it was said, when the woods were young and the winters long, there lived a man in Lynnwood. This man had a wife, and together they had two sons, and each year when the autumn came and the trees turned red he filled their pantry with food. The winter months were vicious. Frost froze the earth, the trees fell bare and all but the strongest forest creatures sickened, grew thin and died. There was no fruit, there were no roots to dig, except for graves, and so the man worked hard to save supplies and make their larder large before autumn ran its course.

Then one year when the winter came and the snow and ice alongside it, the man's pantry was bare. His wife shook as she asked him what had happened. "Where is our food?" she said, still trembling from fear and the cold. "Why is the larder empty?"

And the man wept – he was an old man now, for the seasons had turned many times since he had first come to Lynnwood – and he admitted that he had eaten the larder's contents for himself. "This winter above all has been so very cold, and I so very hungry, and I had hunted much before the first snow so I thought there would be enough to last."

452

But there had not been enough to last. The wife shook her head and cursed that human creature, then grew thin and hard and fell stone dead across the floor. And the husband wept at what he had done.

It was not long before his two sons came, attracted by the sounds of his tears. They saw their mother's figure on the floor and they too wept. They asked their father what had happened.

"I have done a terrible thing in eating our supplies," he said. "Everything that we stockpiled is now gone."

"Then, like our mother, we will starve because of you," replied his sons.

He continued to shake his head. "I will find more food. You will not starve like your mother. I will be back for you." And so saying he climbed astride his shivering horse and called his world-weary hound and he set off from Lynnwood in search of food.

It was a pale, shining place beneath the frosty boughs. Ice cracked across the forest. His horse's hooves broke the glassy sheets beneath their tread. But there was no food to be found in the New Forest. Day stretched into night and the old man grew colder but he would not return until he could feed his sons. He had given them his word, after all, and they were his children.

Then, in that last moment, he saw it: a smooth-flanked stag, white as snow, with antlers twisting branchlike from its brow.

And so he kicked his horse's flanks and they gave chase, a cry of exultation on his old lips. They raced through the icy undergrowth: beneath the oak, the birch, the aller. They passed the shards of Mawley Bog and then the Hanging Tree. But no matter how fast his horse ran or how close they grew to the stag, it was always just out of reach.

The tale had changed through the telling, but Freya knew that to be the nature of stories, as it is the nature of winter to be cold, or the human creature to glut. Some claimed the old man's name was Cernunnos of the Wildwood. Others said he went by Herne, the Hunter. Others still say there was no stag at all; that the old man chased himself through the thin, grey trees and that he continues to do so forever more, a wintry spectre with his hound, his horse and his guilt.

453

CHAPTER FIFTEEN

They felt the change in the air; a subtle shift in the wind and rain that swept through the village. It danced across their skin like the scattered steps of a hundred crawling flies; an interminable itch growing stronger and more irritant with each passing day, until one morning when winter broke and with it the news that three boys had been reported missing.

The village embraced the hunt. Neighbours, not carollers, knocked from door to door and the skies filled with the baying of hounds, a full month before Midwinter, as residents followed their struggling dogs over the heathland. The village resonated with dread feeling, visible in the haunted eyes of the residents, if only they knew what they were seeing.

The boys' names were Andrew Stone, Stewart Foxley and Christopher Savage. The Stones and the Savages were relatively new to the village, having moved here in Freya's lifetime. The Foxleys, by contrast, had lived here for many generations and were an established presence. They were wealthy and owned one of the oldest cottages, near the dairy. A loud, exuberant sort, they frequently hosted parties no less loud or exuberant, though Freya had never been invited to one herself. She had Catherine for those kinds of evenings.

The boys had gone missing on Thursday afternoon. Mr. Sandford's son said he saw them walking down the high street, after school. Catherine, shopping in the village for spices, confirmed this. Mrs. Morecroft had been emptying the upper corridor of the Vicarage of Ms. Andrews's belongings, although she didn't notice them pass outside. It appeared they had turned off somewhere along the high street, through the fields that stretched behind it and crossed over into the Forest.

In the days that followed, Freya's motherly concern reached new depths. If three boys from George's school could go missing in the middle of the afternoon, who was to say the same could not happen to her son? She grew hot with anxiety, unspoken fears burning in her blood and pressing at her skin. She couldn't sleep but was woken each night, and found the tension infinitely worse in the darkness. The walls of her bedroom, the borders of the Forest and the night sky were all canvases against which she painted her worries; Boschian landscapes filled with skeletal figures she knew but could not name, and children, fleeing from them, from the vast blackness of the woods. Nor were these dreams but waking thoughts. Lynnwood seemed taut; as though every scrape of the branches from the ash tree outside her window might snap the tension and bring the Forest crashing down around her bed.

But it did not come. The branches continued to scratch the glass. Each night the tension pulled tighter, echoing the knot in her stomach. There was no relief, no matter how chaotic it would have been. In many ways, she thought, this was worse. She turned to Prozac, not to help her sleep – it was no good for that – but to deal with the places her mind began wandering. She had more than enough of the tablets left over from the months following Robert's absence.

She helped in the hunt for the boys, finding herself in the Forest, where she had sworn not to walk again. How could she not help, a mother herself? Everywhere she hoped to see the three boys, huddled and cold inside a dead tree, tucked into a hollow, or beneath the splayed roots of the felled oak by the bog. They were in none of these places. She doubted they were still of this world, swallowed by the Forest, like so many beforehand.

She had read much folklore in the Vicarage. Stories had existed for hundreds of years, purporting the presence of figures in the Forest; otherworldly creatures, slender and fickle, which made their home beneath mounds of earth or inside fungal elf rings. Superstition said they snatched children who wandered into the Forest unaware; her Bauchan of the trees and the earth.

She knew such creatures were fancy. There were no spirits, no demons, only people with famished features and the insatiable cold. Still she scoured the Forest. In her wakening world, of half-chewed magpies and enduring frost and long, sleepless nights, it was all she could do.

* * *

In light of the missing boys, Lynnwood became a different place. It wasn't an obvious change – there was nothing wrong with the village in any physical sense – but it felt different. Frost lingered longer on the ground in the mornings. The birds in the trees seemed quieter, as if they too sensed that something was subtly amiss. Trees, which she passed every day, looked taller and thinner; the Forest's bones picked clean by the season. The village transformed into a harsh, pointed place, full of sharp edges and sheer surfaces; the starving shadow of the Lynnwood she knew. And there were so many shadows, as though the shade beneath the trees had grown too great and was spilling out, encroaching ever closer on the unsettled soul of their village.

CHAPTER SIXTEEN

The mystery of George's friend in the tunnel didn't stop with his fleeing from the vast magnitude of the opening that morning.

Amid the pangs of the starving season, Freya remembered other traditions: the devotion to family, to friends, good food and good company. Afraid for her son and his detachment from the village she spent as much time as she could with him. They watched films together; festive and fantastic and ringing with Christmas spirit. They took Eaton for long walks, touring Lynnwood's cobbled streets, illuminated with strings of tasteful lights. And she cooked him hearty meals, the likes of which every growing boy needed; dripping meats, crisp, golden skins, thick gravies and sweet sauces, all washed down with carbonated drinks, which sparkled sharp and refreshing in his face and down his throat. After these meals, when she was briefly sated, her mouth coated with the lingering glaze of dinner, she would sit with him and talk. They spoke of many things, which he might not otherwise have disclosed to her. And while some of these things saddened her, or made her hot and anxious, she wasn't upset because through speaking they grew closer.

He still returned to the old Brockenhurst line each afternoon. They often talked about the place, which seemed so special to him. The tunnel frightened him, as the dark frightened all children, but there was a part of him that recognised the darkness and was excited by it.

* * *

One late October afternoon, while visiting the tracks, George had heard shouts behind him. The unwelcome voices startled him, his heart racing in his chest. Still on his hands and knees, where he had been inspecting the sleepers for beetles, he looked around. Three boys were moving towards him from the trees.

"What the hell?" said the closest. He thought it might have been Andy.

"What's he doing up there?"

"He's playing with dirt –"

"No, worms! He's eating worms!"

He lost track of who was speaking because he had turned back around to pack away his things, and then it didn't matter because they started to chant, their ugly voices joined in childish ritual. They reached him just as he was refilling his rucksack. Chris snatched the bag from beneath him while Andy interposed himself between the two. Stewart took the bag from Chris and emptied it onto the grass. His equipment tumbled out.

"So this is where you go after school every day," said Andy.

"You said we should follow him," added Chris. "Look at all this stuff."

"Looks like shit to me." Stewart picked up the polythene bag and emptied the crumbs across the ground. He retrieved one of the jam jars – the clean one – and stared at him through the glass. It did strange things to his eye, making it appear larger than it actually was, multifaceted and sharp. "What d'you use this stuff for?"

When he didn't speak, Stewart hurled the jar against the tracks. The glass shattered against the metal so that only the jagged base remained. "I said what do you use this stuff for?"

Still he didn't answer. His mouth felt dry, powdery, like the wings of those butterflies in the display cabinet at home. This was his place. His private place. And the others had followed him here.

"You're an idiot, Georgie," said Stewart flatly. "Can't speak to save your life, eh?"

"Mouth full of worms, probably," said Chris.

"Mouth full of shit more like."

They taunted him like this for some minutes. He stopped listening after the first, retreating into himself. He wished he were an insect, with glistening black skin hard enough to withstand their words, three pairs of legs, sharp mandibles with which to nip the limbs neatly from the other children, until they were armless, legless stumps, flailing, moaning by the old tracks –

He wasn't sure which one of them pushed him over. He slipped and rolled down the embankment, only stopping when he reached the base. Mud streaked down his back and across his face. His belongings followed after him: some schoolbooks, the second jam jar, his pencil case. His neck ached, his chest constricted. He didn't cry.

"See you tomorrow, Georgie," shouted Stewart. "Don't be late."

He struggled to his feet in time to see Michael hurl his magnifying glass into the tunnel. Then the three of them ran off through the trees.

For a long time he didn't move. A fresh wind played through the orange leaves. Autumn was in full sway, the Forest appearing rich, almost golden, beneath the drab sky, but he saw through that. His was a different Lynnwood, far removed from the village other people seemed to see. Of that much he assured Freya, when they spoke about it.

Eventually he moved, climbing the embankment to the tracks. He found his rucksack and some of his books, which he carefully retrieved from the grass, and was about to leave when he heard it again, as he had before: a scraping sound, of something being dragged against loose rock. He turned to the mouth of the tunnel. The darkness made it near impossible to see and yet he thought he could discern something within: a shape, gaunt and grey in the shadows.

He leant in, his eyes squinting, just as it emerged from the tunnel mouth. Not all of it, but an arm, long and thin. The limb stretched out from the darkness, hurled something through the air, then withdrew in a flash. George stared down at the grass by his feet and at his magnifying glass, lens cracked, which had landed there.

He approached the tunnel slowly. It was darker than he remembered. Colder. It towered over him. There was no more movement, no sign of anything within, except the distant echo of dislodged stones. He stared a moment longer, then spared a backwards glance to make sure he was unwatched. Only the magpie witnessed his actions.

He turned back to the tunnel. His pockets bulged with the collected detritus of the afternoon's efforts: a handful of dead woodlice, a shrivelled earthworm, caught above ground for too long, a small Tupperware box that he had placed two large snails inside. Each of these things he took slowly from his pockets and arranged on the ground before the tunnel. He wasn't so close that the figure inside could reach him; of that he was certain. Friendship was still a strange thing, whatever form it took, and he treated it accordingly.

Seated on the ground, surrounded by his menagerie of insects, living and dead, he opened his mouth and began to talk. He talked about arthropods and habitats and how lonely he felt in a village where no one understood him. He spoke of other things too; the beating inside him, a soft, insistent pulsing, like a pupa pressing at its cocoon.

It didn't matter that the figure in the cave remained anonymous. In fact, he thought, it was better that way. He talked to it, the figure who had watched him when he came to the tracks each day, the figure who had returned his magnifying glass to him. He talked and, though he didn't smile, he was happy because he heard the scattering of tiny stones and he knew it was listening. There were other sounds too; sometimes the sharp, hollow crack of distressed bone, as when Eaton gnawed a chew-treat, and he realised it must be feeding in there, or had fed recently. This didn't bother him unduly, he told Freya, for all things must eat, and he wasn't so alone in Lynnwood anymore.

CHAPTER SEVENTEEN

The brooch's artistic merit was undeniable and Freya was certain it would have stood out among Mr. Shepherd's other wares: the crosses, shield-emblems and burnished crow-shaped pendants displayed each week at market. He was a true craftsman, renowned throughout the village for his Celtic-themed work. She had once commissioned him to make their wedding rings: modest gold bands each sporting a single diamond.

But she had glimpsed the hungry horror inside them all and instead felt only revulsion for the beautiful object in her pocket, which seemed intent on nurturing that nascent wildness. So she sought to return the borrowed brooch to its rightful owner, because it was both the right thing to do and because she wouldn't have it in her house a moment longer.

Stepping out into the village that day, she found the sky white, an uninterrupted stretch of snowy cloud. The village seemed greyer by comparison, a collection of low buildings with dim windows, roofed with dowdy straw. The trees, which surrounded Lynnwood on all sides, had never looked so dense, so dark. And below the blanket of clouds, plumes of smoke, rising from behind the Old Barn...

She hurried down the street in the direction of the Forge. The title was fitting, given the converted cottage's original function. John Shepherd's family, he could often be heard to claim over a pint at the Hollybush, had lived in the cottage for several generations. The parish records confirmed as much, when curiosity led her to inspect the village documents one day: there had always been a metalsmith at the Forge. She still doubted the true ancestry of the Shepherds, knowing what she did about the nature of family names, but that didn't detract from John's claim to the cottage, or the skill of his hand when he turned it to his craft.

She moved through the village, her boots knocking against the icy cobbles. Lizzie was working on her art at a friend's house, so she had asked Catherine to watch George for the afternoon. Catherine had looked after both of her children many times during their infancy.

When Lizzie was first born she had made Catherine godmother; the result of a schoolgirl pact beneath the ash tree in her garden.

* * *

The smell of blossom and motor oil filled the garden. It was the first day of spring. The afternoon growled with sound as Freya's father dragged his lawnmower back and forth, reducing the grass to short, bristly clumps, chewed and spat in the machine's wake. Freya thought the lawn looked worse afterwards, but then grass never grew well in Lynnwood. Her father had explained it to her once; something to do with the Forest roots absorbing all the nutrients, leaving none for the lesser plants. She hadn't wholly understood, at the time.

Catherine and she sat beneath the ash tree as dusk descended. They had been sitting there since school finished for the day and were both still dressed in their uniforms. The year was '78 and they were eleven. They should have long outgrown fairy tales and fancy dreams, though neither of them seemed to have realised this. Having mown the lawn, David returned inside. The girls busied themselves with plucking the yellow grass from the soil.

They swore many things that day. Always to play. To laugh. To live together in Haven House with their dogs and their cats and the sounds of the Forest through the open cottage windows. When Catherine realised they might one day have to marry boys she grew sad, then excited, then thrilled at the prospect of motherhood in the way only young girls could.

"I'm going to have two babies!" she said.

"I'm going to have three!"

Catherine scrunched up her face at Freya's declaration. "You can't have three, there's not enough room in the house."

"I'll have as many babies as I want, thank you very much. And you'll have to help me look after them."

"I don't think so," said Catherine. "I mean, it's a lovely thought, but I'll be far too busy with my own to look after yours. And you'll have a husband for that, anyway."

"I still want you to be there," said Freya coyly. Her cheeks grew hot

461

and she plucked a little faster at the grass.

"I suppose I could be their godmother, if you really wanted."

"Yes!" said Freya. "I mean, I'd like that very much."

At that tender age, words still seemed fleeting. Freya remembered the sharp, sudden pain as she pricked her thumb on a piece of bark from the tree behind her, and the splash of red that had fallen from her thumb to the soil below. The bare earth around the tree grew wet with sisterly blood.

It wasn't until her thirties that Catherine learned she was infertile; that she always had been, and would never have children of her own. They were sitting in the same garden when she broke the news to Freya. Merlot of both kinds – cat and grape – had swiftly followed.

* * *

Though Catherine was godmother to both Freya's children, it was George with whom she got on better. Far removed from the shrill, wine-toting woman Freya had grown up with, Catherine was patient and accommodating with her son. When Freya and Robert used to return home from dinner, on those occasions when they treated themselves to meals out, they would often be greeted by the sleeping pair in the front room. Catherine's strong arms would be wrapped around George, his eyes closed, legs dangling from the sofa, or either side of her knee. Asked about this friendship one day, if it could be called such, George had said simply that Catherine was nice, and that she listened when he spoke.

Freya encountered few people along the way to the Forge. Most, she knew, were still scouring the Forest for the missing schoolboys. It might have reflected well on the village that they had rushed so quickly into the dark places beneath the trees. Once, she could remember, not so long ago, she thought men feared those dark places, or the dogs that raced alongside them through the thickets. Now she knew it ran deeper than that, deeper even than blood memories. If they feared these things at all, it was because they craved them; the darkness, in which to hide and hunt, one part of a bestial pack...

They couldn't speak of it, of course. Speech was a different construct; civil and societal. There were no words to express this ancient exuberance or the primal rush of blood and heat and beating heart that accompanied it. Still the village searched, as Freya had searched until she could go no further for fear of losing herself in the gaps between those haunted trees...

Turning down a gravel path, with a little gate and a low brick wall, she watched as the converted cottage emerged from behind the trees. The yard at the front was white with frost and wild snowdrops. Dark windows with lattice bars lined the ground floor of the cottage and, though the first floor was mostly brick, she remembered from previous visits a small window on the other side, above the workshop. Just to the right of the door emerged a weathered pole, from which hung the smithy's sign of old. It creaked painfully on her approach.

For several minutes she waited patiently, her knocking at the door unanswered. She might have waited longer, too, except that the ornament in her pocket seemed to grow heavier, hungrier, as though sensing its return to the one who had made it. Besides, she knew Mr. Shepherd was at home. By all accounts, he hadn't been seen about the village for over a week now.

Even as she moved back from the doorstep and around to his workshop, consternation gnawed at her. She began to fill with dread. Mr. Shepherd was known to lock himself away, sometimes for several days if working hard at his bench, but to miss the village market, and so close to Christmas, was most unusual. Never mind the search for the missing children, which should have taken priority over anything he was working on.

She moved to the back of the Forge. The gravel crunched beneath her feet. The yard continued around the house, leading to a garden. Though stripped by winter there was still some vegetation to be found; nettles clung stubbornly to life and snowdrops seemed to be flourishing, a bed of pristine petals on delicate green stalks. And behind the garden, joining the side of the house, sat the workshop.

She saw these things in a second. Then she noticed the mouths and her stomach clenched fiercely. Some hung from bird houses; pendants on thin, silvery chains, the shining slip of their tongues extending past their lips. Others were larger; iron emblems hammered into the dusty stone of the residence, teeth like animals' fangs. Still more covered the entrances to those bird houses or littered the leafless bushes and these, she realised with growing horror, were not ornaments but cunning traps; open jaws, spring-loaded and sharp with cruel lips and iron teeth strong enough to break birds or small animals –

Her throat had grown tight, her breaths short, her head light. She noticed strange details in those lasting moments; the grain of the wood used to make the bird houses, hammered and sawed and nailed into a thing of artifice. The aroma of the garden filled her nostrils, fresh and crisp, almost as though she could smell the coldness on the air. She saw the rust-brown stains along the metal teeth of the traps, heard the imagined crash of their jaws as they snapped shut with brutal force –

Then she saw the figure in the window of the workshop. It leant in close, palms pressed outwards, breath steaming the inside of the glass. She had no doubt it was Mr. Shepherd and yet its face was covered by a mask, beaten into the beautiful shape of a beast. Ridges of iron framed its eyes. Ears jutted from either side of the temple, pointed like those of a hound, and its mouth was locked in a horrid howl, which put the meagre brooch in her pocket to shame. The shape of that mouth would not leave her for many days, or the shape of the real mouth beneath, Mr. Shepherd's lips echoing that voiceless howl.

For almost a minute she stared unmoving at the figure in the window, which still pressed, poised, against the glass. Then quite suddenly it lunged, vanishing from visibility like a dog that had grown anxious waiting for its owner to return home, and Freya fled from the garden of mouths. She didn't stop running until she reached the village proper and even then she hurried straight home, not once turning back, not daring, in case that monstrous, magnificent mask dogged her steps, and the man beneath it.

Only once she was safely indoors and tentatively drinking tea did she realise the brooch had fallen from her pocket somewhere when running. Too frightened to be happy, or care that it was lost, she could do nothing but place her lips against the smooth china cup and drink.

CHAPTER EIGHTEEN

The diaries in the Vicarage were more than just informative. Like speech they represented a higher form of communication; structured language, however fragile, amid the hot, chaotic flush of bestial urges. They couldn't hope to tame the hunger that filled Lynnwood; that much was obvious from the volume of literature shelved in the study, the steady accumulation of centuries of guilt. Nor could they explain how or why these urges surfaced beyond Lynnwood's starving origins, and those were mere suppositions. Freya found solace in their pages nonetheless. They reminded her that she wasn't alone. Not now or ever. Hundreds had felt the stirrings of that same hunger; an innate dissatisfaction with the strictures of Lynnwood, of life, where they couldn't run, or pant, or gorge themselves on grease and juice and hot, spitting fat, but were forced to walk and smile and proffer manners and civility as though it was the most natural thing in the world.

Mostly they told her about people. This, more than anything else, continued to draw her back. The same day that she fled from the Forge, she found herself again in the study. Evening light filtered through the window, catching every mote of dust, which floated on the air like grains of mud suspended in Mawley Bog. She read from many different diaries that evening, but her favourite was Ms. Andrews's, to which she always returned. Not the later entries but those that came before, showing their vicar as Freya liked to remember her. That evening, once she had read her fill of hungry poems and horrid deeds, she retrieved the leather-bound diary once belonging to their vicar and turned to a middle page.

* * *

"It was dark when I left Allerwood and started towards the village hall. Street lamps lit the pavement, the rest of Lynnwood a shapeless smudge of grey and black, but despite this I knew it was not late. I pulled back the sleeve of my coat and checked my watch anyway. It read almost six o'clock.

"Huddling deeper into the coat – an early Christmas present, from

Maureen – I struggled on through the cold. The street lights guided my way, as did the sound of carol singers, faint but growing stronger. They carried on the wind. I knew the song instantly, 'Carol of the Bells'. It was a favourite from my childhood. Memories surfaced from the cold crisp of Christmases past and I remembered sitting in the front row at Midnight Mass, watching open-mouthed choristers as they celebrated the Lord with their voices.

"I walked on through the dark, coming to the village green. At first I thought to find it empty this evening. Doubtless the children had been called inside, for their dinner and bed. Then I noticed a solitary man, the homeless sort, sitting on one of the benches. I moved quickly through the darkness, feeling strangely vulnerable for the lack of company. Though never full, Allerwood Church was rarely without one person or another, come to pray, or else just stand in a House of God and be close to Him. Religious souls. 'We are a dying breed in this day and age. The Righteous Damned,' my father would have said.

"My shoes made hollow sounds against the pathway, feet moving in time to the ethereal rhythm of the choir. The church had been especially busy this afternoon, and the green seemed all the more unsettling because of this. Much to my relief it was not long before the hall grew out of the darkness ahead. I glanced back at the man on the bench as I left the green – a cursory glance, out of pity or mistrust I was not sure – but he had not moved from his seat. I thought he must be sleeping. In his own way, I supposed he was a follower of Lynnwood Green, as I was Allerwood Church. The wooden slats of the bench were his pews, the trees his pillars, the empty bottle by his feet a source of inner comfort. And though I loved the Lord, I could not help but feel something for this man and his wide, wild religion.

"My hand found the railings on the north side of the green, the gate between myself and the street swung open, but I paused. There was something more; something about this man tonight, alone on a bench, so cold, so close to Christmas. The wind picked my hair from my shoulders so that it fluttered against my face. I turned, stepped away from the railings and began walking slowly back across the green. The gate whined closed behind me.

"I have walked this way many evenings, on my way to the village meetings. In the spring it made a pleasant route, with the flowering trees, the birdsong, and lush smell of freshly cut grass. Even in the summer, when it was hotter, the walk was not unpleasant. And while the winter stripped it of leaves and life, I did not mind this much.

"I was right to suppose that the man was sleeping. His eyes were closed, his head thrown back, pale, stubbly throat exposed as though with the throes of laughter. I didn't think he had been laughing, not for a long time. Pain – exhaustion – was etched in the lines around his eyes and his shallow, sunken cheeks. I thought of a dog, which had been presented too much food, and eaten until it could not move a muscle. If his religion was the world, it was a hard one.

"Taking a few more steps, I came to a standstill beside him. I stared over him as he slept; this man, uncared for by anyone except God. I felt deeply sad. My eyes picked out more details: a bruise beneath one eye, the tattered collar of his beige coat, crumbs caught in that halfway beard. A label, sewn into his coat, read N. Roach. He was breathing deeply, I noticed; the sleep of the inebriated. I knew the sort well. Unloved, he had turned to drink to get through each day. I had not seen him in the village before this evening but I knew this to be true. What else would have brought him into my path, I, who love everyone with His unbiased eyes? It was never too late for redemption. Even the damned could be saved.

"I slipped the letter knife from around my neck. The cool chain on which it hung felt like ice against my skin. Shaped like a crucifix, I wore the object there always, a cold reminder of the Lord against my chest.

"It was the work of a moment, to press the cross gently to his forehead. I muttered a prayer. The wind rushed through the bare trees as I spoke and I heard His voice between the branches. It was grateful, justifying, and I knew I had done right by Him.

"When the figure on the bench was blessed – at peace, I thought – I replaced the chain around my neck. I wished him Merry Christmas, as across the street 'Carol of the Bells' reached its righteous climax. Then I hurried home through the night, leaving the green and the trees, the voices of the carol singers fading on the wind."

CHAPTER NINETEEN

With morning came snow and the certain knowledge that the three boys were lost to Lynnwood. Freya had known it would snow from the whiteness of the sky, but there was still no preparing for the first icy breath, bearing with it fledgling flakes. Standing in the kitchen doorway with Lizzie, she watched as Eaton and George dashed across the garden, two spirits unbridled by the breath of winter. And though there was no denying the flicker of delight that accompanied those first few flakes, she couldn't ignore the sickening realisation that the snow changed everything. The Forest, the village, the abandoned Brockenhurst line, the Old Barn, Mr. Shepherd's snowdrops and his cruel traps... Beneath the blanket of white they were all the same.

One by one, or sometimes in pairs, villagers emerged from the tree line, trudging slowly through the thickening snow. Their cheeks glowed red, their eyes sharp, narrowed perhaps from the wind, but there was a defeated look to each of them. Not because the snow had driven them inside, she thought – if anything, they looked hungrier, meaner – but because it had stripped them of an excuse to hunt beneath the boughs. Hope of finding tracks faded with the flakes. Hope of finding life faded with the cold. And so the searches were called off.

She stood with her daughter for nearly an hour while child and beast stalked each other through the garden. They talked about many things: the Knightwood Oak, which seemed to have inspired Lizzie to new heights of artistic flare, her time at school, and what the future might hold for her. Lizzie told her then that she wanted to attend university. She had found the perfect course, a Fine Art degree at Winchester. Freya felt proud for her daughter, who she thought had grown into such a strong young woman. The world could teach so much but not that fierce drive; the determination to succeed, to lead the pack through the narrow spaces between the trees of Lynnwood, of life.

She realised she hadn't considered her own future for a long time. She had been enacting routines, daily rituals, but never living as Eaton lived, bounding through the snowy grass, tongue lolling, hunger burning. She liked to think she had felt those things, once, with Robert. But then he had left and with it her appetite for pleasure, indulgence, life... Until now, when she hungered as never before, when she could hardly sleep for the wild dream that filled her night-time thoughts, in which she felt so hot and happy under the trees.

A euphoria settled over her, carried on the cold flakes, until it seemed she wasn't standing in the doorway but floating there. Her daughter had moved from her side, to make them both a hot drink. Screams filled her ears; grievous animal sounds, as Mrs. Foxley stumbled past the cottage, mingled with the savage shrieks of George as he chased Eaton round and round the garden. In that moment she forgot what it meant to be human or to be beast, or whether there'd ever been a difference.

* * *

That night Freya didn't sleep well. Brandy eased the affliction, or seemed to smother it. Her mouth grew warm, her limbs numb, her thoughts slowly blurred. Finally she drifted into sleep, oblivious to the silent snow, which continued to fall solemnly past her window, or the masked figure standing outside Haven House.

* * *

In her dream, winter had settled fully over the brook. Long crystals of ice hung from the branches, which were grey and bare except where algae coated them. Sunlight streamed weakly through the trees, winking faster and faster before fading completely. The last flash caught the frozen brook, then vanished, leaving the lurid blue of twilight in its wake.

She moved quickly through the trees towards the brook. Her feet crunched against the frosty floor, echoing the footsteps of her father behind her. Though the brook was frozen, she could still hear a faint

469

trickling, of a tiny current coursing underneath. It rushed under the ice, weak and wonderful, so that the ice appeared to be moving, or melting, when everything else was still.

At the banks she seemed to stop. The air stung her chest with every needle-breath. Slowly she looked down into the dark, translucent ice. The reflection staring back surprised her; she was not a little girl, as she had first supposed, so many weeks ago. Perhaps in that first dream she had been younger. Such concerns were fleeting. She seemed to have aged with the seasons, so that a familiar face stared back: long blonde hair, pale face rouged with cold, those lupine eyes, almost angled like those of a she-wolf. For what seemed like forever she stared at her reflection, only vaguely aware of her father behind her.

A second silhouette leant over the ice. She didn't need to look to know the Bauchan had appeared at the opposite bank. She glimpsed it from the corners of her eyes; a long, pale reflection in the murky ice, and she fancied a skeleton stood across the brook from her, or something equally thin and bleached.

As before, the silhouette shifted, kneeling to dip its hands in the waters. When it encountered the ice, it paused and seemed to reconsider, hands pressing against the glassy surface. Then, fingers outspread, it began to tap, as if exploring the ice; hollow sounds in time to her beating heart.

A familiar brightness radiated from the Forest, creeping into the corners of her vision. With every tap it seemed to expand, a snowstorm filling her view, until all she could see were the human hands, and it was then, as she pondered the nature of those delicate hands, that she felt another pair on her waist, and a thought struck her as strange: if this wasn't a childhood memory, and she was not a little girl, then it couldn't be her father who grasped her from behind.

CHAPTER TWENTY

Words could hardly hope to convey Freya's primitive urges, yet somehow George managed; her little boy reducing these bold, burgeoning feelings to structured sentences. To hear him speak of them, to see them shaped by the same mouth that kissed her goodnight before bed, was the most monstrous thing...

"Lunch, darling?" she said that afternoon, moving to the refrigerator. Lizzie leafed through a magazine at the dinner table. "I'm happy to cook. Shepherd's pie? Some pork belly? I bought some spices from the market, just last week."

Without looking up from her magazine, Lizzie shrugged. "Don't worry about lunch. I'm going out."

"You're going out?"

"I'm meeting with Rachel, remember? To discuss my art project. School might be shut but the deadline's still looming."

She thought about Lizzie and Rachel. The pair often worked on their art together. Their pieces last year had been selected for an exhibition; complementary collages using media cut-outs, displaying the Forest in summer and winter. Rachel had created the summer piece, although it was Lizzie's that had struck her as the stronger; the tall, silver trees, made from newspaper headlines, stripped of their leaves, their lives, by winter's bite. They had titled the two pieces 'The Forest'. There were still some photographs from the exhibition on the school's website.

"Are you eating with Rachel?" she said.

Her daughter nodded. "I need to leave actually, or I'll be late."

"Stay in the village," Freya said, as her daughter slipped from the kitchen. "Love you." The front door closed on her words and she returned her attentions to the refrigerator.

She felt George before she heard him; the tug of his hand on her sleeve. This in itself drew her attention. She could not remember the last time he had grabbed for her.

"I feel different," he said.

Turning to her son, she pressed the back of her hand to his forehead. "Different how, darling? Is it your stomach? Your sister wasn't very well last week; I hope you haven't caught something from her..."

"No, I mean different inside," he said. "I feel bad."

She knelt to his level, taking his face in her hands. "It's all right to feel bad, George. People feel bad all the time, for lots of different reasons. It doesn't make you any less of a man, to be honest with yourself. Remember what I said before, about honesty?"

He spoke quietly into her ear. "Honesty is good?"

"Yes, honesty is good."

There was a moment's silence, in which neither of them spoke. A car roared past the kitchen window – the third that day – its engine audible long after the vehicle had vanished. The noise was jarring, out of place, belonging to the city, not their little village. Lynnwood's sounds were altogether more penetrating, the high-pitched squeal of burning swine singing again in Freya's ears. She realised George was trembling.

"It's okay, darling. It's okay, I'm here."

"I'm not scared," he said.

"Of course you're not."

"I'm not scared, really. I just feel bad, because of Andrew and the others."

"What's happened is awful, George, but it's not your fault. You must remember that. You can't blame yourself."

"But I know," he said. "I know what's happened to them, and I haven't told anyone."

He looked up at her, his wide eyes revealing many things. She saw every ache, every shining fear, every wild gleam. She saw other things too, revealed for an instant. Then he spoke, and his words were like cold hands on the back of her neck.

* * *

George remembered the afternoon well, recounting many details Freya might have thought insignificant. Was anything significant

472

anymore except the hurried thumping of her heart, the eager wetness of her mouth, her two children?

Mrs. Welham, the woman at the head of the classroom, was a well-fed, well-to-do creature, with broad shoulders and a frame below to match. Like so many in Lynnwood she was partial to McCready's produce: bacon, pressed between slices of thick white bread each morning. In the afternoons she spread the Allwood's jam generously over warm fruit scones and when evening came her kitchen filled with the joyous glugging of Catherine's reds as it sloshed into glasses still warm from the dishwasher. Freya knew these things about the teacher not because she had seen them with her own eyes but because she hadn't; the private, impatient habits of the people of Lynnwood, revealed only through stray seeds caught between teeth, the jagged slash of red wine lips, the quivering light in their eyes.

The subject of the lesson that afternoon was Sin. George told her how animated the woman had been, her fat arms flourishing, her mouth quick. He told her about the mud that was trawled across the carpet from the wet outdoors, the smears of rain against the windowpane. As he said these things, she thought about Sin and her own lessons in the subject. She remembered Ms. Andrews's face as she preached the predatory nature of man at Sunday service, the stained-glass monsters in the windows, the churchyard of twisted statues; human figures bent low and bestial.

In the brightly-lit classroom, with the dreary rain pressing at the windows, they discussed what happened to sinners. They had been taught about Heaven and its fiery opposite lots of times before, never mind from TV and films. It didn't mean they were going to answer. To raise their hands, speak out, act know-it-all. George had long since learned the names for those people: teacher's pet, mummy's boy, tosser. Stooped in their chairs, heads held low, the class stared at Mrs. Welham. Christopher Savage dropped his biro. From the back row, somebody laughed. It was a thoughtless sound.

"You mean prison, Miss? Like that old perve in Southampton?"

"Andrew, I don't think that's appropriate –"

"My dad said he got ten years, 'cause of those photos they found –"

"Stop, Andrew –"

"He said they were all –"

"Stop."

The outspoken boy shrugged, loosened his tie, hunched further over his desk. Shaken, the teacher picked up her textbook. She flicked to a page and began reading aloud, scripture concerning Hell.

George knew the way they treated Mrs. Welham wasn't fair. She was much nicer than most of the other teachers. He supposed that was why they got away with it; the rest of the class, with their behaviour. The talking, the swearing, the sheer contempt. She was sensitive and they had a second sense for such things. Pack mentality, like newly-hatched spiders to their struggling prey, or the wild dogs he had watched on the Discovery Channel last week. They could sniff out the weak and the vulnerable like so much rotting flesh, smell the rank, intestinal tang of their fear. Playground scavengers.

He was reminded of a recent dream, in which he found himself in his classroom. Mrs. Morecroft stood at the front but it was his classmates who held his attention; each of them perched upright at their desks, backs straight, their faces those of famished dogs. Saliva dripped in ropes from their sly smiles, the sort that all dogs can't help but display, and pink tongues lolled from parted jaws. For the longest time it seemed that no one moved, as if waiting some unspoken direction. The air grew moist and rank with the foetid breath of the children.

Then a great horn sounded, reverberating the windows, the walls, the very particles of his blood until it boiled with anticipation and with an unspoken signal burst. He threw himself to the floor and raced from the classroom, his schoolmates hot on his heels. At first he thought he fled from them; the feral light in their eyes, their rancid breath, the yellow rot of their teeth. Then one raced past him, and another, and another, their human hands slapping the linoleum, and he chanced upon his reflection in one of the windows. He too bore the guise of a hound, his ears pricked, mouth dripping with the promise of the hunt...

Shivering, he dismissed the dream, returning his attentions to the classroom. Outside, the rain fell harder, striking the windows at a slant. There was a subterranean sluice as the heating behind him kicked into life. Four rows away to the front, Mrs. Welham continued talking.

"Page thirteen, everyone. Reason and Religion. Are there enough copies? Christopher, stop playing with that pen, please. Now, all together..."

A couple of children mumbled dutifully after Mrs. Welham. Most remained silent. From somewhere outside they could hear Mr. Jones, their haggard, grey-haired PE teacher, his instructive bellows echoing across the playing fields. George stared openly at the rain-flecked windows, losing himself to the bleak, watery sky. The chairs, tables and teacher of the classroom faded into a fugue of nothingness.

He thought about Hell as it was described to him. He imagined a dark place, lit with bursts of flame and shadows. Across this rocky landscape, filled with ruinous monoliths and charred, broken trees, he saw the Damned; the lost souls of the Godless; those same men and women who lied, cheated and killed in his favourite detective dramas on television. They screamed under the black sky, condemned by a higher justice; some pitiful wails, others younger, fresher, more savage sounds.

All things considered, it was strangely disaffecting. Flames weren't frightening. Neither were screams. It all seemed so made-up, so fabricated, so detached from the village he knew.

Something struck his face and he started, as if shocked. He looked around, to the right, and found himself staring into the face of Stewart Foxley. The boy's bright eyes bore into his own and George looked quickly away. His chest ached, his forehead burning from where the paper had struck, as if remembering the pain of heavier missiles; sharper, rougher, or the hot wetness of his blood.

He glanced back as Stewart mouthed something. It might have been "I love you." Or "I'll have you." He concentrated instead on Mrs. Welham.

"The Bible describes a variety of demons, monsters of metaphor used to illustrate sin. Specifically, there were seven lords of Hell. Can anyone remember them? Or find them on the page?"

He knew all about the Sins and their namesakes. He could still remember the first time his mother had explained the concept; of Heaven and Hell, right and wrong, good and bad. He knew she wasn't religious. She had made it very clear to him that their Sunday service was a different tradition. She didn't keep The Bible or The Book of Sin side by side on the mantel like Jessica Morley's parents. But she had done well to explain the concept and he thought he had understood, at least partly.

"The seven demons, anyone? Or their Sins? It's all there, on page thirteen. The first, somebody?"

As before, nobody spoke. Mrs. Welham stared expectantly across the class and George hid his face with his sleeves. The school bell filled the silence and the classroom flew into movement; the scrape of chair legs, slamming books, animated chatter as everyone rose to leave. Chris's biro struck George on the chin, to laughter. He twitched, his face burning, and shrank inside his jumper.

"See you later, Georgie," said Chris as he sauntered behind his chair. He kicked the table, which shuddered on its legs.

"Don't forget your homework, you shit," said Andy. Then Stewart himself strode past. He smacked George on the head.

"Better run, Georgie, your mum'll be waiting at home for you."

The three of them left, surrounded by a crowd of other students, and then George was alone in the classroom. As he finished packing away his things, he realised The Bible knew nothing of Hell. Snatching his rucksack, he ran from the classroom. The school grounds swallowed him up.

* * *

Nobody remembered seeing the three boys beyond the high street, so they couldn't have known that on the day they vanished they had turned off at the disused station, or that they followed a fourth boy as he moved alone along the tracks towards the Forest. Freya only knew these things because George had told her. There were no other witnesses, except the trees themselves.

The rain had churned the grassy embankment into a mound of mud. It continued to fall, dashing grass and soil like pebbles. Winter was upon them and the nights were drawing in. It would not be long, George suspected, before his mother wouldn't let him here at all, for fear of accidents in the dark. He moved quickly, with scientific fervour, studying the gaps between the sleepers for snails and earthworms.

The three boys interrupted George just as he had sat down by the tunnel. He remembered it as though detached from his own body; staring down over the boys as they converged on him. They rushed through the rain, three dark shapes, wet and wild.

He saw himself, rising as they approached, head turned, alarmed by their whooping. His trousers were soaked through with rain and mud. He felt very cold. They were shouting things but their voices reached him distorted, as though travelling through water, or drowned beneath another sound, which was quiet at first but grew very quickly into an ancient roar, droning in his ears like a swarm of bees, except coming from the cave behind him...

He remembered pain as they pushed him back to the ground. He remembered their faces, long and pale and filled with something much older than their physical selves; a sharp disdain for rules and restraint. He remembered burning with heat, blood pounding in his ears beneath that terrible roaring, and another heat against his legs as he wet himself.

The figure emerged from the tunnel, loping across the grass like an ape. He saw pale skin, a childlike face and long arms, which snatched the three boys and broke them. Even as its fingers curled around their flesh and that deafening roaring was cut short by snapping bones, the boys' expressions were those of ecstatic terror. Their lips twisted, their eyes shone with rainwater, wide and unknowing, and then they shone no more.

Silence sank over the clearing. George stared, unmoving, as the figure examined the bodies with its nose. Like a spider it scuttled from boy to boy, back arched, head low. Then it dragged them, one by one, backwards into the tunnel, leaving him alone beneath the empty sky.

A scream shatters the silence that has settled over the village. Nib still pressed into the paper, she pauses. Drawing a deep, tremulous breath, she stands from her note-making and moves to the window. The floor feels cold, almost icy, against her bare feet.

Two birds pick at something in the garden, beside the Griffin sculpture Robert and she had bought together in Lyndhurst. They are crows; great, black birds with marble eyes and shining beaks. Their talons bury into the thing beneath them, puncturing soft flesh, sliding past skin to the wet muscle beneath. She glances at their prey only briefly, before returning her eyes to the birds. It is recently dead, much like the rest of Lynnwood. She notes the steam, which pours from its ravaged stomach into the cold outside. Moments ago it had been one of Catherine's cats. The animals had been the first to go missing. Before Mr. Shepherd, before the boys, even before Ms. Andrews. Of course, no one had noticed at the time.

The crows make short work of the cat until it is unrecognisable. Their talons reduce it to flesh and fur and ropes of intestinal meat. Her stomach's screams join those of the frenzied birds...

She drags herself back to the dining table. Her fingers find furrows in the wood, where her pen has pressed through the paper. She follows the shallow grooves, like a blind woman reading with her fingertips. Blood brail. It is the greatest irony, that she is reduced to reading like the sightless when she sees clearly now for the first time, when words themselves mean so little anymore.

She finds the pen again. It feels strange in her hand; a relic from a different time. Somehow she resumes writing. In her mind's eye she sees only the crows; two broad, black silhouettes. She hears them even as she writes, their hungry cries ringing in her ears...

CHAPTER TWENTY-ONE

Freya knew there were no monsters, no figures in the trees, but still she felt the need to hold George tight. He trembled in her arms, his breath soft against the curve of her neck. She ran her hands down the back of his jumper, as though stroking his story away; his words wiped clean beneath the palm of her hand. At some point she closed her eyes and they stood in silence. She became aware of other things in the absence of sight; the artificial texture of his jumper against her fingertips, the boniness of his slight frame, the warmth of her own breath, over his shoulder.

Then he did a rare thing, his own arms reaching out to hug her back. They joined behind her, his hands locking, and she felt the terror of the unknown in that grasp. A child, young to the world, he was still capable of marvelling at the enormity of the sky, of fearing its emptiness, of feeling the trees and the grass and the swift-footed animals of the Forest in his blood, but was expected to ignore all these things, or deny them, for order and conscience and proper conduct. There was nothing proper, nothing natural about it. That, she thought, was the greatest contradiction of all, the truest irony in this modern world of masked, proper predators.

* * *

For Freya's sixth birthday her parents threw a small garden party. All of the children from her class were invited; her mother and she had spent a whole day making invitations, using paper and glitter and the colouring crayons from the drawer in her bedroom. And what invitations they had been! The colours, the magnificence, the fierce pride she had felt, handing them out to her friends!

She spent the afternoon making a nest from the fresh grass cuttings. The smell of the recently-mowed lawn was intoxicating, as was the sodden feel of it in her hands, the press of the summer sun against her face. Laughter filled the garden as her parents entertained the other grown-ups around the patio table.

The summer sun flashed in Freya's eyes. She began to feel hot and thirsty as she patted the mounds of grass into the nest-shape. She considered getting up to fetch some squash from the table.

A silhouette fell over her, blocking the sun from her eyes. She looked up at a girl who was making a similar grass nest across the lawn. A moment passed while they studied each other.

She remembered the shriek of the adults as their parents drank and ate and laughed into the sky, and the stillness that accompanied Catherine as she stood silently over Freya, as she reached for grass from Freya's nest, the grass that Freya had so carefully amassed for herself. She remembered standing up and pushing Catherine and kicking her; this girl, who sought to steal from her grass nest, where her imagined young would sleep and grow and writhe amid the cuttings. She had shouted and scratched Catherine with her fingers and Catherine had cried and their parents had come running to split them apart, placate them, as all children are meant to be placated. She realised this might be the earliest memory she had of Catherine. The earliest memory of her oldest friend; a memory of damp grass and drawn blood and wild faces.

* * *

Evening soon fell on Lynnwood. Lizzie returned home from Rachel's house in the fading light. Freya cooked them a mighty meal: sausages, smooth mash, mixed vegetables and dense, dark gravy. The hot, rich food would do them good, she decided. Mostly, she needed it herself; the fat, juicy sausages, sweetened with apple, the creamy potato, the crunch of the carrots – still slightly hard – between her teeth.

George and she cleared their plates. Lizzie picked at her food before scattering from the table. Freya finished the leftovers herself. There was never enough.

Alone again with her son, she forbade him from returning to the tunnel. She told him the figure was not his friend, that he was dangerous and might hurt him, if given the chance.

"But he saved me," said George.

"He didn't save you, darling. Those poor boys were in the wrong

480

place at the wrong time."

"They hurt me," he said, "and then they couldn't hurt me anymore."

She strained inside, chest tight, unable to explain the wrongness of what had happened. Perhaps it was because she almost doubted that wrongness herself. He was her baby, after all, and they had struck him...

"They were being very cruel, George, but they needed telling off. What happened to them isn't right..."

He told her he didn't understand but that he would stay away from the tunnel, if it was what she wanted. Then he said he was tired and that he was going to bed. She excused him from the kitchen and resumed her household ritual; clearing the table, hand washing the dishes, losing herself to those chemical suds, anything but contented.

* * *

After that day, George spoke of many dreams. He shared them openly with Freya, having learned the merits of honesty, the relief of unburdening his thoughts with another. She took solace from this realisation. Deception was another artifice. Her son, at least, seemed to have recognised this.

He dreamt first of a copse within the Forest. She knew the place well; recognisable by the Hanging Tree, of local and historical fame. Back in the forties, a village witch – Margaret Roach – had made the tree her haunt. Though she was never charged with witchcraft, it was a well-known fact about the village. Certainly, there was much conflict recorded between her goings-on and those of Ms. Andrews's parents. Allerwood parish, it seemed, did not take kindly to pagans and devil-worshippers. Many were the mornings she could be seen, walking from her cottage in the direction of the tree, a cape around her shoulders, a necklace of animal bones in one hand. She made the grotesque artefact from the remains of her dog, after it was crushed beneath the wheels of a cart, or so the guidebooks said.

Those same guidebooks recounted how Margaret hung herself in the winter of '49. Her body was left to swing from the old oak branches for three days before one resident found her and took pity. It wasn't difficult for Freya to imagine the villagers' relief at the death of the woman and her unwholesome taint on their village – the hypocrisy!

In George's dream there were three figures: the tree, a woman and a solitary magpie. In this dream the figures, which seemed to have been waiting, began to turn on one another as he approached. The magpie moved first, plucking ravenously at the Hanging Tree, drawing strips of bark, like pale flesh, from its trunk. Sap oozed from the wounds, glazing the bird's beak.

Even as the bird's beak grew more frenzied, the woman, tall and thin but glowing so brightly George couldn't see her features, fixed her shining face on the magpie. Moving towards it, like a ghost above the grass, she snatched her struggling prey in one singular motion and stuffed it into her face. There was no eating, no movement of the mouth – there was no mouth – but this didn't save the bird. It was absorbed entirely, with a muffled croak, one glistening green feather falling in its wake.

Then the Hanging Tree, wounded though it was, fixed its hungry eyes on the woman, and the sound that echoed from its broken lips rang with the enormous appetite of the Forest itself. Groaning into the dusk, which grew darker with every moment that passed, it drew the woman into its mouth; that gaping chasm of empty blackness, from which no things escaped...

Another time George dreamt of night and a snowstorm falling over the village. At first he ran outside into the path of the snow, relishing the delicate kiss of each flake against his skin. It built up on the ground and crunched beneath his feet, a cold carpet of pure white. He opened his mouth, tasting the flakes on his tongue.

Other figures began emerging from their homes; thin silhouettes, illuminated in the doorways of their cottages. They too moved amid the snow, faceless and laughing, swaying like dead branches in the wind.

The snow continued to fall, thicker and faster, until it seemed to move against his face and, looking up, he realised the flakes were tiny insects; flies, made entirely from frost. They fell frantically from the night, moving in vast, swirling clouds, swarms of droning ice. They crawled across flesh, their feet scratching skin, and where they landed the villagers grew gaunt until the white street was filled with white bodies; the last dance of the snow dead, grinning under the yellow light of the moon.

He dreamt of the dog-children again, and the wild hunt through the corridors, and often of that afternoon by the tunnel, when the three boys had been taken. Freya tried to console her son, running her hand through his hair and holding him in her arms, but he hadn't finished talking. As though she had unstopped something inside of him, he continued to speak, his lips spilling ever darker dreams.

And each time, he said, no matter the nature of the dream, he would find himself back in his bedroom, in the dark and the cold, with the imagined movement of a figure at his window; a streak of white, glimpsed then gone from where it had pressed up against the glass. His friend from the tunnel, watching over him.

CHAPTER TWENTY-TWO

It was still light when Freya left for Catherine's house. The sun shone salmon pink above the tree line. She moved quickly through the twilight towards the cottage, her boots against the snow the only sound down the street. This time no curtains twitched. The houses stared back at her, somehow older, less cared-for. She wasn't sure that she preferred the stillness.

Relief filled her at the sight of the cottage. She hurried the rest of the way down the street and up the pathway. Catherine would know what to say. They would open a bottle and collapse in her sofas and talk and laugh as they had done for nearly forty years. She could almost smell the robust wine, oaky and delicious in her mouth.

As she stepped up to the door, she realised that she really could smell wine. She noticed the curtains were shut. She also noticed several bottles, nestled in the bushes. She might not have seen them except for the smell and the way they caught the fading light. Anxiety fluttered inside her.

"Catherine?" she called. She knocked against the door, then waited a minute. "Catherine, are you in?"

She entered the cottage using the key Catherine had given her when she had gone abroad last summer and asked Freya to keep an eye on the cats. The key slid smoothly into the lock, turning quickly in her hand.

Movement sounded behind the door as someone sprang back. Only moments behind, Freya heard footfalls against the old wood, glimpsed a pale shape as it disappeared into the kitchen.

"Catherine?" she said, "Catherine, what's the matter?"

When Catherine spoke, her voice was like a hiss. "Go away!"

She followed the voice and the vanishing shape into the kitchen. Her throat was tight, her stomach sick. She felt as though everything she had eaten these past months was swimming inside her, pushing at her skin, threatening to rise up into her mouth. Had the hunger reached her friend? Had it claimed Catherine?

The cottage was in disarray. More bottles, mostly empty, cluttered the work-surface. She noted sheets of paper, scrunched into tight balls beside the bin. A slab of brie festered on a chopping board. Beside it, a cheese-knife glistened blue and green.

"Catherine, where are you?"

"Please, go away," said the voice again. She followed it to the wine cellar. The door was locked. She touched it, lay her head against it.

"You know you shouldn't drink alone, Ms. Lacey."

After a moment, Catherine replied. "You know you shouldn't drink at all, Ms. Rankin."

"Are you going to tell me what the matter is?" she said.

Laughter echoed from the cellar. It didn't sound like Catherine. "The matter? You might as well ask me the point of cats again."

"We never did decide on that," Freya said.

More laughter bubbled up from behind the door. "We decided you were a bitch, remember?"

484

"Ms. Lacey! That's hardly something to call someone from behind closed doors."

"You're a bitch, I'm a bitch, the whole world is full of bitches." Catherine's voice was sharp, acidic. It matched the stench of the kitchen. "Isn't that the point? The point of it all?"

"The point of what?"

"Life!" hissed Catherine. Something smashed in the wine cellar. "To breed, to feel a man between your legs, to drop screaming children, one after the other, to mother them like they're you, like they're a part of you, crawling hungry and bloody across the floor?"

Laughter degenerated into sobs, then bubbled back again until Freya could hardly distinguish between the two. She felt herself beginning to cry. "Don't do this to yourself," she said quietly. "Catherine, don't."

"How can't I, when it's all around me? All I see anymore is the hunger in people's eyes, the desire burning there, a hunger for life that I can never know. I can never know it!"

Freya choked back her voice. "There's other things too, Catherine. Think about it. Think about me."

"Think about you?"

"Think about love."

Freya felt hot and dizzy from the tears and the heady aroma of wine. Reds and whites and half-drunk pinks had mixed into a kaleidoscope of rank smells, which caught in the back of her throat. Her eyes fell back to the brie, rotting slowly on the side. She found she couldn't look at it.

"Love is nothing," muttered Catherine. "Love means nothing."

"Don't you love me?"

"I... can't," she said. "I can't have children and I can't love you! The rest of the village has let go and I can't! So tell me, what's the point?"

Freya sank slowly to her haunches against the door. She pressed her thumb to the wood, remembering a promise, pricked in blood. She thought she might lose herself wholly to tears, but instead swallowed them down. Eventually she managed words.

"Did you ever find Merlot?" she said.

485

"No."

"She's the point, Catherine. Merlot's the point. Follow in her footsteps. Go, be with her." Freya felt herself smiling. "You always were more of a cat woman."

CHAPTER TWENTY-THREE

In the hallway of Haven House the next morning, Freya slipped into her wellies. Her Parka felt dry against her skin and strange, as though she shouldn't be wearing it. It was a moment before she slid it over her arms and zipped it up to her chest.

She had to know the truth of George's story, to verify what had happened to those boys in the tunnel, if not for peace of mind then to sate her own curiosity. There could be no peace of mind, not while she still belonged to the village. There was only her hunger, which she knew would never end. Eaton paced around her legs, his tail wagging, anticipation shining in his eyes. She thought he looked sad. As she attached the leash to his collar, she wondered about the emotional capacity of the dog. Was he really sad? Or was she just imagining the upset in his eyes? He had food, water, shelter and love...

She opened the door and stepped out into the bracing cold. They moved quickly through the village, woman and dog. Snow fell softly around them. She thought of George, of the snow he had dreamt, then insects and hungry swarms, swirling in the air. They passed few people on the way. She exchanged a furtive glance with a teacher from the school. The man was white with cold, his eyes dark, narrow. His vanishing footsteps crunched in the snow behind her. Once or twice a curtain twitched, but when she turned to look it was too late. Once she thought she saw a pale face, staring at her through a window, but only once. All other times there was nobody there, and after that she let the curtains twitch and didn't look again. She passed through the village, across the high street and the abandoned station, and walked towards the trees.

As the last time, she followed the overgrown tracks. They proved slippery with ice, so she walked across the embankment, where the cold and snow had made the mud hard. She released Eaton from his lead. He bolted across the grass after some invisible prey or, she thought, the silhouette of her son, who she pictured running ahead, peering between the metal slats, moving ever closer to the yawning mouth of the tunnel.

She followed the apparition through the snow. Often he stopped to examine the unseen, and she realised she was smiling; her little boy, lost and fascinated in equal measure at the monstrous size of the world around him and the unknown things within. They were all lost, really. No one person truly knew their place in Lynnwood, domesticated by school and society into good, orderly citizens.

It was madness, she realised, faltering in her step. It was insanity, branded the norm. Her eyes studied her son a second longer, then he dissipated under a flurry of snowflakes and she watched Eaton instead as he raced across the heathland. The sadness was gone from his eyes. His paws churned clumps of snow.

The tunnel mouth seemed wider than she remembered. It whistled with wintry breath and an undercurrent of something else. She smelled the foetid stench, so much like spoiled meat, and her face fell. Inside she seethed; the maternal against the hungry, the social against the wild, the wrong against the right.

Another gust of wind brought the stench renewed, and she winced. Eaton must have caught the smell too, for he inched past her, his ears flat, one paw in front of the other. What did it mean, if the three boys rotted in there? They had lives once, futures, mothers of their own. She could still hear Mrs. Foxley's wails from when she had passed Haven House after the searches were called off. They were honest sounds, heartfelt and human as anything Freya had come to expect.

And yet everything had changed now. She saw Lynnwood for what it was, and in the village there were only two sorts: those that hunted and those who were their prey. One fed, the other was fed upon. And in doing so they nurtured the hunters, who grew strong and full beneath the Forest canopy, or the oaken beams of their cottages, bright and indomitable as the constellation Orion itself...

Inside the tunnel nothing moved that she could see. The darkness was dense and velveteen. Frost clung to the tunnel mouth like ravenous spittle and, around the base, more snowdrops broke through the blanket of white. Nature's bouquets, commemorating the three boys who festered within and the role they played in the insatiable cycle of life.

Cold and contemplative, she didn't notice the trap, concealed in the snow. A single, heavy crash echoed across the clearing, followed by Eaton's whimpers. Arms stiff, chest frozen with fear, she rushed towards the wounded dog even as something else darted from the darkness of the tunnel. Much closer than Freya, it reached Eaton first, and seeing the skeletal figure in the overcast light she faltered, slipping in the snow.

It had been Mr. Shepherd, once. She had seen it before, watching her from his workshop. But under the wintry light it looked horrible. Its naked flesh seemed blue and pink. Ribs pressed from its chest, its eyes wild behind that monstrous mask, which was at once ornate and revolting.

She struggled to her feet and started towards Eaton. His head lolled wildly, eyes mad, as the snow became red around him. It was darkest around his forelegs, where the metal had mangled his flesh, becoming paler and icier as it diffused into the flakes.

Long fingers reached for the dog's head. He snapped once, instinctively, yellow teeth flashing from black gums, then the figure grasped his head and twisted. A crack, like thawing ice, echoed in her ears.

Silence settled over the clearing as Freya fell upon the man. She remembered the press of it beneath her, the surprising softness of its skin for one so thin and hard. Her face felt hot, burning with anger and sadness and a thrill she had never known. This was a new instinct and an old one, no less bred into her blood. The figure might have kicked her, or thrown her back, she couldn't be sure. It was strong. It thrashed wildly beneath her, and then she was on her back in the snow, the breath knocked from inside her. Tears ran into her hair.

The roar of the Forest filled her ears. Turning sideways, she watched as the figure dragged Eaton's body into the tunnel. Then a howl emerged from the darkness, half human, half beast, and as she crawled to her feet and staggered toward the village it was answered by another from the trees, and another, and another, until the morning air filled with cries of wild hunger.

* * *

Lynnwood blurred around her as she ran. She might have been moving through banks of fog, or a distant memory. In many ways, the village was a memory now. Lynnwood as she had known it all her life no longer existed. The streets, the trees and the stone-cold tiles of their kitchen floors were all bathed in invisible blood; monstrous deeds committed by monstrous people, dried and flaky in the cracks between the stone, or soaked into the soil beneath their feet. She felt lost, stripped of the society she had been raised to depend on. It had been torn from around her; a lamb, devoured by Aesop's wolves, leaving her naked and vulnerable in the cold and the snow...

CHAPTER TWENTY-FOUR

It might have been midday when Freya found herself outside Catherine's house. The cottage was still. She stared numbly at the building, which meant so much and so little, Eaton's lead hanging limply by her side. She knew Catherine had gone, to be as the others in the Forest. She could tell just from looking at the house. Still she walked slowly up the path to the oak wood door and knocked.

She didn't know quite how old the house was, or how long the Laceys had lived there, only that it had stood for hundreds of years at least. Families had lived out their lives behind the grey stone of its walls; their loves, their hates, their tender moments and cruel words imprinted on that stone for as long as people living remembered. She knew Catherine's pain when, late for school one morning, she had stubbed her toe on a table-leg. She heard the echoes of Catherine's laughter when they had discovered a dirty book in her father's study. How they shrieked at the thought of learned Mr. Lacey, nose-deep in those pages! She remembered the quiet sound of the floorboards beneath their feet as Catherine had leaned in to kiss her, the thrill that had coursed through her as their lips brushed together that first time. It had been their last day of school and her breath was hot with celebratory wine. The taste, she knew, had remained with Catherine for decades afterwards.

She knew the sounds of grief, when Catherine's parents passed away, of joy, when she had bought Merlot, and the animal screams of birth when the cat had produced her litter. She knew tears and smiles and the warmth of desire and the walls knew all these things too. A lifetime witnessed and remembered.

She used her key to enter the cottage. The inside was just as she remembered it. The hallway had been tidied recently. Six empty wine bottles stood beside the door. She smelled lavender and loneliness and realised she was breathing heavily.

She moved into the front room. The scarlet curtains were stark against the whiteness of outside. Some books had been left open on the coffee table, their spaces vacant in the bookcase. They looked like poetry collections. She didn't read them but turned to inspect the rest of the house, revisiting the rooms and retracing the steps she had walked a hundred times.

The bedrooms were perfectly made. The bathroom too appeared to have been thoroughly cleaned. On descending into the wine cellar she found it empty. Where before there had been stacks of wine, cases of bottles older than she, now there was only darkness and the skeletal framework of the racks. The air was sweet and vinegary on her tongue.

The kitchen was cold. The whole house was cold, as though Catherine alone had warmed it with her lips, her eyes, her wild, drunken laughter. On the work-surface, beside the knife block, she found a piece of paper. It was a page, torn carefully from a book. A lipstick had been used to weigh it down.

For several minutes she read silently from the page. Then she turned and walked out of the cottage, closing the door behind her. On the doorstep she smelled the lingering aroma of lavender. She fancied she heard laughter and crying and the mewling of a cat. Then she left.

Marry me, my Lady,
By the Forest's edge,
Hear the trickling of the stream
As we, as one, are wed.

Marry me, my Lady,
By the Forest's side,
Hear the roaring of the trees
As we, as one, are wed.

Marry me, my Lady,
By the Forest's kiss,
Hear the silence of the leaves
As we, as one, are wed.

* * *

She has almost caught up with herself. It could not have been a week, days perhaps, since Eaton stepped in the jaws of the trap. He flashes behind her eyes, his auburn fur matted with blood, as though the colour seeped out of him with the passing of his life into the snow. She misses him more than she can express in words, or through the nib of a pen. A memory resurfaces, which she had thought lost. She is watching a puppy as it crosses their sitting room, head low, ears flat with the curiosity of youth. He is awkward-looking, like the foals born to the Forest in spring. He grew into his limbs, his speed, her love; a constant reminder of that last meal with Robert, when she had first decided they would one day get a dog. And now he has gone. They have both gone. There is almost nothing left, to remind her who she was.

She clutches her chest, feeling the texture of her clothes – these had mattered, once – then the hardness of her chest beneath. She traces her ribs with her fingers, reminding herself that when all else fails she is flesh and blood and sweat and bone and hot, wet breath...

Eaton was all these things, and now he is none of them, even his bones snapped and sucked clean by the man that had been Mr. Shepherd. Her stomach growls, and she hears Eaton in her mind, lips drawn back, teeth bared, and then it is not Eaton but Mr. Shepherd, jaw set, mouth red, and then her son, his eyes sharp in his pale face, mouth open, a hungry shout tearing from his throat.

She does not know for certain if Mr. Shepherd was always in the tunnel. She does not know whether he visited her son at night, whether it was he who bequeathed him the brooch from Ms. Andrews's grave. She does not know whether it was he who protected her son from those boys, who dragged their bodies into the tunnel and ate from them, or whether it was George himself, her little George, who fed on their flesh, every bite a rebuke against their bullying, against school, against uniform and smart shoes and Sunday service and a world that neither loved or understood him, but expected him to comply all the same.

Her chest rises and falls quickly beneath her arms. Her ribs are hard, her body shaking. This is not the first time she has considered his role in Lynnwood's darkness, but it is the first time she has faced it. Inside, she has always known, always suspected. They all grow lean and hungry. Why should her son be any different? Nothing else could have driven her back to the tunnel that day, where the trees grew so close, except to stare with her own eyes into the abyss where her son had simultaneously found and lost himself.

Another figure flashes behind her eyes and she starts as, outside, pink sky turns to midnight blue. It is her daughter's face, so similar to her own. It stirs more feelings inside of her. Pride struggles to surface above the forest of primitive drives, which are so strong now. Pride and sadness enough to dredge her from instinctual descent, for just one moment. One moment is all she needs, before she is free to run as the dogs through the trees. One moment of remembrance for one solitary girl, who, when the rest of Lynnwood succumbed to their wilder instincts, fought a silent battle with her hunger, unnoticed by all.

CHAPTER TWENTY-FIVE

The howling of the figures in the trees showed no signs of stopping. Freya fell against the inside of her front door, silencing the wind and the screams. In the hallway, all was still. Lamplight shone from the kitchen and a soft ticking reached her ears, of the grandfather clock to her right. She realised she still held Eaton's leash in one hand. Her fingers were white, where they clasped it tightly. Slowly she placed it where it belonged, on the coat-pegs with her Parka.

"George," she called. The word was followed by movement upstairs, as he stepped onto the landing. The stairs creaked three times beneath as he began to descend.

"Hello?" he said. His face appeared over the banister.

She realised she didn't know why she had called him. There was nothing she could say to explain what had happened. "Nothing, darling. Just... Nothing."

He stared at her a second longer, then started to withdraw from the stairs.

"George, wait."

"Yes?" he said, reappearing.

"Have you seen your sister?"

"She's in her room," he said.

"Thank you."

She didn't ask him what he was doing upstairs in his room. Nor did she mention Eaton. Alone she moved through the cottage, inspecting every room, as though viewing them for the first or last time. In the sitting room, her eyes lingered over the case of butterflies. She stared at their delicately preserved wings, their withered bodies and fading colours. They were beauty and revulsion, change and growth and colour, captured in the glittering scales of their wings, and she had hung them from her wall, as though to remind herself of these things, to celebrate them. In the kitchen the black mass of the AGA held her attention, a testimony to man's appetite for containment. He bound his hunger to the flames of the cooker in an attempt to manage it, just as he displayed decaying remnants of the wild in cases on his walls.

In the bathroom, she studied herself in the antique mirror, as her mother had done so often before her. She wondered if they saw the same things now, if that was why Harriet had spent so long diligently masking herself beneath make-up and blusher each morning.

The cottage sounded with movement as she exited the bathroom and crossed the landing. She might have been walking through a dream; the haze of outside having followed into her home. George had fallen asleep on his bedroom floor, beside the window. She left him where he lay, curled up like an animal in its den.

She knocked at Lizzie's door. When there was no answer she knocked again. Still there was no response, so she pushed the door open and stepped inside.

The room was dark with night. Strange silhouettes leapt out at her; sculptures, illuminated in moonlight. She looked past the twisted fey figures, the screaming face casts, the abstract shapes that she realised with growing concern might have been mouths; papier mâché versions of the lost brooch –

Her daughter lay on the floor. Where George was curled comfortably into his chest; however, she was sprawled against the wood. Freya saw for the first time how pale Lizzie looked beneath the light of the moon, how thin her arms had become; like sticks of bone, her face gaunt, as though stripped of flesh and life.

She rushed to her daughter and gathered her in her arms. She was cold and hard to touch, and proved horribly light when she lifted her to the bed. A thin line of blood emerged from her nose, where she must have knocked herself. It was brown in the dark and crusty when she tried to wipe it away. How long her daughter had been lying there she couldn't tell. All she knew was the terrible state of the girl, who, it seemed, had denied her simple hunger at every turn, where everyone else had indulged it.

When Lizzie woke some hours later, she shared her private hell with Freya. It was a story of denial, driven to extremes by the growing hunger inside. There was no escaping the cycle of eating and purging. It was, in itself, all devouring; sapping Lizzie's strength, her health, her life. Only her will remained, and what an iron will it was, to maintain such strictures, to uphold her monstrous habits even as they ate her up, pound by pound! If she wouldn't feed the hunger then it would feed on her, until there was nothing left. Mother and daughter wept together, and hugged, and Lizzie unburdened herself further.

At first, she said, she hid the changes easily. They were slow and she was resourceful. She wore loose clothing and blamed tiredness on late nights, or too much pressure at school. Still, her friends looked slimmer than her. The boys at school followed Rachel as dogs to a scent. It seemed demeaning and yet she craved those base attentions, their lingering eyes on her body, their noses sniffing her scents. If only they would look! She couldn't remember a time before A-levels, before reflections in the mirror, before complex carbohydrates and glossy magazines. Reduced to these things, she was not a person. She might as well not have existed.

Food, she said, began to lose its appeal. She noted the way spots of grease swam on the surface of gravy. Meat revolted her. This was no moral choice, no personal preference, as Freya's vegetarianism had once been – how long ago that seemed now. Lizzie spoke of plucked chicken like drowned men's flesh; bare and white and bloated. Sausages glistened with fat. Bacon shrivelled and grew hard. Even as Freya celebrated her new-found hunger with cooked breakfasts each morning these sickened her daughter, so that she barely touched them, and in private regurgitated what little had passed her lips.

"How could you do this to yourself?" Freya said, when her daughter had finished speaking. "Boys don't want *this*. Nobody wants this!"

"It wasn't about the boys," she said, shrinking into her covers. "That was just how it started. But then it became more. I started getting hungrier. It felt like I was losing control and the worse that got, the more I wanted to fight it. And when I couldn't, when I couldn't cut out food altogether, I had to throw it up to get it out of me."

They continued to argue, her daughter's expression so much like the hares', caught in the headlights on the road through the village.

"I don't understand," said Freya. "This isn't normal, darling. Your body needs food to grow, to live. You know this!"

"It's under control!" she said.

"It isn't, Lizzie! Let me get you something to eat."

"No."

"Please," she said, "Lizzie. You're starving yourself."

"I can't lose control! Look at the rest of the village! Look at what they're turning into, at what they've become!"

"It's normal," said Freya, and even as she spoke she realised that she was right. Lynnwood had always taken pride in its rich array of produce. Temptation had always been near. Breads, cheeses, wines and preserves; the village expressed itself through the unique brand of its New Forest flavours, as all places do, unconsciously or otherwise. There were the Allwood's jams, Catherine's wines, McCready's meats, never mind Lynnwood's wilder appetites, which said more about the village than words ever could. The revelation seemed to rise through her, dizzy and distancing. "It's normal to feel hungry. It's normal to want boys, to feel confused and scared, but that's what I'm here for. To talk to you, to help you, to be your mother. The only thing that isn't normal is this." She reached out to touch her daughter's arm. For a second she graced the skin, cold and hard again, before it vanished into the bedcovers.

"It's normal," Freya said, and the last vestiges of doubt faded from her own mind. "You must be starving."

Her daughter's sallow eyes rose to meet hers, and in the darkness of her bedroom, swaddled in her sheets, she nodded.

* * *

Freya stayed with Lizzie all night while she slept. At some point she also fell asleep, her daughter wrapped in her arms. It felt good to hold her close, impossibly good, as though holding her somehow made up

496

for the weeks of disregard. She felt stronger, more whole, completed by the closeness of her offspring.

They woke before dawn to shouting. At first she was confused, still deep in her dream by the brook. Then she realised the shouting was real. Lizzie was recoiled into the bedsheets and the sound coming from outside. Moving to the window, she stared down at the street and the man crouched in the middle of the road. Stripped of clothes and humanity he could have been anyone. It was the mask that betrayed him. He continued to shout; wordless noises, wild and unchallenged.

Then a second voice reached her ears, not from the street or the village but the room next door. It was a small voice, high and raw, like a feral cat screaming into the light blue of dawn. Each scream resonated inside her. Time seemed to slow, everything else fading into the background. All that mattered were those screams, which she realised then came from George's bedroom. She rushed from the window and Lizzie's room, across the landing and into her son's room. George was nowhere in sight. She raced to the open window, tearing back the curtains in time to see him vanishing with Mr. Shepherd into the village.

She stood at the window, watching him as he raced from view. She wasn't especially upset, as she thought she should have been. Nor was she happy. Instead she felt a surge of relief that she couldn't hope to explain. Her son, at least, was free now.

CHAPTER TWENTY-SIX

"A thin, delicate figure, with wings like glass and wide black eyes, Gluttony is the youngest of the Seven Sins. Her Court and she drift languidly through the forests of the world, accompanied by mellifluous music and the intoxicating scent of spring. Yet they are not to be underestimated, for when night falls, a feverish hunger descends on the Sin and they erupt, irresistible as the tide, through the undergrowth with their bows and spears and bloody,

nail-bitten claws. They slash and maul, searching out the beasts of the forest to devour, with bare hands gorging themselves, sating their yearning hunger with raw flesh and slurping down still-warm blood."
Description of 'The Forest' by Elizabeth Rankin, on display at
Hollybush Manor.

* * *

Freya woke again beside her daughter. For one moment of uncertainty, she wondered whether she had dreamt her son's escape. Then she saw the shining white of winter outside, felt her daughter trembling beside her, the clammy heat that prickled her skin, and she knew it had been real.

They left the house together. Lizzie followed obediently and Freya wondered whether the girl was as drained as she. They moved quickly through the morning snow, Lizzie's shoes making compact sounds with each tread. Freya had forgone footwear. Her feet were cold, then painful, then numb enough that she couldn't feel them. She moved soundlessly beside her daughter.

Smoke continued to pour from behind McCready's barn, as it had done now for over a week. The smoke tickled her nose almost as soon as they reached the high street, and she picked up her pace through the village. It smelled of ash and burned flesh, luring her towards the farmhouse, as though she needed encouragement.

When they reached McCready's cottage, they found the door open. She didn't enter to inspect the inside but headed around the back towards the Old Barn.

The structure towered over the farmhouse and she knew from old photographs that it had stood for many years, long before John McCready had come to Lynnwood. To the best of her knowledge he housed his pigs in there, along with various pieces of equipment. Today it was silent.

They spoke of nothing as they approached the place behind the barn. The place where the village children had used to play safely, away from the village but not so far that they intruded on the trees. Her vision blurred as she lost herself to smells and sounds and the growing pressure inside. She took her daughter's hand as they walked.

Rounding the barn, they encountered a field of charred pigs. They stopped where they stood and regarded the sight. Freya's stomach clenched even as her daughter's grasp on her hand did the same. The shapes that dotted the field were black and twisted, their bones buckled from heat, and all of them were grinning where they lay in the withered grass. At the other end of the field they spied McCready. They watched as, bent low, he set light to another of the animals. She could just make out his spidery figure, the can of lighter fluid and the fierce fire that followed. A gust of wind brought the acrid smell and with it the sound of spitting fat. He seemed to be screaming: "Mary! Mary!"

They converged on the old man and his pigs. Those nearest had not yet been burned, their porcine skin pale with cold, with death. Even before they reached him, Freya's mouth began to moisten, her eyes narrow with eagerness. Her daughter shared a similar sharp expression.

This close, the fires were intense. They crackled with ravenous glee enough to match that inside her. Still McCready screamed. The heat pressed against her face, blasting her skin, as mother and daughter fell upon the nearest animal. At first they were tentative, pressing their hands to the pig's swollen belly. Though it hadn't been burned, its skin was warm and dry from the nearby fires. Much of the hair had been singed from its back and sides, so that only a few crisp strands remained. She began to press harder, her fingers sinking into the flesh as though massaging it.

Seemingly satisfied, they gorged themselves on the pig. The field around them faded into nothingness. Freya knew only heat from the fires, the rubbery feel of the flesh in her mouth, tough and slippery between her teeth. Sometimes her daughter's hand met hers, sometimes another pair, as McCready crouched to join them. Her eyes watered, where smoke blew into their faces, but she didn't care. There was no stopping this revelry. She felt free at last; of Lynnwood, of Robert, of artifice and of conscious thought. All she knew was the wild abandon of feasting and the deep gratification that every mouthful brought.

* * *

One by one they broke off from the pig, momentarily sated, and sank into the snow. Much of it had melted from the constant heat, leaving sodden slush across this part of the field. Slowly she returned to herself, her sides aching, mouth stained with worse than blood. Though she remembered herself in these moments, she also knew that she had changed; that she wasn't the same woman she had been before, or her daughter, or the man beside them. They were something less now, or more. She was filled, completed by the flesh of the animal in their midst.

Only once the fires died, and the cold became too much, did she rise to her feet with her daughter. McCready remained on the ground, thin but bloated. He seemed to have stopped screaming, reduced to rasping breaths. The wind took her hair and cooled the stains against her face. She moved sluggishly back through the village with her daughter, to the place that had been their home.

CHAPTER TWENTY-SEVEN

Freya couldn't say what drove her back to the Vicarage in those last days. It felt important to see the place one more time, so that she could leave it fully behind her. As with her own cottage the day before, she moved through the lifeless building, seeing and remembering. Ghosts assumed themselves in the shadows; two women enjoying scones and brandy and civil conversation. Whispered words carried on the dusty air. She found that she felt strangely at home in the darkness, in a building where she had always previously felt stifled.

The last diary she read was her own, "Freya Harriet Heart" written in small letters across the cover. She hadn't been surprised when she found it in the bookcase. She thought that she remembered it, from years gone; the escape of a schoolgirl with a sick father and a mother who both loved and hated herself.

The diary was small, and irregularly kept, as anything required of a child was. She flicked through it, reluctant to read too deeply. She didn't recognise this girl anymore. This was someone else's life, someone else's memories. Still, she couldn't leave without looking inside. She owed herself that much.

There were the accounts of horror that each Midwinter brought. She had expected these, given what she already knew. She read of the figure at their sitting room window, the year Harriet had first taught her to bake. The year after, she noted four children missing from her class. Her parents said their families had left the village but she had found bones and scraps of school uniform, when playing with the dogs on one of their walks through the Forest. She read of the night her bed-ridden father had vanished, and how he had fled from the cottage, Harriet close behind him, howling as he staggered for the trees.

It was not these accounts that struck her but the human details she found most affecting, as though seeing them from the other side and remembering their tenderness.

She recalled the day Catherine and she had followed Marcus Gillingham home from school. His parents had owned one of the bigger houses near to the church, and it was quite a walk from the Manor.

Catherine and she had lusted for him in the way young girls are both intrigued and repulsed by boys. He must have known they were following him but he never turned around. That seemed only to have incited their intrigue further. Why wouldn't he look at them? Why couldn't he see them? She heard her own voice, so much like her daughter's the night before, saw her eyes filled with that same frenetic fear. It didn't matter that the other boys were interested, or that not a week later Robert Rankin, from Mrs. Lovejoy's class, would ask to walk her home, offering his jacket when it started to rain.

She read and remembered the time she had mixed up the salt with the sugar when baking cakes with her mother for the village market. They hadn't realised their mistake until Joan – Ms. Andrews to her, then – had taken a generous bite out of a cherry scone. Freya's laughter, she was told, had been heard as far as the Old Barn.

She had written of the day their Cocker Spaniels, Ralph and Jack, had attacked another dog. After that they had been put down. They were "unsafe," her father had insisted, "what if that had been your dog, Freya? What if they'd gone for you?" She hadn't thought that fair. They were only doing what came naturally. It had made no difference in the end. She was allowed to say goodbye, to stroke them both one last time, their tails wagging, blissfully oblivious to the fate that awaited them at the veterinary centre in Lyndhurst. She thought she had grown up a little that day. She had written as much in the diary.

She glanced over a dozen such intimate moments, until she felt sick from sentimentality and could read no more. Then she placed the diary back where she had found it on the shelf, and she left the Vicarage and didn't return again.

* * *

With night came hunger and the dream that had afflicted her for so long. It began as always; with her running through the trees. Her feet dashed icy puddles. The light glittered in the branches overhead, then flashed and was gone. Shadows rushed from the spaces between the trees, stretching across the floor, reaching for her and the elf rings she knew were there but couldn't see for the snow. Footsteps crunched behind her, as the second figure gained ground.

The brook appeared ahead, frozen but lively with the current underneath. She moved across the bank, to where ice met soil, and knelt, as always, to drink. When her hands encountered the sheet of ice they paused, fingers pressing curiously. She knew without looking that the Bauchan across the brook was doing similarly. She had seen it a dozen nights already; its cold, red fingers testing the dark ice.

She looked anyway. She was helpless not to in this place, this dream, which was nothing compared to the real brook and yet felt so real all the same. Her eyes rose slowly to the figure opposite, expecting whiteness to expand her vision, breaking from the brook or the snow, as it had always done before she could see properly. Only this time, no whiteness came. She looked up, seeing those hands still pressed to the ice, following slender arms, a familiar blouse and then the face, her face, staring back at her across the Forest. She looked drawn, bloodless, as though the cold had numbed her entire body. It was all she could do to stare at herself, crouched like an animal beside the brook, fingers scratching at the ice. She was the figure. She was the Bauchan!

The sound of running feet slowed to a walk. Then the figure, who she had once mistakenly thought her father, strode up behind her and slipped his hands around her waist. She felt those hands, so warm against her stomach, even as she watched them on the opposite bank and she saw that they weren't her father's but Robert's, and it was he who stood behind her.

Fear and uncertainty took hold of her. She couldn't remember this, even as it played out before her. She remembered the blouse though, which she had worn on their last night together, and her bare feet, and the way in which she crouched beside the brook like a thirsty dog. Then she heard him talking in her ear.

"Freya," he said, "Freya. It's me, Robert. It's your Robert."

She squirmed, tried to spin round, wriggling in his grasp, but his arms became something more, a fierce grip on her stomach.

"Freya, it's okay. It's going to be okay. I'm going to look after you. You can fight this. You can fight this!"

She kicked harder now, pushing off from the bank with her feet. They scrunched up against the snow and the hard soil beneath, then lashed out. Through unknowing eyes, she watched as the couple across the brook tumbled to the floor. She snarled, spat, at the mercy of the Midwinter Frenzy all those years ago. It had claimed her once already! Her mind raced with fear. She must have fled the house after the meal. Her hunger must have drawn her to the trees. He must have followed her.

He wouldn't give up on her. His arms said that much, as they continued to grip her tightly. She could hardly breathe in the stranglehold, the figure opposite writhing horribly, and yet she knew he was trying to help. He was trying to contain her, to save her from herself and the others who stalked the trees on this night alone.

Her head flew back and knocked into his face. His grip loosened. She thrust forward, her toes finding purchase on the ground, and struggled to her feet. One foot stepped onto the ice, which cracked beneath her weight.

The man on the ground scrabbled towards her.

"Freya, listen to me. Listen to my voice. This isn't you!"

She heard him and the words that spilled from his mouth, but they meant little to her like this. She had only eyes for the black wetness beneath his nose, the stink of his sweat, the ragged breaths that came from his throat. Looking into her eyes he seemed to sense this. He staggered to his feet, his hands raised in front of him.

"Freya," he said. "Stay with me. I want to help. I'm here to help you. I love you. You know I love you."

She rushed at him through the night, one part remembering, the other reliving. He turned and ran. Every second stretched out as she chased him through the trees. She felt the snow between her toes, the flakes that had begun to fall against her face. Her chest ached with longing; to have him in her hands and her mouth, to feel his skin against hers, his heat, his taste on her tongue. The Forest was a blur of black and white.

She caught him near Mawley Bog, beneath an alder tree. Moonlight reflected off the frozen water, bringing his face to stark relief. She glanced at it only once and then it was forgotten, in favour of hands and teeth and the inescapability of her hunger.

CHAPTER TWENTY-EIGHT

Just as that first taste of meat had driven her to Allerwood Church, so Freya found herself once more among the headstones. Statues rose around her; some weeping angels, others Sin in its various guises. She moved between the angels and the demons, knowing full-well that neither were honest depictions. There were no divine forces, no hellish creatures, only beasts of the earth, with their feelings and their drives, however base or noble. It didn't matter. None of it mattered. The church was another lie, founded to keep the residents of Lynnwood happy in their lives, to keep them placid, when underneath they seethed with instinct.

She left the statues behind and moved across the churchyard. There, on the very outskirts, just off the gravel path, one headstone stood, no higher than a boy. A bouquet rested at its base, withered with frost. Engraved into the modest stone, just above the hard flower heads, there was a single name, and below that an epitaph. She read both slowly, as though for the first time, though she was sure she had seen them a hundred times before and not remembered:

HERE LIES ROBERT RANKIN

"A MAN SEES IN THE WORLD
WHAT HE CARRIES IN HIS HEART"

She thought for a long time about the wording of the inscription. She supposed she had chosen it herself. She must have felt something, even then; a stirring of uneasiness at the idyllic village. Guilt might have played a part in its choice. She might just have liked the statement. Either way, it resonated now more than ever before.

Her eyes fell to the bouquet of flowers at the headstone's base. Frost had done terrible damage to them, but it still roused her to see something there. She wondered who might have brought them, who continued to replace them, year after year. Ms. Andrews has been responsible for this place once. Freya hoped that, faced with the question, she might have remembered if it was her. There was still much she could not recall, or ever would. She was almost free...

Many were the times George had stood before the headstone. Perhaps he had sensed something, the bond of blood between father and son; an ancestral connection, drawing him back to the grave when he passed it. Robert had passed on the hunger, as his father before him, and his father before that. It was not so hard to think an instinctual love coursed through the same blood.

She lingered a moment longer, then turned from the grave and left. It was all superfluous now. She visited the spot with the detached nostalgia of someone who has moved on. There was no other way for it. She didn't even know if there was anything left to bury after that night. The ritual of mourning was just that; another needless ceremony. So she said her goodbyes and walked from the churchyard for the last time.

* * *

A restlessness filled the empty village, as a clutch of insect eggs eager to hatch. She sensed that tonight was Midwinter. Time and dates were reduced to night and day now, but the wind and trees and the empty houses spoke to her as she moved through them and they told her that tonight was the night when instincts raged and Lynnwood filled with howls.

When she arrived home Lizzie had gone. She could only imagine where the girl ran, now that she was freed. The village had driven Lizzie half to death, but in the end her hunger had saved her. The hunger, which was so normal in their insane world of rules and regulations, laws and limitations, schools and streets and manners...

The soft pink of fading afternoon crept into the sky, and she realised this was her last day as Freya. So much of her had gone already, lost the night she had chased Robert through the trees, then covered up; replaced with propriety and false smiles and a lifetime of habits designed to keep her satisfied. But there was no satisfying that hunger for life, no sating that appetite. It lived always, under her skin, growing stronger with each passing year.

She found herself food, which she ate ravenously. Seated at the dining table, she stared out of the window. The cottage opposite was still. Empty. Nothing stirred – there was no one left to stir, except hungry ghosts, and they would come soon enough. She knew she would forget soon. It did not seem to matter now that everyone was gone, and their mild manners, their modesty, with them. The village was full of these things before. To forget them would be bliss. She was so close to forgetting, and to the freedom forgetting brings.

But others might come, one day in the future. They would come when the village was silent, its occupants missed. So she must write, before she forgets. She must write this for them. She had never written anything before, beyond schoolgirl diaries, and those seemed so long ago now.

* * *

She no longer remembers things, but lives them. She moves through the shadows of the undergrowth. Branches scratch her, each nick, each flare of pain real and sensuous. Her blood, so hot, cools rapidly against her skin. She can smell it, coppery and rich on the night air. She moves quickly through the Forest.

Her nose fills with other scents. This low to the ground, she can smell the soil, even beneath the layer of snow. It is earthy, regenerating. She smells the cold air, the frozen Forest, the salty sweat of other animals. They are invigorating aromas. They bear no traces of town life, the vagaries of village existence. This is home now. It always has been. She has returned to the dark beneath the trees, where all things hunt or are hunted.

She thinks of very little but the wind in her face and the pull of the moon, high above. It does not illuminate the Forest – there is no piercing that darkness! – but it glances from the branches, throwing them into black relief. She pushes through these thickets, past tall trunks, and slinks through the hollows of trees, faster, faster, her eyes wide and watering.

The Forest feels endless. She cannot see past the trees, only vaguely aware of other things; muddied water, frozen into a swathe of ice, the crunch of the snow beneath her hands and feet, spotted brown where she has bled. Her wild eyes scour the undergrowth. Her breath is ragged in her throat. Her fingers scrabble through the snow, grow numb and become red. The feeling that drives her seems to swell inside. It gnaws, growing desperate, pushing at her chest, turning her stomach with sickness. She might have had a name for this feeling once. Now it is beyond names. She knows it only as a part of her, pressing against her skin, filling her heart, her eyes, her mouth, until she collapses beneath a tree and it erupts from her, a singular shriek...

The sound fills the Forest, then is swallowed by it. She sinks to the base of the tree, where she lies amid snowdrops. Her hurried breathing becomes slow, shallow, as though stolen by the snow. Her bright eyes dim and something stirs in the depths of her mind. Memories of former times: shapes skipping through Forest paths, green wellies, laughter lighting up a child's face. Headstones, warm wine the colour of blood, the insect hum of the refrigerator. Muddy fur against her fingertips, a smiling man's face, the Forest, cut and stuck and pasted with poignancy against a blank piece of paper...

Another sound slips past her lips. Low and forlorn, it seems to last forever, before finally trailing off.

Then she hears something, which causes her head to rise, her eyes to widen, her breath to catch. An answering howl, off through the trees. It echoes into the night, followed moments later by a second. Her heart is racing now, as though clawing to escape her chest. She pushes from the tree and begins to run again.

The Forest slides past. She moves quickly through the trees, looking but not seeing. Her senses are tuned elsewhere. She listens for the howls, which rise erratically into the night. Sometimes they sound nearer, other times further off. The cold air fills her nostrils and for one brief moment she loses herself completely to the Forest. It is transcendental. She feels the cold, sees the night, hears the trees and the pulsing of her blood in her head, and she is complete...

Two shadows slink from either side of her, running at her heels. They are smaller, thinner, but no less wild, filled with the ecstasy of the hunt. Together, mother and offspring race between the trees, hungry and alive.

Sparkling Books

We publish:

Crime, mystery, thriller, suspense, horror and romance

Non-fiction

All titles are also available as e-books from your e-book retailer.

For current list of titles and direct links to stores visit:
www.sparklingbooks.com

@SparklingBooks

www.ingramcontent.com/pod-product-compliance
Lightning Source LLC
Chambersburg PA
CBHW030845030726
47495CB00005B/1383